John Beveridge Mackie

# The Life and Work of Duncan McLaren

Vol. II.

John Beveridge Mackie

**The Life and Work of Duncan McLaren**
*Vol. II.*

ISBN/EAN: 9783337062675

Printed in Europe, USA, Canada, Australia, Japan

Cover: Foto ©Raphael Reischuk / pixelio.de

More available books at **www.hansebooks.com**

# THE
# LIFE AND WORK
## OF
# DUNCAN M<sup>c</sup>LAREN

BY

J. B. MACKIE

---

## Vol. II.

---

THOMAS NELSON AND SONS

*London, Edinburgh, and New York*

1888

# CONTENTS.

## CHAPTER XV.

### *RELATIONS WITH ENGLISH LIBERALS.*



## CHAPTER XVI.

### *INDEPENDENT LIBERALISM IN EDINBURGH.*

## CHAPTER XVII.

### *THE DUTIES OF CITIZENSHIP.*



## CHAPTER XVIII.

### *PARLIAMENTARY WORK.*



## CHAPTER XIX.

### *POSTAL REFORM—COUNTY ROADS.*

## CHAPTER XX.

### *THE MEMBER FOR SCOTLAND.*




## CHAPTER XXI.

### *FRANCHISE REFORM.*

## CHAPTER XXII.

### *NATIONAL EDUCATION.*



## CHAPTER XXIII.

### *OVERTHROW OF THE HERIOT FREE SCHOOL SYSTEM.*



## CHAPTER XXIV.

### *CHURCH-RATES AND DISESTABLISHMENT.*

## CHAPTER XXV.

### *RETIREMENT FROM PARLIAMENT.*



## CHAPTER XXVI.

### *IRELAND AND HOME RULE.*



## CHAPTER XXVII.

### *LAST ILLNESS AND DEATH.*

# THE LIFE AND WORK

OF

# DUNCAN M<sup>C</sup>LAREN.

# CHAPTER XV.

## *RELATIONS WITH ENGLISH LIBERALS.*

Mr. M<sup>c</sup>Laren's active participation in the Anti-Corn-Law 1842
agitation made his name almost as well known in political
circles in England as it was in Scotland. When he went
to London on League business in 1842, he was in correspondence with Lord Brougham, probably the most distinguished amongst the statesmen and jurists who had left
Scotland for the wider sphere of English public life. To
this period belongs the following note, dated Tuesday, 8th
February 1842 :—" The Edinburgh Conference petition
will be presented in the House of Lords this evening soon
after five. If Mr. M<sup>c</sup>Laren wishes to be present, and will
come then, Lord Brougham will take care to have him
admitted below the bar." Lord Brougham did not co-
operate with the League, and was opposed to, rather than
a supporter of, the thoroughgoing nature of its policy ; but
he welcomed Mr. M<sup>c</sup>Laren as a citizen of Edinburgh whose
work and character had gained his esteem, with whom he
had held confidential political correspondence, and who,
in former years, had engaged his humanitarian sympathies
in the cause of Prison Reform in Scotland. Thus in
1839, in forwarding a petition from the Convention of
Royal Burghs in favour of a bill for the improvement of
prisons and prison discipline in Scotland, Mr. M<sup>c</sup>Laren
wrote :—" The truth is, that the state of the Scotch jails is

1842

a disgrace to the country. In the great majority of cases, the sole expense of their erection and maintenance, and of the maintenance of prisoners, fall on the boroughs, without any aid from the county population, and their revenues being very inadequate to support them, as they ought to be, on an improved scale both of accommodation, classification, and discipline, nothing could be done of any consequence under the present law to remedy the existing evils. Hence the jails have been for years the *grand nurseries of crime*. I hope the death-blow will be given to the system by the passing of the present bill into law. You will do an essential service to morality by devoting your great talents to the cause ; and I feel confident, if you do so, there will be no fear of the measure being longer delayed." Lord Brougham was interested in this subject, and in full sympathy with his correspondent.

New work brought new friendships and imposed new duties and responsibilities. These proved neither few nor light. The English Radical party, with whom Mr. M<sup>c</sup>Laren now cast in his lot, welcomed him as a valuable ally. During the Anti-Corn-Law agitation he was frequently appealed to by English Radicals to assist their candidates to seats in

Mr. Joseph Hume.

Parliament ; and in 1842, after Mr. Joseph Hume's defeat at Leeds, Mr. M<sup>c</sup>Laren willingly and successfully used his influence with the Anti-Corn-Law party in Forfarshire to obtain for Mr. Hume, who had previously been mentioned in connection with Edinburgh, Leith, and Fife, nomination in the Montrose Burghs. Sir John Bowring especially was urgent on the subject of obtaining a seat for Mr. Hume, and wrote to Mr. M<sup>c</sup>Laren that the Whigs had plotted Mr. Hume's exclusion from Parliament. He was greatly pleased with the victory that was secured. " You never had a better recompense," he wrote Mr. M<sup>c</sup>Laren, " than that you have obtained for your admirable exertions—an excellent lesson to every *cunning* tactician and an invaluable service to the good cause. I hope you will tell your fellow-labourers in the boroughs, that Hume's return is better than a mere *local* triumph, and that we are all sincerely thankful to them." The result of the election, too, confirmed the friendship with Mr. Hume, which had been begun several years before from sympathy on public questions; and the Member for the Montrose Burghs became a most energetic and sympathetic parliamentary correspondent of the leader of the Advanced Liberal party in Edinburgh, keeping him informed of all the movements and plans of the English Radicals, and reporting progress in the discussion of the Corn-laws, Church questions, national expenditure, &c. Probably enough Mr. Hume's letters intensified Mr. McLaren's distrust of the Whigs and their ways. More especially he gave early warning of the surrender of both parties in the state to the demands of the Roman Catholic clergy. He believed that Whigs and Tories were equally prepared to accept the principle of concurrent endowment in order to gain the political support of the Roman Catholic clergy. In 1843 he wrote to Mr. McLaren:—"I am sick of party strife. The public interest seems to be sacrificed to party. It is evident that the Whigs are of opinion that they would gain Ireland by buying the clergy, and, regardless of the principles of religious equality, they will, when they have the power, make that one of their schemes." Mr. McLaren was doing his utmost to secure that, so far as Edinburgh and the Scottish Dissenters were concerned, no encouragement should be given to the party to play fast and loose with their principles on the question of the Maynooth grant. In 1844 Mr. Hume was still more apprehensive of danger. He wrote Mr. McLaren assuring him that a measure for the endowment

1842

Parliamentary correspondence.

of Roman Catholicism would certainly be proposed as a buttress for the Established Church, and earnestly counselling the formation of a League or Union of all Dissenters after the manner of the Anti-Corn-Law League. "I reason thus," he wrote. "If Sir Robert Peel thinks it right to waste a million of money in maintaining a force of 50,000 men in arms, and all for the *support of a sinecure Church*, he will not scruple to propose £300,000 for bribing the priests, if he can succeed in removing their hostility to the Established Church."

Mr. M<sup>c</sup>Laren had every reason to be gratified with the result of his intervention in the Montrose Burghs. On the day of Mr. Hume's unopposed return (14th April 1842), Mr. David Binny wrote him from Forfar reporting the happy issue. "Mr. Hume," said Mr. Binny, "was nominated by his old and intimate friend ex-Baillie Clerk of Montrose, a brother Seceder, and seconded by our Provost. I moved, and Mr. Buchanan seconded, that a vote of thanks be tendered to you and Dr. Bowring for your powerful and well-timed support of Mr. Hume, which was unanimously carried at a full meeting of Mr. Hume's Committee." But though in this case the result was in every respect satisfactory, Mr. M<sup>c</sup>Laren was extremely chary in after-life about interfering personally with local elections outside of Edinburgh. He knew that the independent electors, who formed the mainstay of the Advanced Liberal party in every constituency, were ready to resent anything like outside dictation; and sympathising with this feeling, he was careful not to attempt to assume the rôle of intermediary. Up to the close of his life he was frequently applied to by political sympathisers and admirers in nearly every constituency in Scotland and by Advanced Liberal candidates for information and guidance. But whatever faults were imputed to

him by political opponents, he never was accused of acting
the part of a parliamentary election wire-puller; and when
consulted, he generally confined himself to giving an opinion as to the merits of the candidate, without seeking to
influence the choice of the electors.   He always insisted
on local initiation and action, recognising as supreme the
right of the constituencies to chose their members for themselves.

Mr. McLaren had no difficulty in responding to appeals
for the aid of his advocacy in organising public political
work in harmony with his convictions and sympathies.   His
head and heart continued throughout with the Liberalism of
Mr. Cobden and Mr. Bright; and though he felt that these
friends had formed an exaggerated estimate of his power to
help, he never failed them when the opportunity for effective
co-operation occurred.   The most important of these occasions after the abolition of the Corn-laws was the controversy
regarding the maintenance of a British naval squadron off
the coast of Africa, presumably as an Anti-Slavery Police
Force.   The subject was introduced to his notice by the
following letter :—

MANCHESTER, *January* 15, 1851.

MY DEAR SIR,—It is very odd that when a Whig job is to be
done, the political whippers-in turn their attention to Scotland.
The upholders of the African squadron, with Palmerston & Co.
at their head, have been lately pulling the wires of the clubs, and
setting the cliques of Glasgow, Aberdeen, &c., to work to get up
public meetings, calling on Government to enforce the treaties
for putting down the slave traffic, which means that the Whigs
shall continue to spend £700,000 or £800,000 in literally doing
mischief.   I am surprised that people so far north should play
into the hands of the tax-gatherer.   No such meeting could be
held in Manchester or Leeds, or if it were, common sense would
carry the day.   Can you warn any of our sound-headed friends

to be on their guard ?   Make use of my name or show this note
if you like.

Let the Scotchmen who join in the foolish cry not blame the
Government, but *themselves*, if they have still to read taxed books
and papers, and wash themselves with taxed soap.   The worst of
it is they are lending themselves to a job which involves the
taxation of us Englishmen as well as themselves.   A word from
you may put some of our friends on their guard ; and believe me
truly yours,                                   R. COBDEN.

   D. McLaren, Esq.

*P.S.*—The worst of it is, that the parties who are moving in
support of the slave squadron are passed off by Government in
debate as the Anti-Slavery party, whereas, on the contrary, the
British and Foreign Anti-Slavery Society have for several years
been protesting and petitioning against the slave squadron, which
they denounce as having aggravated the miseries of the traffic.
My friend Sturge of Birmingham, who is the very soul of the Anti-
Slavery party, is resolutely opposed to the squadron.

As an ardent friend of human freedom, he had been pre-
disposed to regard with favour the maintenance of a British
squadron on the African coast for the suppression of the
slave-trade ; but he was quickly undeceived.   His investigations showed that, on account of the immense line of coast
to be watched, the operations of the squadron were and
must be hopelessly ineffective.   According to the *Times*, the
slave-trade squadron was a hypocritical humbug and a
philanthropic sham; and while it imposed on Britain a direct
burden of from £700,000 to £1,000,000 per annum, and
indirectly much more, it enforced on the slave-trader pre-
cautions and overshipments that immensely increased the
horrors of the " middle passage."   " If," said Mr. Gladstone,
" in order to set at liberty 5000 or 6000 persons, we caused
the death of 9000 and aggravated the sufferings of many
thousands more, he was justified in saying that the sum of

human misery as regarded slaves carried across the ocean was increased by the repressive system." Mr. McLaren saw the force of these views, and in order to educate the public mind on the subject, he prepared an exhaustive statement of the result of his investigations, and published it in the form of a letter addressed to Councillor Gray. He supported his conclusions by quotations from the reports of two Parliamentary Commissions, *Times* editorials, and the testimony of the Anti-Slavery Societies, and even that of the commander of the squadron himself. The array of condemnatory opinion which he presented, formidable both in bulk and authority, was quite conclusive as to the futility and the mischievousness of the squadron. But in full sympathy with the Anti-Slavery sentiment, which then beat strong in the country, he proposed a substitute policy, based on the principle that this trade, " the sum of all villanies," could be most successfully attacked, not at the source of supply, but at the source of demand—in other words, at the slave-trading ports of Cuba and Brazil.

"Spain and Brazil," wrote Mr. McLaren, " have most shamefully violated their treaties with this country, after receiving our money and other advantages as the price of compliance with our wishes. In 1817 we paid Spain £400,000 as an indemnity for abolishing the slave-trade. She retains our money and yet refuses to perform the contract. If our cruisers must be employed, why not order them to blockade the ports of Cuba as strictly as they recently blockaded Athens for a much less important claim, until Spain shall either repay us our £400,000 with interest since 1817, or perform the conditions for which that sum was paid ? And in like manner, if Brazil shall still systematically violate the treaties she made with us, and if a squadron must be employed, why not blockade her principal ports till she fulfils her engagements ? There can be no doubt that a strict blockade of this kind would result in abolishing the slave-trade within six months, while there is no prospect of the present system producing the same result in a century."

Immediately on the publication of this statement, Mr. M<sup>c</sup>Laren wrote to Mr. Cobden, and forwarded him a copy. In reply he received the following letter :—

LONDON, *February* 12, 1851.

MY DEAR SIR,—Many thanks for your letter and the accompanying newspaper with your communication upon the African squadron, which contains a masterly summary of the arguments upon that question. I hope you will prevent your Councillors from falling into the Whig trap. Really you ought to devise a political *detective force* to protect the Scotch lieges against the insidious efforts of the Whigs to convert them into the tools of the Government. *London and Scotland* are the favourite fields of the tactics of Whiggery.

I am glad to see that you are moving in the new agitation against State Churches. This Papal outcry must come to *that*. But the English Dissenters as a body (particularly the ministers) seem to have forgotten their principles, and are willing to let Parliament undertake to *protect* them from Popery, forgetting that, if it be the duty of Parliament to put down by Act one sect, it must, by the same principle, have the right to set up another. You will have observed that the ministers of the Congregationalists (three denominations) in London have presented addresses to the First Magistrate on her throne against Popery ! This comes of allowing priests of any denomination to act apart from the laity. It ought to be laid down as a rule that the ministers of no religious sect ought to be allowed to act in the name of their congregations on any public question, unless in conjunction with laymen in proportion of at least two of the latter to one of the former. I hope, when your Anti-State Church Conference meets, you will adopt as a fundamental principle a resolution repudiating the right of Parliament to interfere, either to promote or to discourage any religious faith, by temporal rewards or penalties. This principle must embrace the Roman Catholics, or it is not worthy of the name of religious freedom. I exhort you to try to turn the tide of intolerance, which threatens to endanger our liberties in more ways than one. The Whigs are dragging nearly all our good men through the mire. If we go on at this rate, there will be no public principle which professing Liberals will not have violated, and the Tories will by and by be again welcomed into power by the masses.—Believe me, yours truly,

R. COBDEN.

Mr. McLaren's statement, though it did not prevent the adoption of the Lord's Provost's motion in favour of the continuance of the squadron, soon had the effect of changing the opinion of the Scottish Anti-Slavery party as to the value of the service, in which they had on mistaken grounds felt a pride.

As regards the Church question, on which Mr. Cobden asked for aid and gave warning, it was in one form or another seldom out of Mr. McLaren's mind, and his relation to it has been described in a previous chapter. By and by another question arose which completely effaced for the time being all recollection of the African squadron from the public mind. Russia quarrelled with Turkey, and Britain began to drift into war with Russia. Mr. Cobden and Mr. Bright, as resolute opponents of the war policy, seemed to forfeit their once commanding influence with the great mass of their fellow-countrymen. But, heedless of their lost popularity, and convinced of the justice and wisdom of their political views regarding war, they bravely confronted the storm, and applied themselves to the conversion of the nation to the ways of peace. Again they appealed to Mr. McLaren for counsel and aid. Could he repeat the service of the Anti-Corn-Law Conference? Could he organise a national demonstration in Edinburgh in favour of peace when the thoughts of the people were full of war, as he formerly did in favour of Free Trade

1853

when the public sentiment was beginning to run strong against Protection?   Mr. M<sup>c</sup>Laren was not by any means sure.   But he felt that the task ought to be attempted, and he did not stay to count the cost to himself in personal popularity and authority as Chief Magistrate of the capital of Scotland.   He knew the temper of his countrymen—that they were being misled by a strong antipathy to the Czar Nicholas as a supposed foe of human freedom; and recognising that a conference of the friends of peace in Edinburgh would provide a valuable education for them, and in that respect, at all events, prove helpful to the Peace policy advocated by his accomplished and trusted political friends, though it might not immediately arrest the war feeling, he resolved to promote the meeting.   His promise of aid was joyful news to the Peace Society; and Mr. Cobden, full of appreciation of the courage of his Scottish ally, wrote him the following letter, containing as clear and as convincing a statement of the principles of the Peace Society as has ever been penned:—

Bognor, Sussex, *September* 19, 1853.

My dear Sir,—You are going to do a very good but courageous act in giving your countenance to the Peace Conference.   Nowhere has the movement fewer partisans than in Scotland; and the reason is obvious.   First, because your heads are more combative than even the English, which is almost a phrenological miracle; and secondly, the system of our military rule in India has been widely profitable to the middle and upper classes in Scotland, who have had more than their numerical proportion of its patronage; therefore the military party is very strong in your part of the kingdom.

In this Peace Conference movement we have not the same clear and definite principle on which to take our stand that we had in our League agitation.   There are in our ranks those who oppose all war even in self-defence; those who do not go quite so

far, and yet oppose war on religious grounds in all cases but in
pure self-defence; and there are those who, from political, economical, and financial considerations, are not only the advocates of
peace, but also of a diminution of our costly peace establishments.
Amongst the latter class I confess I rank myself; for, without
ignoring the religious aspects of the question, which are so well
advocated by others, I must admit that I have been led to an
active co-operation with the Peace party from a conviction that
their views and principles harmonise with my Free Trade and
economical plans.  And it is probably the best augury for the
complete future triumph of the Peace principle that we have
attained **that age** in the world's progress when man's secular policy
in his international relations is, from motives of interest and
state necessity, brought to the **confirmation of the** truth of revealed
religion.  But unfortunately very few of those who join in the
advocacy of Free Trade understand the moral bearing of the question.  They cannot see that Free Trade throughout the world and
peace and good-will amongst all nations are really convertible
terms.  Besides, we cannot disguise from ourselves that the military spirit pervades the higher and more influential classes of this
country; and that the court, the aristocracy, and all that is aping
the tone of the latter, believe that their interests, privileges, and
even their very security, are bound up in the maintenance of the
" Horse Guards."  Hence the very unfashionable character of our
Peace movement, and hence the difficulty of inducing influential
persons to attend our meetings.  Nor must we lose sight of the
eminence and social power which is given to the military party by
not merely the rank but the emoluments which are bestowed on a
great and united body, having their connections throughout the
length and breadth of the land, thus spreading their roots into
almost every family of influence in the kingdom.  Recollect that
we spend annually in England and our colonies, including India,
*nearly thirty millions sterling* for our military and naval establishments—certainly twice as much as any other country in the world
excepting France, and 50 per cent. more than in that country.
And although in India the expenditure is partly upon the native
regiments, yet *all the commissioned officers are British.*  This vast

amount of income going into the pockets of the military class gives it a money power which is felt in the House, and for which the press will be naturally found to cater. If we add to all this that the character of the English people is arrogant, dictatorial, and encroaching towards foreigners, and that we are always disposed to believe that other nations are preparing to attack England, it must be apparent that, in seeking to diminish our warlike establishments, we have to encounter as tough an opposition as we had in our attack on the Corn-Law monopoly, whilst we look in vain for that powerful nucleus of support which gave us hope in the latter struggle of an eventual triumph.

The tactics of the enemy have hitherto been cunning enough. The soul of the Peace movement is the Quaker sentiment against all war. Without the stubborn zeal of the "Friends" there would be no Peace Society and no Peace Conference. But the enemy takes good care to turn us all into Quakers, because the "non-resistant" principle puts us out of court as practical politicians of the present day. Our opponents insist on it that we wish to totally disarm, and leave ourselves at the mercy of Louis Napoleon and the French,—nay, they say we actually invite them to come and invade us. Now in this respect the enemy is much more exacting than our "Friends," for the latter do not insist upon all who join them in the Peace agitation declaring themselves advocates of the non-resistance principle. The object of this Peace Conference movement has been to construct a platform (as the Americans say) on which all may meet who want to diminish in the slightest degree the chances of war or to reduce to the smallest extent the amount of our military establishments. Nothing is required by the Quakers (who are the most practical and the most tolerant of agitators) beyond the abstinence from all acts or resolutions on the part of the Conference in violation of the principle which they conscientiously advocate. They do not, in fact, insist on our professing their faith—all they ask is that we do not call on them to join in condemning it.

My own connection with the Peace movement arose from no

abstract or theoretical notions on the subject. It occurred thus :— On my return from my long tour on the Continent in 1847 (in the autumn), I found the newspapers filled with the cry of our *defenceless* state· and the dangers of a French invasion. The Duke of Wellington's letter to General Burgoyne was published about the same time, which added fuel to the flame. There was a senseless panic created, which I denounced at several public meetings, and was well abused for it. However, when Parliament met, Lord John proposed an increase of our armaments, the mustering of the militia, and at the same time laid before the House and the country his plan of increasing the income-tax. The country was at the time in great distress, and there was a universal opposition to an augmentation of taxation. He was obliged to withdraw his Budget. Now bear in mind that all this took place during the financial year 1847, in which it will be found we expended upwards of nineteen millions for warlike preparations (including the Kaffir war), and whilst Louis Philippe, the "Napoleon of Peace," was still on the throne. There never was a more impudent attempt to impose upon the public, and it was followed by a *reaction* which led to a *reduction* of our warlike establishments. But then came the advent of Napoleon III. to the imperial throne, and again we heard the cry of our "defenceless situation " and the danger of an "invasion." This time the cry was more successful. The country was prosperous ; there was a surplus revenue, and the Whigs again revived and carried their old project of a militia. From that time to this we have had a succession of appeals to the military spirit of the country in the "camps," "reviews," and public funerals of martial "heroes ;" and never was there a more warlike feeling in England than has been witnessed during the last two years, and never was there' less occasion or justification for such a feeling. It has been under these circumstances that I have been battling against an increase of our armaments. I may add that every pretence for the augmentation of our forces has been invariably exploded within six months of the time when it was put forth, and yet our opponents are as confident and impudent as ever in their tone. In fact, they know they have the prejudices of the people with them, and it is to

gain the people to the side of common sense that we hold these
Peace Conferences.  I have no doubt that we can triumphantly
meet our opponents at a public discussion, and I hope they will
venture to appear at the Edinburgh gathering.  I feel little
doubt about being able to popularise our Peace principles after
a time, and the result of the Edinburgh Conference will have an
important bearing on the future success of our agitation.  I hope
you will induce as many influential people as possible to meet
us on the platform, and it is with a view to place you in a
position to be able to explain to them the character and objects of
our " Peace Congress " that I trouble you with this long letter.

My wife desires to join me in kind remembrance to Mrs.
M<sup>c</sup>Laren and yourself, and believe me ever yours sincerely,

R.  COBDEN.

D. M<sup>c</sup>Laren, Esq., Lord Provost
    of Edinburgh.


It was during the second year of an unprecedentedly busy
Lord Provostship that this call came to Mr. M<sup>c</sup>Laren ; and
though burdened with other public work to an extent
which would have been sufficient for any ordinary man, he
found the time and means of doing for the Peace Society
as abundant service as could have been expected from him
if he had had no other occupation.  Under his vigilant
superintendence arrangements were at once made to organise
a national demonstration.  A local committee was formed
with William Miller of Millerfield and John Wigham at its
head, and a London committee, directed by Henry Richard,
ably assisted them.  Two hundred thousand pamphlets and
tracts were distributed throughout the country ; and the
United Presbyterian Church again cordially and efficiently
co-operated in this preliminary advertising and educational
work.  The Conference, which was held in the month of
October—a few days after the Sultan, assured of British and
French support, had declared war against the Czar—attracted

sympathetic visitors from all parts of Scotland, and a large contingent came from England. Mrs. McLaren was keenly interested in the work, and she was zealously supported by what a contemporary journal described as a small circle "of elegant and cultivated women, who would lend attractiveness and grace to any cause which they might espouse, and who have long taken the cause of peace to their hearts, and whose influence contributed materially and in various ways to the success" of the demonstration. The hospitality of these ladies was severely taxed, but the demands made upon it were met with pride and pleasure. An interesting gathering assembled at Newington House on that occasion, of men and women distinguished for philanthropy and Liberal politics.

The meetings were successful beyond expectation. They extended over two days, including conferences during the day and public meetings in the evening. The committee had engaged the Queen Street Hall for the conferences, but as the hour of the commencement of the proceedings approached, it was evident that the accommodation provided in Queen Street would be insufficient for the increasing host of members and visitors. An adjournment was made to the Music Hall in George Street, and this larger building was quite filled during the day and was densely packed at the evening meetings. The chair on the first evening was taken by Mr. Cowan, one of the Members for the city, and Mr. McLaren presided at the other gatherings, and conducted the proceedings with his usual skill. His opening speech was in harmony with Mr. Cobden's letter, and proved the keynote of the whole demonstration.

"The Peace Conference," he explained, "consists, in fact, of two sections—those who hold the principle that war, in every form, for every purpose, is unlawful, as being opposed to the precepts of Christianity and to the holy spirit of the New Testament. Many members hold these principles as broadly, as strongly, and as unqualifiedly as it is possible to express them; but other members do not hold them, though they cordially concur in deprecating the war spirit, wherever it may be found, in doing everything in their power to repress that war spirit, and in thinking that the armaments, not only of this nation, but of all the nations of the world, are far too powerful; that they lead to war inevitably from the great preparations always made to meet it; and though, no doubt, they are said by our opponents to be made for the preservation of peace, still we believe, however good the intentions of the parties are, they do have the effect of fostering the war spirit. We believe they lead to an enormous waste of the national resources in employing men, who are not required, for no really useful purposes. We therefore agree in thinking that everything should be done in our power to promote the peaceful spirit, to repress the war spirit, and to keep down those great armaments—to act in such a way to all the world that no other nation is likely to have any just cause to quarrel with us. Then, above all, we hold that one great means of preventing war would be an arrangement made between nations when they are in a friendly position towards each other, by getting clauses inserted in the national treaties, providing that any dispute arising may be solved, not by the parties themselves, but by arbiters named in the treaties, to whom the questions shall be referred. In that way those feelings of bitterness and wounded pride, often arising from trifling incidents, but which are blown upon by those who wish to propagate a war spirit, would be kept in abeyance, and the arbiters, irrespective of such feelings, would decide those questions as they arose."

Thus in 1853 Mr. M<sup>c</sup>Laren laid down the principle which Mr. Gladstone and the Liberal party applied in 1871 to the settlement of the controversy with the United States arising out of the depredations of the *Alabama* privateer.

Mr. M<sup>c</sup>Laren, as in the case of the Anti-Corn-Law Conference, was ably and heartily supported by the United Presbyterian ministers. The venerable Dr. John Brown invoked the divine blessing upon the proceedings, and the first resolution was proposed by his accomplished and warm-hearted colleague, Professor McMichael of Dunfermline. The Rev. Dr. George Johnston, of Nicolson Street Church, Edinburgh, the Rev. Henry Renton, of Kelso, the Rev. Dr. Joseph Brown, then of Dalkeith, afterwards of Glasgow, likewise took part in the proceedings, and sustained the reputation of the denomination in those days for public spirit and patriotism. The chief speakers were Mr. Cobden and Mr. Bright. Mr. Edward Miall, Mr. J. B. Smith, Mr. Hadfield, Mr. Charles Hindley, Mr. Lawrence Hayworth, all Members of Parliament; Mr. Biggs (Newport), Mr. James Bell, Mr. Samuel Bowly (Gloucester), Mr. Joseph Sturge, Mr. Thomasson, Mr. Henry Richard, with Bailie Fyfe, Dean of Guild Blackadder, Mr. W. Miller, Mr. H. Wigham, and other prominent citizens, assisted in the discussion. At the concluding meeting the following resolution, proposed by Mr. William Crosskill of Beverley, and seconded by Mr. Richard, was adopted:—

"That the sincerest thanks of this meeting be presented to the Right Honourable the Lord Provost, for the great judgment and ability with which he has presided over this Conference, for the kind and generous welcome he has accorded to its members, and for the cordial manner in which he has lent his great personal and official influence in promoting the objects of the Conference."

Three ringing cheers, led off by Mr. Cobden, emphasised this vote of the Conference. In his reply Mr. McLaren spoke of the work he had rendered as a labour of love, and recalling the humble origin and ultimate success of the Free Trade movement, in which he had locally been associated with Mr. Wigham, he expressed his unbounded conviction in the ultimate, though it might not be the early, triumph of the Peace principle.

"Believing," he said, "as I firmly do, in the Scriptures of truth, I am often amazed how men can appeal to these records and throw ridicule upon the present cause, when they remember that one of the prophecies that we have, and which I for one most sincerely believe, is that the time will come when men shall learn the art of war no more. If men will learn the art of war no more, assuredly the cause of the Peace Conference will then be promoted. I think that everything indicates the growing importance of this great cause, and I will just counsel our friends to follow the same course which was followed in the case of that confederation for Free-Trade which has proved such a blessing for this country, to go on perseveringly, straightforwardly, and determinedly, neither turning to the right nor left, abusing nobody, going into no collateral question, but just holding right at it and keeping it before the public mind. The public mind will be in the end enlightened; your members will be enlightened; and Parliament will then give effect to the wishes of the constituency. The Government of the day will give way; they will exercise their influence in this direction; and the influence which they will have on the other Governments of Europe will be such, that I have no doubt there are persons in this meeting at the present time who will live to see this cause all but triumphant."

According to the testimony of the press of the time, whether friendly or unfriendly to the objects in view, the Conference was a magnificent success; and its representative character, as well as the high tone and ability of the speeches, powerfully affected public opinion throughout the country. The *Herald of Peace* regarded the Conference as certainly equal in interest and importance to any "of the series of remarkable meetings for the purpose of promoting international peace which during the last five or six years have been taking the round of the European capitals;" and after reciting various causes which contributed to the great success achieved, the official organ of the Peace Society concluded :—

"But perhaps more than all other circumstances of a local nature was the fact that we had as Chief Magistrate of the city a gentleman of rare abilities, and of a commanding weight of character, who did not hesitate to identify himself with the Conference, not only by presiding over several of the meetings with admirable wisdom and tact, but by giving to us the advantage of his counsel and experience in private, and by welcoming with the most large-hearted and generous hospitality the strangers who visited the city on the occasion. Nor must we forget the characteristic frankness and cordiality with which Mr. Cowan, one of the Members for the city, consented to bear part in our proceedings."

This Conference undoubtedly proved influential in steadying public opinion in Scotland, and more especially in encouraging the Nonconformist clergy in their fidelity as public teachers of the gospel of peace. But in England the war feeling strengthened as the terrible struggle in the Crimea proceeded, and the Peace party found their political position increasingly precarious. Mr. M<sup>c</sup>Laren's sympathy, however, did not fail, though he declined an earnest invitation from Mr. Sturge to go with him on a Peace Mission to St. Petersburg.

Mr. Bright's steadfastness also remained unshaken. Throughout he was irreconcilably opposed to the Crimean War. In a letter dated March 5, 1855, he wrote to his brother-in-law :— Mr. Bright and the Crimean War.

"I am one of those who believe the fundamental error to be in the *policy* rather than the management. The latter may be bad, but no management could have repaired the idiotic blundering of the policy. To go to the Crimea was lunacy, and no amount of *method* will make lunacy anything but lunacy. . . . The death of the Emperor of Russia is supposed to be favourable to peace. I believe he was for peace, and that his opponents were not. I shall rejoice, however, if this startling event shall put an end to the war. My speech for an armistice met the feelings of the House, and probably more than fifty members on both sides have told me so in private. I hope it will have done something to make peace more possible. . . . The Peelites sit on our bench—have, indeed, taken our seats—but I know not if they have any notion of acting with us. Lord Aberdeen, I believe, advised them to consort with us, though he was opposed to their resignation of office. I suspect, however, we go too *straight* in our course, and too uncompromising to permit of our ever becoming a numerous party. We can pioneer, but we cannot lead, when there is so little principle and so much self-seeking abroad."

But the secession of the Peelites from the Government caused no sensible diminution of the strength of the war party. On the contrary, it seemed to strengthen the authority of Lord Palmerston, who, in popular estimation, was the head and front of the war policy, and who, after the close of the Crimean War, made himself in public estimation increasingly necessary to the nation by his management of the controversy with China which then emerged. More and more he became master of the situation, and more and more did the seceding Peelites and the Peace party feel their political influence as friends of peace decline.

Defeat of the Manchester School.

In anticipation of the general election of 1857, Mr. M<sup>c</sup>Laren wrote to Sir James Graham, as one of the leading Peelites, for his view of the situation. Sir James in his reply, dated House of Commons, 12th March 1857, did not conceal his apprehension that a terrible defeat was impending. " The reports," he said, " which I receive from the country lead me to believe that the Liberal party will give effect in these cases to a blind confidence in Lord Palmerston, which I cannot express, because I cannot feel it." This prognostication was only too fully verified. Sir James Graham himself retained his seat for Carlisle, though not without a struggle; but the Peace party, then generally described as the Manchester School, was temporarily banished from the parliamentary arena.

1857

The reaction soon came, and one of the first signs of the change was Mr. Bright's unopposed return for Birmingham. The general election which proved so disastrous to the Peace party was fought in April, and by the following August the rejected of Manchester was the unanimously chosen of the capital of the Midlands. The unexpected vacancy in the representation of Birmingham was caused by the death of Mr. George F. Muntz. At this time Mr. Bright, shattered in health by the prolonged strain of his conflict with the war party in Parliament, deeply suffering, too, from the patriotic grief caused by the profound conviction that a disastrous national blunder—in his eyes a great crime—had been and was still being committed, was resting at Newington House after his return from a holiday in the South of Europe. The telegraphic despatches urging Mr. Bright to accept nomination at Birmingham reached him there, and were followed by a visit from Mr. Joseph Sturge to press the request still further. Both Mr. and Mrs. McLaren earnestly and affectionately advised compliance with the call, and Mr. McLaren promptly offered to abandon his other engagements for the time, and to place himself unreservedly at his service till the election should be over. Fortunately for Birmingham and the country, Mr. Bright yielded, and Mr. McLaren accompanied him to Tamworth, where they met representatives of the Liberal party from Birmingham. There Mr. Bright penned his election address; and feeling unfit at the time to face the ordeal of a personal canvass or a public meeting, he gladly and gratefully consented to let Mr. McLaren go to Birmingham as his deputy. To the general surprise, no opposition was offered.  A Conservative candidate had been spoken of, but when it was known that Mr. Bright had consented to solicit the suffrages of the constituency, Mr. Adderley, the then local leader of the Tory party in Birmingham, wrote intimating that the seat would not be claimed, and courteously invited Mr. Bright to accept the hospitality of his house.  Mr. McLaren, speaking from the hustings on the day of nomination, made graceful acknowledgment of this generous behaviour on the part of a political opponent.  He likewise, in Mr. Bright's name, very cordially thanked the constituency for the high distinction which had been so handsomely conferred upon him.



"They were aware," he said, "that Mr. Bright, in the careful and toilsome attention he devoted to the duties of his office, in his painstaking and conscientious attendance in committees by day and at the debates of the House by night, had so seriously impaired his health that it was impossible for him any longer to take part in public matters.  His affection was not merely a physical ailment; it was the result of an overworked brain in the service of his country.  His medical advisers said, that although he might seem to be pretty well, although he could read and speak as well as ever he did in his life, that he must give his brain at least two years' repose before he ventured into any kind of excitement, and they laid down a strict injunction, that not only should he refrain from public speaking, but he should not appear at public meetings, where exciting circumstances might occur to bring back the disorder, which, he trusted and hoped, a merciful Providence had now removed.  Eighteen months of that period had now elapsed; the two years will have expired ere he could be called upon to take his seat in Parliament, and it was his (Mr. McLaren's) firm belief, and Mr. Bright's own hope, and the hope of his friends, that when Parliament assembled he would be able to take his place and to advocate their interests in the Commons House of Parliament."

Few of Mr. M<sup>c</sup>Laren's public acts afforded him more
genuine satisfaction than this participation in the introduction of Mr. Bright to a political connection which has
been maintained unbroken for more than thirty years.
He welcomed the unopposed return at Birmingham not
merely as a personal compliment to Mr. Bright, but as
the sign of a healthy change in public opinion; for, referring to his friend's address penned at Tamworth, he
showed the change was not with him. "Mr. Bright," he
said, "came forward with no apology, with no retractations,
with no expressions of sorrow, and with no promises of
amendment; but he came forward saying that he had
been advocating his country's interests and the rights of the
working-classes, that he was the supporter of good legislation of every kind; so he would continue honestly to
advocate the views which he believed to be right, whether
they should be consonant or not with the popular opinions
of the day."   But possibly Mr. M<sup>c</sup>Laren's chief satisfaction
was derived from his knowledge that Mr. Bright was at the
time turning his attention to a work dear to his own heart,
viz., the enfranchisement of the working-classes; and he
was assured that the new Member for Birmingham would
make use of his commanding position and his commanding
talents for the advancement of this cause. "They knew,"
said Mr. M<sup>c</sup>Laren on the hustings, "that a Reform Bill was
talked of, and that Government intended proposing one;
but John Bright would have no sham measure of reform;
and he would be supported by the power of Birmingham in
devoting his time, his talent, and energy to the promotion
of the enfranchisement of the great body of the people."

In a speech previously quoted at the Edinburgh Peace
Conference of 1853, Mr. M<sup>c</sup>Laren confidently anticipated the
recognition by the country and the Government of inter-

national arbitration as the only right and satisfactory means of settling international disputes.  Public opinion, however, ripens slowly.  It was not until twenty years afterwards that a resolution was passed by the House of Commons affirming the principle of international arbitration, although in the previous year the British Government had so far entered into the views of earnest Liberals on this question as to concur with the United States in a reference of the " Alabama " claims to an International Court of Arbitration at Geneva. This resolution, brought forward by Henry Richard, was passed on the 6th of July 1873, on which day Mr. and Mrs. M<sup>c</sup>Laren celebrated their silver wedding.  This coincidence is recorded in one of Mrs. M<sup>c</sup>Laren's interesting letters :—

" . . . You will be sorry to hear of the disappointment which attended the celebration of our silver wedding.  We had expected to have had a very interesting 'at home,' as so many of our friends seemed interested in it, and I was especially pleased that so many of our parliamentary friends had agreed to come, as this gratified your father.  But there is often a law of compensation in our disappointments, and certainly it was so in this case.  Henry Richard, the Member for Merthyr-Tydvil, had a motion in favour of arbitration, and on that very night the debate came on.  He made an admirable speech.  Mr. Gladstone replied, but the motion was carried by a majority of 10 in a House of nearly 200 members.  This kept all our parliamentary friends tied to the House, but I wrote to Henry Richard congratulating him upon having had the great honour of carrying, for the first time in the House of Commons, a vote in favour of arbitration, and said I would rather have had our silver wedding associated with that event than with the most brilliant assemblage London could have gathered together." [1]

---

[1] Congratulations were sent to Henry Richard from Garibaldi, Senator Sumner, &c., &c., and he afterwards travelled to the Continent to receive support for his views, and a banquet was held in his honour in Rome.

# CHAPTER XVI.

## *INDEPENDENT LIBERALISM IN EDINBURGH.*

1841

ALTHOUGH Mr. M<sup>c</sup>Laren never lacked among his fellow-citizens recognition of his talents and services, as expressed on one occasion by a public testimonial, at other times by elevation to local offices of dignity and authority, and at all times by the confidence of friends and the respect of the citizens generally, yet the distinction of parliamentary representative was withheld from him longer than his political associates in England and his admirers in Scotland expected. His special aptitude for parliamentary service was known and acknowledged beyond the limits of the constituency of the Scottish capital, long before he appeared in the parliamentary arena. That he did not sooner obtain the opportunity through the natural and legitimate channel, the suffrages of his fellow-citizens, was the subject of frequent remark, and of much regret amongst statesmen who had been brought in contact with him through Edinburgh business, and who knew his influence and power, and especially among the Anti-Corn-Law Leaguers and members of the Manchester School, who valued him as one of their most accomplished allies, and also among the Scottish Dissenters and Radicals, who trusted him as their leader. But Mr. M<sup>c</sup>Laren was not, in the ordinary sense of the term, an ambitious man. To him public service was at once a duty and a pleasure, to be sought not merely for the gratification of personal ambition or the promotion of personal interests, but from a patriotic regard for the public welfare. He diligently strove to qualify himself for the highest form and sphere of this service. But as a public man his aspirations were not centred in St. Stephens. We could cite many of his letters, written to his public friends as well as those of a private character, to show how steadfastly he resisted all proposals that he should enter Parliament. The applications for him to do so were frequent both in England and Scotland; but he never yielded, even where there was an assurance that his election expenses would be paid. He occasionally said to those to whom he could speak in confidence that he could only be tempted to enter Parliament under one condition, namely, as Member for the city of Edinburgh, which would be to him a proof of the trust reposed in him by his fellow-citizens. And when at last this proof was so abundantly given, no one ever entered St. Stephens with a greater feeling of pride and pleasure.

He was resolved that, if he ever entered Parliament, it should be as an independent Member. It was this sterling quality of independence, possibly carried in some instances too far, which aroused against him antagonisms of which less single-minded men know nothing. In Edinburgh the forces of the great parties were organised under a system approximating to military discipline, and under such a system no place could be found for one who thought for himself, and who even flouted the opinions of " heads of the party." Monopolists and sinecurists of course regarded him as an inveterate and incorruptible enemy, and Mr. M<sup>c</sup>Laren had reason to know better than most men the hold which privilege had on Edinburgh under the restricted franchise, which was maintained until 1868.

When, therefore, proposals were made to him to accept nomination as a candidate—as they were on the occasion of every vacancy that occurred after the elevation of Mr. Abercromby to the peerage and of Sir John Campbell to the Lord Chancellorship—two considerations naturally presented themselves to his mind, though he did not parade them. First, there was the economic difficulty, because Mr. McLaren was at no time a wealthy man; and secondly, he had to consider that the upper classes, and all the partisans of privilege in "Church, Army, Physic, Law," would, under the guidance of the political committees, array themselves against him, and that he could only look for success when the Liberal sentiment of the constituency was sufficiently strong and the Liberal party sufficiently organised to overbear the combined forces of Whiggery and Toryism. These considerations forced him to resist the innocent stratagems of eager friends to allure him into acquiescence in nomination on the resignation of Sir John Campbell in 1840, and again when they judged it necessary to oppose Mr. Macaulay in 1846 and 1847, and to wait until time should declare itself on his side.

*[Margin: 1841]*

To the removal of these hindrances to Radical progress he for many years applied his talents and energies as a political leader and organiser. He set himself to establish an Independent Liberal party in Edinburgh—a party comprehensive yet compactly knit together, combining the various cohorts of Dissenters, Free Traders, and Social Reformers, into one invincible legion, deriving its strength from conviction and mutual sympathy, as well as from discipline and loyalty, and making its influence felt in the constituency and in Parliament as representative of men in earnest about Liberal principles.

*[Margin: Organisation of Independent Liberalism.]*

At the time of the changes in the representation of the

city caused by the elevation of Mr. Abercromby and Sir John Campbell to higher spheres, Mr. M<sup>c</sup>Laren had not yet broken with the Whigs, and he was a consenting party to, though not an active promoter of, the selection first of Mr. Macaulay and afterwards of Mr. Gibson-Craig; but he had given expression to his dissatisfaction with the close system of nomination by committees, and his desire that the representation of the capital of Scotland should be in the hands of men independent of Ministerial influence and official rank. Without causing any breach of friendship, he had frankly told his views to Mr. Abercromby on his elevation to the peerage as Lord Dunfermline; and on this and cognate subjects he continued to receive from him for many years afterwards long and elaborate letters. With Sir John Campbell, then Attorney-General, he had been equally frank, and when, in 1841, the Attorney-General was suddenly transformed into the Lord Chancellor of Ireland, Mr. M<sup>c</sup>Laren received from him the following note :—

LONDON, *June* 21, 1841.

MY DEAR SIR,—I am exceedingly solicitous that you should have no misgivings respecting the sincerity and good faith with which I have acted with a view to the coming election. When I sent down my address which has appeared in the newspapers, I do solemnly assure you that I had not the remotest notion that anything could have occurred to prevent me from offering myself as a candidate, and if chosen, serving as your representative. It was not till within a few hours of my farewell address that I knew to the contrary. And now I will cordially thank you for all your kindness to Sir J. Campbell, although the Attorney-General has lately thought himself a little hardly used by you. Of course I cannot in the smallest degree interfere in the choice of my successor, but I do most earnestly hope that the constituency of Edinburgh will long enjoy their present reputation for purity and independence, for public spirit and moderation, and for the steady pursuit of attainable objects.—I remain, dear Mr. M<sup>c</sup>Laren,                                        J. CAMPBELL.

Mr. M<sup>c</sup>Laren in his answer appears to have expressed his wish that the city should have the service of two Independent Liberals, and the Lord Chancellor in his letter of acknowledgment said :—

" I must ever take a hearty interest in Edinburgh affairs, and I thank you most cordially for the explicit avowal of your sentiments and intentions.

" But I cannot help hoping, that if you find that you have two Members who vote for all the public measures you wish to support, and satisfactorily transact all the private business of the city, you will be contented with them although they are called Whigs."

In anticipation of Mr. M<sup>c</sup>Laren's nomination for one of the seats, a Church and Tory writer referred to him as " long the pet of the Whig clique " and " now to be the protegé of the Whig Government." The separation, however, as has been shown, was in actual process at the very time the Church and Tory party thought the union fastest. Mr. M<sup>c</sup>Laren's robust and progressively Liberal principles were becoming increasingly masterful in determining his political course and relationships, while the Edinburgh Whigs, falling more and more under the domination of officialism, were disappointing and offending old friends by the adoption of a time-serving rest-and-be-thankful policy. This divergence, as has already been seen, was greatly accelerated during the Free Trade struggle, and, like the old Secession fathers, Mr. M<sup>c</sup>Laren was forced by stress of conscience to go " without the camp." Henceforth his former political allies became his bitterest opponents. Tory opposition remained, and he never sought to conciliate it ; but it was a toothless, harmless thing compared with the animosity of the men who professed a creed similar to his own, yet feared to apply it lest they should injure party interests. Mr. M<sup>c</sup>Laren, on his part, was equally resolute and active, and proved a foe of indomitable courage and ever-growing strength, who plainly meant to win, and had no thoughts of acquiescence in his own suppression. His first great battle with the Whigs was a sufficiently notable success. Mr. Macaulay's Liberalism was of a different type from his. It had shown itself irresolute and compromising during the Free Trade agitation; it was comparatively apathetic with regard to parliamentary reform; and it looked at concurrent endowment, and not at disestablishment, as the means of meeting the irresistible demands of religious equality. Those leading Liberals in the constituency whom the Whig chiefs had estranged not unnaturally applied to the gentleman whom Mr. Macaulay had indicated as his probable antagonist. A deputation, consisting of Sir James Forrest, Mr. Thomson of Banchory, and Mr. Campbell of Monzie, waited on Mr. M<sup>c</sup>Laren and offered him the support of the Free Church party; but, for the reasons already referred to, he declined nomination. He, however, readily entered into the proposed opposition, and Mr. Charles Cowan, a prominent Free Churchman, and long an intimate friend of Dr. Chalmers, was named as a candidate. Mr. M<sup>c</sup>Laren, willing to bring Dissenters and Free Churchmen together on the common platform of resistance to endowments, organised the coalition, which, while it secured the return of Mr. Cowan, also laid the foundation of the future " Independent Liberal " organisation, which, under Mr. M<sup>c</sup>Laren's leadership, became the dominant political force in Edinburgh.

At the general election of 1852 the first serious reverse was sustained. In anticipation of the election, and in the knowledge of Sir William Gibson-Craig's withdrawal from parliamentary life, the committee which had secured the return of Mr. Cowan at the previous election met to consider whether they and the opposition Liberal Committee could not agree to the unopposed return of Mr. Bouverie as Mr. Cowan's colleague. At this meeting Mr. M<sup>c</sup>Laren, who was then Lord Provost, moved and carried a resolution to the effect that the Independent Committee should prefer a candidate who favoured vote by ballot and triennial Parliaments. This resolution was interpreted by the Whigs as tantamount to the rejection of the candidature of Mr. Bouverie; and most of Mr. Cowan's " Moderate Liberal " friends, taking alarm, withdrew from the committee. Meanwhile the friends of Mr. M<sup>c</sup>Laren in the Independent Committee pressed him to accept nomination for one of the two seats about to be declared vacant, and they received the following reply :—

EDINBURGH, *June* 10, 1852.

GENTLEMEN,—I feel much gratified by the information you have conveyed to me, that, at a numerously attended meeting of the Independent Committee, specially called for the purpose of considering my claims, it was resolved, by a nearly unanimous vote, to request me to allow myself to be nominated to represent the city in Parliament, in room of Sir William Gibson-Craig, who, to the general regret of the inhabitants, has declined again to solicit their suffrages, and that the meeting pledged themselves to use every legitimate effort to secure my return.

I have, at the same time, carefully considered the opinions expressed to me, to the effect that the same degree of unanimity which was manifested by the committee may be fairly assumed to exist amongst the great body of the independent voters, by whom that committee was elected at the different ward meetings throughout the city, and that the feeling in my favour amongst other sections of the Liberal party, not connected with

the Independent Committee, is such that I may reasonably calculate on the cordial support of a large majority of the whole
Liberal electors.

Assuming that these anticipations were well founded, I should
feel it to be my duty, in the circumstances, to respond to the
call; and if elected, I would do my best to represent the interest
of the inhabitants of all classes.  If, however, it were found that
my nomination did not meet with that measure of support from
the Liberal party generally which you have anticipated, and that
some other candidate could more successfully unite the different
sections than I could hope to do, in that case I should greatly
prefer remaining in my present position to being returned by a
narrow majority, or by any merely sectional influence; for without the moral power which would flow from being returned by a
decided majority of the whole Liberal electors, I feel that I could
not fill the office either with advantage to the public or comfort
to myself.

In these circumstances I place myself in your hands, leaving
it to you to ascertain the feeling in my favour in such a way as
you may think best.

With the most grateful feelings towards you, and all the
other members of the committee, for your kindness, and for the
great honour which has been done me, I am, gentlemen, yours
faithfully,                                    D. M<sup>c</sup>LAREN.

To Wm. M'Crie, Esq., Chairman, and the other Members<br>of the Independent Committee.

Five days afterwards a public meeting of the electors held
in the Music Hall confirmed the committee's invitation,
and Mr. M<sup>c</sup>Laren decided to go to the poll.  By this time
he had discovered that an active effort was being made to
withdraw support from him on the ground that his opposition to the Maynooth grant was based on Voluntary, and
not on "sound Protestant principles."  Mr. M<sup>c</sup>Laren,
in taking note of this objection, boldly and successfully
vindicated his consistency as a Protestant and a Voluntary.

He declared " without qualification or hesitation " that he held as decided Protestant principles as any man in Edinburgh; that his Protestantism and the Protestantism of the United Presbyterian Church, with which he was connected, was based on the New Testament, which is " opposed to the whole spirit and genius and scope of Popery; " that he considered Popery scripturally wrong and most injurious in its effects on civil and religious liberty, and that these convictions had been greatly confirmed by personal observations of the operation of Roman Catholicism in Madeira and Spain.   But he was opposed to the Maynooth grant on the ground of the injustice of all Government grants to religious bodies, and not only because of his objection to the endowment of error ; and he was ready to vote against all grants as he had opportunity. He continued :—

" The body to which I belong has no grant.   It desires none. It would take none.   I am prepared to put other bodies having grants in the same position.   Therefore I will do what I can to abolish the Maynooth grant; but I repudiate the principle which some gentlemen hold, that unless you class them altogether, the Maynooth grant, the Regium Donum, and all other grants— unless you put them, as it were, in a bag and set fire to them altogether, you are not to touch any of them.   I repudiate any such principle, and will hold by the Scripture precept to do good as I have opportunity ; and, opposed as I am to all these grants from the Consolidated Fund, apart from the question of Church Establishments, which stands on its own footing, I will vote against them all as they turn up, without regarding which comes first or which comes second.   If the Maynooth grant comes up alone, I will vote against it ; if it comes up with the Regium Donum, I will vote against them both ; if the Regium Donum comes up first, I will vote against it.   If the grant for the Episcopal clergy in the West Indies comes up, I will vote against it; and let them come in whatever form or shape they please, I will vote against them all."



The supporters of Mr. Cowan generally refused to be conciliated, and a second Free Church candidate, Mr. Campbell of Monzie, was started, apparently for the purpose of preventing the second votes of Free Churchmen going to the Lord Provost. At this election Mr. Macaulay was nominated without his consent being asked. It was felt by many Liberals that Mr. Macaulay's high position and past services to Liberalism marked him out as a suitable Member for the metropolitan constituency, and that, since the Corn-laws were repealed, minor differences might on this occasion be overlooked. And although the two men differed so widely as to the basis of their Liberalism, some of the most intellectual and earnest Liberals in Edinburgh supported the candidature of Mr. Macaulay and Mr. McLaren, on the common ground of political integrity, knowledge of affairs, and ability to serve the country.

The Conservative party, of course, supported their own candidate, the Hon. T. C. Bruce: of these, only 35 gave their second votes to Lord Provost McLaren, while Mr. Cowan received 398 Conservative votes, and Mr. Macaulay 186. A large number of the Tory electors kept themselves in reserve until the last hour; but about three o'clock they held a meeting, and finding from the state of the poll, which was, in those days of open voting, known from hour to hour, that Mr. McLaren stood second, and would be returned as Mr. Macaulay's colleague, they went in a body to give their votes for Mr. Cowan, and thus secured his return; a proceeding which called forth a strong condemnatory expression even from Mr. Cowan himself, whose high moral nature shrank from the position of owing his seat to an electoral manœuvre, and entering the House of Commons by the power of the Tory vote. Considering the unfortunate effect of the cross-voting on his candidature, it is not surprising that Mr. McLaren only came out third at the declaration of the poll. The result of the poll was: Macaulay, 1872; Cowan, 1754; McLaren, 1559; Bruce, 1066; Campbell, 626. Mr. McLaren was undoubtedly the popular candidate. He obtained the "show of hands," which in those days preceded the actual election, and he found comfort in the fact that he had received the support of the majority of electors who claimed to be Liberals. At the declaration of the poll he said:—

*1852*

*Popular candidates defeated.*

"I have the honour of having had recorded in my favour the votes of 1559 independent electors, not gathered together from all the corners of the globe, but the very heart's-blood of the Liberal party. All of us are united as the friends of civil and religious liberty. We recognise no large parties among us—neither the Conservative party, nor the old Whig party, nor the Church party, nor the Catholic party, nor the Free Church party, nor any party, but the citizens of Edinburgh, who wish to support me irrespective of party combinations. The great effort," Mr. McLaren added good-humouredly, "that has been made to keep me out is the greatest compliment that was ever paid to me. The fact that the Tory party thought it worth while to come forward at the end of the day, and thought fit to make this effort to throw me out, was the greatest compliment that could be rendered to me. I feel exceedingly proud of the distinction that has thus been conferred."

*The hostile coalition.*

A point in Mr. McLaren's character that often extorted the involuntary admiration of his opponents was that throughout ife he was able to maintain an even temper and a cheerful exterior under adverse circumstances. On this occasion Mr. McLaren, unmoved by defeat, returned to the congenial duties of Lord Provost, which, as shown in another chapter, he discharged with unsurpassed efficiency and popularity. In a letter referring to his defeat he said, " The disappointment is greater to my friends than to myself; the result has not cost me five minutes' sleep."

A bye-election.

Shortly after the expiry of the Lord Provost's term of office, the retirement of Mr. Macaulay from the representation of the city was announced, and Mr. M<sup>c</sup>Laren was again earnestly pressed to accept nomination. He explained in a letter to the chairman of his electoral committee, Mr. W. M<sup>c</sup>Crie, that he did not feel the call of any urgent public question with which he was closely associated at that particular moment, and that the conditions which observation and experience had convinced him were essential to a successful candidature did not then exist. The wounds inflicted by the Independent Liberal party on themselves were indeed beginning to heal, but the party organisation was far from satisfactory; and besides, it was not at a bye-election, when only one seat was vacant, but at a general election, when the question of the whole representation of the city was to be decided, that he intended again to enter the field. He wished, if sent to Parliament at all, to go with a like-minded colleague, and with a definite popular commission to serve the city in the House of Commons during the full lifetime of a Parliament. Many of his friends were more confident than he, and they persuaded Mr. Francis Brown Douglas to accept nomination as an Independent Liberal against Mr. Adam Black, proposed by the "Aggregate Liberal" or Whig committee. Mr. Brown Douglas's candidature quite coincided with

Mr. Brown Douglas's candidature.

Mr. M<sup>c</sup>Laren's scheme of party reconstruction. As a trusted Liberal, and as a loyal energetic Free Churchman, Mr. Brown Douglas brought the larger sections of the Nonconformists once more to the same political platform, and prepared the way for the ultimate union.  His disinterested attempt to keep together the "Independent Liberal" organisation proved advantageous to the party with which he connected himself, but it did not, unfortunately, reward him with the personal success which, under other circumstances, his talents and high character might have attained.  The name and record of Mr. Black's services to the city outweighed the claims of the Independent Liberal candidate, and secured for the Whig committee another decided victory at the poll.

Mr. M^cLaren did not initiate the opposition to Mr. Black, but he openly and energetically supported it.  In his letter written to Mr. Black's sons after the publication of the "Memoirs" in 1885, he thus explained and defended his action :—

"The account given of your father's election, in so far as my agency in the matter is concerned, is calculated to mislead.  I am made to appear as having acted from personal motives against Mr. Black.  Nothing could be more incorrect.  I was opposed to him on all the pressing questions of the day.  He was a staunch old Whig, and one of the leaders of that party.  I was a staunch Radical.  I was opposed to him about the Maynooth grant and the extension of the suffrage.  I was for the total abolition of the Annuity-tax; and I had been, as a member of the Anti-Corn-Law League, in favour of *total and immediate repeal,* while Mr. Black took the part of the Whigs, who would be content with a fixed duty, as is explained in Mr. Macaulay's letter printed in the 'Memoirs.'  Mr. Black was in favour of the *principle* of total repeal, but could not persuade his friends to go for it; and he did not go against the Government or Whigs on that point, as we of the League did.  It was because I was opposed to the candidate on all the leading political questions of the day that I opposed him.  He did not represent my political opinions, and therefore I did not support him.

"Again, it is in effect stated that I had personally managed to bring together all the political sections who are said to have combined to oppose Mr. Black and support Mr. Brown Douglas. I was very active in the cause individually. I have no recollection who proposed Mr. Douglas, but I am quite certain that I never met with or canvassed any of the separate sections who are said to have combined against Mr. Black. My belief is that they did not act as separate bodies, but as men each acting on his own opinion. I acted with the Voluntaries, and perhaps as their head. I believed that Mr. Brown Douglas would better represent my opinions than Mr. Black, and therefore I gave him all the support in my power, as it was my duty to do as an honest man. Mutual friendships imply mutual obligations and mutual rights, equal on both sides.

"One of the brothers whom I have the pleasure of addressing recently made a speech in entire accordance with my opinions,[1] and if my relative, Mr. Renton,[2] had held old Whig opinions, I should certainly have voted for Mr. Black, if I had possessed a vote. In like manner I should certainly have voted against Mr. Goschen, and in favour of the Radical candidate, who holds my opinions. I entirely disapprove the principle in vogue in some quarters, that a vote for an M.P. may be dealt with as a mere matter of personal friendship or liking or disliking. I hold it to be a great moral wrong for a voter to act on such views. In 1852, when I stood, Mr. Black did not give me his influence or even his personal vote, but exercised some influence—I don't know how much—against me, as is substantially admitted in the 'Memoirs' (p. 165); but I never complained, publicly or privately, of this, believing that Mr. Black acted according to the dictates of his own conscience. Why, then, should I not have equal liberty to exercise any influence I might have from pure motives for the supposed public good against him?"

In 1857 Mr. Cowan and Mr. Black were returned with-

---

[1] Mr. Adam W. Black, who stood as a candidate for the Central Division of Edinburgh at the general election of 1885.

[2] Mr. James Hall Renton, who contested the same Division.

out opposition; and in 1859 Mr. Moncreiff, then Lord Advocate, taking the place of Mr. Cowan, obtained, in company with Mr. Black, a tenure of the seat till 1865. The two Members had thus a long period of probation, and during its course they did not succeed in winning the support of the Independent Liberals. It may be doubted whether any efforts of theirs would have achieved such results, because there was the element of personal preference of Mr. M<sup>c</sup>Laren as a representative. Matters were still further complicated by the well-meant but unsuccessful efforts of the city Members to settle the Annuity-tax. Against this so-called settlement of the Annuity-Tax controversy thousands of persons protested as an aggravation of the evil, which made roupings (distraints) for ministers' money in the midst of exasperated crowds a painfully frequent occurrence. In the next place, Mr. Black, veteran reformer though he was, had, in opposition to one of the established articles of the Liberal creed, spoken and voted against schemes of franchise extension submitted to the House. Nor had the growing desire of constituencies that Members should give an annual account of their stewardship been met by Messrs. Black and Moncreiff, who abstained entirely from addressing the electors during the existence of this Parliament. This neglect, combined with other sources of dissatisfaction, added to the unpopularity of the Members.

In the summer of 1865 a few resolute men, with the Anti-Annuity-Tax Association as a nucleus, recognising Mr. M<sup>c</sup>Laren as the true leader of the Advanced Liberal party, raised again the standard of independence. During his absence at Clifton, near Bristol, whither he had taken up his winter residence on account of the health of one of his children, these friends promoted a requisition calling on

1865:  him to accept nomination as a citizens' candidate.[1] The first intimation of their intention was conveyed by a letter from Mr. Josiah Livingston ; and before Mr. M^cLaren could return to Edinburgh the requisitionists had obtained upwards of three thousand signatures, had induced Mr. Miller of Leithen to accept the position of second candidate along with Mr. M^cLaren, and had organised themselves into a powerful electoral committee.  Mr. Hugh Rose, one of the ablest representatives of one of the most resolute sections of Liberal Dissenters, and Mr. W. M^cCrie, the genial-hearted chairman of the electoral committee who fought the battle of 1852, were joint-chairmen of Mr. M^cLaren's committee, and Mr. John Wilson (afterwards Member for one of the present divisions of the city) was honorary secretary.  Associated with them were staunch friends like Bailie Fyfe, Mr. David M^cLaren, Mr. T. Ireland, Mr. James G. Marshall, Mr. Millar of Sheardale, Dr. Moir, Mr. Josiah Livingston, and. Mr. Thomas Nelson, prominent citizens and influential Free Church laymen; Anti-Annuity-Tax irreconcilables of the stamp of Councillor Stott, Mr. James Richardson, Mr. George Laing, Mr. J. G. Tunny, Mr. George Burn, Mr. J. H.

---

[1] Subjoined is a copy of the requisition which was presented to Mr. M^cLaren asking him to stand as a parliamentary candidate in 1865 :—

" *To Duncan M^cLaren, Esq., of Newington House.*

" SIR,—We, the undersigned electors in the city of Edinburgh, in view of the approaching general parliamentary election, hereby request you to allow yourself to be nominated as a candidate for the representation of the city; and in the event of your compliance with this requisition, we pledge ourselves to give you our active support.  (Signed) Francis Richardson, G. Burn,* Andrew Fyfe, John Cochrane, William Paterson, J. H. Stott,* Archibald Young,* David Lewis,* A. E. Macknight, Thomas Menzies,* Robert Murray, A. Alexander, Peter Methven,* John Richardson, James Tunny, Hugh Wetherston,* George Laing,* James Richardson.* "

[The asterisk after the name denotes that those affixing it had had goods sold at the market-cross for non-payment of the Annuity-tax.]

Balgarnie, and Mr. Pirrett; Mr. Thomas Knox, Mr. David Lewis, Mr. David Dickson, and Admiral Peat, honourably distinguished as social reformers and enjoying deserved popularity; outspoken Councillor Ford, Mr. Fullarton, publisher, Mr. John Weir, Mr. James Young, Mr. Robert Goodsir, Mr. John Greig, Mr. Hugh Brown, and many others known to be true to the Independent Liberal programme. The spontaneity and unanimity of this summons, the evidence of thorough organisation which was afforded, and the provision of a second candidate, meeting as they did all the requirements of success for which he had formerly stipulated, gave Mr. M*Laren much gratification; and on his return from England he unhesitatingly and unconditionally placed himself in the hands of the requisitionists. Shortly afterwards, at a crowded and enthusiastic meeting of citizens in Queen Street Hall, the action of the requisitionists was fully endorsed, and the candidature of Mr. M*Laren and Mr. Miller formally approved.

At this meeting Mr. M*Laren delivered a telling electioneering address. He reminded the electors that he had not of his own accord come forward to claim the seat for himself and Mr. Miller against the Lord Advocate and Mr. Black, but he had been called forth by the rightful owners of the seats. Mr. Black and the Lord Advocate, he said, "were elected for a definite term of years. The present Parliament has lived longer than any Parliament in our recollection. The term is expired, the seats are vacant, and it is not for them to say 'The seats are ours.' The seats are yours, and it is for you to say whom you want to represent you." Ringing cheers, again and again renewed, welcomed this vindication of free popular election against the monopolising claim of " the Government Whig party, by far the smallest party in the city."[1] Quite as hearty and resolute was the applause which enforced the speaker's protest against the objectionable Annuity-Tax Act of 1860, and "the arbitrary and despotic manner" in which that Act had been enforced upon the community. Specially effective was the exposure of Lord Advocate Moncreiff's supposed inconsistency in accepting as a colleague one who, as a Member, had opposed the Government's Reform policy. Pressing home this inconsistency, and daringly testing popular opinion as to the sincerity of the Palmerstonians as Reformers, Mr. McLaren continued :—

"Now, if the Lord Advocate be regarded as the head and organ of the Government in Scotland, I would like to put this question, which I hope he will answer at his next meeting. How comes it that he allies himself with a man who has so strongly opposed the Government on these important occasions? and how does it happen that he links himself to Adam Black for the purpose of

---

[1] It is perhaps not too much to say that the popular dislike of the Whig committee, or "clique," had as much to do with the electoral defeat which it sustained in 1865 as the personal popularity of Mr. McLaren or the jealousy of official influence, supposed to be represented in the persons of Lord Macaulay, and afterwards of Lord Moncreiff. This committee maintained itself by co-optation, pure and unadulterated. Its meetings were strictly private, the names of its members were unknown outside its charmed circle, and it was even said that Liberals who would have been admitted by the "Reform" or "Brooks's" were liable to be unceremoniously blackballed by the chairman or secretary for the time being of this irresponsible *junto*. It is needless to add that the gentlemen who composed the committee were in their private capacity estimable, and probably perfectly inoffensive, citizens. A good deal of the animosity created by the alleged "domination of the Whig clique" was perhaps founded on misconception; and impartial history, should its notice fall upon this curious product of Reform legislation, will perhaps pronounce the "Whig clique" of Edinburgh a corporation of very innocent persons; at worst, a court of registration for carrying out the decrees of the Government Whips, who had relegated Edinburgh to the category of nomination burghs.

opposing me, who supported the Government on these occasions, for I attended the public meeting in the city which supported the Palmerston Reform Bill ?   I think it would be well for the Lord Advocate to answer this, for if he does not, the impression will get abroad that, if he be the accredited exponent of the opinions of the Government, the Government must be very hollow and insincere in regard to its professions in favour of Reform.   (Loud and continued applause.)   If that be true of the Government—if it be the tactics of the Government, through the Lord Advocate as their exponent in Scotland, to oppose all those candidates who have supported Reform, and to support all those candidates who have opposed Reform, like Mr. Black—(laughter)—then I say that the sooner the Government is turned out and another put in its place the better will it be for the country.   (Loud applause.)"

The grounds of opposition to Mr. Moncreiff and Mr. Black, it will thus be seen, were sufficiently broad and distinct. Referring in his letter on the "Memoirs" to the loss of popularity sustained by both Members through the Act of 1860, Mr. M<sup>c</sup>Laren remarked :—"The Annuity-Tax Bill, in my opinion, did more to lose Mr. Black's seat than any *one* point.   The tenpence-halfpenny per pound on the *real* rents of the police-roll was computed to be equal to the six per cent. on the lower roll of the stentmasters (taken usually as four-fifths to three-fourths), and was made *part of the police-tax*, so that no one could thereafter resist it as a direct ecclesiastical tax ; and this avowedly was done with that view.   The inhabitants were infuriated against it, and I was a most willing leader, although I never refused to pay the original tax, or wished to have my goods distrained for it, as not a few of my friends did—as Bailies Russell and Stott and Mr. Tait, by going to prison rather than pay.   By the arrangement which my efforts ended in, the direct taxation is altogether abolished, and the stipends of thirteen ministers are fixed at £550; but by the voluntary liberality of their flocks they get more than £600 a year." Certainly the reports of the election proceedings in 1865 bear out Mr. McLaren's view of the keenness of feeling and resoluteness of purpose excited against the Act of 1860. One example, taken from the *Caledonian Mercury's* report of Mr. Hugh Rose's speech at the public meeting which first endorsed the candidature of Messrs. McLaren and Miller, may be given :—

"We live in an age," said Mr. Rose, "when, from the vast amount of difference of opinion in regard to the religious questions of this country, the time has gone by when a single shilling of the public money should be voted for the support of any religious sect whatever—(tremendous applause)—whether these votes or this class legislation bear upon the endowment of Roman Catholic colleges or upon the continuation of taxation for ecclesiastical imposts, whether dignified by the name of church-rates in one country or police-rates in another. (Great cheering, continued with deafening effect.) I trust the time has come—(renewed cheers and hisses)—I trust the time has come—(here the excitement was tremendous, the chairman's voice being completely drowned)—when we will endeavour to send from this city— (renewed applause)—men who will say to the Legislature, 'Gentlemen, the thing does not work.' (Loud and prolonged cheering.) We are not here, gentlemen, either to accuse or defend the gentlemen in this city who are giving their strong opposition to the clerico-police rates. This is not a place for such a subject of consideration ; but I hold the scenes which late legislation have caused to be enacted in this city are a disgrace to this age of civilisation. (Tremendous applause.)"

Mr. Black's opposition to the lowering of the franchise likewise operated most adversely against his candidature. It tended to alienate from him the class of voters who were not deeply interested in politico-ecclesiastical questions. Mr. Black's views on the subject of reform (conscientiously held and maintained against his own immediate electoral interests) may be best given in his own words :—

"Though he was not bound," he said, "to the support of Lord Palmerston's or any other Government, he was generally found voting along with the Lord Advocate, and that on the question of the franchise, as no Government would now introduce a bill for a mere lowering, apart from the accompanying safeguards of education, taxation, or property, he was perfectly certain that on that question too they would be found acting together. It was a gross misrepresentation to say that he was opposed to the extension, or even the lowering, of the franchise ; he only wanted that some qualification other than mere rental should be required in any large addition to be made to the constituencies."

Such a declaration could hardly be regarded as reassuring by the parliamentary reformers who formed the mass of the Liberal party in the city. The reports of the canvassers showing that many electors who had voted for Mr. Black in 1856 as a reformer were now resolved to divide their support between Mr. M<sup>c</sup>Laren and Mr. Moncreiff, led Mr. M<sup>c</sup>Laren to say more than once during the canvass, that whoever might be placed at the head of the poll, Mr. Black would not be that man, and this statement he repeated with much emphasis on the hustings on the day of nomination. Two days later, when all parties were again on the hustings to hear the declaration of the poll, Mr. Black, referring to this remarkable testimony to Mr. M<sup>c</sup>Laren's accuracy, said : "I confess that when I heard Mr. M<sup>c</sup>Laren on Wednesday state so strongly that he was sure to be at the top of the poll, because he had tested the lists by every means in his power, and was perfectly certain of the fact, I knew that Mr. M<sup>c</sup>Laren would not speak in that way unless he believed it, and I felt that he must have had some good ground for saying it."

The canvass was carried on with great vigour on both sides, but the reception awarded to Messrs. M<sup>c</sup>Laren and Miller at the numerous public and ward meetings which they held, and also at the hustings, proved beyond the possibility of doubt that they were the popular candidates, that the great mass of the citizens were on their side, and that whatever might be the issue of this election under the restricted £10 franchise, the extension of the franchise, for which all reformers pleaded, would be fatal to Whig supremacy in Edinburgh. Mr. M<sup>c</sup>Laren, as an old electioneering adept, confidently calculated on the success both of himself and his colleague even under the £10 franchise. The canvassers reported 4561 pledges for himself, and 3829 pledges for Mr. Miller ; and with the experience of previous elections in his mind, he was satisfied that these pledges, obtained by honest voluntary workers, secured the success of the Independent Liberal party. If these expectations were only partially realised, it was not because the promises obtained were to any material extent unfulfilled, but because of the unprecedentedly heavy vote recorded, and because of the united support given by the Tories to Mr. Black and the Lord Advocate. In anticipation of the polling, the Conservative Association advertised the following resolutions :—



"(1.) That at the ensuing election, there being no Conservative candidate, Conservative electors ought to give their support to Mr. Black.

"(2.) That, in present circumstances, Conservative electors should not pledge their second votes; and that unless in the case of any Conservative electors who have resolved to vote for Mr. Black alone, or who may have already pledged their second votes, it will be expedient to abstain from voting before twelve o'clock, by which time an opinion may be formed whether it will be possible to give second votes without endangering Mr. Black's return."

This policy was strictly followed out, but the Conservative vote which defeated Mr. M<sup>c</sup>Laren in 1852 was happily unavailing against him in 1865.[1]

The return of the voting made by the Sheriff showed this to be the result :—

| M<sup>c</sup>Laren | . | . | . | . | . | 4354 |
| Moncreiff | . | . | . | . | . | 4148 |
| Black | . | . | . | . | . | 3797 |
| Miller | . | . | . | . | . | 3723 |

Referring to this election in his letter previously quoted, Mr. M<sup>c</sup>Laren said :—

"The polls were then published every hour or every half-hour, and I was always at the head from the opening to the close. My colleague, Mr. Miller, was next to me till about one o'clock, when the leading Tories, who had by agreement abstained from voting, held a meeting at which they resolved to vote for our opponents as the least of two evils; and they were thus rapidly advanced, and my colleague lowered on the poll till he was the lowest. My opponents got nearly all the Tory votes, and this was what Mr. Black expected, as he told Mr. Bright.[2]

"If all the Tory votes were deducted, my majority of Liberals must have been very large indeed, thus proving that I had the

---

[1] In the remarks made here and elsewhere regarding the Tory policy at Edinburgh, no disparagement of the Conservative party is intended. Being a minority in Edinburgh, and unable to carry a candidate of their own, they had of course a clear right, and even a duty, to espouse the cause of the candidate whose views came nearest their own on the questions of the day.

[2] After Mr. Black's repeated votes in Parliament against Reform, he was sarcastically asked by Mr. Bright how he was getting on in Edinburgh, and if all the Tories would support him; to which he replied, "I hope so."

confidence of the Liberal party in an overwhelming degree.  I
need add nothing about the general principles involved in the
contest, as these are amply discussed in the case of Mr. Black's
first election.   There is one other point I may notice.   It was
rumoured, and generally believed among my friends, that Mr.
Black did not wish to stand at this election, but that his party
over-persuaded him to stand against his own judgment.   This
report is in effect confirmed (p. 227 of his 'Memoirs').[1]

"The town gossip went further to say that the Whig party
urged Mr. Black to stand in order to keep me out, as they
believed no stranger would have a chance of being returned
against me." [2]

To show how strongly his candidature was opposed by
those who had hitherto ruled over the political situation in

---

[1] "Very much perplexed about retiring from Parliament at the approaching election, or leaving it to the committee to decide."

[2] The subjoined analysis of the polling shows which were the Tory and
which the Radical wards in the city.  It likewise shows that the "New
Town" went most largely for Mr. Moncreiff and Mr. Black, that the "Old
Town" was the stronghold of Mr. M<sup>c</sup>Laren and Mr. Miller; while the
residential suburb of Newington was almost evenly divided between the
four candidates:—

| Wards. | M<sup>c</sup>Laren. | Moncreiff. | Black. | Miller. |
|---|---|---|---|---|
| 1. Calton | 316 | 287 | 259 | 263 |
| 2. Broughton | 189 | 228 | 237 | 159 |
| 3. St. Bernard's | 280 | 355 | 336 | 233 |
| 4. St. George's | 115 | 356 | 352 | 91 |
| 5. St. Stephen's | 232 | 372 | 352 | 172 |
| 6. St. Luke's | 278 | 346 | 307 | 224 |
| 7. St. Andrew's | 242 | 328 | 315 | 201 |
| 8. Canongate | 433 | 345 | 312 | 385 |
| 9. St. Giles' | 392 | 292 | 256 | 328 |
| 10. St. Cuthbert's | 522 | 348 | 296 | 448 |
| 11. George Square | 434 | 259 | 228 | 382 |
| 12. St. Leonard's | 554 | 272 | 227 | 503 |
| 13. Newington | 367 | 360 | 330 | 334 |
|  | 4354 | 4148 | 3797 | 3723 |

Scotland, the late Rev. Dr. Guthrie said to Mr. M<sup>c</sup>Laren :— "It would surprise you to see the number of letters I have had begging me not to give you my vote; but when I saw that all the Catholics and all the publicans were against you, I asked myself how could I, as a Protestant Christian minister and an avowed Temperance man, shirk my duty as a citizen and withhold my vote? And," he added, "I never knew what it was to be persecuted till after I had voted for you; it only shows how much it was felt by the 'ruling classes' that you were the champion of true Liberalism in opposition to class and privilege. I never voted before in any parliamentary election, but I have never regretted giving you that honest vote."

This victory was a great triumph for the Independent Liberal party; it was also a high personal distinction for Mr. M<sup>c</sup>Laren. Being highest on the poll, he was placed in the position of senior Member for the capital of Scotland, with the chief Scotch representative of the Ministry as his colleague. And he had gained this position in open and honourable contest. He could say on the hustings :—"I have taken no pledge; I have catered to no prejudices. I go free and independent into Parliament." But this assertion of independence in no way diminished the confidence of his constituents. "You'll no' turn your coat," shouted an elector from the crowd; and he did not. In the House of Commons he was faithful to the principles of Independent Liberalism as he professed them, namely, the general and hearty support of the policy of the party, with a reserve veto in case of conscientious disagreement. His conduct in Parliament, and the respect and authority he quickly gained there, caused him to be generally accepted as the future, and in a manner permanent, representative of his city. The conspicuous success of his parliamentary service greatly strengthened the position of his party in Edinburgh. Mr. M<sup>c</sup>Laren, however, did not attain this position until he had fought in more than one electoral campaign. In anticipation of the general election of 1868, and encouraged by a slight schism in the ranks of the Reform Union—an association of which Mr. B. F. Dun, an honest and outspoken Radical, was the chief orator, and which had organised the Reform Bill demonstrations of the preceding year — the Edinburgh Tories promoted a requisition to Lord Stanley (now Lord Derby, then one of Mr. Disraeli's Ministerial colleagues), under the impression that that political *rara avis*, the Conservative working-man, largely abounded amongst the newly enfranchised householders, and on the representation that Mr. M<sup>c</sup>Laren and Lord Stanley were political friends.



At an excited and noisy meeting held in the Music Hall in July 1868, Mr. M<sup>c</sup>Laren gave the finishing stroke to these dreams and also to the Stanley candidature. He ridiculed the Conservative working-man idea, and roundly declared that the requisition, to which it was said 6000 signatures had been obtained, was not a *bona fide* production, but the work of hirelings. "Do you think," he asked, "that Lord Stanley, who is far too acute to be taken in by paid hirelings—£3 per week for working-men is, I understand, the rate at which they are paid—do you think that Lord Stanley would be so gulled as to go to the poll and be ignominiously defeated with 6000 votes on his side, and probably 16,000 on the other? For my part, I do not believe that his friends in this city would ever allow such a thing to take place. I believe all this opposition will end in smoke, notwithstanding the turmoil which it has occasioned in this city."

With reference to his alleged sympathy with Conservatism (apparently founded on the support which Mr. M<sup>c</sup>Laren gave to the Disraeli Household Suffrage Bill), Mr. M<sup>c</sup>Laren was equally emphatic. " If the Conservatives can vote for me as an honest man who has tried to do his duty to the best of his ability, good and well; but if they resolve to vote for me because I am of the same political opinions as Lord Stanley, I beg them to keep their votes to themselves, or at all events not to give them to me." As a matter of fact, a few Tories had always supported him, both in municipal and parliamentary elections, on the ground on which he valued their help, " as an honest man who had tried to do his duty to the best of his ability," and whose devotion to the interests of the city and of the nation could be recognised in spite of political differences. But as a party, the Tories had always been, and he knew must always continue to be, his natural opponents, if he continued faithful to his political creed.

Exhausted by the fatigues of the session, he had gone to Harrogate to recruit immediately after the prorogation of Parliament. But the needed rest came too late. He became dangerously ill, and he remained there in a critical state for some months. Thanks, however, to his own sound constitution, the careful nursing of Mrs. McLaren, and most attentive medical skill,[1] the progress of the sickness was stayed; and the first task attempted during his convalescence was a letter written by his own hand to the Independent Liberal Committee in Edinburgh. In this letter he reminded the committee that the Stanley opposition was really directed against Mr. Miller, and intimated his wish, if a contest should take place, and there should be a splitting of votes on the part of any, that the split votes should be given

1868

Serious illness.

---

[1] During this illness he was greatly indebted to the generous kindness of his friend Dr. Macleod of Ben Rhydding, who frequently came to give help and encouragement, and to watch over the invalid during the night.

to Mr. Miller rather than to himself. But, as he formerly predicted, the Stanley requisition ended in smoke, and when the day of election under the household franchise approached, neither ancient Whig, modern Conservative, nor any combination of reactionary politicians ventured to show their faces. Mr. Moncreiff retired, frankly confessing that he did not possess the confidence of the electorate on the Annuity-Tax question. Recognising that their main difference was on this local question, Mr. M<sup>c</sup>Laren took an opportunity of commending the candidature of his former colleague as Liberal competitor for the suffrages of the newly-created constituency of Glasgow and Aberdeen Universities, as in 1852 he had commended his candidature for Leith. In Edinburgh the Independent Liberal party were left in undisputed possession of the field, and Mr. M<sup>c</sup>Laren and Mr. Miller were returned without opposition. On the hustings, after his election, Mr. M<sup>c</sup>Laren renewed and extended his declaration of independence. "In the past," he said, "in more cases than nineteen out of twenty, I have given a most zealous support to the Liberal party, but in some instances, when I thought they were wrong, I gave effect to my own opinions and not to theirs, and I know from very good sources that I met with your approval. I intend to follow the same course when I go back to Parliament. . . . In acting as I have done, I have sought no favour from the Whig Government when in office, and none from the Tories when they were in office, either for myself or any one connected with me. I have been independent of all parties and all men, endeavouring to take an honest view of everything for the good of the public."

The Independent Liberal party undoubtedly made good use of their victory, and one of the most notable results was the pacific settlement of the Annuity-Tax controversy, with its two-century history of grievance and dissension. But on one occasion a section of the party were tempted, by the consciousness of the giant strength they possessed, to try to use it tyrannously, and against their own friend and victorious leader, Mr. M{c}Laren himself.   In the summer of 1873 a disagreement broke out between a number of working-men representatives and Mr. M{c}Laren.   The Criminal Law Amendment Act, particularly those clauses which were directed against "picketing" workmen who disowned the authority of the Trade Unions, gave great offence to the Trade-Unionists; and an extensive and formidable agitation arose for the repeal of the recently enacted law, which sought to protect Non-Unionists from this form of intimidation, practically a combination for the purpose of preventing workmen from accepting employment during a strike authorised by the Union.   Mr. Miller sympathised with this agitation, and promised to support repeal.   Mr. M{c}Laren, as an economist and Free Trader, and, it may be added, one who illustrated in his own career the principle of "individualism," could no more tolerate or connive at social tyranny amongst working-men than he would accept it from the political coteries from which he had suffered.   He therefore offered an uncompromising opposition to the proposals for the repeal of the "picketing" clauses.   A movement, headed by Mr. Paterson, the secretary of the Amalgamated Society of Joiners, was set on foot for the purpose of coercing the refractory Member into compliance with the Trade Union demands.   An "Advanced Liberal Association" was formed; an imposing trades demonstration was organised; and on the platform of a trades meeting held in the Queen's Park Mr. M{c}Laren was denounced as a "traitor." Later in the year a deputation was sent to Newington House, where the whole question was discussed with great

1874

just and
gene-
s at-
ks.

earnestness, without, however, changing the position of either of the parties.

Matters came to a crisis at the next annual meeting of the electors with their Members, which took place in Queen Street Hall. The meeting was chiefly composed of working-men interested in the desired trade legislation, and who were much irritated at the position Mr. M^cLaren had maintained. Mr. M^cLaren spoke amidst considerable interruption and uproar, and in the end Mr. Paterson moved and carried a resolution to this effect—"That this meeting of the electors of Edinburgh, being dissatisfied with Mr. M^cLaren's answers to questions put, and with his conduct and irregular attendance in Parliament, has no longer confidence in him as their representative; also awards a vote of thanks to Mr. Miller for his past services, and for his clear and explicit statement on the laws affecting working-men."

A characteristic incident occurred at this meeting, which caused a momentary reaction in Mr. M^cLaren's favour. At the close of his speech he was subjected to the usual "heckling," which in this case took the shape of a string of prepared argumentative questions, put seriatim by Mr. Paterson amidst the cheers of the Trade-Unionists. Mr. M^cLaren answered them all with courage and clearness; for in his platform appearances he never showed to greater advantage than in meeting opposition and interruption. When the last question was reached, a voice from the gallery was heard to exclaim, "No shuffling, Duncan! Answer the question." Mr. M^cLaren fixed his keen eye on the interrupter and instantly replied, "I have answered all the questions. I fear no question, and I fear no man!" An enthusiastic cheer burst from the audience, proving that the author of the random shot had signally missed his mark. The reference to irregularity of attendance was also quickly resented by

the meeting amid cries of "Shame," as Mr. McLaren was 
well known for his constant devotion to his parliamentary
duties, and Mr. Paterson, seeing that he had gone too far,
offered to withdraw the offending words.

The controversy caused Mr. McLaren some pain. His
heart had always been with the working-classes. He knew
the hardness of their lot, and had striven to mitigate it.
He had sympathised with their honest and healthful aspirations after social advancement, and he had helped them with
what was to many of them the priceless boon of free education. He had always striven to secure for them the benefit
of equal laws, and to accomplish their political emancipa-
tion. And now he saw them making use of the power and
the franchise he had laboured to secure for them in days
when parliamentary reform had few active friends, for the
purpose of exercising a form of social tyranny upon their
fellow-workmen. Mr. McLaren did not, however, accept
the view of the Trade Union leaders that they had the
whole working-class population at their backs, and he
prepared to defend his seat, in full consciousness of the
strong opposition that was awaiting him. He, however,
recognised the perfect right of the meeting to pass a vote
of want of confidence if it thought it right to do so; but
he frankly said that he would not accept the decision
of a one-sided meeting in Queen Street Hall, but should
submit his case to the judgment of the 25,000 electors
of the city. "I distinctly deny," he indignantly said, "that
I have acted against the true interests of the working-
classes in this matter. My whole life has been a refutation
of it. There is no one who has done more for working-
men than I have done in my own sphere, and all the alle-
gations to the contrary are incorrect." He had confidence
that, notwithstanding this demonstration, the working-men

of Edinburgh would do him justice, and the event justified his confidence.

Nearly all his old electioneering friends, with Mr. M<sup>c</sup>Crie and Mr. Hugh Rose as joint-chairmen of his committee, rallied around him ; the ward committees were reorganised ; and Mr. M<sup>c</sup>Laren, appealing to his past conduct and opinions as the credentials of the character of his Liberalism, and promising to do in the future as in the past, went on his own course, apart from Mr. Miller and the seceding Liberals.   In his address soliciting re-election Mr. M<sup>c</sup>Laren said :—

" Forty years have elapsed since I first entered the service of the city, during which period I have filled many important offices, and devoted much time and labour to promote the best interests of my fellow-citizens of all classes.   The experience thus acquired has been of great value in enabling me to form a calm and dispassionate judgment, not only on local, but also on Scottish questions generally."

Mr. James Cowan, then Lord Provost, was nominated by the " Aggregate Liberal Committee."   The Tory party, seeing three Liberals in the field, asked Mr. J. H. A. Macdonald (now Lord Justice-Clerk), then a popular Volteer officer and leading Tory politician in the city, to champion their cause.

Mr. Cowan received a considerable share of support from Mr. M<sup>c</sup>Laren's friends, and Mr. M<sup>c</sup>Laren had the general support of the Liberal party of all sections, including many individuals who had hitherto actively opposed him.   The result was a complete triumph for Mr. M<sup>c</sup>Laren.   This was the first election in Edinburgh under the Ballot Act, and Mr. M<sup>c</sup>Laren, in spite of the Trades Council opposition, obtained the extraordinary poll of 11,431 votes ; Mr. Cowan was chosen his colleague with 8749 votes ; Mr. Miller obtained 6218 votes; and even in this year of Tory reaction, in spite too of his popular gifts, Mr. Macdonald was left at the bottom of the poll with 5713 votes. When, in 1876, the Tories, in their eagerness to conciliate the working-classes, introduced amending legislation, which the Trade-Unionists accepted, Mr. McLaren found that the principles he maintained in 1874 were substantially the same as those embodied in the new Act.

The severance between Mr. McLaren and Mr. Miller was greatly regretted by many of their mutual supporters, as Mr. Miller was a faithful and earnest Liberal, and probably the Independent Liberalism of the city has never been so well represented as during the six years from 1868 to 1874, when these two Members sat side by side below the gangway of the House of Commons.

As colleagues Mr. McLaren and Mr. Cowan worked well together. The Liberalism of the new Member was less advanced than that of his senior; but Mr. Cowan had a genuine respect for the political acquirements and knowledge of Mr. McLaren, and the two Members were seldom found in different lobbies. But when the next general election came round in 1880, many ardent Liberals desired to provide a politician of more robust type than Mr. Cowan as a colleague for Mr. McLaren. Mr. Cowan met this demand to some extent by accepting the principle of Disestablishment, and Mr. McLaren, while not personally interfering in the action of the new United Liberal Committee, was glad to find that it resulted in the continuance of their confidence to Mr. Cowan, who certainly had not done anything to justify them in encouraging opposition to his candidature. The result was that, after consideration and discussion, the United Liberal Association, under the presidency of Mr., afterwards Sir George, Harrison, unanimously adopted Messrs. McLaren and Cowan as the Liberal candidates; and as Mr. Macdonald was again induced to enter the field in the Conservative interest, the Liberal Association proceeded to organise and carry through, with a minimum of expense, a most efficient canvass on behalf of the two candidates. The greatest of all Mr. M<sup>c</sup>Laren's electoral victories, and the greatest of all the Liberal victories at the election of 1880, was then achieved. Mr. M<sup>c</sup>Laren was again placed at the top of the poll, but this time with 17,807 votes; Mr. Cowan was next, with 17,351; while Mr. Macdonald was left with even a smaller vote than he obtained in 1874. He polled 5651 votes, and Edinburgh thus pronounced in favour of the Advanced Liberal candidate by the unprecedented majority of 12,156 votes. Mr. M<sup>c</sup>Laren was deeply moved by this splendid manifestation of the confidence and regard of his fellow-citizens, and he felt specially indebted to Mr. Harrison for his services as chairman of the great organisation which contributed to this decided success. His period of public service had now extended to forty-eight years, and of the many encouragements and distinctions that cheered him during almost half a century of unceasing struggle, often against tremendous odds, for the public welfare, none afforded him livelier gratification than the act of homage rendered him in the eighty-first year of his age by the 17,807 voters who so zealously and disinterestedly supported him in his last electoral contest.

# CHAPTER XVII.

## *THE DUTIES OF CITIZENSHIP.*



WHEN he first took his seat as Member for Edinburgh, Mr. M‘Laren found that his new position opened for him a greatly extended field in which to labour. But, faithful as he was to the House of Commons, he did not give up his interest in those Edinburgh institutions which had engaged his attention in former years. His idea of the duty of citizenship was never dimmed by the wider sphere of duty to which he was called. While his active participation in work which came within the province of the Town Council naturally ceased, or was limited to watching over the municipal interests of the city in Parliament, he continued to take a leading part in the transactions of such bodies as the Chamber of Commerce and the Royal Infirmary. Of the Merchant Company he had been a member ever since 1826, when he had just commenced business, and of the 500 or 600 members belonging to it at that time, he survived all except one, Mr. John Miller, of 26 Nelson Street, who was admitted a member in November 1825. Mr. M‘Laren had served as an Assistant-Master of the Company in the years 1841–42, and also as Governor of George Watson's and James Gillespie's Hospitals;[1] but he never took a prominent part in directing the Company's affairs,

---

[1] Educational institutions under the control of the Company.

though he kept himself intimately acquainted with them, and gave a hearty support to the husbanding policy pursued during the mastership of Mr. Duncan, and also to the scheme for the conversion of the " Hospitals " into high-class secondary schools, a reform devised and carried out mainly by the exertions of Sir Thomas Boyd, afterwards Lord Provost of Edinburgh, and Mr. Thomas Knox.

In the Chamber of Commerce, however, Mr. McLaren had greater scope for action. Here, as in the Merchant Company, he found not a few colleagues thoroughly conversant with and interested in the discussion of commercial questions in their relation to public interests. The more prominent of those with whom Mr. McLaren found pleasure in co-operating were his predecessor in the chairman's office, the late Mr. James Richardson, his immediate successor, whom he nominated for the presidency, the late Sir George Harrison, Mr. David McLaren, and Mr. Josiah Livingston. Without claiming too much for Mr. McLaren in this connection, it may be said with truth that it was during his chairmanship, extending from 1862 to 1865, that the Chamber of Commerce first acquired the position of authority which it now holds as one of the institutions of the city. It was not without some hesitation that he consented to remain in the chair for so long a period, but the following letter and other similar assurances induced him to waive his objections :—

7 Roxburgh Place, Edinburgh, *March* 2, 1864.

My dear Sir,—Mr. Harrison and I had a little conversation yesterday as to the arrangements for the Chamber of Commerce next month. I see Mr. Harrison feels very strongly, as well as myself, the great desirableness of our getting you to retain the chair, and I can hardly tell you how important I feel this to be. I am sure you would be gratified did you know how cordially all, even those who have been your keen political opponents, express

their satisfaction at seeing you at the head of the Chamber, and 
their perfect confidence in your judicious management; and every
member of the Chamber feels that all is going well so long as
you are in the chair.   I do not think we ask anything unreason-
able when we ask the favour of your continuing as chairman for
another year, and your consenting will be highly esteemed both
by the Chamber and the public.   To myself it will be an obligation; in matters of that kind I would rather act under you than
under any other man.—I am, my dear sir, yours faithfully,

Josiah Livingston.

On his initiation the Chamber united the Town Council, Reduction<br>of railway<br>rates.
the Merchant Company, and the Trade Protection Society
along with itself in a common effort to protect the public
interests against the proposed amalgamation of the Caledonian
and Edinburgh and Glasgow Railway Companies.   It was
his diligence in collecting and skill in presenting facts and
statistics bearing on the passenger and traffic rates that
made the case of the public against the powerful railway combination irresistibly strong.   His correspondence with the
chairmen of the Companies, and his intimate association with
the negotiations and struggle both in Edinburgh and London,
gave to the result the appearance of, for him, something
like a personal triumph.   For several years thereafter the
Chamber made the careful examination of all Scottish Railway Bills one of its special duties.   In his successive positions
as chairman of the Chamber and Member for the city, Mr.
McLaren was at least as jealous of the interests of the city
when affected by these measures—more especially the North
British schemes in the days of Mr. Richard Hodgson's dictatorship—as of the interests of the commercial community.   His
experience as a railway director at an earlier period had
made him conversant with the arts by which a corporation
of capitalists can attract to itself public and parliamentary

influence, and he was more concerned to guard the public from the rapacity of companies than at any time to champion their cause. When, at a later period, a ruinous competition arose between the North British and Caledonian Railways, and a joint-purse agreement or amalgamation was proposed in the interests of the shareholders, whose dividends had become a vanishing quantity, he advised the Chamber not to entertain a motion submitted by Mr. Charles Cowan recommending some arrangement between the companies; his view being that the railway directors and shareholders might safely be left to look after their own interests, and that the public welfare was more likely to be advanced by fair competition than by combination and monopoly.

Before leaving the presidential chair of the Chamber of Commerce to carry on his public work in the more responsible position of a Member of the Legislature, Mr. McLaren invited the Chamber to make recognition of the splendid services Mr. Gladstone had rendered to the mercantile classes as well as to the general community by his great fiscal reforms, based on the Free Trade principles, which the country had now finally accepted. The following correspondence ensued :—

EDINBURGH, November 6, 1865.

DEAR SIR,—I have the honour to send you a minute of the Chamber of Commerce, from which you will perceive that you have been elected an honorary member of that body.

It is the first case in which we have availed ourselves of this power of appointment under our new rules and regulations. I may state that the Chamber was incorporated by royal charter in 1786, and consists of nearly 500 of the principal merchants, manufacturers, and other traders within Edinburgh, Leith, and other towns in the county of Midlothian, and that your election was quite unanimous and most cordial. Enclosed is a slip cut from the newspapers of the proceedings of the meeting which took place on the occasion.

I enclose a printed copy of a petition presented to Parliament by this Chamber in 1820 in favour of Free Trade principles in all their breadth ; and the result of a good deal of inquiry has proved that this was the first petition ever presented to Parliament broadly advocating the principles of Free Trade.   Shortly after our Chamber had sent off their petition, a meeting of traders in London was held on the same subject, and a petition was also presented by them about the same period.

I have only to add that it gives me great pleasure personally to have the honour of making this communication.—I have the honour to be, dear sir, yours very respectfully,

D. M<sup>c</sup>LAREN.

The Right Hon. W. E. Gladstone, M.P.,
    Chancellor of the Exchequer.

11 CARLTON HOUSE TERRACE,<br>
*November* 9, 1865.

MY DEAR SIR,—I have to thank the Edinburgh Chamber of Commerce for the high honour they have done me in placing my name upon their roll, and I beg you will take a suitable opportunity of conveying to them my grateful acknowledgments.

I have to thank you also, and very much, for the documents you were kind enough to send me.   The petition is a composition of peculiar interest.   Great indeed is the honour due to those who move *early* in the right direction, and all the more because, at the moment of the eventual triumph, they are too commonly forgotten.—I have the honour to be, my dear sir, faithfully yours, W. E. GLADSTONE.

D. M<sup>c</sup>Laren, Esq., M.P.

As a Member of Parliament Mr. M<sup>c</sup>Laren continued to take an active interest in the work of the Chamber, and its testimony in favour of Free Trade principles was continued and emphasised.   In November 1868 the Chamber elected Mr. Bright its second honorary member, on the occasion of his receiving the Freedom of the City during the Lord Provostship of Mr. William Chambers. It was in his speech [1] acknowledging the civic distinction that the eloquent champion of Free Trade sounded the new cry of " A Free Breakfast Table." Mr. David M<sup>c</sup>Laren—no relative, but in almost complete agreement with Mr. Laren's political views, and an ardent upholder of the doctrines of the Manchester School —at once began in the Chamber of Commerce to explain and to popularise the Free Breakfast Table policy. The senior Member of the city assisted him in many speeches. Many other politico-commercial questions were discussed in the Chamber from time to time, such as the French bounties on shipping and on sugar, gambling on the Stock Exchange, mercantile morality, the amalgamation of the Board of Customs and Excise, the law of bankruptcy, the exemption of private property from seizure at sea during war, the Board of Trade and railway management, the law of partnership, the assimilation and codification of the mercantile laws of the United Kingdom, not to speak of numerous local and Scottish subjects. On these and kindred questions it may be said generally that Mr. M<sup>c</sup>Laren, while contributing much valuable information, advocated views in harmony with Advanced Liberal principles, and tending to the purification of our commercial system. In 1872, in his examination before a Select Committee of the House of Commons on the Trade Partnerships Bill, he gave an interesting and suggestive explanation of the refusal of the Edinburgh Chamber to join the Associated Chambers. " I will state the reason why," he said to the chairman, Mr. Norwood. "The custom has now become so inveterate of putting a line in bills that ' this bill shall not apply to Scotland,' that our Chamber found that they would have very little in common with other Chambers, and therefore they would not join. Our

---

[1] See Mr. Bright's Addresses, vol. iii. p. 106.

Chamber not only petitioned in favour of this bill, but they **1868**
wish it to be extended to Scotland." By way of explanation,
Mr. Norwood interjected, " You remember me telling you
last year that the reason I could not accede to make my
bill apply to Scotland was that the legal machinery of
England and Scotland were not identical." Mr. M<sup>c</sup>Laren's
reply was characteristic : " The Chancellor of the Exchequer," he dryly remarked, " has never any difficulty when
laying on the taxes to adjust the clauses so as to make
them applicable to Scotland."

No public-spirited man can reside long in Edinburgh and The Royal
remain uninterested in the noblest of its institutions—the Infirmary.
Royal Infirmary. Mr. M<sup>c</sup>Laren's first connection with the
management of the Infirmary was almost contemporaneous
with his entrance into the Council ; and from that time forward, through a period extending to over half a century, he
laboured to promote the efficiency and prosperity of this
institution, alike in relation to the public and to the Medical
School of the University. With characteristic zeal he threw
himself into the front of every controversy which affected
the financial well-being or the public usefulness of what he
regarded as a national and not merely a local charity.

In 1868–69, by the exertions mainly of Sir Thomas Boyd, The battle
Mr. John Millar of Sheardale, and the Directors of the of the sites.
Infirmary, a large sum of money had been subscribed by the
public for the rebuilding of the Infirmary on its original site.
An opinion then gained ground that the Infirmary ought to
be transferred to a more airy situation. Mr. M<sup>c</sup>Laren was
one of the earliest and staunchest supporters of its removal
to the site of George Watson's Hospital, adjacent to the
" Meadows," which was strongly advocated by Mr. Syme,
then Professor of Surgery in the University of Edinburgh.
Although the physical strength of that brave-spirited man

and world-famed surgeon was then visibly declining, he continued by speech and pen, always forcibly but temperately, and with the firmness that generally characterises moderation, to plead for the Watson Hospital site, on the double ground of humanity and economy. Mr. McLaren was prevented by his parliamentary duties in London from attending the deciding meeting of the subscribers. He therefore addressed an open letter to the ladies and gentlemen entitled to vote, disposing of the objections urged against Mr. Syme's plan, such as "the alleged great distance from the College," "the low level of Watson's grounds," "the difficulty of drainage," "the insalubrity of Watson's ground," &c., and he reminded them that the original site, when selected in 1738, was in the country. "There was," he said, "no South Bridge then, there was no Nicolson Street, and no Drummond Street. There were no houses between Potterrow and the Pleasance; and the space between the Infirmary and the College was all garden ground." He continued :—"The town has now extended a mile to the south of the Infirmary of 1738. Why should not the poor inmates of 1869 have as free air as the inmates of 1738? Place the poor patients of 1869 as nearly as you possibly can in the same relative position as their predecessors of 1738; and if you cannot remove the Hospital to Liberton, where the authorities of old placed their lepers ('Leperton') for sanitary and curative purposes, do the best you can in existing circumstances by placing them in the grounds of Watson's Hospital, removed from all the insanitary influences of the Cowgate and surrounding districts."

As soon as the battle of the sites had been decided in favour of removal, so far as the contributors to the Infirmary were concerned, the opponents of the Watson Hospital site transferred the scene of conflict to the Merchant Company, who were the owners of the institution. Here they seem to have changed their grounds of opposition. Influenced largely by the objections of residents in George Square and the neighbourhood, they disputed (1) the advantage of the offer made to the Merchant Company, and (2) the powers of the Company to sell the land. At a meeting of the Merchant Company Mr. M<sup>c</sup>Laren successfully answered both objections—the first by a reference to the unsuitability of Watson's Hospital to the educational schemes of the Company, then in contemplation, and to the ease with which far better accommodation could be secured for a less sum than the purchase-money offered by the Infirmary, and the second by showing that the George Square proprietors had no right to object.

" Watson's Hospital," he said, "never paid a shilling for the land, but merely paid a feu-duty, which last year (1868) amounted to £47, there being £5 additional paid to the Town Council for a strip of ground at the north. Surely, then, if they got £43,000 for the property to be retained as one holding (which was the condition on which it was originally got), this would be a far better and more honourable course to follow than (even if they had the power) to cover the ground with buildings. George Square property was feued out on the same day with Watson's Hospital property. In both cases the parties were bound never to put any houses upon their respective garden-plots ; each was to be retained as one holding. Lord Ross was the superior of the George Square and Park Place districts, and after the lapse of thirty years the feuars set to work to thwart the conditions of his grant. It was therefore Watson's Hospital that ought to go to the proprietors of George Square and say, ' You and your predecessors have violated the equal conditions which we and you came under ; the moral obligation lies on you to pull down your houses and make an open space. After you have done that, then we will both be in the same position ; for each of our feu-charters binds us to preserve a great open space near Heriot's Hospital.' "

These and similar arguments prevailed, and the controversy seemed to be at an end, when a new difficulty arose, which gave another proof of Mr. M<sup>c</sup>Laren's unceasing watchfulness over the interests of the poor. The Infirmary Managers, having acquired the Watson Hospital site, proceeded to arrange for the disposal of the property they were about to quit, and as the University authorities were at the same time considering a scheme for the extension of their buildings, Mr. M<sup>c</sup>Laren was one morning startled to learn that the Managers had agreed to sell the whole grounds and buildings of the Old Infirmary to the University for £20,704 16s., a sum fixed upon by mutual valuation. Regarding the bargain as a disastrous surrender of Infirmary interests, he hastily consulted a few private friends, Mr. Josiah Livingston, Mr. Hugh Rose, and others, and having with them satisfied himself that the property in open market would bring a much larger sum than £20,704, he and Mr. Rose, on 21st January, applied to the Court of Session for an interdict against the Managers carrying out their agreement with the University. Two days afterwards he wrote a letter offering, on behalf of Mr. Livingston and himself and five other gentlemen, an upset price of £30,000 for the property, the offer to be held binding for three months, and afterwards extended to six months. A protracted controversy ensued, embittered by an indiscreet attack made on the interdictors by Sir Alexander Grant, Principal of the University, at the annual dinner of the Royal Scottish Academy, and complicated by a second arrangement, whereby, as a compromise, the University increased its offer to £25,000. In October, the Judge who heard the case in the first instance (Lord Gifford) decided in favour of the interdictors and against " the sacrifice of £5000 of the Infirmary funds " by the Managers. In his judgment Lord Gifford said :—" The course which the Managers ought to adopt in the unfortu-nate circumstances which have arisen is to expose the whole subjects for sale by public roup "—he assumed that Mr. M<sup>c</sup>Laren would renew his obligation to offer at the public sale £30,000—" and thus a great benefit will be secured to that important charity, which, notwithstanding the past liberality of the public, stands in need of all the funds it can obtain." The Managers acquiesced in this judgment, and they after-wards wrote Mr. M<sup>c</sup>Laren, asking whether he would abide by his offer, although the period of six months during which it was to be held binding had expired. On 30th November Mr. M<sup>c</sup>Laren replied :—

" We are of opinion that the proper time to make the inquiry will be when the committee has reported, and the Managers have adopted the report, and resolved to expose the property to public sale in the manner recommended by Lord Gifford, as being the proper rule to be followed in such cases. When these matters are all fixed, and also the date of delivery, we will be glad to hear from you on the part of the Managers, addressed to Mr. Living-ston, when a meeting of the parties to the former offer will be held ; and any such communication will be favourably considered, with the desire to prevent the property from being sold for less than £30,000. I may say, on the part of my two friends and myself, that we think no property can be so advantageously sold as when the seller is able to deliver it within a short time after the sale ; and that, if this rule be followed, the property will not be knocked down at the upset price of £30,000, but will bring a larger sum for the benefit of the Infirmary, the interests of which alone induced us to interfere in the matter."

The Managers thereupon wisely declined " to take any steps at present towards a sale," and their decision, while proving of great financial benefit to the Infirmary, saved Mr. M<sup>c</sup>Laren and his friends from any temptation to become property-jobbers ; for subsequent events proved that if they had acquired the property at the price of £30,000, they, if so disposed, could have far more than recouped themselves for their outlay.

Another controversy arose at this time of much wider interest—that regarding the medical education of women in the University. This is not the place to give a detailed account of that episode in the history of the University of Edinburgh, which its best friends would doubtless wish to leave unwritten. It is sufficient to say that in 1869 Miss Jex Blake and four other ladies (the number being afterwards somewhat increased) applied for permission to study medicine at the University. The Medical Faculty of the University, in a momentary impulse of liberalism, and influenced by Sir James Simpson, Professor Hughes Bennett, and Professor Balfour, granted the application, subject to the condition that the lady-students were to be taught in separate classes. The Senatus and the University Court confirmed the resolution of the Medical Faculty, and regulations were inserted in their Calendar, of which the first was, " Women shall be admitted to the study of medicine in the University." During the session which followed all went well, and had the ladies been wise enough not to achieve any marked success in their classes, their opponents, who probably counted on their failure, might have acquiesced in their continued studies. The ladies, however, gained some of the highest honours open to them, and this proof of coming success roused the smouldering animosity of the hostile faction, or, let us say, the professional jealousy of the medical students. Every possible difficulty was now put in the way of the lady-students, and after they had attended the classes of the few medical professors who bravely stood by them, and the four extra-mural classes that were allowed by the rules of the University, they found the path to all further progress hopelessly barred. One necessary part of the education of a medical student is the giving attendance in the wards of an hospital of a certain size for two years. The Edinburgh students have always received this part of their education in the wards of the Edinburgh Infirmary, and here the ladies also applied for admission; but the influence of the hostile professors, led by Professor Sir Robert Christison, was now paramount alike in the University and in the Infirmary, and the Infirmary Managers refused to admit them. The lady-students appealed to the Court of Contributors, *i.e.*, the subscribers to the Infirmary, who elect annually a certain number of the Board of Management. In January 1871 a stormy meeting was held to elect the new Managers, when the chief question at issue was the admission or non-admission of lady-students to the Infirmary wards. Neither party spared any effort to ensure the success of their candidates, many subscribers coming considerable distances to vote; but the hostile professors won the day, and the ladies were kept out of the Infirmary.

Both Mr. and Mrs. M<sup>c</sup>Laren had warmly sympathised with the ladies from the commencement of the struggle, and actively helped them in this Infirmary contest. Mr. M<sup>c</sup>Laren attended various meetings in their favour, and publicly identified himself with the movement, only stipulating for separate classes for the ladies in some few subjects.

"There were some classes," he said, "which, if he had a say in the matter, he would not have mixed, but separate. In regard to a large proportion of the medical classes, however, he saw no reason whatever why they should be separate. He saw no more reason why ladies should not walk into certain gentlemen's classes than why they should not walk into church and sit beside gentlemen there.　In old times ladies sat on one side of the church and men on the other.　He believed the opposition manifested in the present case was just the remains of that sort of feeling; and as men and women now sat together in places of worship—with the single exception of that small and highly respectable body the Friends, who still kept to the old plan—he did not see why any separation should exist in the class-rooms of the University except in the case of particular classes which he should not name.　He was therefore quite in favour of a lady paying her fee and walking into any ordinary class in the University, and being subjected to the same examinations and getting the same honours and degrees as a man was entitled to get.　The strong point to his mind was, that there were thousands of women of all classes in this country who earnestly wished to have highly educated women as their medical advisers.　It was not merely a question of the seven—or even if it were seven hundred—women applying to be medical students; it was for the women who would wish to consult female practitioners that the committee were attempting to legislate.　In the case of the former, there might be personal hardship in their not being allowed to follow the calling for which they thought they were peculiarly fitted; but in regard to the latter, the course pursued amounted to punishing one half of the whole human race for the supposed benefit of a small close body like the professors of the University of Edinburgh, who imagined that they had a right to put up this barrier to stop the progress of education. He thought the thing was altogether indefensible on any sound principle."

On every occasion his advice and help were at the service of the ladies, and, in company with Professors Masson and Calderwood and others, he strenuously fought year after year for justice and fair-play in the Infirmary contests.　At one time, indeed, they obtained the victory, but they were not able ultimately to make headway against the prejudices of the medical profession.　The following letter testifies to the valuable help given :—

10 REGENT TERRACE, *January* 1, 1872.



DEAR MRS. M<sup>c</sup>LAREN,—I cannot let this evening pass without saying to *you* how much I feel we were indebted to Mr. M<sup>c</sup>Laren to-day. The number of strong points on our side he brought out (that about the firms especially), and the calm acuteness, wisdom, and force with which he brought them out, struck me particularly. Without his presence and interposition at critical points, we should have lost much of our strength to-day. Doubtless he will watch all the immediate sequel; but I would fain convey to him, through you, my hope that he will follow up what he has done to the uttermost, by observing every point for us, and giving his advice.—Yours very truly,

DAVID MASSON.

The ladies had many friends of whom Edinburgh may be proud, both among the citizens and in the University, as well as among the students, and they received the greatest help from the press. An action was eventually brought in the Court of Session to try the question whether lady-students were entitled to be enrolled with the view of qualifying for a medical degree. It was determined in the negative—a decision much regretted at the time, but which did not prevent the opening of the medical profession to women through other universities and medical schools.

As Mr. M<sup>c</sup>Laren was never lacking in the discharge of the duties of citizenship, such objects as the relief funds in connection with the distress in Lancashire during the American civil war, the Indian and China famines, and the City of Glasgow Bank failure engaged Mr. M<sup>c</sup>Laren's administrative skill in addition to his platform advocacy. As he had opportunity or as he perceived necessity, he gave personal aid, but always unostentatiously. An illustration of the extent of his private beneficence was unexpectedly revealed in 1865, eight years after its spontaneous and generous bestowal. A journalist having, with what was

1872

at the time characterised as "unexampled impertinence,"
called for a catalogue of Mr. M<sup>c</sup>Laren's acts that were not
purely selfish, elicited from Mr. John Gray of Edinburgh
an unexpected reply. Mr. Gray felt called upon to refute
the sneer, and he most effectually did it by the publication
of a simple but touching narrative :—

"I was," he wrote, "a partner in the Western and Edinburgh and Glasgow Banks when they failed, and by the calls
made upon the shareholders of the former I lost my all—the produce of forty years of hard labour. Mr. M<sup>c</sup>Laren, hearing of my
misfortune, called at my house, kindly sympathised with me, and
presented me with the handsome sum of £100. I may state
that this was the first time Mr. Duncan M<sup>c</sup>Laren ever entered
my dwelling, and I never obliged him in any way whatever. I
am only his neighbour as to our residences. I leave the public
to judge whether this was an unselfish act or not."

Instances of his unobtrusive generosity might be multiplied in cases where he had known that fidelity to duty in the
public good had involved pecuniary difficulties, for he could
warmly sympathise with those who sacrificed material advantages for the sake of principle. But although many cases
of a similar nature might be cited, matters such as these
are best kept private, except where, for public reasons, such
as those that influenced Mr. Gray, they are made known.

An interesting occasion of public jubilation in which
Mr. M<sup>c</sup>Laren took part was the celebration of the marriage
of the Duke of Edinburgh with the Grand Duchess Marie
Alexandrovna in January 1874. The marriage was extremely popular, and was generally and gratefully accepted
as a pledge that the great and costly blunder of the Crimean
War would not be repeated. The British public were willing to believe that at the coming of the Russian Princess,

the Czar's "own imperial flower" and his "people's pride," clouds would disperse—

> "And some diviner air
> Breathe through the world, and change the hearts of men."

In the universal jubilation, Edinburgh, as the giver of their popular title to the Prince and Princess, heartily participated. The citizens held a soirée, which the late Lord Gifford happily described as "a wedding party," and Mr. McLaren, as one of the wedding-guests, proposed a resolution expressing "the citizens' loyal and unfeigned attachment to the throne and person of the Queen, and their grateful acknowledgments of the manifold blessings which under God have accrued to the British Empire from her Majesty's long and happy reign."

From citizens' meetings for the consideration of burning questions of the day which might be regarded as non-partisan and non-municipal Mr. McLaren was seldom absent. In this category may be placed demonstrations such as those which denounced the proclamation of martial law in Jamaica by Governor Eyre in 1865, the Fugitive Slave Circular issued by the Tory Government in 1876, and the Turkish atrocities in Bulgaria at a later period of the same year. At the meeting held in condemnation of the Jamaica massacres he vindicated the missionaries, prominent among whom were United Presbyterian ministers, from the Governor's reckless charges of complicity in rebellion, arson, and murder, and he demanded that Mr. Eyre and the three subaltern officers he had employed as a summary tribunal for the conviction of Mr. Gordon and his friends should themselves be brought to England and arraigned for murder;—"three young men," said Mr. McLaren scornfully, "who, it is very likely, if they were asked the difference between treason, conspiracy, and sedition, would not be able to tell." "We know," he proceeded, "how the last great rebellion in this country was put down by the Duke of Cumberland when he burnt Highland cottages and slaughtered people, but there were not so many lives taken then, even after the Highlanders had fought two battles with the Queen's troops and gained one—there were not so many put to death in that great rebellion as at this paltry outbreak in Jamaica." He concluded by demanding that Governor Eyre and his three petty officers should be recalled, and that they should never again be employed in her Majesty's service. In this demand Mr. M<sup>c</sup>Laren only anticipated the verdict of public opinion, on which the "services" were compelled to act.

The Fugitive Slave Circular meeting was a noisy and excited gathering. The Tory party in the city attended in force to defend the circular, and thus associated the Conservatives with the new policy to a greater extent than even the promoters of the demonstration were disposed to do. But the result was none the less satisfactory because the proceedings were stormy; and Mr. M<sup>c</sup>Laren at the close, in moving the vote of thanks to the Lord Provost for presiding, expressed himself well satisfied. "The meeting," he said, "called to remembrance old times forty or fifty years ago, when Edinburgh exhibited an Anti-Slavery sentiment that was well known throughout the United Kingdom. There was another reason too which pleased him, and that was that the speaking had been strictly to the question of slavery, and that the occasion had not been made one for attacking the Government or for attacking anybody. They had simply asserted the principle that British ships of war should be used, so far as they were used in this connection, in mitigating the horrors of slavery, and in certain circumstances in allowing poor slaves to escape."

At the Turkish Atrocity meeting he again raised his voice in favour of human freedom. He proposed the leading resolution condemning the misgovernment of the Turks, and in concluding his speech he thus outlined the policy which most harmonised then, and still most harmonises, with the best traditions of British policy and the happiness of the people of South-Eastern Europe :—" I have no hostile party feeling against the Tory Ministry. If they would use their influence to get good government for these Turkish provinces; if the government were to be of such a nature that practically it would be self-government, as suggested by Mr. Gladstone, with only a tie of union with Constantinople by payment of an annual sum as tribute—if our Government could accomplish that—enfranchise the Christians and free them from those horrors to the end of time, my opinion is that they would be forgiven for all that has been done in the past."

In 1874 Mr. M<sup>c</sup>Laren was present in Westminster Abbey at the funeral of Dr. Livingstone. Few lives ever touched him with the enthusiastic sympathy that he felt for the simple heroism of the great African missionary and explorer who had begun life as a poor factory-boy ; and he was deeply gratified at being asked to act as one of the pall-bearers when the last sad honours were paid to his distinguished countryman. Twenty-two years before, in his official capacity as Lord Provost, he had attended the funeral of the Duke of Wellington in the same historic sanctuary. On both occasions the nation mourned a hero " without fear and without reproach," who had gone through life facing death obedient to duty, and true to the principles each held dear. But even the obsequies of the great Duke, laid to rest in his ripe age, with the highest in the land among his chief mourners, had not for Mr. M<sup>c</sup>Laren the holy and

1876

The Turkish atrocitie

pathetic interest which surrounded the grave of the African missionary. Struck down in the midst of his work, and dying alone in the far-off desert, with the quiet courage that had characterised his life, he little dreamed how his earnest longing to rest in his own country would be thus marvellously fulfilled. Two years later Mr. McLaren joined in the unveiling of the statue of this great man by Mrs. D. O. Hill in Princes Street Gardens. Mrs. McLaren was greatly interested in this work, both from her love and admiration for Dr. Livingstone himself, and from the pleasure it gave her to see the work of a distinguished woman thus honourably recognised. In a letter dated August 1876, she thus describes the ceremony :—

" Dr. Moffat (Dr. Livingstone's father-in-law), who Christianised the Bechuana tribe in South Africa, was the centre of interest among those assembled. Eighty years of age, he stood there, noble, erect, with a face and eyes that seem to have all the fire of a tropical sun—those splendid eyes, that tell you they have looked upon the grand wilderness of Nature, and looked with noble courage upon the wild heart of the desert, and yet beam with all the tenderness for mankind and hope of the future which his love for his Saviour had called forth, and which the conscious possession of a Saviour's love has beautified and deepened. I never saw a finer face. I liked to see him and papa stand together—so different, and yet so like in the grand realities of devotion and courage. I once saw them and William Chambers sitting—the three side by side, at a meeting of Gavazzi's; and I felt that Scotland did certainly produce wonderful men. Mrs. D. O. Hill [1] wished me to unveil the statue, and so did Mrs. Falshaw, as I had been so much interested in the work. I said it was the Provost's wife who should do it; but they kindly made me take part. It was a pretty sight to see the young ladies place the wreath upon the statue. Your

---

[1] The sculptor, sister of Sir Noel and Mr. Waller H. Paton.

father had the pleasure of driving Mrs. Hill and her sister afterwards to a meeting of the Livingstone Memorial Committee in George Street, where we had cake and wine, and he, as Member for the city, proposed a vote of thanks to the gifted sculptrix in a beautiful little speech which came warm from his heart, and which she seemed much to appreciate. We afterwards lunched with Mrs. Hill, and I sat next one of Livingstone's sisters, and watched her countenance with intense sympathy. There was no face there with half the expression *hers* wore. I knew so well all she felt, and turned to tell her so. I said, 'No one can feel like a sister, not even a wife.' She said, 'I believe you are right.' I added, 'I see in your face all the memories of the past; the thought of your father, your mother, the early home; you trace everything in your brother's life, and think what he and all those who lived with him would feel could they see the present; none can enter into all this but yourself.' She pressed my hand, and seemed glad of my sympathy. How my heart went out to her she could scarcely know!"

1876

# CHAPTER XVIII.

*PARLIAMENTARY WORK.*

Mr. M<sup>c</sup>Laren was sixty-five years of age when he entered
Parliament.  Most men, when they reach this mature age,
think themselves entitled to seek repose; but in 1865, when
he was chosen by his fellow-citizens to represent them in
Parliament, Mr. M<sup>c</sup>Laren had no such desire.  He had been
at work since boyhood; for more than thirty years he had
held a front place among the public men of Edinburgh, and
his holidays had been few.  Notwithstanding all the wear
and tear to which it had been subjected, the spring of his
mind retained its elasticity unimpaired.  Experience had
taught him wariness and wisdom, but it had not closed his
mind against susceptibility to new impressions.  He was
quick as ever to observe and learn, to gauge public opinion,
and to respond to the spirit of the times in so far as it was
progressive and healthy.  The enthusiasm which makes early
manhood chivalrous had not left him when he entered the
House of Commons.

And while no young man could have been inspired by a
fresher ardour than Mr. M<sup>c</sup>Laren, it may safely be said that
in other respects he enjoyed qualifications for parliamentary
service greater than many new Members possessed.  Time
had brought him knowledge and experience.  Few possessed
a wider and more intimate acquaintance with political
questions.  He was familiar with parliamentary manners

and with the forms of the House; he was unhampered
by official connections or the desire of office.  Occupying
the corner-seat on the third bench below the gangway,
which had formerly been occupied by Mr. Bright—a part
of the House in which a sturdy band of Scottish and
English Radicals usually sat—he found himself among
associates and friends, old Free Traders, disciples of the
Manchester School, uncompromising Liberationists, who appreciated his talents and welcomed him as an ally.  Mr.
M<sup>c</sup>Laren soon found that he was almost as well known in
the imperial senate-house as on the public platform of an
Edinburgh citizens' meeting.  It is not to be wondered at
that, in these circumstances, he achieved in his own way a
parliamentary success.  A more enthusiastic gathering than
that which he addressed when rendering an account of his
stewardship at the close of the first session could rarely be
seen.  Its tone throughout was one of triumph.  The electors recognised that the conduct of their senior Member,
the work he had done, and the influence he had acquired,
had falsified all the adverse predictions of his opponents.
" Mr. M<sup>c</sup>Laren," said Mr. Rose, " had been the Member of
his political opponents as well as of his friends, the representative of the poor as well as of the rich ; " and on more
occasions than one the Town Council had felt themselves
called upon to thank him for the efforts he had made on
behalf of the city.  " We did great service not only to
Edinburgh, but to Scotland and to the United Kingdom, in
returning Mr. M<sup>c</sup>Laren," was the testimony of Mr. David
Dickson in proposing the vote of thanks at the close, and
the crowded meeting most heartily assented.  Mr. Charles
Seeley, then Member for Lincoln, writing to Mr. M<sup>c</sup>Crie,
the co-chairman of the Independent Liberal Committee,
said :—

"Mr. M<sup>c</sup>Laren is a man whose judgment is much esteemed, and he is listened to in the House whenever he speaks with great respect. Firm, temperate, and courteous, he is of course much liked and respected. It is a great honour for any man to represent Edinburgh, but Edinburgh will not lose in position by having Mr. M<sup>c</sup>Laren for its Member. If we had a hundred and fifty M<sup>c</sup>Larens in the House, we might not have such long speeches, but there would soon be a considerable improvement in the management of the public business."

votion
luty.

But though the conditions under which he entered Parliament were highly favourable, Mr. M<sup>c</sup>Laren had to work hard to win and to maintain his parliamentary reputation. He applied to the discharge of his duties all the methodical business habits and self-exacting scrupulousness he had displayed in the municipal sphere. He shirked no duty imposed upon him either by the Committee of Selection or by his constituents; and while as a member of parliamentary committees he showed himself alike faithful and useful, he left no municipal deputation unattended, and no elector's letter unanswered. His correspondence, which related to nearly every Scottish subject discussed at Westminster, and which extended to every constituency in Scotland, was in itself a heavy burden. In a long letter dated Park Hotel, St. James Street, 8th March 1866, Mrs. M<sup>c</sup>Laren gave to their eldest son, now Lord M<sup>c</sup>Laren, then recruiting his health at Algiers, a graphic account of the family life in London, and of Mr. M<sup>c</sup>Laren's work in Parliament. That work engrossed Mr. M<sup>c</sup>Laren's whole time and energies.

"   .   .   .   .   .   You will excuse his silence," she wrote, "when I say he has about a score of letters to answer every morning, besides reading up for the House. . . . I never saw any one so persevering and conscientious, and who had so few

selfish wants to supply.  I have often been very anxious about
him lest his health should give way.  He looks thin; but he
enjoys his new sphere of duty; and I am well satisfied to have
some self-denial to practise for the sake of his being put, though
as it were at the eleventh hour, in his right place.  But when
I see his wonderful adaptation to fill the highest post, that not
only his own city, but parliamentary life could confer, I regret
that a longer time has not been given him to prove his power to
advance the interests of the nation."

His place was seldom vacant when the House assembled
at four o'clock, and in the earlier portion of his sixteen years'
service he generally waited till the adjournment.  Mr. Seeley,
in the letter previously quoted, said :—" Mr. M<sup>c</sup>Laren was
so constantly in his place in the House, that I pointed out,
I believe on more than one occasion, that his health must
necessarily be impaired if he gave up so much of his time
to his parliamentary duties."  This warning was unheeded
session after session, until the doctors intervened and autho-
ritatively forbade late attendances.  In 1868 Mr. M<sup>c</sup>Laren,
during his convalescence after his serious illness at Harrogate, already referred to, writing to his committee, said :—
" I have indeed been stricken very low; and the wonder
is that I have survived to profit, as I hope I shall, by the
warning to be always ready, not knowing when our time
may come."  But this warning did not cause him to make
any relaxation in his round of duties.  Happily his recovery
was rapid; and by the time the new Parliament reassem-
bled, he was as eager for work as the youngest Member of
the House.  It was not till some years after this illness that
he consented to withdraw his attendance at the House shortly
after midnight.  But he always broke the half-past twelve
limit when any Scottish or other special business or any
important division required his presence; and unfortunately

many calls of this kind were made upon him. During his last parliamentary session in 1881, this legislator of more than fourscore years was frequently seen in the House as late as two or three o'clock in the morning, waiting to defeat the efforts of the Education Department to push forward their Educational Endowments Bill at some unexpected, and therefore, for them, auspicious moment; and on his arrival at home he would briskly relate the night's proceedings to his wife before retiring to rest.

Mr. M<sup>c</sup>Laren's parliamentary work with reference to educational, ecclesiastical, and to some extent also municipal questions, is fully described in other chapters. But that work, important and extensive though it was, formed only a fraction of his parliamentary service. He was essentially a practical politician, and though warmly interested in imperial questions, he mainly concerned himself with home affairs; and the poorer and humbler classes were his peculiar care. To befriend individuals or sections of the community beyond the circle of official influence, and neglected because of their comparative helplessness, afforded him true pleasure. Such instances as the following were by no means uncommon. During his first session of Parliament, a widow, whose son had enlisted in the Royal Marines, and who had with difficulty raised the redemption-money, brought her case under the notice of Mr. M<sup>c</sup>Laren. He at once prepared a statement of facts; he went with it personally to Sir John Pakington, then First Lord of the Admiralty, who could not have paid more attention to it " though it had been the case of a colonel or an admiral; " and by and by he was rewarded by a call from the man to thank him for his successful exertions to secure his release, and to tell him that instead of getting 3s. 6d. per week as a marine, he was earning 25s. 6d. per week as a plasterer in Edinburgh. On another occasion, Eliza Wigham, also a friend of the friendless, directed his attention to the injurious operation of the hawkers' license against the weak and the aged, who could earn a living by hawking during the summer months, but were unable to carry on their trade during the cold and inclement winter season; and after some patient and persistent negotiation at the Treasury Office—for evil is sometimes done more by want of thought than by want of heart—he succeeded in obtaining an alteration of the law, allowing the issue of licenses for the summer six months, and saving the humble but honest people referred to half of the outlay for which they had been formerly held liable. A deputation of coach-workers brought under his notice a one-sided and vexatious application of the duty on cabs and hackney-carriages, under which the poorer classes of coachmasters were required to pay a heavier proportion of duty on each cab than their wealthier neighbours. He called on Mr. Gladstone, and afterwards sent to the Treasury a full statement of the grievance. The inequality was quickly redressed, and soon afterwards Mr. M<sup>c</sup>Laren, when being driven home one evening, received the thanks of his cabman, who said he had been saved £5 by the alteration of the regulation. In 1870, on the representation of his philanthropic friend Mr. George Laing, of Edinburgh, he exerted himself to secure a modification of the stamp-duties exigible on the conveyance of land for workmen's houses of £10 rental and under, and ultimately he induced Mr. Stansfield, then Secretary of the Treasury, to adopt the following clause in his Consolidated Stamp Duties Bill:—" No lease, or tack, or agreement for a lease or tack in Scotland of any dwelling-house or tenement, or part of a dwelling-house or tenement, for any definite term not exceeding a year, at a rent not exceeding

the rate of £10 per annum, is to be charged with any higher
duty than one penny." In the following year, with Mr.
Baxter at the Treasury, he obtained the abolition of another
still more inequitable and vexatious stamp-law, that, namely,
which rendered people who obtained valuation merely for
their own information liable in a ten-shilling stamp duty.
In this session also he found opportunities of letting
the poor Highlanders know they had a friend in Parliament. Mr. Lowe was then Chancellor of the Exchequer,
and Mr. M<sup>c</sup>Laren pleaded hard though unavailingly with
him to secure the exemption of the Highland crofters from
the 15s. duty on ponies and carts, which, in addition to
agricultural work, were employed in conveying them and
their families to church, frequently a long distance from
their homes.

But, as Mr. Rose justly pointed out in the passage quoted,
Mr. M<sup>c</sup>Laren was Member for the rich as well as for the
poor. The wealthier classes and the learned professions
gladly availed themselves of his willingness and his power
to serve them. When the Lunacy Bill was before Parliament, the College of Surgeons and the College of Physicians
represented to him the injustice to which they were exposed
under the existing law, which enabled any man who had
been placed in an asylum under a medical certificate to bring
an action of damages for false imprisonment, even after all
the witnesses who could have spoken to the case were dead;
and they quoted in illustration a case which had been raised
ten years after the death of the necessary witnesses. Mr.
M<sup>c</sup>Laren framed a clause which satisfied the Colleges, limit-
ing the time of raising such actions to one year after the
liberation of the patient, and this clause was afterwards
embodied in the Lunacy Act. When the Life Assurance
Companies' Bill was passing through the House in 1870,

he, as representing a constituency largely interested in
life assurance, gave the measure a cordial support; but he,
always proud of the reputation of a great Scottish Institution, promptly contradicted an injurious misrepresentation
made in debate, to the effect that the Scottish Widows'
Fund had undervalued its liabilities by £179,000. "The
Scottish Widows' Fund," he said, "was the largest life
assurance office in the world, it having an annual income
of above £600,000, and its accumulated capital amounted
to four and a half millions. Any actuary, therefore, who
should have the boldness to come forward and assert
that the business of the office was based upon erroneous
calculations could never expect to receive the least credit,
and would only show his own incompetence for his profession." As regards the Scottish banks, while he had no
sympathy with English attacks, and while he cordially
assisted them in their claim to open branches in London,
which the English bankers so stoutly resisted, he complained of the monopoly, which was ever getting closer,
enjoyed by these institutions; and when the Committee on
Banks of Issue was appointed in 1875, he made an unsuccessful attempt to get two Members added as representatives of
the public outside the banks. In the various attempts at
legislative reform regarding the courts of law which were
made from time to time, he cordially co-operated in the
interests of the public, which he also believed to be the
true interests of the profession, He advocated, as desirable
changes, the abolition of the double sheriffship; the reduction of the number of sheriff-substitutes as vacancies should
occur; the enlargement of judicial areas, through which the
sheriffs should travel on circuit, after the manner of the
English County Court judges; the increase of salaries as
compensation for the increased work; and above all, the

1866

The law-
courts.

prevention of delay and the limitation of expense in sheriff-court procedure. In 1877 he supported a motion for the abolition of the double sheriffship; induced the Lord Advocate to extend the limitation of choice for the sheriffship to advocates of not less than five, in place of three years' standing at the bar, and earnestly counselled the adoption of an arrangement under which merit, and not political service or party preference, should be the ground on which the appointments of all judicial officers were made. But he never favoured the elevation of the dignity and the enlargement of the duties of the sheriff at the cost of diminished efficiency in the work of the Court of Session. He wished law and justice to be made easily and cheaply obtainable in the supreme court as well as before the subordinate tribunals. He therefore jealously guarded the status and efficiency of the Court of Session, objecting more particularly to proposals for the reduction of the number of judges from thirteen to eleven, and fortifying his position by statistics showing that the Scottish judges were not only fewer in number than their Irish brethren, but that they did more work and received less pay.

The successive projects of reform in the interests of the tenant-farmer which took practical shape after Mr. McLagan's return for Linlithgowshire enlisted his ready sympathy. He attended meetings of the Chamber of Agriculture and of the Highland Society, to hear the views both of the tenant-farmers and of the landlords; and all that he heard then confirmed the Radical opinions he had early entertained respecting hypothec, the protection of game, primogeniture, and the whole series of questions involved in the land laws. But while seeking to secure for the tiller of the soil a free hand in conducting its cultivation, and suitable security

alike for the crops he raised and the capital he expended
in fertilising his fields, Mr. M⁰Laren as a Free Trader was
constantly on the watch against the re-establishment of
anything like protection of this industry at the expense of
other trades.   Repeatedly during his parliamentary career
the Tory landlords attempted to introduce the thin end of
the wedge of Protection, generally in connection with cattle-
trade regulations, and latterly in the name of reciprocity;
but Mr. M⁰Laren was never thrown off his guard by these
devices.   In his first session, in connection with the Cattle-
Plague Bill, he found professed Liberals as well as Tories
connected with the landed interest making use of the panic
which had been excited to obtain arrangements under which
in large districts the cattle-plague, instead of proving a
calamity to the cattle-dealer, really contributed to his en-
richment because of the amount of compensation from the
taxes voted to him for slaughtered animals.   Mr. M⁰Laren
and other sound Liberals were not able to defeat this particular scheme for the protection of the landed interest at
the expense of all other interests; but one development of
this reactionary system he was fortunately able to check.
In explaining this particular service at the annual meeting
with his constituents he said: " In another part of the bill
it was proposed to lay a tax on the burghs of Scotland.
On that question I resisted the motion, for I was the first
speaker on that occasion—divided the House on it, and beat
Sir James Fergusson, who brought it forward.   He tried it on
a second occasion in regard to still smaller burghs—those
having less than 10,000 inhabitants—and again I had the
pleasure of opposing and beating him on the question.   To
show how adversely it works, I may mention an instance
of which I was told by a friend of mine, who represents
the burgh of Stockport in Cheshire, where the cattle-plague

1866

—

en's
k.

was very severe. In one of the clauses of the bill, Stockport was held to be part and parcel of the agricultural county of Cheshire, and liable to be taxed as if it were land; and the consequence was that the share of taxation for the cattle-plague falling on the burgh of Stockport was above £80,000, in addition to its being taxed enormously by the enhanced price of butcher-meat. Stockport and the other towns in the county have lately passed through a very grievous famine—the cotton famine—and it was never proposed to lay a rate in aid on the neighbouring counties. But Stockport did not want to have its rates aided by the agriculturists; and this is the way Stockport has been repaid for its patriotism."

To purely local questions, apart from those arising out of municipal administration, Mr. McLaren gave most careful attention. His efforts to secure the Queen's Park for great public political demonstrations may be quoted as instances of his zeal and pertinacity in this respect. During the Reform Bill agitation of 1866 a proposal to hold a demonstration in the Park was mooted; but some difficulty having arisen as to the right of admission for such a purpose, Mr. McLaren addressed the following letter to the Surveyor of the Board of Works for Scotland:—

EDINBURGH, October 27, 1866.

DEAR SIR,—A deputation of working-men applied to me, as one of the Members for the city of Edinburgh, to get the proper sanction for holding a great public meeting in the Queen's Park on the subject of Reform, similar to the meeting held in the same place and for the same purpose in 1832, when, according to the most reliable estimates, 50,000 men were present. I am not sure who has the right to grant or refuse the request in any Government department, and therefore I write to you as the principal Government resident officer in that department here, and if you have not full power to decide the matter, I will feel obliged by your forwarding the application to the proper quarter, with a request for an early answer, as the meeting is proposed to be held within three weeks from this date.

I may mention that I was personally present at the first meeting in 1832, and that it was conducted in all respects in the most orderly manner, and no injury was done to the Park or in any other way. And I have no doubt that the meeting now contemplated will be equally orderly and careful in all respects.

I need hardly remind you that there are no plants, or flowers, or trees in the Park which can be destroyed, and that beyond the memory of man it has always been regarded by the inhabitants of Edinburgh as an open common, to which they had the right of access.—I am, &c., D. McLaren.

R. Mathieson, Esq.

On the 1st of November Mr. Mathieson was enabled to inform Mr. McLaren that no hindrance would be put in the way of the proposed meeting, and the demonstration passed off without the slightest disturbance. But the question was not then settled. The Parks Bill for the United Kingdom, introduced in 1872, contained general provisions which threatened the old privileges, if not the rights, of the citizens of Edinburgh. In the House of Commons Mr. McLaren moved the insertion of a new clause in the Government bill, protecting the citizens' claim to hold public meetings in the Queen's Park, subject to regulations to be prescribed by the Board of Works. He maintained that the Park really belonged to the people, and not to the Queen. "It was at one time," he said, "held by the Earl of Haddington at a rental of £400 a year, but in order to settle the question in dispute, an arbitration took place with reference to the acquirement of the Park by the people of Edinburgh, and the arbitrators awarded £30,000. Everything about it for the benefit of the people was done

at an extravagant price long before the Crown acquired
their present position with respect to it." The Government, however, refused to accept the proposed clause, and
a few days afterwards a meeting held in Edinburgh under
the presidency of Councillor, now Bailie Cranston, passed
resolutions strongly condemnatory of the bill, and plainly
intimating that any law passed for the purpose of closing
the Queen's Park against public meetings would be delibe-
rately ignored or defied by the people. To this meeting,
convened by the Advanced Liberal Association, Mr. McLaren
sent a letter explaining his view of the position of the citizens, and the effect of the proposed measure.

"At present," he wrote, "if a meeting be held, the Crown
could not punish those engaged in it except for trespass, just
as any other landlord could for trespassing on his grounds. But
when this bill passes, every one engaged in such a meeting could
be fined £5 under the provisions of the Act, unless a strictly legal
right could be shown. Edinburgh has a far stronger claim
than London, for London has contributed nothing to lay out or
enclose the Parks, whereas the Council of Edinburgh from 1552
to 1555 laid out large sums (for that period) for these purposes.
We levelled the slopes of the Park of Holyrood, and built the
whole of the enclosing walls from the Palace round to Dud-
dingston. This appears from the minutes of the Town Council
and the Treasury accounts of that period, which are still in
existence. These facts make us in effect joint-owners of the
Park, for these outlays never would have been made except on
the understanding that all means of enjoying the Park for any
purpose whatever would be preserved to the citizens in all time
coming."

The speakers warmly commended Mr. McLaren for his
efforts. It behoved the citizens, said Mr. Cranston, to do
everything in their power to back him up; and Mr. David

Lewis, speaking with gratitude of his services, gave an
effective illustration of his indomitable courage. "On one
occasion," said Mr. Lewis, " when Mr. M<sup>c</sup>Laren was ordered
by his medical advisers to abstain from parliamentary work,
a measure being expected in which the interests of the
citizens were at stake, he refused to absent himself from the
House.  He stuck to his post, and rested on a couch night
after night in the lobby of the House of Commons, waiting
until this measure came up for discussion."  Eventually an
arrangement was effected practically carrying out the proposal embodied in Mr. M<sup>c</sup>Laren's clause, and the threatened
danger was averted.  Since 1872 various political demonstrations have been held in the Park under the regulations
prescribed by the Board of Works;  and the first important gathering after the privilege of public meeting had
been secured through the exertions of Mr. M<sup>c</sup>Laren was
the imposing trades' demonstration against the Criminal
Law Amendment Act in 1873, which some of the speakers
endeavoured to convert into a demonstration against Mr.
M<sup>c</sup>Laren himself.

Mr. M<sup>c</sup>Laren was always a jealous guardian of the status
of Edinburgh as the capital of Scotland, and as one of its
Members he heartily joined in every movement for resistance to changes which seemed to threaten the metropolitan claims of the city.  One of these occasions occurred in
1872, when proposed new postal arrangements, ostensibly in
the interests of Glasgow, seemed designed to reduce Edinburgh to the level of a provincial office.  Along with his
colleague, Mr. Miller, he accompanied an influential deputation from Edinburgh to Mr. Lowe, then Chancellor of the
Exchequer, and Mr. Baxter;  and a revision of the arrangements was secured, under which Glasgow, as a great postal
centre, obtained greater freedom of action, while the dignity

of the Edinburgh office as a metropolitan institution suffered
no diminution.   As opportunity presented, too, he made use
of his position in Parliament to illustrate the stinginess of
Government in their relation to Edinburgh institutions compared with the treatment of corresponding offices in London.
He was a severe economist, but he was a Scottish patriot as
well ; and his sense of justice and his patriotism induced
him to make frequent complaints in the House of the neglect
from which the capital of Scotland suffered at the hands of
the Imperial Executive.   In 1875, when the vote for the
Science and Art Department was under consideration, he
drew a contrast between Edinburgh and London arrangements for scientific instruction which vividly illustrated the
partiality of the Government.   Honourable members, he
said, were apt to think that out of London everything was
of little importance, but while the number of visitors annually to the whole of the London museums was 2,100,000, the
number of visitors to the Industrial Museum in Edinburgh,
still uncompleted, was 336,000, and yet it only received
one twenty-fifth part of the money spent in the English
capital.   Professor Huxley lectured to some fifty students
in the School of Mines in Jermyn Street, but during the
absence of Professor Wyvill Thomson in the " Challenger "
expedition he conducted the class of natural history in Edinburgh University, which consisted of 350 students.   Yet
during the preceding five years the payments to Jermyn
Street for education votes and salaries had been £25,181,
while the whole votes for the same purpose to the Edinburgh Museum had been £15,169.   " The same principle,"
Mr. M<sup>c</sup>Laren added, " runs through other grants."

Mr. M<sup>c</sup>Laren was in general sympathy with the objects
of the Peace Society.   He believed in defence, not defiance,
and claimed reasonable security for the persons and pro-

perty of his constituents. He accordingly assisted Mr. Macfie, the Member for the Leith Burghs, in his efforts to direct the attention of the Government to the "defenceless state of the Firth of Forth," and in a brief speech delivered in the House of Commons in 1871, he stated the claim of Edinburgh and Leith with great clearness and conciseness, and indicated the simple means of defence which were required. He pointed out that, while the iron-clads of a hostile naval power could not approach Glasgow, or Liverpool, or Hull for want of deep water, they could sail to within three miles of the Scottish capital and bombard it. And a tempting prize was within their reach. He reminded the House that the funds of the Banks of Scotland were kept in Edinburgh, and there was generally in store from three millions to four millions in gold; while the rental of the city, amounting to a million and a quarter per year, was greater than the gross rental of thirty or forty boroughs in England each returning the same number of Members to Parliament as Edinburgh. He claimed, therefore, that there should be reserved for the Firth of Forth a portion of the large sums expended on coast defence elsewhere, more especially in the South of England; and he added :—" When we know what was done in former times, without the advantages of steam, by the predatory raids of Paul Jones and his associates, and what these proceedings cost the country, we must feel that the Government are bound to take a special interest in this matter, and do something for the defence of Edinburgh, irrespective of the general question of the defence of our ports and harbours." He directed the attention of the naval engineers to the island of Inchkeith, situated midway between the Fife and Midlothian coasts, and suggested that the construction of fortifications on this island, supplied with a few heavy guns,

1871

The Inchkeith fortifications.

"would be all that would be required, together with a small body of men to conduct defensive operations." During the war panic in 1878, when the Government of the day obtained a vote of credit to the amount of six millions, Mr. M<sup>c</sup>Laren called on Mr. Hardy, now Lord Cranbrook, who was then Secretary of State for War, and directed his attention to the requirements of Edinburgh and Leith. The result was the almost immediate adoption of the simple plan of defence he had advocated seven years before.

On all questions affecting municipal and local administration, Mr. M<sup>c</sup>Laren, with his unrivalled personal experience and knowledge, was recognised as an authority on both sides of the House. In his first session he was appointed a member of the Select Committee which investigated the subject of the erection of houses for working-men, and when Mr. Disraeli was declaring that *sanitas sanitatum* was the foundation of his policy, he gave valuable aid to Mr. (now Lord) Cross in his conduct through the House of Commons of the legislative measures to which the Premier looked as the means of improving the condition of the working-classes and popularising his party. In numerous discussions on the vexed question of Poor-Law Reform he took a prominent part, and his sturdy opposition to the one-sided legislation promoted by the Irish members attracted general notice and commendation. When, in 1875, Mr. Downing moved the second reading of his Poor-Law Removal (Ireland) Bill, Mr. M<sup>c</sup>Laren delivered a speech which "scotched" the measure with facts and arguments, quite as effectually as the old Border warriors were wont to scotch their Southern invaders with their hooked axes. "What did this bill do?" he asked. "If a person from the most remote part of Scotland, say from Orkney, Shetland, or the Western Isles, came before the poor-law authorities of

Edinburgh or Glasgow, and wanted to be put upon the poor-rates there, so as to get indoor or outdoor relief, the question asked him was, ' How long have you been residing here—five years?' and if he said 'No,' then he was sent back to his parish. But if this bill passed, an Irishman would come, and he would be asked whether he had resided, not five years, but *one year*, and he would reply, ' I am an Irishman. I am a privileged person, entitled to a right of settlement after one year, and you are bound to take me because I have resided one year within your jurisdiction.' That was not equal right. Then if a poor Scotchman went to Ireland and told the same story—if he said, ' I have lived for one year in Ireland, and I want poor-law relief,' what did the poor-law authorities say to him? They said, ' We have no system of settlement in Ireland, and you cannot get any relief.' The authorities would not give that man a settlement in Ireland though he had been one year there, or even two, three, five, ten, or twenty years; in fact, they would not give him a settlement under any circumstances." In referring to this subject in his annual address to his constituents, Mr. M<sup>c</sup>Laren analysed a return he had moved for, which showed that in December 1874 there were only 100 Scotchmen in Ireland receiving parochial aid, while 13,510 Irishmen were the recipients of relief in Scotland; that there were only 14 Scotch lunatic paupers in all Ireland, while there were 487 Irish lunatic paupers in Scotland; that Scotland was saving the Irish landlords £11,688 per annum for the maintenance of lunatics, and only receiving £336 in return. It is to be hoped that, small though the number of Scottish paupers in Ireland was in 1874, it is even less now. After the publication of his return, Mr. M<sup>c</sup>Laren received a letter from a gentleman in Dublin stating that he was the honorary secretary of a society for looking after poor

1865

Scotchmen in Ireland. He was greatly surprised to hear that there were even a hundred Scotchmen in Ireland in receipt of parochial relief, and he asked for the particulars, in order that the society might investigate the cases.

Mr. McLaren was a master of the details as well as of the principles of finance. He generally spoke on Budget nights, and was one of the few men whose opinion on these subjects was respected, if not always deferred to, by the Treasury experts. When in 1871 Mr. Lowe was rejoicing over his lucifer-match-tax, which bore the ingenious device *Ex luce lucellum*, Mr. McLaren was one of the first critics to warn the briiliant Chancellor of the Exchequer that his self-congratulation was premature, as " the tax upon lucifer-matches would never stand the test of investigation," and that if the lucifer-stamp were insisted on, the authorities would need to build new reformatories to accommodate the youthful vendors who would systematically break the law. In numerous speeches, both within and without the House, he advocated a radical readjustment of the incidence of local taxation, and a radical rearrangement of the system of local government, based on the principle of popular representation and control. In 1870 Mr. Campbell, the Member for the Stirling Burghs (now Mr. Campbell-Bannerman, one of Mr. Gladstone's most successful lieutenants), won his parliamentary spurs by proposing, in an able and eloquent speech, that the principle of representation should be applied to the government and financial administration of counties. Mr. McLaren heartily supported Mr. Campbell. " My honourable friend," he said, " has explained in detail that there is not a vestige of representation in county government in Scotland, although there is a little in England. The Commissioners of Supply were originally a body created by

Parliament, consisting of a few gentlemen who were deputed to collect the taxes in the case of war, and to see that the supply so raised was duly paid into the Exchequer, and hence the name. It is a mere farce for these bodies to try and regulate the whole affairs of Scotland."

At Westminster, as well as at home, he was avowedly and consistently " on the side of the Ten Commandments." He strove to conform the legislation of Parliament to the requirements of the moral law, and to Christianise, and therefore humanise, the whole system of imperial and local administration. It was regard for public morals that induced him in 1868 to claim and obtain the extension to Scotland of the provisions of the bill requiring that the death-sentence should be executed within prison, and not on a public scaffold. As a magistrate he had had the painful duty imposed upon him of attending two executions, and his observation on these occasions had produced the strongest conviction that publicity did harm instead of good. It was a growing conviction of the indefensibility of capital punishment that induced him afterwards to allow his name to be added originally with Mr. Gilpin, Mr. Fowler, and Sir John Gray, and at a later period with his friends Mr. Pease and Mr. Leeman, to a bill for the abolition of the punishment of death for murder, and the substitution of the punishment of penal servitude for life. And in the same session, moved to indignation by reports of atrocities said to be committed in the Medical School of Edinburgh in the name of scientific teaching, he cordially supported Mr. Holt's measure for the prohibition of vivisection. Doubtless his Scottish Puritanism influenced him as much as his views as an economist in obtaining the suspension for one year of the vote for the Queen's Plates for Scotland, with the view of attacking the vote for the Queen's Plates for Ireland in the following

1865

Capital punishment.

Betting laws.

1881

year; and the same motives likewise guided him in helping to secure the passing of the bill for the suppression of public betting—a measure which the sporting fraternity have fortunately been less successful in undoing than they were in their agitation for the restoration of the Queen's Plates. His experience of the beneficial influence produced in Scotland by the working of the Forbes-Mackenzie Act made him an efficient as well as a hearty supporter of the Sunday-closing bills for Ireland and for various counties in England, introduced at different times into the House of Commons. He was a resolute opponent of the opium trade; and in his advocacy of the suppression of this odious traffic he gave to and received much help from his friend Mr. David M<sup>c</sup>Laren, now of Putney, whose name is honourably identified with the anti-opium agitation.[1]

Contagious Diseases Acts.

He was one of the earliest and throughout one of the most unflinching denouncers of the immoral legislation known by the name of the Contagious Diseases Acts. He regarded these Acts as a disgrace to the statute-book; and in him Mr. Stansfield, the self-denying parliamentary

---

[1] Mr. David M<sup>c</sup>Laren writes:—"I remember a very characteristic incident of Mr. M<sup>c</sup>Laren. He was asked, along with a number of public men throughout Scotland, lay and clerical, to sign a protest against the opium trade not long after the second Chinese war, when there was a strong feeling among all who informed themselves on that painful subject. The language of the protest in some passages was perhaps, in consequence, somewhat high-flown. Mr. M<sup>c</sup>Laren signed it, but in doing so remarked that it was not without some hesitation on account of the characteristic noticed. He said, 'I have always avoided the use of such language myself. I had recently a letter from Mr. Hill, the Recorder of Birmingham (a well-known authority in matters of crime and prison discipline), a gentleman I have never seen, with reference to some public matter, in which he says, "I have always admired your speeches in one point especially—you never have any peroration." I considered that one of the greatest compliments ever paid me.'"

leader of the movement for their repeal, found one of the staunchest and most fearless of his allies. In his attitude of uncompromising resistance he was in close accord with the kind of public sentiment which he most respected. He knew that good men and good women, irrespective of religious denomination or of party, were on his side; and he was warmly supported, even at the commencement of the struggle, by meetings in, and petitions from, his own constituency, one being signed by 7200 working-men. When the public first became aware of this legislation, which had been passed silently and secretly as a departmental bill, a monster petition was signed throughout the country expressive of indignation, and was signed by over a quarter of a million women. The petition was intrusted to Mr. M<sup>c</sup>Laren for presentation, and in this work he was assisted by the late Mr. Candlish, then Member for Sunderland. This bulky declaration of the opinion of the country was borne up the floor of the House with considerable difficulty by the two Members by means of handles attached to it, and was regarded with interest and astonishment by the numerous Members who were present, and whose curiosity had been excited regarding it by the receipt of a circular the same morning announcing the intended presentation.

The following letter, written by Mr. M<sup>c</sup>Laren after attending a large meeting in Newcastle, shows the deep interest he took in this subject :—

NEWCASTLE, *September* 28, 1870.

DEAR MR. GLADSTONE,—I take the liberty of sending you some remarks I made last night on a parliamentary paper issued by authority of the Government, which were very strong, but not nearly so strongly condemnatory as were my real feelings. The occasion was mainly a working-men's meeting here, which I came from Edinburgh last night for the purpose of addressing, at the

1865

A monster petition.

urgent request of the Ladies' Association established in London for the repeal of the C. D. Acts. You will see that a crowded meeting of over one thousand persons unanimously desired the repeal of the Acts, and have no desire for any inquiry. I likewise enclose a report of discussion at the Social Science Meeting on the same subject, in case you would like to see it, but I have not been a member of that body for many years. It also unanimously came to the same conclusion. I know personally nearly all the ladies forming the London Committee, and I am satisfied that they feel these Acts to be such an outrage on their sex that they will never desist from this agitation till they be repealed, and they will carry the war into every election until their object be accomplished. My own opinion is, that a speaker last night was correct in saying that if the Acts were not repealed next session, they would be repealed by the next parliamentary election.— I am, dear Mr. Gladstone, yours very faithfully,

D. M<sup>c</sup>Laren.

For Mrs. Butler and the other ladies who bore the brunt of the arduous struggle, which lasted till 1886, Mr. M<sup>c</sup>Laren ever retained the highest admiration, and he constantly aided them by speech and pen. Though he was no longer in Parliament when victory crowned their efforts, his sympathy remained undiminished, and he received with joy, during his last illness, the tidings that the Acts, so far as they related to Great Britain, were totally repealed.

Enfran-
chisement
of women.

When Mr. John Stuart Mill, in 1867, brought forward his amendment to the Reform Bill of Lord Derby's Government in favour of extending the parliamentary franchise to duly qualified women, Mr. M<sup>c</sup>Laren gave it an unhesitating support, and his influence also led others to do the same. At the close of the debate a distinguished statesman turned to him and said, "M<sup>c</sup>Laren, how are you going to vote?" "I shall vote for it, and I don't see how a man who had a good mother can do otherwise,"

Priscilla Bright McLaren

was the reply. "I had a good and noble mother also," was the rejoinder; and the two went into the lobby together and voted for the amendment. From that time the cause of the enfranchisement of women had no more steadfast friend than Mr. M<sup>c</sup>Laren. But he did not regard it merely as a woman's question. While admitting the strictly logical argument that so long as the qualification for the franchise is the payment of rates, a woman who paid rates was as much entitled to a vote as a man in the same position, he was disposed to advocate women's suffrage on the broader ground that it was a desirable measure in itself, for he believed that the influence of women in politics would tend to peace, temperance, and a policy of social and moral reform, from all of which men would gain equally with women. His house became the centre from which all Scottish agitation on the subject was conducted; for Mrs. M<sup>c</sup>Laren was the president, and Miss Agnes M<sup>c</sup>Laren and Miss Wigham were the secretaries, of the Edinburgh Society for Women's Suffrage. Meetings throughout Scotland were got up by these indefatigable secretaries, and addressed by Miss Jane Taylor of Stranraer, one of the first lady speakers on this subject, who always found that Mr. M<sup>c</sup>Laren's name acted as a talisman in ensuring a favourable hearing at that early stage of the question. At the first annual meeting of the Society, in 1870, when he presided, he was surrounded on the platform by the leading men in Edinburgh, including the Principal of the University (Sir A. Grant), Professors Kelland, Masson, and Calderwood, Sir Lyon Playfair, M.P., Sir David Wedderburn, M.P., Mr. Miller, M.P., the Rev. Dr. Wallace, now M.P. for the Eastern Division of Edinburgh, and many more, while Mr. Jacob Bright, M.P., was also among the speakers. The following annual meeting was honoured with the presence of Mr. John Stuart Mill, who was induced by the high regard he had for Mr. McLaren to visit Edinburgh for the purpose. It was the only meeting out of London that he ever addressed on the subject, and the Music Hall was crowded on the occasion. Mr. McLaren, in introducing Mr. Mill to the meeting, was able to assure him that public feeling was so cordially with him that the whole parliamentary strength of the Burghs and County and University had been put forth in favour of the movement, and that the Edinburgh Town Council had the distinguished honour of being the first public body to petition for his bill. Many years afterwards, in 1884, a still more remarkable meeting on this subject was held in Edinburgh, the only one, during his long life there, at which Mr. McLaren would not have been qualified to speak. It was a meeting entirely composed of, and addressed by, women. The Viscountess Harberton presided, and the Synod.Hall was crowded to its utmost capacity by Edinburgh women, assembled to declare that they asked for the franchise on the same conditions as men. This was one of a series of women's demonstrations held in many large towns in the kingdom, at three of which, in Manchester, Bradford, and Glasgow, Mrs. McLaren had presided, and, so far as public meetings can settle anything, they may be said to have settled in the affirmative the question whether women want the suffrage or not.

Besides giving his vote regularly in Parliament in favour of this measure, he cordially supported the admission of women to the School-Board and Municipal franchises, and advocated the election of women to School Boards and Poor-Law Boards or Boards of Guardians, feeling strongly that, in institutions where women and children were specially concerned, it was imperative that women should have a large share in the control. With Mr. Anderson, M.P. for Glasgow, he joined in introducing and carrying the first Married Women's Property (Scotland) Act, which was, in its day, a very important step in the direction of reform, though much wider measures have since been successively passed for Scotland and England. The Scotch Act was prepared by a Select Committee of the House of Commons, of which Lord McLaren, then Lord Advocate, was chairman, and became law in 1881. The English Act was introduced into the House of Lords in the following year by Lord Selborne, and passed both Houses in the same year.

1870

# CHAPTER XIX.

## *POSTAL REFORM—COUNTY ROADS.*



ONE of the first important extra-municipal works in which Mr. M°Laren engaged was the reform of the postal system. When he began business in Edinburgh, the postal rates and arrangements were practically prohibitory of mercantile and family correspondence, and the need for reform was universally acknowledged. When Mr. Rowland Hill published his pamphlet recommending a penny-postage, the Chamber of Commerce, the Merchant Company, and the Town Council all passed resolutions in favour of a reduction in the rate. And when, in May 1838, Mr. M°Laren, then Treasurer of the city, went to London—sailing from Leith, and reaching his destination in about forty-three hours—to give evidence before the Select Committee on Postage, of which Mr. Wallace, the Member for Greenwich, was chairman, he felt he was at liberty to say that, in earnestly recommending the penny-postage, he was not merely conforming to the views and desires of the public bodies named, but was likewise expressing " the general feeling that exists on the part of the community." He gave his evidence clearly and boldly, and it was no secret at the time that the facts and considerations he presented to the Committee produced a powerful impression in favour of the practicability as well as the advisability of the reform—confirming, as a personal result, a friendship formerly begun with Mr. Wallace, whom Mr. M°Laren always regarded in after years as entitled to as much credit for the introduction of the penny-postage as Mr. Rowland Hill himself.   As a witness, Mr. McLaren spoke with the knowledge and authority derived from personal experience and observation.   He was then in the prime of life, thirty-eight years of age; but he was a veteran in business.   " How long have you been in trade?" asked the chairman; and the prompt reply was, " Since I was a boy — I think about twenty-six years — con- stantly."   He frankly told the Committee that the post- age law was systematically and extensively evaded, and that public opinion countenanced and justified the evasion. For the purpose of saving the heavy postal rates, letters were made up in the form of parcels and given to the care of carriers; in nearly every parcel received or sent by merchants letters were enclosed for delivery; when any one was known to be contemplating a journey to any part of the country, for pleasure or on business, he was, *nolens volens*, converted into a letter-carrier; and while the Committee were sitting, Mr. Crouch, the well-known carrier, openly conducted an agency for the transmission and delivery of parcels in London for 1s. 3d. per parcel, in which everybody knew that possibly as many as thirty letters were enclosed. Mr. McLaren even did not hesitate to confess that he was himself an evader of the law.   " I may mention a circum- stance," he fearlessly said to the Committee, " that occurred the very afternoon I left for London.   I met a friend in the street in Edinburgh, to whom I mentioned that I was going; he pulled a parcel of letters out of his pocket and said, ' Here are some letters for London; I was just going to Mr. So-and-so, the bookseller, to get them enclosed in his parcel; will you have the goodness to take them?'   I put them in my pocket, and said to him jocularly that I would inform the Postage Committee through Mr. Wallace, whom I had the pleasure of knowing. He stated that he did not pay for one-tenth part of the letters which he either sent or received; that he was regularly in the habit of sending and receiving them in booksellers' parcels, and that it was the practice of the trade."

Mr. McLaren was thereupon asked if the same system of evasion would be continued if the postage were reduced, and he answered, with a claim to prescience in the matter which subsequent experience fully justified, " The advantage of putting a letter into the post-office, and thus securing its rapid delivery, in place of going to ask anybody to get it carried free, would be so great, that nobody would think of any other mode of conveyance than by the post-office." As illustrations of the bad effects of high postages, he gave instances of evasions resorted to by societies for religious and benevolent purposes in communicating with their contributors and sympathisers. He therefore advocated cheap postage as a great advantage to the social and religious world, as well as to the mercantile community. But his strongest plea was on behalf of the poor. " It would do a great deal of good," he said, " in a moral point of view, especially in facilitating correspondence amongst the poorer classes, and thus keeping up a kindly feeling between distant relatives, which is to a lamentable extent cut off by distance, in consequence of the difficulty of communicating arising from the high rate of postage. Poor people, of course, have not the same facilities in getting letters sent by mercantile houses as those engaged in business have, and I believe the effect in many cases is that relations who live at such a distance as between Edinburgh and London never correspond at all, and do not know whether their friends are living or dead."

As a picture of the condition of Edinburgh life fully half a century ago, as well as a further illustration of the advantages Mr. McLaren expected to flow from the adoption of the reform, of which he was one of the earliest and most effective advocates, this additional quotation may be given :—

"I observed, in reference to another inquiry in which I was recently engaged, that according to the last census in 1831, there were in Edinburgh 17,000 females more than males. On analysing the classified tables, I found that there were upwards of 12,000 female servants, which I have no doubt accounted for a considerable part of the difference between the males and females; and those servants, to a very great extent, would be taken from the country around Edinburgh, the three Lothians, Fifeshire, Stirlingshire, and Perthshire. The parents and friends of those servants would be delighted to have an opportunity of keeping up a correspondence with them; and I have no doubt that in very many cases it would be exceedingly beneficial, even in a moral point of view. When female servants come to large towns from a distance, they must feel themselves completely isolated beings, without a person that cares for them or sympathises with them, and the means of correspondence by letter, next to that of personal communication with their friends, is most likely to counteract the effect of such circumstances, and to keep alive those kindly feelings which ought to exist amongst relatives."

After an interval of a generation Mr. McLaren assisted in another important postal development. In March 1870 he was a member of a deputation who waited upon Lord Hartington, then Postmaster-General, to urge the introduction of the halfpenny-postage. He assured him of the financial soundness of the arrangement, telling him that private traders were willing to undertake the delivery of circulars at the halfpenny rate, and entreating him to keep the Post-Office from the dog-in-the-manger policy of neither adopting

1838

The half-penny-stamp.

the halfpenny rate itself nor allowing anybody else to do it. But while satisfied that the Post-Office Department would be a gainer by the change, he pleaded for the reform on the ground of public advantage. " It would certainly," he said, " be a great business gain to the people, and their moral gain would not be less, as the inhabitants of every hamlet in the country could then enjoy their newspapers daily, instead of having, as now, to wait a week for one."

The abolition of the county tolls Mr. McLaren regarded as the fitting corollary to the cessation of the burgh petty customs, and in the early stages of the Road Reform agitation he was one of the first supporters of the late Mr. William Pagan of Cupar-Fife, an astute lawyer, who long held a position of great influence in Fifeshire, and who, in 1845, initiated the Road Reform movement. Little sign of progress was observable, however, until, in 1858, Lord Elcho (now Earl of Wemyss) introduced a bill into the House of Commons. The measure obtained small support, and Lord Elcho, recognising that public sentiment was not sufficiently informed or matured to encourage the hope of satisfactory legislation, was content to accept a compromise in the form of a Royal Commission of Inquiry. Mr. McLaren, who for twelve years previously had been carefully studying the question, and who, in the Merchant Company, the Chamber of Commerce, and Town Council, had by public discussion been endeavouring to gain converts to the principle of free roads, was appointed a member.[1]  Twenty years afterwards he thus described his fellow-commissioners :—

---

[1] This was seven years before his entrance to parliamentary life. It is a noteworthy circumstance that this, the only honour or employment under the Crown ever offered to Mr. McLaren, came from a Conservative Government. In the numerous Commissions issued by Mr. Gladstone's Governments relating to subjects which had been the study of Mr. McLaren's life, his name was " conspicuous by its absence."

"The chairman was Mr. Smythe of Methven Castle, chairman of the Commissioners of Supply, Perthshire—a county in which, I believe, there was the largest number of trusts of any county in Scotland—a man of great experience, formerly connected with the Poor-Law Board, and deservedly enjoying the confidence of the great county in which he held this important position. Had no other man than Mr. Smythe been upon the Commission, his report alone, from his local knowledge and experience in the management of roads, would have greatly outweighed the report of any secret Commissioner. But Mr. Smythe was not alone. One of his colleagues was Sir John McNeil, a man so distinguished as to have been selected to go to the Crimea to investigate into the difficulties and abuses which had existed there [in the campaign against Russia], who made a report which was received with great satisfaction, and for which he received high honours from the Crown, having refused to accept any pecuniary compensation. A third Commissioner was Sir James Fergusson, a gentleman who was long a Member of the House of Commons, who had occupied the position of an Under-Secretary of State, and who had afterwards been appointed by Her Majesty's Government Governor of two of the greatest colonial dependencies. Sir James was a man of known experience and ability, and I have no doubt that, if he were again fortunate enough to secure a seat in the House,[1] his services would be taken advantage of in some important office by her Majesty's Government. A fourth Commissioner was Sir Andrew Orr, who had been Chief Magistrate of Glasgow, and who was a landowner in the county of Stirling; and all the four were large landowners."

It was an Ambulatory Commission. It visited various parts of the country, and held its courts of inquiry in presence of the public; but Edinburgh and Glasgow were its chief centres. At the former place no fewer than thirty-seven witnesses were heard, and at the latter as many as thirty-

---

[1] Sir James Fergusson is now M.P. for a division of Manchester, and Under-Secretary of State for Foreign Affairs.

three.  The evidence given left no room for doubt that
the prevailing opinion was in favour of the abolition of
tolls, and of the maintenance of roads by an assessment
on all lands and heritages within the counties and burghs
—the counties maintaining the roads outside, and the
burghs the roads inside the parliamentary boundaries of the
burghs.  The Commissioners reported accordingly, and a
large public meeting held in Edinburgh in 1860, under the
presidency of the late Sir John Forbes, energetically urged
the embodiment of the Commissioners' proposal in an Act
of Parliament.  A general Tolls Abolition Bill, introduced
in the following year by Lord Advocate Moncreiff, failed,
however, to pass; and though, by Mr. Pagan's unwearied
vigilance, the promotion of successive County Permissive
Acts discussions in the Chamber of Agriculture and other
public bodies, the holding of large and influential public
meetings, and a long series of interviews with Lord Advocates and Home Secretaries, the subject was kept constantly
before the country and before Parliament, Liberal Governments did not again show any strong desire to promote the
legislative reform required.  The formation of the Scottish
National Toll Association, of which Mr. M<sup>c</sup>Laren was one
of the leading spirits, gave an impetus to the movement
in 1872, and at last, in the following year, a deputation,
including more than one-half of the Scottish Members of
Parliament, arranged by Mr. H. Murray, the indefatigable
secretary of the Association, secured from Mr. Bruce (now
Lord Aberdare), the Liberal Home Secretary, a recognition
of the existence of a strong desire for a general bill, and
a promise to represent to his colleagues " that this was one
of the questions that eminently required to be dealt with at
their hands."  During the recess, at a representative meeting held in Edinburgh, Mr. M<sup>c</sup>Laren earnestly counselled

the friends of the movement to press the advantage they had gained; and encouraged by his advice and sanguine expectations, the Association carried on the agitation with increased resolution. But 1874 witnessed the termination of the first Gladstone Government and the beginning of the six years of Lord Beaconsfield's rule. At the earliest possible opportunity the reformers sought and gained the ear of Mr. Cross (now Viscount Cross), the Conservative Home Secretary. Mr. M<sup>c</sup>Laren introduced to the new Minister a deputation from the Convention of Royal Burghs, and in a long and masterly speech explained and enforced the case for abolition. "Then the burghs," said Mr. Cross towards the end of Mr. M<sup>c</sup>Laren's long and cogent argument, "would have free use of the roads in the counties;" and the rejoinder was quickly and effectively given, "Yes; and the counties would have free use of the burgh roads." He continued:—"In old times we travelled over the county roads, by coaches, to London and Manchester and elsewhere in England, and to country towns and districts, and it was then equitable that we should pay for them by the tolls on these coaches. But now we use the railways, and there is no longer any equitable claim on us to pay for these roads." In concluding, he assured the right hon. gentleman that if he enabled the Lord Advocate to promote "good and useful legislation" of the kind indicated, he would be rewarded with the gratitude of the people of Scotland.

Immediate legislation did not follow, but enough had been done to show that the Government "meant business;" and the attention shown to him in connection with this and many other subjects gradually forced Mr. M<sup>c</sup>Laren— strong partisan of the Liberal cause though he was—to the conclusion that Ministers of a Conservative Government listened with more consideration to the representations of the Scottish Liberal Members, and were in many respects more accommodating to those who were their political opponents in matters of administration, than a Liberal Government. During the recess Mr. Cross visited Scotland, and took pains to consult local opinion. Several bills followed, but it was not till 1878 that the work of legislation was seriously undertaken by the Conservative Government, represented by Lord Advocate Watson and Mr. Secretary Cross. Unfortunately this 1878 measure, notwithstanding the time the Government officials had had for consideration, was far from satisfactory, and Mr. M<sup>c</sup>Laren found it necessary at first to offer direct opposition. In his view, it unduly favoured the counties at the expense of the burghs, setting aside the equitable principle unanimously adopted by the Commissioners of 1858—no Radical Commission, as he reminded the House, but one appointed by a Conservative Government, and having himself as the only burgh representative—that burgh and county should accept the parliamentary boundary as the dividing-line, and each support the roads on its own side of the line. He ably and persistently defended the rights of the burghs, more especially of Edinburgh and Glasgow; and, in the interests of the smaller burghs stretching alongside the main turnpike roads, used almost entirely for county traffic, he proposed a special amendment, securing for them the option of merging themselves into the counties, so far as the maintenance of roads was concerned, in the same way as they had been merged as regards the management and maintenance of the police. Subsequently, in speaking to his constituents in explanation of his attitude to the Government measure, he said :—

The Ministerial Bill.

Mr. M<sup>c</sup>Laren's amendment.

"I had the honour of being one of its strongest opponents in its original state. It was a bill which, while professing to

abolish tolls, kept them up for ten years certain, and as long
thereafter as Parliament might think fit. The badgering which
it got resulted in this, that the Home Secretary agreed to
restrict the period to five years, and that without any parliamentary power to continue the tolls after that date. We who
opposed the bill in its original state thought this a very great
gain, and that the effect would be to have all tolls very soon
abolished, because parties might agree to abolish them before
the five years, as they could have agreed before the ten years;
but then the fact that the five years are soon at an end would
make them much more reasonable in their negotiations than they
would have been with the ten years before them. Then another
great improvement that we made in the bill was this. As it
stood originally, the burghs were entirely ignored; they had
no power to move hand or foot. Everything depended on the
Commissioners of Supply for the county. But supposing them
to be the fairest men in the world, these Commissioners could
only move by a majority of two-thirds. Well, I put it to any of
you who have knowledge of the world, whether it is a common
thing to get two-thirds of any body of men to agree on anything;
and the fact I think is, if that clause had stood, there would not
have been a county in Scotland in which, by whipping-up, you
could not have provided one-third to have opposed the abolition
of tolls. Well, by opposing the bill we got the majority reduced
to one-half—the ordinary common-sense majority."

Mr. M<sup>c</sup>Laren also mentioned various minor improvements; among others, one effected by himself in the interests of the smaller burghs, " requiring the Sheriff to inquire
and take into account the extent of traffic belonging to
the county which passes through the streets of the burgh."
In short, he helped to make the Government bill at once
more efficient and more equitable; and three years afterwards this love of equity brought him forward as a
witness on behalf of the city when Sheriff Davidson held
his inquiry on the application for a Provisional Order

under the Act of 1878, which was made by the Commissioners of Supply for Midlothian. Previously, in 1874, he had defended the rights and interests of the city before a Select Committee of the House of Commons appointed to examine the Edinburghshire Roads (No. 1) Bill, and had at the same time expounded and advocated the recommendations embodied in the report of the Royal Commissioners of 1858. His habit of referring to this report, which it may here be explained was written, not by himself, but by Mr. Smythe of Methven, as though it were " the law and testimony" on the subject of road reform, evoked from a member of that committee the question, " May I take it from you that you think the more a bill is prepared in conformity with the terms of that report, the better bill it is—is that your view?" Never was sneer more happily met. " No," quietly replied Mr. M<sup>c</sup>Laren ; " the lapse of time changes everything, and I am not a believer in the infallibility of Royal Commissions." The official report of his examination on this occasion occupied upwards of thirty large-sized pages in print, and it discloses not merely a perfect mastery of the elaborate statistics evolved during the controversy, but a marvellously accurate knowledge of local and imperial Acts bearing on the subject of road administration. His management of the case for the city before Sheriff Davidson, though a less onerous task, was equally successful, and gave welcome proof to his fellow-citizens that, notwithstanding he had then passed the fourscore years' limit of human life, he was still as unassailable as ever in the domain of figures, however elaborate and complicated ; that his mental powers were no less active and strong than was his devotion to the interests of the city, after half a century of service, fresh and self-sacrificing.

# CHAPTER XX.

## *THE MEMBER FOR SCOTLAND.*

" A' the world kens that the Duke of Argyle is his country's friend; and that ye fight for the right and speak for the right, and that there's nane like you in our present Israel, and so they that think themselves wranged draw to refuge under your shadow." This was Jeanie Dean's beautiful description of the character and of the popular estimate of the Scottish patriot, to whom his fellow-countrymen in London were wont to uncover their heads, saying, as he passed, " There goes the Prince of Scotland—God bless him ! "

*1865*

*" His country's friend."*

Mr. McLaren, also an Argyleshire man, won for himself in London a similar distinguishing appellation. He had not been long in Parliament before he was known there as his " country's friend," ready to fight for the right and speak for the right, the willing champion of the humble and oppressed, ever standing up for Scotland's cause. By his extraordinary knowledge of everything connected with his country, and his special devotion to its interests in Parliament, he gained the title of " The Member for Scotland."

Numerous illustrations of the national character of Mr. McLaren's parliamentary services have been given in previous chapters. His ruling idea in the House of Commons was " Justice to Scotland," and he set himself to obtain it

*National character of services.*

if possible. His familiarity with every detail connected with Scotch government made this work at once congenial and natural, while the almost exclusive attention he bestowed on it soon gave him the prominent position just described. The most obvious injustice under which Scotland suffered was lack of adequate representation in Parliament. To make this abundantly clear, Mr. M<sup>c</sup>Laren moved for various returns—for he loved to appeal to statistics on any subject —which brought out the fact that, judged either by the standard of taxation or population, Scotland should have a larger number of representatives. The first return, in 1867, showed that at the time of the Act of Union the fair share which Scotland had to pay in direct taxation was one-fortieth part of what was due from England, viz., £48,000 to £2,000,000, but that now Scotland contributed to the Exchequer one-fifth. It was also shown that Scotland did not get back her fair share in the public expenditure, while Ireland got much more than that to which, judged by the same test, she was entitled.

Claim for additional seats.

In the discussions on the redistribution of seats in the Reform Bills of 1867–68 he kept this subject constantly under the notice of the House and the country. He showed that under the Act of Union the treatment of Scotland was liberal and generous when she received 45 members. In 1832 the number was increased to 53, on the ground that the revenue of Scotland had increased thirty-eight-fold, while that of England had only increased tenfold. In 1868 the taxation of England yielded £51,300,000 ; of Scotland, £7,740,000 ; and of Ireland, £6,015,000 ; and though he did not desire that revenue should be the only basis for adjusting the representation, he showed that, if it were, Scotland would be entitled to 78 members, and Ireland to only 61. " Why," he asked, " should Scotland only have one-twelfth of the members when she pays one-eighth of the taxes?"

He recognised, however, that population must also be considered, and striking the average between the two, he claimed that the Scottish representation should be increased from 53 to 68.  This view he was most anxious to impress on Mr. Disraeli, who then led the House of Commons, and had charge of the Reform Bills; but a deputation from Edinburgh, which came for the purpose, failed to secure an introduction, even though Mr. Moncreiff exerted himself to obtain one.  Mr. M<sup>c</sup>Laren, however, always on the watch, succeeded in his object, and one evening, when the Speaker left the chair for his usual brief interval for tea, seeing Mr. Disraeli alone on the Treasury bench, Mr. M<sup>c</sup>Laren went to him, and asked permission to state his case.  Consent being readily given, Mr. M<sup>c</sup>Laren went fully into the subject. In describing this interview at a meeting of the Chamber of Commerce, he said he found Mr. Disraeli a very good listener, the few remarks he made were fair and candid, and he had no ground to complain of him.  Mr. Disraeli professed anxiety to obtain information, saying he would be happy to receive memorials on the subject; and he indicated that to meet the difficulty he would add seven members to the number of the House.  Mr. M<sup>c</sup>Laren saw the difficulty that the Tories felt in this matter, for any additional Scotch members would probably be Liberal, and therefore the Government could not feel very anxious to add to their numbers.  Such being the case, it is not remarkable that the Act of 1868 only gave Scotland seven more members, but Mr. M<sup>c</sup>Laren's arguments carried conviction, and in due time bore fruit.  When the greater and juster bill of 1885 was passed, Mr. Gladstone, accepting Mr. M<sup>c</sup>Laren's principle of rearrangement, came to

1867

the same conclusion, that Scotland was entitled to sixty-
eight members, in addition to the two previously assigned
to the Universities by Mr. Disraeli. This was naturally
accepted as a fair and reasonable settlement, and a full
recognition of the principle embodied in the amendment
which Mr. M^cLaren had moved in 1867, viz., "That no
arrangement respecting additional members can be just or
satisfactory which does not treat Scotland, as respects the
number of its representatives in Parliament, as an integral
part of the United Kingdom, entitled to be placed on a
footing of equality with England and Ireland, in proportion to its present population and the revenue which it
yields to the national exchequer, as compared with the
present population and revenue of England and Ireland;
and that to establish this equality, at least fifteen additional
members should now be provided for Scotland."

al
ern-
t.

Mr. M^cLaren was equally prominent in the agitation for
the reform of the government of Scotland. That agitation
was started during his Lord Provostship, and he continued
to be its chief guide and advocate until it bore fruit in
the creation of a Secretary for Scotland, on conditions and
charged with duties very similar to those he described in
the speech delivered by him at the first National Convention in 1853, at which the reform was pressed upon the
Government on the ground, not of party advantage, but of
national right. Indeed, the speech he made on that occasion
might, with perfect appropriateness, have been repeated at
the second and greater Convention, held more than thirty
years afterwards in the Free Assembly Hall, Edinburgh,
when the reception accorded to him by a gathering more
representative of the public life of the country than any
previous assembly in Edinburgh was itself a most impressive
demonstration of national gratitude.

At the earlier meeting held in connection with the National Association for the Vindication of Scottish Rights, under the presidency of the Earl of Eglinton, Lord Provost M<sup>c</sup>Laren proposed a resolution in favour of the restoration of the office of Secretary of State for Scotland, "with all the rights and privileges formerly appertaining thereto." Scotland, he said, had her great officers of state before the Union, and she had her Secretary of State after the Union. What was now asked was that this state of things should be restored; "that we should · have this important officer, who should be directly chargeable with the legislative and other business belonging to Scotland, and that we should not be obliged to send deputations from one functionary to another." He complained of the scant amount of attention Scotland received from the Legislature and from Government, and as an illustration mentioned that the Home Secretary, when memorialised regarding a Scottish bill, confessed that he knew nothing about it, although his name had been on the back of it for six weeks previously! He complained further, that, as the result of this indifference and neglect, Scotland did not get a fair share of the Imperial expenditure; and he laid the foundation of his future claim, for which, as has just been seen, he ultimately gained practical recognition, that having regard to her revenue, contributions, and her population, Scotland was entitled to a largely increased representation in the House of Commons.

The consistency he maintained during the prolonged agitation, with new men and new notions periodically springing up with new developments of the movement, illustrates not only his remarkable tenacity of purpose, and his power of influencing political thought, but likewise the maturity of his convictions before he gave them public expression.   He did not join the Association for the Vindication of Scottish Rights merely in obedience to a patriotic impulse.   He had carefully studied the question, both historically and in its practical bearings, long before this Association was formed; and though he was to the end of his days always open to new light—though his mind continued fresh, acquisitive, and active, and never gave way to the natural conservatism of old age—the claim he formulated in 1853 he steadily maintained, and it remained substantially the national claim, supported alike by Tories and Advanced Liberals, until it was fully recognised by the creation of the Scottish Secretaryship in 1885.   Still less ground was there for the charge, not unfrequently made in the excitement and heat of local political contests, that antagonism to Mr. Moncreiff inspired his efforts to terminate the reign of the Lord Advocate as " King of Scotland," as the holder of that office, in former days, was often called; for, as has been seen, he was connected with the movement long before he came into personal conflict with the author of the Annuity-Tax compromise. He objected to the political supremacy of the Lord Advocates solely on public grounds.   He recognised the professional talent of the leaders of the Bar, but, so far from acknowledging this professional pre-eminence as a qualification for political service, he regarded it as a distinct and serious disqualification, because of the heavy demands it made on the time and energies required for the efficient discharge of Ministerial duties.   In the next place, he objected to the limitation of the selection for state service to one profession, and held that political prizes in the form of Ministerial position and influence should be open to the best men of all classes and professions.   Again, he advocated the reform on the ground of economy.   He wished to see business principles applied to the whole system of national administration, and busy lawyers, accustomed to the receipt of large fees, were not, in his estimation, the men best qualified for this kind of work. Besides, he judged the old Parliament House system by its fruits, and found that they condemned it. Not only was it extravagant, but it was also inefficient. Its chief, as one of the leaders of the Bar, was overladen with private business which detained him in Edinburgh when his presence was required in London, and which claimed for a multiplicity of clients much of the time and talent that State service needed. Accordingly, a system of costly devolution was constantly in progress. Board after Board was being created, and each Board was giving birth to well-paid offices that were more or less sinecures and beyond public control. In Mr. M<sup>c</sup>Laren's claim that Scotland should receive her fair share of the Imperial expenditure, he never suggested or desired that the balance should be restored by means of unproductive outlay. All he asked was that the State should get value for its money in real and efficient service.

A more pliant and accommodating " senior Member " for Edinburgh than Mr. M<sup>c</sup>Laren would doubtless have been well content to exhibit a good-natured benevolence towards these Edinburgh Boards. Their officers were his own constituents, and, men of talent and influence themselves, their family and social relations surrounded them with a host of powerful friends. But Mr. M<sup>c</sup>Laren did not regulate his public work by the dictates of private interest. Regardless of the personal hostilities and the unpopularity in influential official quarters which he well knew his action would excite, he assailed the Edinburgh Boards, and associated a demand for their curtailment and revision with the agitation for the appointment of a Secretary of State for the transaction of all the non-legal public business of the country, personally responsible to the House of Commons for the work done and the policy carried out in his name.    Accordingly, when the question was revived in 1869 by a representation to Mr. Gladstone from more than two-thirds of the Scottish Members in favour of the appointment of a Secretary, Mr. M<sup>c</sup>Laren wrote to the Prime Minister the following letter, which was afterwards published as a parliamentary paper, in explanation of the issue of a Commission of Inquiry regarding the management of the public Boards in Edinburgh :—

DEAR MR. GLADSTONE,—When I had the honour of waiting on you to urge the appointment of an additional Government functionary for Scotland as Secretary, or under some other name, you suggested that I should write to you on the subject.   This I have always deferred doing, partly from knowing how deeply you were engaged with more important matters, and partly because I feared to enter in writing into the wide field which the question naturally embraces.   It has, however, occurred to me this evening to write you in the shape of brief notes on different points, and that in this way some good might be done.   I shall now, therefore, state such matters as occur to me in this desultory way.

(1.) *Duties.*—The new officer should attend to all Scotch bills other than legal ones, both as respects framing them and carrying them through Parliament; should have a seat in Parliament; should look carefully at all English bills, and, where practicable, should engraft clauses on them making them apply to Scotland, by giving a Scotch interpretation of legal words in addition to the legal one, as was done in the Act of last session for appointing English judges to try election petitions in England.   A long list of Scotch equivalent meanings was appended to the bill at the last stage, making it apply to Scotland ; and this should be done with nearly every bill, otherwise what becomes of the " United Kingdom "?   In other two bills I got the Tory Government to do the same thing—the Artisans Dwellings Bill and the Execution within Prisons Bill.   In the former bill, I proposed the Scotch clauses, and any one could easily do this with a multitude of bills.



(2.) *Future Absorption of Duties.*—The new officer shall be the head of the new Education Board for Scotland, and answerable in his place in Parliament, as is the President of the Poor-Law Board, for the conduct of his department. The new President, when in Parliament, might get £2000 a year. In Scotland he might get £1500 if he were to act just as the Lords have sent down the vote for education only. The only additional expense would thus be £500 a year for his salary. The Lord Advocate's secretary gets £350. The new man's secretary would require the same; I mean for the secretary to be with him in London. Then the office-keeper would get about £100, and the office-rent in London, say £250. This would be £1200 in excess. In Edinburgh he would of course require no separate office, as he would have rooms in the School Board apartments, and would work with the resident secretary there and other two members of the Board when Parliament was not sitting; that is, assuming that other two paid members were required, which I object to.

(3.) *Assistance in London.*—After the passing of the Reform Act of 1832, a Scotch solicitor was, for the first time, appointed in London. The salary, to cover all work of whatever kind, was fixed at £1000. It is an office that changes with the Government, and therefore no one has any vested interest in it. Like all Scotch appointments, the cost has gone on increasing; and this year I see in the estimates the emoluments thus stated:—" Preparation of bills for Parliament under the direction of the Lord Advocate, £1000; for business relating to Scotland, £1400." I have personal knowledge of the fact that nearly all the Scotch bills are prepared in Edinburgh, and separately paid for; and the cost is included in the accounts of "the Crown Agent." The office of London solicitor should be suppressed altogether, and two draftsmen appointed, one for the Lord Advocate and one for the new Secretary, and to give their whole time in the two offices to this and such other duties as they might be required to perform in connection with Scotch business. Excellent men could be got for £800 a year each.

This would set free £800 of the solicitor's emoluments.   If taken from the increased expense of £1200, the difference would be only £400 for the public to pay by the new arrangement; or the £800 might be applied in some other way when it was required. In the present way the expenditure of £2400 is quite a waste of the public money.

(4.) *Other Duties.*—The new officer should absorb that of Chairman of the Board of Supervision.  It was established as a temporary Board to set in motion an improved system of poor-law administration, and it should now cease.  The cost of the establishment is now £6867.  Two or three clerks and two visiting officers, to be amenable to the new Secretary, would be amply sufficient.  The Lunacy Board was also temporary when established.  It costs £6206.  Two Assistant-Commissioners are all that are required to visit and report to the Lunacy Commission in London.

(5.) *Economy in other Departments.*—The new officer would take a general oversight to the extent of inquiry into any matters of proposed new expenditure, when requested by the Treasury to do so.  There are great extravagance and waste in nearly all the departments of Government in Scotland, and great savings could be made.  For example, last year, when Mr. Hunt was Secretary of the Treasury, there was a demand from Edinburgh for three additional clerks, with considerable salaries, in the Inland Revenue Office in Edinburgh.  I know from two persons of undoubted credit in the office that they were not required, because there were men getting from £400 to £800 who had not one-half of the work required to fill up their time, and some of them were often absent for hours during the day from their offices.  All that was needed was a rearrangement of work.  I went to Mr. Hunt in the interest of the public, and told him this. He promised to inquire.  I also told Lord Advocate Gordon. The head of the Inland Revenue in London wrote to the head of the office in Edinburgh, and was told that they were required; and as I refused to give my authority (in order not to injure the parties), three new men were appointed.  The head of the office in Edinburgh is a very good man.  He was appointed first as a solicitor with a small salary, and has now £1600 a year. You could get men of first-rate talent for £1000 in Edinburgh. My informants told me that Mr. Fletcher sat nearly constantly in his own room, and did not personally know about the details of the office, and honestly reported what he was told and believed, but that he was misled.

*Fishery Board.*—This should be suppressed altogether. It exists on the exploded theory that our herrings would not sell in foreign markets unless each barrel had the Government brand. This requires a swarm of clerks in Edinburgh, and inspectors out of it, and it costs £6073 nett, after deducting nearly £4000 as branding fees for the work done.

To go through the abuses about the swarm of clerks in the courts of law, highly paid, and the Sheriffs and Sheriffs' clerks, and the number of solicitors employed by the different departments, would require a long report to do justice to the subject and show the waste and extravagance that go on. Suffice it to say, that, as a general rule, each department has a solicitor and advocate, all paid by salaries, although there is little to do. One, or at most two, ought to suffice for the whole business of the Crown in Scotland. Then, as to other offices, there is generally a big man with a large salary who does hardly anything. Then there is an " assistant " or " depute," with a smaller salary, who does a large portion of the work; but often there is a third man to assist the " depute " who does the rest of the work, and in some cases nearly all the work. This process has been going on for many years, and the number of persons should be cut down as vacancies occur.

If you appoint a new officer well qualified for the duties, he would save ten times the additional cost of the new office in a few years.—I am, &c.,

D. M<sup>c</sup>Laren.

This letter produced its desired effect, and a Commission, with the Earl of Camperdown as president, was appointed to make full inquiry into the operation of the Edinburgh Board system of management. Before this Commission,

1869

Mr. M<sup>c</sup>Laren gave evidence in support of, and greatly
amplifying the illustrations of the costliness and needless-
ness of the Boards presented in his letter to the Prime
Minister.   He re-stated his objections to the supremacy
of the Lord Advocates, adding, however, a cordial acknowledgment of their ability, whether Whig or Tory; and he
prefaced his detailed condemnation of the Local Boards by
a general plea as to the healthy influence of publicity and
parliamentary responsibility, from which the Edinburgh
bureaucracy was largely exempt.   "The very fact," he
said, "of parties knowing that it is in their power to get
questions put in Parliament and answers readily obtained,
I have always held as one of the best parts of the working
of our Constitution in small matters for securing a good
administration—I mean the system of parliamentary publicity.   But in Scotland all the Boards are worked in
secrecy; public opinion is never let in upon them; public
light never shines upon them; no man knows what is done,
or who advised certain things to be done, till it is ordered."
He repeated his objections to the Board of Supervision, and
held that the Lunacy and the Prison Boards were both over-
manned.   The necessary duties of the Fishery Board, such
as the supervision of small piers and the protection of the
fisheries, he thought could be transferred to the Board of
Trade; and if that were done, there would be no need of a
Fishery Board; for its other work was objectionable, "as the
last fragment of monopolist and Anti-Free-Trade principles
that remains in Scotland."   "The Board," he continued,
"assumes that nothing can certainly be good unless it has
the Crown stamp upon it—that every barrel of herring
must be branded by a red-hot iron having a representation of the Queen's crown: this is supposed to give it a
value on going to foreign countries, as containing fish that

1869

are well cured under public inspection, and the proof of
the public inspection is this branding. Now I object to
that as altogether opposed to modern notions. I think
it is not the fact that public departments can take better
care of the affairs of traders than traders themselves can
do; and I think the thing is altogether wrong in principle,
even if it did not cost the public a shilling, in place of
costing, as it does, several thousand pounds." He explained
that the Board of Manufactures was founded on a grant of
£2100, agreed upon at the time of the Union for the encouragement of manufactures. But Scotland, he said, had
outgrown that kind of nursing; and though he did not
object to the transference of the grant to the promotion
of the fine arts, as arranged a number of years previously,
he suggested that the payments should be made directly
from the Exchequer, and not through the intermediary of
a Board of Manufactures.

To the office for the registration of births, deaths, and
marriages he did not object, but he could not conceive how,
for the conduct of its business, three highly paid officers
should be required—a chief with £1000 a year, a secretary
with £500, and a chief-clerk with £337. Similarly, with
regard to the office of Queen's Remembrancer, he suggested
that one man could do the work efficiently for £900, in place of
the two employed—the Queen's Remembrancer with £1250,
and his first clerk with £610—provided that the new man was
bound to attend during the whole office hours, and to engage
in no other business, either by himself or through a partnership. He illustrated the kind of service he desired for
Government offices by a reference to the habits and customs
of a former official. He said :—" The late Remembrancer,
Mr. Henderson, whom I knew very well, was a model of a
public officer. He came to the office every morning at ten

1869

A model
public ser-
vant.

o'clock.   He walked several miles  to it, and he was so punctual that the poor people on the road used to set their watches by the time he passed their cottages ; and until the last two years of his life, when he became a director in a bank in addition to his office, he never was absent during office-hours ; he was in the office from the moment it was opened till it was shut.   Now you ought to require every man who gets Government pay to do that ; and I would exclude him from being director of a bank or anything else except serving her Majesty during office-hours."   He suggested that the Lord Lyon King-at-Arms and the Lyon-Clerk, who also had a deputy, should be merged into one office ; he advised the entire abolition of the Bible Board ; but other smaller payments, such as those to her Majesty's Limner and Historiographer, given to painters and historians as marks of public approbation, he did not object to.   The substance of his evidence amounted to this :— The abolition of all the Boards, with the exception of that for Lunacy, whose organising work in 1870 was scarcely finished ; the retention of the Lord Advocate at his present salary, but with his work restricted to legal affairs ; and the appointment of a Secretary with a status equal to that of the Lord Advocate, charged with responsibility in and out of Parliament for the work of the departments now transacted through the costly machinery of the Boards.   "The legal man," he proceeded, "should have all that pertains to legal matters, and the non-legal man all that pertains to non-legal matters.   I think the Scotch Members generally would approve of that division. There is a feeling among many of them who have no connection with Edinburgh that Edinburgh and its lawyers rule everything.   Altogether the system is becoming more and more disliked.   At present, no man, let his talents be

The legal
and non-
legal
Ministers.

what they may, can ever be Minister for Scotland unless he becomes not merely a lawyer, but a successful lawyer, and gets to the head of his profession; then he may become Lord Advocate, and he may retain the office for a long term of years, thus stopping all promotion. In the other way, the office will be open to men of talent who are not lawyers, and there would be a natural and pleasant emulation between the two chiefs to do good to their country." Looking at the question from the standpoint of a rigid purist, he estimated that, on the existing arrangements, the expenditure might be cut down, without the slightest risk to efficiency, to the extent of £31,500 per annum, while the new arrangements could be maintained in efficient operation for an outlay of £7062—a net annual saving of £24,438.

No immediate result followed this inquiry. The Commissioners prepared a report in defence of the existing arrangements, saying they could not suggest a cheaper or more efficient form of administration than Boards. Yet, since that report, the Bible Board has been allowed to lapse, and other changes in the direction advocated by Mr. M<sup>c</sup>Laren may be looked for as new appointments fall to be made, more especially under Liberal Governments pledged to economy and reform. Nor did the Commissioners speak in a kindly way even of the proposed Secretary of State. They saw no necessity, they said, for the appointment of " an independent and highly-paid officer answering to the Chief Secretary for Ireland," who " would supersede, rather than act together with, the Lord Advocate, while the government of Scotland would be removed from the Home Secretary." In brief, they looked at the question from the point of view of Ministerial convenience, and not from the point of view of a Scotch grievance. They said, Let the Home Secretary be made in fact what he

1869

Estimated
saving fror
new plan.

A non-re-
forming
Commis-
sion.

is in theory, Minister for Scotland, with two advisers—
the Lord Advocate, and a civil parliamentary officer or
Under-Secretary attached to the Home Office; and they
remarked that " the appointment of a civil officer, even if
he would relieve the Lord Advocate from none of his duties,
would at all events silence the complaint that the business
of Scotland is conducted too much in deference to legal
ideas, and with an undue preponderance to the legal
element."



Of course, a makeshift reform of this kind gave no
satisfaction, and it was not accepted.    Eleven years
afterwards, when the agitation was revived, the Camperdown " remedy " was revived with it; and Lord Rosebery
submitted himself to the operation of this specific.    But
his Lordship's experience as " a piece of Home Office fur-
niture "—a subordinate Minister with no power of effective
initiation or authoritative settlement — proved the ineffi-
ciency of the arrangement, and the necessity of such a
secretary as Mr. McLaren and those who sympathised with
him had all along contended for, viz., an official practically
independent of any English department, controlling, if not
superseding, the Edinburgh Boards, directing the administration of Scottish education, approachable by deputations
as the one man necessary for them to see, and directly
responsible in his place in the House of Commons (membership of the Lower House being specially insisted upon)
for the conduct of the whole civil portion of Scottish
business.    Lord Rosebery's resignation led to the movement which culminated in the great National Convention
of January 1884 already referred to.    At this meeting



all parties agreed in demanding the new Secretary; Lord
Stair and Lord Lothian, Lord Aberdeen and Lord Bute,
Lord Elgin and Lord Balfour, the Liberal Members for

Glasgow, Mr. A. J. Balfour, and the chief Tory Members for Scotland.



On the 19th of February 1884, Mr. McLaren accompanied the deputation who, as representing the Edinburgh National Convention, waited on Mr. Gladstone to urge immediate legislation on the lines laid down in the resolutions adopted by that large and representative gathering. He delivered a brief speech testifying to the continued insistance of the demand for a Scottish Minister and a Scottish Department for a period of fully thirty years, and to the maturity of public opinion in favour of the reform. He advised the Government to simplify legislation by abandoning the bill of the previous year, the framework of which was " decidedly objectionable," and to start afresh. He likewise discouraged a suggestion which had been made, that the new Scottish Minister should take the office of Lord Privy Seal, in order to save a salary. " It is not desirable," he said, " to mix up the duties of the Scottish Minister with those of another office, and I think, upon the whole, the Government, knowing the large sum which Scotland pays in the form of taxation, is entitled to make suitable financial provision for the new office, apart from any other." The Prime Minister expressed special satisfaction at seeing Mr. McLaren with the deputation and appreciation of his helpfulness in promoting a satisfactory settlement. " We feel," he remarked, " an obligation to Mr. McLaren, whom I am glad to see here in a green old age, as fresh as, perhaps rather fresher than when he lived more in the atmosphere of the House of Commons, for having placed his views in a definite form, and we feel that such proceedings are a real service rendered to the progress of the question."



In accordance with the suggestion made by one of the speakers, Mr. McLaren framed a bill giving effect to the

1884

resolutions of the Convention, printing it in parallel columns
with the rejected Government measure, and sending copies
to all the Scottish Members of Parliament and other prominent men interested in the question.  Many of his suggested
amendments were accepted ; and by means of his draft bill,
which commanded in the House of Commons an amount
of attention and consideration befitting the experience and
devotion of its author, Mr. M^cLaren contributed almost as
effectively to the ultimate settlement as if he had been personally present in Parliament.  Though he had resigned his
seat in 1881, his name and reputation as an authority on
all Scottish questions were in 1884 still recognised and deferred to in the parliamentary arena with which he was so
long familiar.

Another Scottish grievance—the scandalous cost en-
tailed on local authorities in promoting local or private bills—
Mr. M^cLaren frequently illustrated and protested against.
He had difficulties and doubts as to the devolution by
Parliament of its power to subordinate bodies ; but he
always felt that the arrangements for the management of
private bill legislation—requiring the presence in London
of local witnesses, who might easily have been examined in
Edinburgh, if not in their own localities, and the employment of English counsel, with all the attendant costly
machinery—constituted an intolerable burden as well as
proved a serious hindrance to municipal reforms and local
improvements.  A few weeks before his death he was induced by the agent for the Convention of Royal Burghs
to prepare a statement of his views on the subject of local
government, which had been brought before the Convention
by Mr. Vary Campbell, advocate, in a memorandum which
Mr. M^cLaren described as " an able paper," although he
himself had " never thought of any plan of reform for

Scotch affairs of so extensive a character." Mr. M<sup>c</sup>Laren's statement, which is dated 10th March 1886, was afterwards circulated by the Convention, and contained a summary of the author's views on various questions of local government. In dealing with the subject of private bill legislation he made the following suggestion, to which, as his last scheme of constructive reform, a special interest attaches :—

"An idea has passed through my mind as to how a good local council could be formed in Scotland to promote the passage of any such local bills through Parliament as did not impose any rate or other burden except on the locality which desired to have the measure passed and at its own expense. This Council should not be large. We have 72 Members of Parliament ; one-half of this number would, in my opinion, be sufficient to form an excellent Scotch Council for parliamentary and other Scotch affairs. At every parliamentary election I would suggest that thirty-six additional men should be elected as parliamentary councillors, and by means of the same voting papers, to save the trouble and expense of separate elections. This could be done by taking the votes for this purpose in *two* contiguous burghs, or divisions, or counties, who would thus represent the united electoral body. This Council might meet in Edinburgh or elsewhere. It should be empowered to appoint three committees, consisting of four of their own number, to whom all bills should be referred after being read a first and second time ; and one ordinary Judge from each Division of the Court of Session and one of the Lord Ordinaries shall be told off in rotation to act as chairmen of these committees, which could thus all sit at the same time if required. When a committee passed a local bill, it should then go before the Council to be read a third time, if approved of, and passed. It should afterwards be laid on the table of both Houses of Parliament, and if not disapproved of within forty days, it should become law, in the same way as provisional orders and schemes by Royal Commissions and other bodies are now passed. These committees should act in all respects according to the Standing Orders of the House of Commons and the practice of its committees, and should

have the same powers respecting the taking of evidence and in all
other matters. In particular, the chairman should be allowed to
vote only in cases where the four members of committee were
equally divided. When any proposed measure was intended to
apply to Scotland generally, it should be dealt with only by the
Imperial Parliament."

Mr. McLaren's national services did not lack popular
recognition outside the limits of his own constituency. One
of the most gratifying of these expressions of public appreciation came to him in 1879. As a Scottish Member, and
more especially as a Scottish Highlander, who had served
his country with fidelity and distinction, Mr. McLaren was
asked to accept the Freedom of the Burgh of Inverness.
He was spending the autumn recess at Dunain Park, Inverness, where he was joined for some days by Mr. Bright.
The Council of the burgh proposed to take advantage of
the presence of the English and Scottish Reformers in the
capital of the Highlands, and to express the public appreciation of their character and services by conferring on
them the highest municipal honour it was in their power
to bestow. Unfortunately Mr. Bright's arrangements did
not permit him to stay for a public ceremony, but Mr.
McLaren was able to accept the invitation; and, without
distinction of party, the leading citizens and their lady
friends assembled in the court-room of Inverness Castle
to witness the presentation of the burgess ticket. The
Provost of Inverness, in a happy, graceful speech, recited
the more prominent services Mr. McLaren had rendered,
not only to the city of his adoption, but to the whole of
Scotland. Inverness, he said, could not claim local connection with Mr. McLaren, but it was the capital of the
Scottish Highlands; and Mr. McLaren was " a Highlander
who, leaving his native glen in Argyllshire when a boy,

won his way in our Scottish capital, by the sheer force of his talents, perseverance, and unswerving loyalty to conviction, to the widespread esteem and influence which he now enjoys;" and it was surely seemly and right for the Council to recognise his services to the country. Mr. M<sup>c</sup>Laren in his reply rapidly reviewed his relation to the public and political questions referred to by the Provost ; but the most personally interesting, and perhaps also the most valuable portion of his speech was that in which, earnestly commending municipal service to the patriotic regard of his fellow-countrymen, he said : " As an old Town Councillor, I venerate very much municipal institutions, and I think they should be cherished and respected, whether in small, great, or middle-sized towns. But I am sorry to say that there are some people who affect to despise Town Councils, and think they are too great to have anything to do with such small things. I don't suppose that feeling exists in Inverness, but it does exist in some towns, and exists to a very large extent in the town with which I have the honour to be connected. Nothing can be more suicidal than feelings of this kind, for a great part of the liberties of this country is owing to the training of men in municipal institutions, be they Town Councils, Police Commissions, Harbour Trusts, School Boards, or any or all of those things for which local management is required. In such bodies, men, I think, are trained up to be useful citizens, to think well of public institutions, and to do a great deal of good. This principle of local management is opposed to the spirit of centralisation, which appears to be growing, and which is exhibited, I am sorry to say, in far too many of the Acts of Parliament now being passed. To that state of things I am very much opposed, for I do not

think that it is for the benefit of this country to encourage centralisation." At the conclusion of the speech the
Provost put a gold ring on Mr. M^cLaren's finger; and
three hearty Highland cheers were given for the youngest
burgess, with one cheer more for Mrs. M^cLaren.

# CHAPTER XXI.

## *FRANCHISE REFORM.*



PARLIAMENTARY reform was the first public question which engaged Mr. M<sup>c</sup>Laren's attention at the threshold of his career. At the beginning of the present century it engrossed the public mind. To earnest-minded young men, more particularly among the class with whom Mr. M<sup>c</sup>Laren was associated, it represented the cause of human freedom. It spoke of the rights of man—rights withheld, but which must be asserted if patriotism were to be preserved and religious faith vindicated and maintained; for it appealed not only to the love of freedom innate in the Scottish character, but likewise to the sense of responsibility to God. It was an outcome of the Reformation—a development of the Protestantism which had established in Scotland a democratic, self-governing Church. It was a political manifestation of the Scottish Presbyterianism, which in its purer and intenser aspects had secured the ecclesiastical franchise for the members of Christ's Church, without respect of social status or of sex.

To this early adopted faith Mr. M<sup>c</sup>Laren proved true to the end of his life. He laboured to secure the parliamentary franchise for every member of the commonwealth—for every man and woman householder, as a right as well as a trust, just as the ecclesiastical franchise was regarded as part and parcel of the membership of his church.

In his private memoranda, written in the spring of 1886, he thus described his introduction to political work :—

"I had never been an active working politician up to 1833. I was too obscure a man to be thought of in this connection. But I was in heart an earnest Reformer, and had attended all the great Reform meetings held in Edinburgh since the agitation commenced, both those in halls and the great meetings in the Queen's Park, Grassmarket, and other places. I had also attended the first purely political meeting ever held in Scotland. It was held in the Pantheon Circus on 16th December 1820. All open-air meetings were then illegal under one of Lord Castlereagh's Acts, and all the public halls in the city were withheld through the influence of the local Tory aristocracy, who then ruled Scotland with a rod of iron. Through the kindness of my employer I was allowed to attend this great meeting. The building was filled to overflowing, and large numbers were shut out. Mr. James Moncreiff, advocate (father of the present Lord Moncreiff), was in the chair. Francis Jeffrey was the leading speaker. But all the Liberal lawyers who afterwards arrived at such great celebrity were present, and most of them took part in the proceedings. Resolutions were passed praying the King to dismiss his Ministers, and 17,000 names were affixed to the petition, while only 1700 names were got to the Tory opposition petition. On this day Edinburgh took up its position as a Liberal city, and has never returned a Tory to Parliament. The effect of this meeting was to imbue my whole heart and mind with Liberal principles, so indelibly fixed that no change has ever occurred except in an onward direction."

At the great public dinner given to Earl Grey on 15th September 1834, with the Duke of Hamilton in the chair, the Earl of Rosebery as croupier, and attended by nearly every Scottish nobleman and county gentleman who then belonged to the Reform party, Mr. M<sup>c</sup>Laren was one of the acting stewards. After the Reform Bill was passed, and the first flush of victory was over, while the bulk of the party was disposed to "rest and be thankful," his energetic spirit perceived that this feeling of languor was fatal to effective organisation for further reforms. He endeavoured to rouse his friends to a recognition of their duties and to hasten them to the new fields waiting to be conquered. Even in the midst of his onerous municipal labours, he actively engaged in political work; and in 1839 he was the chief promoter of the "Reform Union," an association based on the principles adopted by the modern Caucus— "open to every Liberal voter on the parliamentary roll, without regard to his peculiar views on any of the questions about which Reformers are at present divided." But though the Liberal party continued in the ascendant in the city and generally throughout Scotland, its reforming zeal was not active. It was disinclined for anything like heroic legislation; and Mr. McLaren found it necessary to turn from the leaders and wire-pullers to the people to find the enthusiasm needed for the inspiration of the party.

One of these pioneer reform agitations was what was described as the Scottish Freehold Movement. Mr. McLaren was associated in this work with the Rev. Dr. Begg. In the desire to elevate the working-classes and to strengthen the national spirit of independence through the possession, by prudent householders, of a property qualification for the franchise, as well as in the endeavour to widen the bounds of freedom as these were defined by the Act of 1832, the two men, though differing widely on many ecclesiastical questions, found a common platform, and for several years they carried on the work together with equal enthusiasm and energy. Dr. Begg approached the question chiefly from the point of view of the social reformer.  He wished the working-classes in their aspirations after self-advancement to associate independence with manhood ; and the first and most necessary step towards the acquisition of this independence was the possession of a house as an absolute property.  The spirit embodied in the old song—

> " I'll hae a hoose o' my ain—
> I'll tak dunts frae naebody,"

animated the social and political economy he taught to working-men.  Mr. M<sup>c</sup>Laren ardently sympathised with this teaching, and frequently in his speeches and writings he cited one of the objects of the movement in these words : " To promote the elevation of the working-classes in the social scale by encouraging amongst them habits of industry and economy for the purpose of thereby acquiring freehold dwellings for themselves."  But in his advocacy of this reform he devoted his arguments and illustrations mainly to the political aspects of the question.  This department of the subject he discussed with his accustomed thoroughness and lucidity.  He surveyed the whole field of political representation in England and Scotland from the beginning of the fifteenth century, in order to show that the forty-shilling freehold was part and parcel of the British Constitution, and by elaborate illustrations of the inequalities in representation in respect of population and of contributions to the imperial revenue, from which Scotland, and especially the Scottish burghs, suffered under the first Reform Act settlement.  He further enforced his contention that injustice had been done to Scotland by the discontinuance of a franchise preserved in England.  He stated these views in detail at a meeting held in Queen Street Hall, Edinburgh, 25th December 1856, at which Dr. Begg and he were the chief speakers, and which the two city Members, Mr. Charles Cowan and Mr. Adam Black, attended. Dr. Begg and he afterwards received pressing invitations from " men in earnest " to address meetings in all parts of the country; and it is interesting here to note that when, amongst other places, they visited Ayr in May 1857, Mr. M<sup>c</sup>Laren was then regarded as an old man. Colonel Shaw had doubtless in his mind the long period during which Mr. M<sup>c</sup>Laren had already occupied a prominent place in the public life of his country, and must have had little idea that nearly thirty years' good, or rather better work, remained before him. After a complimentary reference to Dr. Begg, he proceeded :—

"The meeting had also before it a venerable gentleman, who, after having performed with distinction the civic duties of the capital city of his native land, could not yet rest from labours of love towards his fellow-men. His great and loving heart still sought to elevate his countrymen in their social, moral, and political capacities; and for these great and glorious objects he had come here to-night." [1]

The movement, though decidedly popular, was opposed by Liberals as well as by Tories—by some on the opportunist plea that it was fitted to hinder a general measure for the extension of the refranchise, which many eager Reformers had been vainly expecting for years; by others on the ground

---

[1] "Mr. M<sup>c</sup>Laren wound up the proceedings with a series of statistics which will be found unanswerable on two points. First, that the whole tendency of recent legislation for Scotland has been, by joining burghs together, to cut out their population from county constituencies; and, secondly, that these burghs by themselves have nothing like the representation, as compared with English burghs, which they ought to have, either in regard to the numbers of their electors or representatives. One fact may here suffice: 60 English burghs, with a gross population of 392,278, have 22,548 voters and 94 members, while 69 Scotch burghs, with a population of 392,343, have only 14,907 voters, and only 14 members!"—*Ayr Advertiser, May* 7, 1857.

that the franchise established under the forty-shilling free-hold qualification would be dangerously low ; and by others again under the fear that the burgh forty-shilling free-holders with their county votes would swamp the ordinary county electors, forgetting that the existing county constituencies swamped the proper electorate, and would have been reinforced by forty-shilling freeholders from the counties as well as from the burghs. Mr. McLaren sturdily combated these and many other objections. He was particularly resolute in his refusal to limit to the counties the reform he advocated.

Encouraged by the result of this meeting, Mr. McLaren framed a bill, the precise object of which, as well as of the Freehold movement, is clearly explained in the subjoined letter to his partner in the agitation :—

EDINBURGH, *January* 22, 1857.

A bill drafted.

My DEAR DR. BEGG,—I have now the pleasure to enclose the draft of a bill, which you requested me to prepare, and which, if passed into law, would carry the forty-shilling freehold franchise, which you have so ably supported, into practical effect. . . .

The first enacting clause, you will perceive, is, except as regards the amount of the franchise, taken in substance from the Scotch Reform Act (as I stated at the public meeting on Saturday it ought to be), but with certain modifications and additions, which appeared to me to be necessary to make our forty-shilling property franchise the same in substance and in spirit as the English forty-shilling freehold franchise ; and to prevent the creation of fictitious votes in Scotland, which, judging from past experience as regards the £10 franchise, might be accomplished on a great scale, if proper safeguards were not provided, by requiring, as the clause does, the actual possession of a *bona fide* interest of not less than forty shillings yearly in perpetuity, secured by infeftment over the lands on which the claim of enrolment shall be made.

1857

The English Reform Act recognises " rent-charges " and " annuities " secured on freehold land in perpetuity as forming proper freehold qualifications when of the value of forty shillings yearly ; and although it might be argued that the word " feu-duties " in the Scotch Reform Act would give substantially the same right, and be sufficient for our purposes, I have thought it advisable to include in the clause the words of the English Act also, which may apply in cases where the other words would not be sufficient.

My object has been, as you will perceive, to make the clause clearly describe *the thing wanted in Scotland under the name of the forty-shilling property franchise ;* and if we shall obtain this under any other form of words which our legal friends shall think better adapted to accomplish the purpose, I shall be quite satisfied, as I am sure you, and all the friends who act with us, will be. Meantime, I have thought it right to print the bill as it stands, on my own responsibility, without waiting for any legal revision.—I am, my dear Dr. Begg, yours very truly,

D. M\ :superscript:`c`LAREN.

At another public meeting held in Queen Street Hall in January 1857 he remarked :—

"That if they extended the franchise to the forty-shilling free-holders in counties, so many of whom were in a dependent position and liable to be influenced by the landlord and farmer to a very great extent, without including the town element, he had very great doubts whether the present state of subserviency to the great landed proprietors would not hereafter be increased to a greater extent and in a more intense degree than under the present law. So strongly did he feel that view of the matter, that, if it were in his power, with the present information he possessed, to obtain the forty-shilling freehold franchise for the counties alone, excluding the element of town representation, he would not accept it as a blessing at all."

A somewhat unexpected rebuff was received from the Convention of Royal Burghs, which, at its meeting in

Discour-agements.

1857, refused by twenty-two votes against thirteen to adopt Mr. McLaren's motion for a petition to Parliament for an "assimilation of the law of Scotland to that of England as regards the right of forty-shilling freeholders to vote in the election of representatives for shires in Parliament."

The temper of Parliament, too, was apathetic. But Mr. McLaren refused to be turned aside from his purpose; and if he encountered disappointments, he likewise received encouragements. His public meetings in Edinburgh or in the larger prominent towns of Scotland were all remarkably successful, and testified to the popular interest felt in the agitation. His political friends in England likewise gave him hearty support, and more and more, as in the Anti-Corn-Law days, he found himself entering into co-operation with them. As soon as the English Radicals began to move, Mr. McLaren put himself in line with them. He did not abandon the forty-shilling freehold scheme, but with his advocacy of this particular measure he associated the general question of reform for the United Kingdom and Ireland. At a public meeting in Perth, held in December 1858, under the presidency of Mr. Lawrence Pullar, he thus described the platform of the Reform party, then headed by Mr. Bright :—

The Reform platform.

"A vote to all owners of property in counties whose properties are worth any sum above £2 a year: a vote to all occupants of dwelling-houses in counties of the yearly rent of £10 and upwards: the Ballot to protect those who are in circumstances of dependence: that Parliament be elected for the ancient constitutional period of three years: that, in regard to burghs, the privilege of voting, instead of being restricted to occupants of premises of £10 rental, should be given to every man who pays his share of the rates for the support of the poor throughout this country."

In his Perth speech, Mr. M<sup>c</sup>Laren gave special prominence to the subject of the redistribution of seats. He
foresaw that no bill could pass which did not disfranchise
many "rotten boroughs," and he counselled his countrymen
to claim a share of the representation in proportion to their
numbers and contributions to the imperial revenues.

The Perth Reformers passed a resolution heartily supporting the platform recommended by Mr. Bright and Mr.
M<sup>c</sup>Laren; and, in response to these and many other calls,
the Member for Birmingham framed his bill, conferring the
franchise on all burgh householders rated for relief of the
poor; reducing the county franchise to £10 rental; establishing a £10 lodger franchise; discontinuing the creation
of freemen; placing the expenses of returning officers as
a charge on the rates; introducing vote by ballot; disfranchising the smaller boroughs, and distributing the seats
thus liberated among the larger towns and county constituencies in proportion to their population. This measure,
in the framing of which Mr. Bright was materially aided
by Mr. M<sup>c</sup>Laren, was defended by the great popular leader
in a series of speeches delivered in the English manufacturing towns and in Edinburgh and Glasgow.

The share which Mr. M<sup>c</sup>Laren had in the preparation of
this bill may be inferred from the following among many
letters written to him by Mr. Bright:—

LLANDUDNO, *November* 15, 1858.

MY DEAR M<sup>c</sup>LAREN,—The Manchester banquet is fixed for
December 10, nearly a month hence. We propose to go home
on the 24th, which will give me sixteen days between my arrival
at home and the banquet. I proposed to come down to Edinburgh for a week, or for as much of it as might be needful, and
you wished me to make a speech there. I don't know how all
this can be arranged. I am disposed to speak at two or three

places between this and the meeting of Parliament, but nothing is fixed. What is your aim about Edinburgh? Would a speech there help Scotland to rouse itself, or would it be fire thrown away? or would Glasgow answer better? Let me know what you are thinking of. I have got Locke King's return as to the £10 occupiers in counties, and will bring it down with me; also the complete Suffrage Bill proposed by Sharman Crawford some years ago in the House of Commons, which may help us. The Whig papers are not very friendly to us, but I hope there will be sufficient expression of public opinion to keep the press right. The *Times* will go with us the moment it sees any real life in the question—this I know. I see your Lords are angry, the Duke of —— and Lord —— especially; "small pot, soon hot," as the proverb says. I have written a long letter to Cobden giving him my notions of a bill, and asking him for advice on any point. I hope you are giving your mind to the question, so that with your *head* and my *tongue* we may make something of it, as we are in the strife.—Your affectionate brother,

JOHN BRIGHT.

ROCHDALE, *December* 5, 1858.

MY DEAR M<sup>c</sup>LAREN,—I do not think the Manchester meeting will be a good occasion to go into the particulars of the bill, as there will be other speakers, and I shall not have much time. I may, however, indicate something of what we propose, so as in part to meet your views. After the Manchester meeting I shall have Edinburgh and Glasgow, and I hear they are making some move at Bradford for a West Riding meeting, and with the intention of asking me specially to attend it. I do not wish to state any particulars till I have gone through all the figures and material points carefully with you. To-morrow week or Tuesday week I hope to be with you. When we have settled the large points of the bill, I wish to consult certain persons before they are laid before the public. I think I am bound to do this to avoid any appearance of egotism, and to secure unanimity and support. Reserve the *notes* for my speech in Edinburgh, for I shall be in a mess with it so soon after

speaking in Manchester.  Perhaps we may have the bill ready
for the West Riding meeting, if an explanation be then thought
desirable.  So far as I see of the result of your labours, they will
be very important in any attempt to frame a bill.  I see, however, so many points of doubt and difficulty, that I am in no
degree ready to go into any explanation of details till I have
talked them fully over with you.  I shall be glad any time to
see you here, but there is no need for you to come now.  There
will be plenty of time to tell everything we have to tell after we
have had a cabinet council at Newington House.  If we could
get the support of the active and leading men in Edinburgh,
Glasgow, Newcastle, Bradford, Manchester, Birmingham, Shef-
field, and London, we should be able to raise an expression of
opinion that would make it very difficult to carry a worse bill
than ours.—Yours very sincerely,          JOHN BRIGHT.


The draft bill here referred to was explained in detail at
the Bradford meeting, as suggested, and formed the basis
for future agitation on the Reform question.  A few months
later Mr. Bright again wrote :—

ROCHDALE, *May* 27, 1859.

MY DEAR MᶜLAREN,—I agree with you entirely.  I have a
letter from Mr. Gibson some days ago, telling me what was
doing, and one from Lord John yesterday, wishing me to go up
on Tuesday to have some talk with him on the present and the
future.  I have written to say that I have to be in Birmingham
on Tuesday, but expect to be in town on Wednesday, and will see
him on Thursday.  I have told him that I think it desirable to
impart confidence to the more advanced section of the Liberal
party by some very distinct assurance on the question of Reform,
and on a strict neutrality as to the war now begun ; and that
without these I don't see much use in a change of Government,
and that these are views which are held by a considerable number
of members on our side of the House.

I have written at greater length to Gibson to the same effect,
and have urged him to let it be well known that we are not to be

the cat's-paws for the old concern, and that we will be no party
to a change of Government except on conditions that promise
good from the change.

With regard to the £6 rental, in all our great towns I
believe the Liberals would be well satisfied with it as a great
gain, and in all our manufacturing towns of the size of Rochdale
it would be a very substantial improvement. In Scotland, and
no doubt in Ireland also, it would be much less important; and
I agree with you that either something lower should be fixed
upon, or that a difference should be made with regard to Scotland and Ireland, or with regard to all towns in the United
Kingdom under a certain population. I don't think there will
be any insuperable difficulty in this, but I will not forget it. I
wish any business, or some business, would bring you to London
in the week the labour of the House begins. I am not very well
off for advisers, and I think to discuss what may happen with
you might be of great use to me. Perhaps the fine weather may
tempt you to come up for a few days.—Ever yours sincerely,

JOHN BRIGHT.

Mr. Disraeli's first bill, introduced in February 1859, with
its "fancy franchises," was regarded by the Reform party
generally with strong dislike and distrust. Mr. M<sup>c</sup>Laren
was one of those who did not consider the measure as
an honest attempt to settle the question; and after consultation with his English friends, now organised as the
London Parliamentary Reform Committee, he prepared an
elaborate statistical return, or rather a series of returns,
which he entitled "Information for Reformers respecting
the Cities and Boroughs of the United Kingdom, classified
according to the Schedules of the Reform Bill proposed by
John Bright, Esq., M.P.; and also showing the Results of
the Government Bill." [1]  The object of this paper was to

---

[1] London, Effingham Wilson; Edinburgh, W. Oliphant & Co.

illustrate the merits of Mr. Bright's and the demerits of 1860
Mr. Disraeli's plans, alike as regards redistribution of seats
and enfranchisement of new voters.

"It must be obvious," remarked the *Morning Star*, after a Revival
careful analysis of Mr. McLaren's parallels and contrasts, "that form pla
Mr. Bright's plan for the distribution of seats, instead of being
too favourable to the large boroughs, as has been asserted by his
opponents, is far below their fair claims, whether these be based
on population, wealth, taxation, number of voters, or any other
possible principle on which a fair distribution of Members could
be professedly founded."

And again, as to the enfranchisement side of the question,
the same authority observed, in sympathy with the author's
efforts to reassure the timid political Ready-to-Halts :—

"One remarkable fact is clearly proved by these tables—the
gross exaggerations of the opponents of Mr. Bright, who declare
that his rating franchise would 'swamp the boroughs,' and would
increase the number of voters three, four, and five-fold. These
exaggerations were, of course, devised and circulated in order to
alarm the present voters, and to induce them to oppose the bill
of the honourable Member for Birmingham. It now appears that
the ratepaying franchise adopted by that gentleman does little
more than double the number of voters, on an average, in all the
boroughs of the United Kingdom."

Mr. McLaren's masterly compilation was conclusive of
the fate of Mr. Disraeli's bill and its fancy franchises. The
Reformers treated the Government measure as a trap and
a snare, and it was rejected by a majority of 39—a vote
which not only killed the bill, but led to a dissolution of
Parliament and a change of Government. The hopes of
the Reformers, however, were doomed to disappointment.
The restoration of Liberals to office did not inaugurate a

period of legislative activity.  Lord Palmerston was master of the situation ; and, as in former years the Crimean War, and afterwards the Indian Mutiny, directed public attention from home questions, so Lord Palmerston made use of the interest excited by his foreign policy enterprises and his personal popularity still further to stave off urgent domestic legislation, and to baulk the Reformers of their expected triumph.  The popular agitation, however, recommenced in 1864 with redoubled energy; the general election of 1865 was fought on the franchise question ; and the Reformers won—Mr. McLaren enjoying a great personal triumph by his return as Member for Edinburgh.  Lord Palmerston died before the new Parliament met ; and Lord Russell, who was popularly and rightly supposed to be a more advanced Liberal than the talented and daring Minister for Foreign Affairs, succeeded to the Premiership.

Notwithstanding all his experience of the obstructive power of the Whigs, Mr. McLaren was one of the most sanguine Reformers who entered the new House of Commons in 1866.  Himself victorious over the Whigs in Edinburgh, he concluded that the aristocratic section of the Liberal party had not only sustained a general defeat throughout the country, but that their political ascendancy in the councils and policy of the Liberal party was broken.  He believed that a majority of genuine Reformers had been returned to Parliament, and that the chiefs of the party, Lord Russell and Mr. Gladstone, were in thorough accord with the aspirations of their followers and supporters.  In his view the time had come and the men.  " When," he said, speaking at a great Reform meeting held in Edinburgh in the middle of January 1866, " when we have a new Government and a new Parliament, and two such men as Earl Russell and Mr. Gladstone at the head of affairs, I think this must be

the right time." He repeated this expression of confident
expectation at another and greater demonstration held ten
days afterwards at Glasgow, where he was welcomed with
an enthusiasm and an affection which told him that his victory in Edinburgh was regarded as a triumph for Advanced
and Independent Liberalism everywhere. Proceeding to
Paisley, where he was received with, if possible, still greater
cordiality, and where, as the home of a sympathetic Radicalism, he found himself still more at ease, he again declared
his faith in the triumph of the cause and the loyalty of its
leaders. "We have," he said, "just got a new Parliament
elected, and many staunch thoroughgoing Reformers have
been returned to that Parliament. Then we have Lord
Russell, who is a Reformer of the very first water, and who
has done more in that cause than most living men. And
although his Lordship, unfortunately, as I think, has now
gone to the House of Peers, yet we have as leader of the
House of Commons Mr. Gladstone, who is certainly next
to him in power, and not inferior to him or to any man in
talent."

Still more had he faith in the classes to be enfranchised.
Though personally prepared to welcome household suffrage,
he was unwilling to claim a larger measure of Reform than
the general conviction of the Liberal party would concede
or sustain. He therefore advocated a £6 franchise, as the
highest franchise likely to be acceptable to the country,
and the lowest which the Liberal party was likely to be
able to carry. He at the same time sought to remove
honest but prejudiced and not very intelligent opposition
to such an extension of the franchise, by contending that
it would prove a really Conservative measure, by including
in the ranks of full-fledged citizenship the industrious and
thrifty members of the working-classes.

Probably, of all sections of the community, he placed the greatest confidence in the industrial classes. He believed them fully prepared for, as well as entitled to, the trust about to be placed in their hands. In his Paisley speech he said: "A generation has passed since the last Reform Bill. During that period, education has increased to an extent which it would be difficult to calculate or to define; the wealth and influence of the working-classes themselves, as measured by their weekly wages, have enormously increased all over the country, in almost all branches of business; and the establishment of the free press and the penny newspaper has diffused an amount of information on political and economical questions which makes the working-man of the year 1866 a more intelligent man on every question relating to legislation than was the £10 householder of the year 1832." Himself a man in earnest and a Reformer, he recognised political kinship with the working-classes. After having, at the Edinburgh demonstration, exposed the hollowness of the cry that extension of the franchise would prove the prelude to revolution and anarchy, and inaugurate a reign of political ignorance, he continued:—"I believe a great many of those who object to votes being given to the working-classes do so not because they believe in their hearts that the working-classes have not enough of intelligence, but because they believe that they have too much. They know quite well that they would not answer the whip at mere party calls; that it would not be enough if a candidate called himself a Whig or a Tory or a Radical, but that they would weigh him, measure him, scrutinise his motives as far as they could for getting into Parliament; they would consider his character and his trustworthiness, and they would vote for the best man, not caring a fig whether the candidates were sent down by the Carlton or some other club in London, or by some little coterie at home. It is because of that measure of intelligence joined to independence which the working-classes possess that so many men are afraid of giving votes to them."

1866

The Government themselves were less sanguine than Mr. M<sup>c</sup>Laren. They did not believe they could carry even Mr. M<sup>c</sup>Laren's suggested minimum of a £6 franchise for boroughs and a £10 franchise for counties. Their bill proposed £7 franchise for boroughs and a £14 franchise for counties. Mr. M<sup>c</sup>Laren, though somewhat disappointed, recognised the measure as an honest attempt at Reform, and resolved to give it his hearty support, clearing the way as far as he could by withdrawing the Forty-shilling Freehold Bill, which he had prepared eight years previously, and which he had introduced as his first legislative proposal after entering Parliament. In one of the letters to their eldest son, John M<sup>c</sup>Laren, then at Algiers, from which quotation has formerly been made, Mrs. M<sup>c</sup>Laren thus described the first speech on Reform delivered by her husband in the House of Commons :—

Devotion to parliamentary duties.

" Your father's efforts in connection with parliamentary reform have won him considerable approbation from the press both in England and Scotland. The *Pall Mall Gazette* and the *Telegraph* say he quite or more than came up to what was looked for from him. I can't remember all the papers which praised him. The Members on the Treasury bench listened to his first speech very attentively, and he quite gained the ear of the House. I daresay they were also a little arrested by his Scotch, which I think is the nicest Scotch I ever heard ; his voice softens and enriches what in so many seems hard and dissonant. And he spoke quite on the spur of the moment, not having heard any of the speech he followed except for about four minutes, having only just entered the House, so that he must have seemed wonderfully at home with his figures. They happened to be what he had prepared for his speech at Glasgow."

Passing on in this letter to describe her own experiences and observations, Mrs. M^cLaren presents an interesting glimpse of the House as it appeared to her in the spring of 1866, and tells of her interview with her brother, Mr. John Bright, after his speech against the suspension of the Habeas Corpus Act on 17th February, proposed by the Russell-Gladstone Government in answer to the Fenian conspiracy :—

"I have only been once in the House since coming, and it was to go with David M^cLaren's daughter and my niece Anne Frances Ashworth. It was not an interesting night—all about Hunt's bill for the cattle-plague. I was astonished to see how men have changed since I saw them eighteen years ago. Disraeli sat unmoved as a statue, yet gave one the impression that he had wonderful faculties which might be unfolded for the good of his country, and wariness—'biding his time'—ready to do the unexpected whenever occasion should arise. My brother (John Bright) looked like one ennobled by constant fight in every good cause. I daresay you read his magnificent speech on the passing of the Habeas Corpus Act. I was not in the House, but Charles and Walter were, though they could not see their uncle, they were so far back. Every one said it was the finest speech he had ever made. His voice was splendid, and his bearing like a prophet of old. I shall never forget his coming in here on the evening after he had made that speech. It did not require a sister's eye to be struck with the more than usual nobility of his head. I write reverently when I say he looked almost inspired as he told us, in a subdued voice, how he had lain awake the night before full of solemn thought about what they were going to do, and the reasons why they had to do a work so serious and unpalatable. 'But,' he said, 'there are times when one lies awake in the stillness of the night, in the flickering light of the lamp, when the imagination and memory become exalted, as it were, and things

—thoughts come into the mind, you hardly know how or whence —a sort of inspiration. It was so with me last night, and in the morning I endeavoured to jot a few of these together.' The result was that beautiful thrilling speech Gladstone was so struck with, but pronounced inconvenient. Ireland might seem to have been placed among the nations to be a perpetual demonstration of the fallibility of man's judgment in the art of governing. Light may yet be given to do justice to that beautiful island.''



The second reading of the Government Reform Bill was carried only by a majority of five, and Mr. M<sup>c</sup>Laren afterwards reflected with satisfaction that his vote, or rather his choice by the electors of Edinburgh in preference to an anti-reformer, saved the Government from the necessity for immediate resignation. Speaking to his constituents in October he said: " If by your favour I had not been returned, the second reading would have been carried only by a majority of three. . . . I think no one will doubt that if the majority had only been three, the Government would have resigned. That was the first way in which my election interfered with the question of Reform, and I think you will say it was not in the way of hindering it." But his timely vote secured only a short respite for the Ministry. The discontented Whigs formed themselves into a parliamentary group—pungently satirised by Mr. Bright under the name of the Cave of Adullam—and quickly succeeded in their hostile combinations against the Reforming Ministers and their bill. The Government were ousted and the Tories under Lord Derby and Mr. Disraeli took their place.





Having, as a financier and reformer, long regarded the Liberal Chancellor of the Exchequer with trust and admiration, Mr. M<sup>c</sup>Laren on this occasion undertook his defence against some of his party allies, who had attributed the Ministerial defeat to bad management. No accusation such as that of bad management and want of tact brought against the party leader by his critics could, as he said, be more unjust. "Mr. Gladstone," he said, "sat there from the first hour to the last, a perfect monument of patience. I was often amazed to see how, when pelted by foes from the opposite side, and by those who called him their right honourable friend who were sitting behind him—and those honourable friends on his own side generally pelted him with the greatest severity—I was amazed to see how he could reply to those attacks with the degree of calmness and good-nature he manifested, and how he always avoided ascribing any improper motives to them, but, on the contrary, frequently went out of his way to say how satisfied he was that Mr. So-and-so was stating what he cordially believed."



But though the Franchise Bill of 1866 was defeated, Mr. McLaren did not lose faith in the cause, nor even in its early triumph. He comforted himself and his friends by reminding them of the Anti-Corn-Law struggle—how the Conservatives, who had rejected a moderate measure which the League were prepared to accept as a temporary compromise, were shortly afterwards compelled by the logic of facts and the strength of political necessity to yield the League's enlarged and uncompromising demand for total and immediate repeal. His wide experience and keen political insight enabled him to make an accurate forecast. "I should not be surprised," he said, "if a similar result were to take place in regard to the franchise; if a measure were introduced and carried, probably going farther than the measure which was rejected last session." As a Reformer rather than as a partisan, he offered what encouragement he could to the Tory Government to attempt a thorough-going and satisfactory settlement. Mr. Gladstone had promised to give "a fair and candid consideration" to a good Reform Bill if the Tories brought in such a measure. "And that," said Mr. M<sup>c</sup>Laren, "will be my course. I do not care who brings it in; by me it shall be judged according to its merits or demerits." In the succeeding session he conscientiously and courageously fulfilled that pledge.

Mr. M<sup>c</sup>Laren's first impressions of Mr. Disraeli's bill, with its endless qualifications and reservations, did not inspire him with much regard for the measure. In its original state he thought it the most objectionable Reform Bill he had ever seen, and he was prepared to give it the most resolute opposition in his power. But the Tory leader's speech in introducing the measure, and his attitude of accommodation, modified his opinion of the Government's proposal, without, however, in any way lessening his opposition to its objectionable features. He could not overlook the broad fact that the bill was founded on the principle of Household Suffrage, so far as the borough representation was concerned, and Mr. Disraeli's language and known tendencies suggested to him the possibility, nay, the feasibility, of stripping the bill of every fetter and restrictive device introduced by the draftsman for the purpose of neutralising this general principle. In afterwards speaking to his constituents he thus explained his interpretation of the Tory leader's position and described his own line of conduct:—

"Mr. Disraeli said in effect, 'We know our party cannot carry a Reform Bill without the assistance of the opposite side, and the Opposition know from the experience of last session that they cannot carry one without our assistance. Let us then agree that a joint action shall take place, that the House of Commons and the Government may frame a good bill in Committee, both parties making concessions in order that one may be carried this session.' Now, this proposal seemed to me a fair and reasonable one, and also a very safe one for the Liberal party ; because, if the promises thus made were not performed, the Liberals, having a large majority in the House, could extinguish the bill on report, when it came out of Committee, or on the third reading. But it was objected by some that this was not a dignified course for a Government to pursue. I thought, however, that it was a wise course for the cause of Reform. Besides, you did not send me to Parliament to watch over the dignity of any Government, and I thought they were the guardians of their own political honour."

It will thus be seen that party interest in its narrower sense—that is to say, as respects the immediate resumption of office—was not in Mr. M°Laren's mind at all. What concerned him was the settlement, on a broad and liberal basis, of the franchise reform, for which the constituencies had declared ; and he was willing to co-operate with Mr. Disraeli in effecting such a settlement, even although the temporary coalition meant the retention by the Tories of office without power.

By the adoption of this attitude Mr. M°Laren gave keen offence, not only to the official section of the Liberal party, but to some of his personal friends, who had lost all respect for and confidence in Mr. Disraeli, and who thought the possession of place by the Tories under such circumstances a grave national peril. But neither the pressure of the Whips nor the entreaties of friends, with whom difference was to him acute pain, could move him from the position which his sense of public duty constrained him to take up. Although perhaps he did not fully realise it then, he had reached a crisis in his political history similar to that which overtook him at the beginning of the Anti-Corn-Law agitation. He was forced to choose between party advantage and public interest ; and though party advantage meant for him also increase of personal influence and opportunities of

1866

usefulness, he put personal considerations entirely out of view and decided in favour of public interest. As the struggle proceeded the painfulness of this difference increased, but Mr. M<sup>c</sup>Laren steadily and fearlessly maintained throughout both his integrity and his consistency.

Opposit to Liber leaders.

When the Liberal party was first summoned to Mr. Gladstone's house to consider the policy to be pursued, Mr. M<sup>c</sup>Laren was one of the Members whose influence prevented the adoption of a resolution to throw out the Government bill on the second reading. He attended a second meeting held a few days before the bill was to enter Committee, at which Mr. Gladstone intimated that Mr. Coleridge, now Lord Chief-Justice, had been selected to move an instruction for the substitution of a rating franchise for household suffrage. But Mr. M<sup>c</sup>Laren did not approve of this policy. The adoption of the instruction would, of course, have proved fatal to the bill; the defeat of the Ministers on such a point would have been followed by dissolution; and the popular cry which the Tories would use as the defenders of household suffrage would have greatly strengthened their position in the next Parliament. He considered the tactics of his party mistaken, prejudicial alike to the cause of Reform and to their own interests, and accordingly he endeavoured to prevent their success.

How loyally and ably he was sustained by intelligent home sympathy in this period of trial, when many esteemed Liberal friends forsook him and blamed him, will be shown from the subjoined extract from a letter written by Mrs. M<sup>c</sup>Laren to a valued and intimate correspondent who had taken offence :—

" Whilst I do not wish to speak boastfully of what we did, I may say that the more I look back upon it, the more I am convinced we did right in considering during that anxious moment measures rather than men. And, without any undue self-complacency, I may be permitted to add that they who were far-seeing enough to join the Tea-Room party can afford to smile at any derogatory remark which may be thrown out by those who may have been less earnest in the cause of the people than in that of party, believing, as we do, that light is equally to be valued whether it penetrates a cottage or a palace, the mind of the humblest member of the House of Commons or that of its most distinguished statesman.

"The country was tired of Reform bills, woven, like Penelope's web, only to be unravelled again and again. As in almost every other great struggle, neither the Whig nor the Tory party *alone* could lead on to victory. Disraeli himself acknowledged this to be the case with the Reform Bill. The Tea-Room party saw how useless it was to fight against the inevitable, and, trusting to Mr. Disraeli's promise that the House of Commons should carry the bill, after moulding it in the best form its united efforts could achieve, the Tea-Room party decided the bill should go into Committee; and you know the result—the long-vexed question of the franchise has been settled, as we believe, for some time to come.

"We all know, and posterity will fully acknowledge, *who* rolled the stone up the hill. Although at the last great push nearly every one lent a helping hand, many putting their shoulders to the work, it is true, not from choice, but for self-preservation.

"The triumph is a great one for the working-classes. Many are anxious as to how they will use their newly acquired powers, and predict at first many mistakes. I would ask, Have their richer brethren made no mistakes? Why, the Legislature, nearly ever since the previous Reform Bill was passed, has been unmaking bad laws made by those we have been accustomed to call the privileged classes. It was said long ago, by One who is no respecter of persons or classes, 'Let my people go, that they may serve *me.*' I have faith in the newly enfranchised that they will consider the freedom they have gained as a trust, by the exercise of which they can help in a vcry large degree the extension of a righteous legislation, and thus bring down blessings upon themselves and our common country."

Here is Mr. M<sup>c</sup>Laren's own account of the formation and of the policy of the " Tea-Room " party :—

" When the facts respecting this second meeting at Mr. Gladstone's got abroad, many of the friends of Household Suffrage became alarmed at the idea of Members voting against that principle, even although then imperfectly developed in the bill, and it was resolved to hold a meeting of members in the Tea-Room on the Monday afternoon on which the instruction was to be moved; the meeting at Mr. Gladstone's house having been held on the preceding Friday. No circular was issued calling this meeting. It was a spontaneous gathering, by one Member telling another what had been suggested. I had been confined to bed for two days, when Mr. Seely called and informed me of what was intended. Although very unwell, I approved so much of the desire to defeat the proposed instruction, that I made an effort to get to the meeting, and after expressing my opinion in favour of the movement, returned home without being able to enter the House of Commons. There were nearly fifty Members there in the Tea-Room, and it has been generally agreed that about other thirty, who were absent from not having heard of the meeting in time, and from other causes, would have voted with them, and thus have rendered the success of Mr. Coleridge's amendment impossible. A deputation instantly waited on Mr. Gladstone and informed him of the state of matters, and he at once agreed that Mr. Coleridge's amendment should be withdrawn."

Seventeen years afterwards Mr. M<sup>c</sup>Laren wrote a more detailed account of the Tea-Room meeting and of its policy in a letter addressed to his friend Mr. Seely, long Member for Lincoln, to whom he attributed the chief credit of a work which he never recalled without satisfaction :—

EDINBURGH, *June* 19, 1885.

MY DEAR MR. SEELY,—I am greatly pleased to observe that you are to stand again for Lincoln, which you have served so long and so well as an Advanced Liberal. When I entered the House a few years after you, and was introduced to you as holding your advanced views, I was very kindly received, and on many occasions had the benefit of your experience and wise counsel, which I greatly valued and profited by. I have often told my friends, here and elsewhere, that I consider you, more than any one Member of Parliament, the father of the Household Borough Franchise Bill as carried in 1867. I well remember all the facts connected with the passing of that measure, because it had always been a part in my political creed.

Mr. Disraeli's revised Reform Bill included household suffrage, in order, as Lord Derby afterwards said, 'to dish the Whigs.' That party, and many other Liberals as well, were alarmed at the extent of the proposed change, and resolved to oppose it. They accordingly arranged that Mr. Gladstone should move an amendment to the effect that a £4 rating franchise should be substituted, equal to £6, 5s. of real rent, so that all persons occupying houses of less value should be excluded. This would have made an enormous difference in the number of the new electors. Mr. Gladstone's amendment was to be moved on a Monday, and was thought certain to be carried, as the Liberals had a considerable majority in the House, and the result would have been to dish the Tories and secure the advent to power of the Liberal party. I well remember your having called on me on the preceding day and found me confined to bed. But I saw you notwithstanding. You explained the great importance of the pending issue, and advised that as many of the Radical party as were earnest friends of Household Suffrage should be got to support Mr. Disraeli's proposal, because he could get it carried through the Lords, which the Liberal party could not expect to do, even if they should afterwards introduce a similar bill. You told me that you had already seen a number of Members who had agreed to meet on the Monday for consultation in the large Committee-room of the House of Commons an hour before the meeting of the House.  I promised, if at all able, to join your party, and you left hurriedly to call on as many other Members as you could overtake.  I was able to attend, although at some risk.  The result was, that, owing to your personal exertions alone, forty Members attended, and unanimously resolved to support the Household Suffrage clause in opposition to Mr. Gladstone's amendment, and they sent a deputation to Mr. Gladstone to inform him of the fact.  I remember that my friend Mr. Fawcett was one of the deputation, but I am not quite certain as to the others.  The result, however, was—and by your exertions alone—that Mr. Gladstone did not move his amendment.  Household suffrage was carried, and the Whig Government did not come into power as was expected.

I have no doubt you remember how we were abused by the press for our conduct.  We were stigmatised in the most opprobrious terms, and threatened with the loss of our seats at the next election.  I well remember a favourite epithet bestowed upon us, "The Forty Thieves."  I always felt proud of the small part I had in the transaction as one of your followers, and did not mind the abuse, which did me no harm.  Your constituency have great cause to be proud of the conduct of their Member on that memorable occasion.  I will conclude with an important question, deserving serious consideration at the present time, namely, if household suffrage in the boroughs was defeated in 1867, as it would have been but for your exertions, could we have carried household suffrage for the counties in 1885 ?  I think not.

I am thankful to say that, although three or four years your senior, I still enjoy good health, as you will probably infer from my handwriting.  I have written this letter with my own hand. —I am, my dear sir, yours very sincerely,

D. M<sup>c</sup>LAREN.

As already seen, the policy of the Tea-Room party prevailed.  The Liberals, instead of seeking the displacement of the Tory Ministry, laboured to improve their bill, and the result was the practical adoption of household suffrage—a basis of settlement Mr. M<sup>c</sup>Laren had long desired, and which he now welcomed without the slightest misgiving. To secure at once the improvement of the Government measure and the attainment of household suffrage, Mr. M<sup>c</sup>Laren worked, through good and evil report, with the most painstaking zeal and assiduity. Attempts were persistently made to represent him as a factious sectary, a disloyal Liberal, a Tory in disguise, and so on; but his own conduct and the success of his efforts to liberalise the Government bill baffled the malignity of his critics. While the bill was before the House, he was seldom out of his place. Of fifty divisions which took place, he was absent from only one; and that one, suddenly and unexpectedly called for, was simply on a question of adjournment. So far from being a supporter of the Government, he voted almost steadily against them; so far from being an opponent of Mr. Gladstone's party, as his critics represented, he excelled in the fulness and cordiality of his co-operation with the Liberal leader in his efforts to improve the bill. "The Conservative Whigs," he afterwards said, "were the great defaulters. Many of them did not desire a really good bill, and left Mr. Gladstone in the lurch, declining to attend or to vote with him." Mr. M<sup>c</sup>Laren's record of his votes most conclusively shows the emptiness of the charge that he was a deserter from his party and an opponent of his party's leader :—

"In forty-one divisions I voted against Mr. Disraeli, and in eight I voted with him. On five of these occasions Mr. Gladstone also voted with him. In other two of these divisions, Mr. Gladstone was absent, but I know he would have voted as I did had he been present. One of the two was carried by 259 of a majority, composed of the Government supporters and Liberals, against 25 of the extreme Tory party, who wished joint-occupants to vote under the Household Suffrage franchise. The other division was carried by 159 to 87, not to preserve the existence of Lancaster and Yarmouth by merely suspending the writs for a term of years ; and Mr. Gladstone had both spoken and voted for the disfranchisement of these burghs on another occasion. My third and most important vote with Mr. Disraeli was given in the spirit of the Tea-Room meeting, to prevent the bill from being altered on a point to which the Tories attached so great importance, that it was understood they would have abandoned the bill if they had been beaten. It was on the more celebrated than well-understood question of the compound householder and the opposing proposals of Mr. Disraeli and Mr. Hibbert. Believing that there would be very little difference between their practical working in enfranchising electors, I gave my vote to Mr. Disraeli to save the life of the bill. The majority was 322, including most of the Tea-Room party, against 256. The only other vote I gave against Mr. Gladstone was on the Women's Suffrage clause; but Mr. Gladstone voted with Mr. Disraeli in three of the forty-one divisions in which I voted against him. One of these was on a clause providing for vote by ballot, which I supported, while the leaders of the two parties voted against it."

Mr. M<sup>c</sup>Laren believed he was far more in harmony with Mr. Gladstone's political views than the official party men who sought to shelter themselves behind the name and fame of the great party leader. In his address to his constituents in October he said :—

"From what I have seen and heard of him since I entered Parliament, I am satisfied Mr. Gladstone is by far the fittest man to be the future Prime Minister of this country; and I believe the Radical Members, although lamenting his short-comings on certain questions, would hail his advent to power with far more cordiality than the Conservative Whigs. But with all my admiration for his talents and character, I cannot admit that the main improvements in the Reform Bill were carried by Mr. Gladstone or by his influence, far less by the influence of the assailants of the ' Tea-Room ' party, who have so strangely magni-

1867

—

> real
o.

Ballot.

fied their own importance. The fact is, that in the thirty-five divisions in which Mr. Gladstone voted against Mr. Disraeli, he was beaten in twenty-seven and successful only in eight; and I leave you to judge whether it was the men who constantly attended and voted with him, or the men who remained at home attending to their own business, who were the cause of these defeats. It was neither Mr. Gladstone, nor Mr. Disraeli, nor the Whigs, nor the Radicals, that carried the bill in its improved form; for nearly all the bad clauses were dropped out without a division. I will inform you, in the words of an eminent Whig lawyer, but not of the present Edinburgh school of Whiggery, how the bill was carried. Mr. Coleridge (the present Lord Chief-Justice), to whom I refer, says: 'They knew perfectly well that they owed their great measure not to the Chancellor of the Exchequer, but to the fervour of popular enthusiasm, and they knew how, through one great man, above all others in the land, whose conduct last session had shown him to be one of the greatest statesmen of the day, it was that the fervour of popular enthusiasm was raised to such a height as to make it irresistible—and that man was John Bright!'"

Mr. McLaren was not only in advance of his party in advocating an extension of the franchise and in preparing the public mind for household suffrage; he was equally far ahead of it on the subject of secret voting. He was an advocate of the ballot long before the Liberal party generally was educated up to an acknowledgment of its value as a protection for the humbler class of voters. The bill carried through Parliament in 1871 by Mr. Forster received from the first his heartiest support. All cognate reforms, such as the extension of the hours of voting, the suppression of corrupt practices at elections, the lightening of expenses with the view of facilitating the admission of comparatively poor though otherwise thoroughly qualified men into the House of Commons, were from time to time advocated by him, as opportunity

1867

offered. He held that every householder was entitled to the rights of citizenship, and to be protected in the exercise of these rights. He believed the franchise to be a security for, and an agency of, national stability, linking the mass of the people in affection to the State, giving them a sense of self-interest, and a consciousness of participation in the control of national prosperity. And he supported the ballot, the Corrupt Practices Act, and other protective measures, with a view to the preservation and effective use of the new Magna Charta.

But though few men more heartily welcomed or more highly appreciated the great enfranchisement measure of 1867, with its supplementary reforms, Mr. M<sup>c</sup>Laren did not accept it as a final settlement. He had no faith in " finality " measures; and in this case, unexpectedly liberal and comprehensive though the new franchise was, it fell short of his early ideal. To that plan of universal household suffrage he was still faithful, for experience and knowledge of his fellow-countrymen had confirmed his conviction that in Scotland, at all events, the county householder was on the whole better qualified for the franchise than the average borough householder. Accordingly, alike by speech and vote and personal influence, he encouraged Sir George Trevelyan in the earliest stages of the movement which he headed for the purpose of inducing the Liberal party to adopt a uniform parliamentary franchise for boroughs and counties as one of the acknowledged planks of the Liberal programme.

County franchise reform.

The steady progress of this movement afforded him the liveliest satisfaction, and when the time for settlement approached in 1884, recognising the supreme importance of the issue, he counselled all his fellow-reformers, however ardent they might be in the advocacy of their particular schemes, to subordinate everything to the question of the hour, as not only embracing them all, but as giving the assurance of their earlier success. When spending an autumn holiday at Strathpeffer in 1884, he, as a Highlander and as a Reformer, attended a meeting at Dingwall in connection with the candidature of the young Laird of Novar for the representation of Ross and Cromarty, which had just become vacant by the resignation of Sir A. Matheson. He wished the election to be used as a means of strengthening the hands of the Liberal Government in their struggle with Lord Salisbury and the House of Peers, which was then plainly impending; and, much gratified by Mr. Munro Ferguson's speeches, assured of his fidelity to the Liberal cause, he earnestly counselled the electors of Ross and Cromarty to return him to Parliament by a decisive majority, in testimony of their determination to have, as in the times of former franchise struggles, the bill, the whole bill, and nothing but the bill. He also attended another meeting during the same election at Invergordon, driving sixteen miles to it, to raise his voice in favour of the youthful candidate. But the effect of his words was seen elsewhere and otherwise than at the poll. Speaking at a great county demonstration at Dingwall, held two months later, Mr. Peter Macleod of Stornoway happily recalled the incident, and presented a view of Mr. M<sup>c</sup>Laren's life at once striking and true, which revealed the secret of his extraordinary influence among the Bible-loving Highlanders :—

"The last time," said Mr. Macleod, "I had the pleasure of appearing on a Dingwall platform, I heard Mr. Duncan M<sup>c</sup>Laren dispose of this sophistry of the Tories, viz., that they had not opposed, but had simply refused to accept, the County Franchise Bill. We were then on the eve of achieving a great and memorable victory in the county, and Mr. M<sup>c</sup>Laren's appearance that evening I thought augured well for Novar's success.

It reminded me most forcibly of, to me, one of the most touching incidents in Holy Writ, where Paul the aged, having fought a good fight, having finished his course, and having kept the faith, enjoins his son Timothy to fight the same fight, to walk the same course, and keep the same faith. Mr. Duncan M<sup>c</sup>Laren, the grey-haired veteran, the hero of a hundred fights, the ex-M.P. for all Scotland, pronounced his benediction on the head of young Novar, and the victory was ours."

Throughout a long lifetime, in many arduous and protracted conflicts, Mr. M<sup>c</sup>Laren had indeed kept the faith; and in the evening of his days his heart was gladdened by the crown which, as a political reformer, he had most desired and had consistently striven to obtain—the full establishment of his fellow-subjects in their political rights as the free citizens of a free country.

# CHAPTER XXII.



## *NATIONAL EDUCATION.*

His long and intimate association with the Heriot School system made Mr. McLaren recognised as an authority on questions of educational administration. Many of the visitors from England, the Continent, and America who inspected the outdoor schools sought interviews with their founder, and often engaged him in correspondence. By governors of other hospitals his advice was frequently asked, and he spared himself no trouble in supplying information and counsel to applicants whom he believed to be acting in the public interest, and from an anxiety to secure an extension of the benefits of the foundation.

But the administration of Heriot's Hospital was not the only educational work with which he was associated. He took his share, though not the leading place, in the struggle for the retention of the Town Council's management of the University. He believed that the connection had proved good for both institutions, and it was regard for the interests of both that induced him, during the two periods of his civic administration, and on the public platform as well as in private counsel, to contend for the continuance of the patronage. When the bill of Lord Advocate Inglis was introduced in 1858, he, while friendly to reform and to the development of self-government within the University, objected strongly to the with-

1858

Appeal
Lord Al
deen.

drawal of the patronage from the Town Council, not only without evidence of misuse, but even without inquiry—" a thing which he believed was without a parallel in the annals of Parliament." On the strength of a personal acquaintance formed during his Lord Provostship with the late Lord Aberdeen, whom he regarded as " one of the fairest and most upright men in Parliament," he personally wrote to that distinguished statesman, asking him to use his influence in Parliament to prevent the threatened injustice. The following was Lord Aberdeen's reply :—

ARGYLL HOUSE, *July* 20, 1858.

MY DEAR SIR,—I should have supported with great pleasure the claims of the Edinburgh Town Council to preserve their patronage of the professorships, for I well recollect being struck by the admirable manner in which, on the whole, it had been exercised. Not being able, in consequence of illness, to attend the House of Lords yesterday, there was no opportunity of my saying anything. I understand, however, it was urged that a compromise on the subject had taken place in the House of Commons, and that any change now effected would be regarded as a breach of faith. I trust the modifications introduced into the bill may ultimately prove satisfactory on this point.—I am, my dear sir, very truly yours,				ABERDEEN.

Seven years afterwards, in speaking at a meeting of the members of the Mechanics' Library, Mr. McLaren renewed his testimony in favour of the old in comparison with the new system of professorial elections. He was contrasting the advantages working-men possessed as politicians compared with more learned men in their greater freedom from prejudices and scholastically acquired fallacies, and he thus proceeded :—

" He would give as an instance, to show the application of this principle, the Act of Parliament which was passed taking the patronage of the University from the Town Council and conferring it on a small body of excellent men. He had seen the working of both systems; he knew a great deal about the one, and he believed he knew a little about the other; and his opinion was, that there never was a greater error made than that change. Not one member of the Town Council, perhaps, was himself qualified to say who would be the best professor to fill a vacancy in the Senatus Academicus. They did not profess to be qualified; but they listened to the testimonials of those who were qualified, each man considering himself one of a jury of thirty-three impannelled to try the cause. It was a jury indifferently chosen—not a jury of professional men, mathematicians, and lawyers. . . . The University throve under this system. In the case of the smaller number of men who now held the patronage, being all of them men of mark, and themselves mixed up in University affairs, and being good judges, they necessarily relied more upon their own opinions, and did not always reflect the opinions of the scientific community. He was quite sure the Town Council and the Senatus could not do a better thing than to return to the old system of appointments." [1]

As a member of the Town Council of Edinburgh when that body had practically the control of the University in its hands, and as on several occasions one of the Council's representatives on the Board of Curators after the Universities Act of 1858 had changed the administrative arrangements, he proved himself as faithful a guardian of the higher education as he did of the technical education in connection with the Watt Institution, and of the elementary education in connection with the Heriot outdoor schools. In

---

[1] We give this opinion because it is characteristic of Mr. M<sup>c</sup>Laren, and because it illustrates his unvarying confidence in the working of representative institutions. Most people will agree with him that the patronage of the Town Council was, on the whole, exercised wisely and well. As much, and no more, can be said for the exercise of patronage by the present Board.

each of these departments his chief concern was the well-being of the pupils.   When Sir David Brewster, the gifted and accomplished Principal of the University of Edinburgh, renewed, in 1864, a frequently-presented plea for increased parliamentary grants, and complained, more especially, that the Scottish Universities were unjustly dealt with, in comparison with the Queen's Colleges in Ireland, Mr. M<sup>c</sup>Laren, while admitting that the complaint was well founded, and while emphasising and enforcing it, made this somewhat severe rejoinder: " What is most wanted in Scotland are scholarships or fellowships for the benefit of the meritorious students, and not additional grants for the benefit of professors.   The recent grant of £10,000 a year all went into their pockets, without lessening the fees formerly payable by the students.   The next grant, if one should ever come, ought to be exclusively for the students, since the last was exclusively for the professors."   While the exercise of University patronage in Edinburgh has on different occasions excited keen feeling and sharp discussion, it may safely be affirmed that Mr. M<sup>c</sup>Laren's votes were uniformly given on public and scientific grounds, and that in no instance had he occasion to regret the choice in which he took a part.   Speaking in the House of Commons on March 13, 1879, in opposition to a motion condemnatory of mixed classes or colleges, which was proposed by an Ultramontane Irish Member, he gave the following illustration of the principle which guided him as a patron of University chairs, and which recalled the interesting fact that he was largely responsible for the connection of Professors Kelland and Blackie with the University of Edinburgh :—

" More than forty years ago," Hansard reports him to have said, " he was a member of the electing body which appointed the professors in Edinburgh, and he remembered taking deep

1858

Election of
Professors.

interest in promoting the return of a clergyman of the Church of England who was a candidate for the professorship of mathematics, because he believed him to be the best qualified of all the candidates. He remembered another instance, when, at a later period, about twenty years ago, a gentleman who was a very distinguished Greek scholar offered himself as a candidate for the Greek chair. That gentleman was, he admitted, opposed by certain parties on the ground that he was not sufficiently orthodox for the prevailing Presbyterian sentiment. That objection was strongly urged, but it did not prevail; and he was glad to say that that gentleman was appointed, although by the very small majority of his (Mr. McLaren's) casting vote. He was proud of having been the means of appointing a distinguished scholar, although objected to by some on account of his supposed religious views."

National
Education.

Mr. McLaren was an early and earnest advocate of a national system of elementary education. Yet for many years, as occasional legislative measures were proposed, he exerted himself as a critic rather than as a supporter. He was asked, but did not see his way, to co-operate with the Royal Commission appointed in 1858. He was quite sensible of the difficulties arising from denominational jealousies and class-interests that obstructed the path of any practical statesman who attempted a settlement, and he was prepared for a certain amount of compromise. He was sensible, too, of the urgency of the case. But the

Criticism
of Govern-
ment mea-
sure.

measures framed by Lord Advocate Moncreiff on the basis of the report of the Commissioners made, in his view, too complete a submission to these difficulties, and also came so directly in conflict with democratic principle, that he felt obliged to offer strenuous opposition, saying once and again, "Better no bill than such a bill." A letter he published in 1862, declaring that the bill of the year, in its rating provisions for the future maintenance of the schools, gave an amount of relief to the landowners equal to a grant of £1,000,000 sterling, caused at the time no small sensation, and was angrily controverted. He summed up his contention thus :—

"By this bill the landowners of Scotland will get an addition made to the net rental of their estates amounting to £30,000 a year; and as land now sells at about 33¾ years' purchase, this will be equivalent to a grant of £1,000,000 made to them from the Consolidated Fund at the expense of all other classes in the United Kingdom."

Mr. McLaren was equally severe in his condemnation of the machinery by which the new system was to be carried out :—

"An irresponsible Commission," he wrote, "is appointed by the bill, consisting of sixteen University functionaries and four members to be appointed by the Crown, but not one member to represent the people or any local authority. They are not to be appointed, as the English Education Commission was, to examine and report to Her Majesty, but they are appointed to act at once, without the knowledge or consent of Parliament, and to expend £75,000 a year of the public money, which is to be appropriated annually for ever as this irresponsible body shall be pleased to direct; and this appropriation is to include the annual payment of £30,000 a year to the landowners, or whatever sum, less or more, the one-half the salary and other expenses may amount to; and in return for this the people are to get nothing whatever from the landowners. The latter have now the sole appointment of the schoolmasters and the management of the schools, and they are not only to retain all the power they now have, but to obtain more, by getting the same power over all the ' rural ' schools to be erected under the bill, the one-half of the expense of which is to be laid on the Consolidated Fund, and the other half to be raised by a local rate levied in equal portions from the whole occupiers and owners of all lands and houses within the parish or district down to the very smallest cottages."



*Margin notes:*
1862
Objection to relief of land-owners.

Irresponsible Commissioner

Through the ten years' controversy that ensued he firmly maintained his objection to the transfer to the ratepayers from the landlords of burdens under which their estates were acquired, or which were imposed by the Act of 1667. Illustrating his position by a reference to the case of a parish near Edinburgh, he said :—

" There are twenty heritors who pay the whole cost under the Act of 1667 ; the result of passing this bill (1871) will be that these twenty heritors, instead of paying the whole sum, will pay little more than £27, and the rest of the contribution will be spread over the villagers and poor people around, who never paid a farthing before. In short, the effect of this bill would be to put nearly £140 a year into the pockets of these heritors, and to make their estates so much the more valuable in the market."

With equal pertinacity and more success he objected to the attempt to introduce the principle of indirect representation, for which the Education Department and the Royal Commission on Educational Endowments afterwards showed such a marked partiality. He claimed for the ratepayers of both sexes complete control of the local funds, and it was on this ground that he consistently protested against the device of the cumulative vote. In a speech delivered in Parliament in 1871, he described the retention of the cumulative vote as the one blot in Lord Advocate Young's Education Bill. " I always thought that," he said, " a most extravagant and absurd proposition ; and I now maintain in regard to it, that Scotland ought not to be tied to the heels of England in everything. Merely because England made a blunder, I see no reason why Scotland should be made for uniformity's sake to repeat the blunder." After the School Board of Edinburgh began its operations he frequently felt called upon to criticise its administration and its policy, and he seldom missed the opportunity of pressing home his conviction that the cumulative vote sheltered, if it did not encourage, extravagance, owing to the denominational zeal and activity evoked during the elections. It seems not unlikely that public opinion on this subject may lead to the adoption of the simpler system of election by majority, as recommended by Mr. McLaren, who in this, as in other controverted points, proved himself a Liberal in advance of his time.

Mr. McLaren was opposed to the establishment of a Scottish Central Board of Education. He frankly admitted that the prevailing sentiment in Scotland (influenced, perhaps, by his own persistent advocacy of Scottish rights and claims) was in favour of a Central Board as a concession to the demand for " justice to Scotland," and as a counterpoise to some extent to the exceptional educational privileges given to Ireland. The two questions, however, are really quite distinct. Mr. McLaren had on different occasions objected to the extension to Ireland of special pecuniary advantages, virtually at the expense of England and Scotland, and more than any man he had exposed, and continued to expose, the injustice done to Scotland through the smallness of the Treasury grants for education and in aid of local taxation in proportion to her population and to her contributions to the imperial revenue, when compared with the grants made to Ireland out of her relatively smaller contributions to the public exchequer. In a speech delivered in the House of Commons after the Education Act was in operation, and while Lord Beaconsfield's Government was in office, he pointed out that while Ireland had received £447,000 for educational purposes, Scotland had received only £130,000, though Scotland contributed to the imperial exchequer about a million a year more than Ireland. But he would not justify waste in Scotland on the ground of the existence of extravagance in Ireland, and the proposed Central Board in Edinburgh he regarded not only as so much waste in itself, but as an encouragement of waste in the Local Boards. The system of administration through intermediary Edinburgh Boards [1] had not commended itself to him, and he distrusted the proposed Central Education Board on economic grounds, as well as from regard to the freedom of the Local Boards. He wished the real power of management to remain with them, as most directly representative of the ratepayers and parents. It may here be noticed that, on the expiry of the time for which its members were appointed, the Scottish Board was allowed to lapse. It had not many friends in Parliament or in the press, but it may be admitted that it performed the preliminary work intrusted to it fairly well, and it may be doubted whether the Education Office in London would not have encountered even more opposition had this work been intrusted to it.

Mr. McLaren was strongly in favour of making the Local School Boards as representative as possible. With this object in view, he proposed to make the State Church clergy liable to the education rate, so that, in conformity with constitutional principles, the parish minister might be eligible for election as a ratepayers' representative. He had in former times vigorously opposed the bestowal of a special parliamentary franchise on university men incorporated in different districts as learned guilds; but he was equally opposed to the exclusion of any class either from local or imperial representation, and therefore he asked that the State clergy, by being made liable to assessment, should

---

[1] This subject is more extensively dealt with in the chapter describing the movement for the reform of the government of Scotland.

be given a valid constitutional right not only to representation on, but to service in, the School Boards.

Again, as a national educationist, he was an out-and-out opponent of State-aided denominationalism. He considered that no sectarian system could fairly claim to be supported by Government aid. At the same time he refused to allow the Protestant translation of the Bible to be placed in the category of prohibited books. He believed that in Scotland the religious difficulty had assumed a magnitude in the eyes of statesmen and politicians which it did not really possess. The mass of the people were Protestant, and Catholic parents would not allow their children to attend the national schools. In these circumstances it was absurd to object to the use of a version of the sacred writings as to which all interested were agreed. While personally ready to accept the Shorter Catechism as a confession of faith, he was not satisfied of its suitability as a class-book for children ; he thought it " too abstruse for the general run of children," and therefore he believed it could be withdrawn from the public schools without loss to religion of the Presbyterian or any other faith. Moreover, in considering this question, he bore in mind that the imperial Parliament had to legislate for three kingdoms, and that the Presbyterians of Scotland could not claim the Shorter Catechism for their schools without giving to the Church of England a strong title to claim Church of England teaching in the English schools, and to the Roman Catholic Church denominational teaching in Ireland, and without thus sanctioning what he regarded as the obnoxious principle of concurrent endowment. But he held that the reading of the Bible stood in an entirely different position. He denied that a book accepted as the common text-book of Christianity could be fairly regarded as sectarian, and he argued that it could be

1872

Bible-
teaching.

The
Shorter
Catechis

taught without a sectarian bias. " I should like," he said, " to see the Bible read, and its grand moral precepts and its scriptural history and biography impressed on the minds of the children." On another occasion the words he employed were :—" I hold that the Bible should be taught, and not read merely. A simple reading of the Bible to young children I have always held, and I have often expressed that view in public, to be a mockery. I am in favour of the Bible being read and taught in good faith, like any other book of instruction. I do not believe that there is a school-master in the whole of Scotland who would pervert his office in order to draw children from one church to another." And this was the position he occupied during the whole controversy.

prove-
its and
icts.

The various bills, with their various editions, which were introduced to the House between 1862 and 1872, approximated, with occasional partial exceptions, more and more to his ideas of a practicable national settlement, and to the general consensus of Scottish opinion, which during forty years he had done much to form and to guide. Accordingly, his attitude to the more recent bills was distinctly friendly. He yielded none of his former points of contention, but in the bills of 1871 and of 1872, more especially the latter, he perceived concessions so large to liberal principles, and such hopeful prospects of a peaceful and satisfactory settlement, that of each he said : " The bill has faults which we must try to remove or modify, but better that it should pass with all its faults than that it should be lost." Perhaps no public man in Scotland had striven more strenuously than he to secure for his country a really liberal measure of national education ; and when such a measure was at last framed and offered, no Scotch Member employed his influence more loyally and effectively to promote its enactment. His closing words, as the bill of 1872 was about to be read a third and last time in the House of Commons on June 28, 1872, were:—"He had proposed several amendments to the bill, some of which had been accepted, while others had been rejected. He was satisfied, from all the information he had been able to obtain, that no measure could be passed in the House which would be more acceptable to the people of Scotland. With one exception, he thought that the bill was all that it should be, and that it would work wonders for the people." The single exception in his mind was probably the unwarrantable concession Mr. Forster had made to the denominationalists when the bill was passing through Committee, against which Mr. M<sup>c</sup>Laren and the Independent Liberal members earnestly and persistently protested as an incitement to and support of proselytism—an objection which, in the practical working of the Act, has proved only too well founded. Other defects were unfortunately introduced by the amendments subsequently carried in the House of Lords.

In his speech to his constituents in December 1872, while renewing his general expression of satisfaction, and complimenting Lord Advocate Young on the ability he had displayed in framing and carrying the measure, Mr. M<sup>c</sup>Laren made a last protest against the relief given at the expense of the ratepayers to the landowners (amounting, according to his estimate, to £48,000 a year), adding characteristically that "it was no doubt intended as a bribe to the great landowners to induce them to agree to the other parts of the bill."

# CHAPTER XXIII.

*OVERTHROW OF THE HERIOT FREE SCHOOL SYSTEM.*

THE general satisfaction with which Mr. M<sup>c</sup>Laren welcomed
the establishment of a national system of elementary education would doubtless have been modified if he had foreseen
that it was to prove the foundation of an attack on the free
system he had been able to set up in Edinburgh. He
expected and was prepared for further reform in the educational work of Heriot's Hospital, but in the direction of,
and on the general line of, the system he had marked out.
The outdoor free schools, and indeed the whole administration of Heriot's Hospital, Mr. M<sup>c</sup>Laren regarded with
justifiable pride. He knew that the elementary schools
had been examined by German and American educationists,
as well as by Her Majesty's Government inspectors, and
had invariably excited the highest commendation. He felt,
with respect to the financial investments and accounts of
the Hospital, that whatever record was brought to light,
the Governors, from the time of his first connection with
the Trust, had nothing to be ashamed of. He believed
that official inquiry would discover no trace either of waste
or of jobbery, and that through the operation of the Act of
1836 the surplus funds of the Trust, after the fulfilment of
the express and special requirements of the founder, had
been utilised to the greatest possible advantage. Accordingly he courted inquiry, convinced that investigation of

the affairs and administration of the Hospital and its enor-  1869
mous revenues, would disclose results redounding to the
credit of local self-government, and encouraging reform in
the case of other similar institutions on the lines he had
laid down and tested.

In the House of Commons in 1869 he seconded Sir  Inquiry
Edward Colebrooke's motion for the appointment of a Royal  courted.
Commission " to inquire into the nature and amount of all
endowments in Scotland, the funds of which are devoted
to the maintenance or education of young persons ; also to
inquire into the administration and management of any hospitals or schools supported by such endowments, and into
the system or course of study respectively pursued therein ;
and to report whether any and what changes in the administration and use of such endowments are expedient, by which
their usefulness and efficiency may be increased."   In the
same session he also supported Lord Advocate Young's bill
" to make provision for the better government and administration of hospitals and other endowed institutions in Scotland."   But his eyes were soon opened.   In the following
year, 1870, in a remarkable book entitled " Recess Studies,"  " Recess
issued by several of the University professors, which ex-  Studies."
cited no small interest in educational as well as in municipal circles, the late Sir Alexander Grant, two years after
his election as Principal of the University, made a violent
attack upon the Heriot Hospital administration on financial as well as educational grounds, contemptuously speaking
of the £4500 expended on the outdoor schools as so much
money thrown into the streets, and practically claiming the
bequest on behalf of the University.   The constitution of
the Royal Commission he had himself helped to create also
disappointed Mr. M<sup>c</sup>Laren.   He had expected it to consist
of perhaps three persons acquainted with Scottish affairs,

1870

and he and his parliamentary colleague, Mr. Miller, had recommended Mr. George Harrison, then chairman of the Chamber of Commerce, as one of the three members.

unsatis-
tory
umis-
¹.

But the Commission actually appointed consisted of six gentlemen, most of them Whigs—that is to say, connected with the party which the election of 1868 had shown to be "the smallest and least influential of the three political parties in Scotland." [1]

Speaking of the members of the Commission some time afterwards Mr. McLaren said :—

"I know most of them, and I hear good accounts of those to whom I am not personally known. I could not desire better men to be arbitrators in any matter in which I was personally concerned; but in such an arbitration there would be agents or counsel employed on both sides, and the result would be that the facts would be fully and fairly explained before the arbitrators. I lament that this cannot be done by the present Commission. The members of the Commission have been all appointed—I say it with due deference—because of their ignorance of the matter about which they are to inquire. They know nothing about the endowments of Scotland. They are neutral persons. They know nothing about the institutions of Edinburgh, and know nothing about the feeling of the citizens. There are no agents or counsel to bring the facts fully and fairly before them, and no agent or counsel who know the facts to cross-examine the witnesses. . . . I lament this fact, and that there is not even the element of publicity."

It was a hole-and-corner inquiry, and Mr. McLaren's public life was a consistently maintained contention that hole-and-cornerism ought to have ended with the rotten close burgh system, and that government by the people and for

---

[1] The members of the Commission were Sir E. Colebrooke, Lord Rosebery, Sir W. Stirling-Maxwell (who died in 1878), Mr. C. S. Parker, Mr. J. Ramsay, M.P., Mr. H. H. Lancaster, and Mr. A. Craig-Sellar.

the people should be conducted under the public inspection. Further cause for dissatisfaction and disquietude was furnished when, after the Governors of Heriot's Hospital had framed, in compliance with the Lord Advocate's Act for facilitating the reform of the endowed institutions of Scotland, an extremely liberal Provisional Order, the Government withheld their consent. Under this order the Governors proposed to convert the Hospital into a day-school, to continue and extend the outdoor primary schools, to complete a graduated system of education by the erection of a higher or secondary school, to enlarge the provision made for the supply of industrial or technical education, and to increase the benefaction to the University by means of bursaries and fellowships. This plan of reform, while it obviously rested on a well-grounded anticipation of a continued growth of revenue to supplement the sum liberated by the conversion of the Hospital building to a day-school, did not satisfy the suddenly developed scheme of the University reformers. And when, to other provocations already mentioned, the Government added secret negotiations with the chief opponent of the Heriot Schools, Mr. M<sup>c</sup>Laren went definitely and resolutely into opposition. He declined to give evidence before, or further to facilitate, the work of a Commission which he believed to be prejudiced as well as imperfectly constituted. He called attention to the delays sanctioned by Mr. Bruce (now Lord Aberdare), the Home Secretary, which staved off acceptance of the Provisional Order, notwithstanding the ready compliance of the Governors of the Trust with his succession of contradictory demands. Mr. M<sup>c</sup>Laren summoned the citizens to open conference, and before a large meeting held in the Literary Institute on December 16, 1872, he delivered an able address, which afterwards was published by request in pamphlet form.[1]  He complained at the outset of the "underhand" tactics of the Government in their opposition to the Heriot Hospital scheme of reform.  "When," he said, "the Provisional Order was applied for by the Governors to improve the Trust, which was so unjustly opposed by Her Majesty's Government, the Secretary of State for the Home Department, in place of referring the various matters to a public inquiry before the Sheriff in Edinburgh, as was required by the Act of Parliament, did, most unconstitutionally, as I think, send his private secretary to Edinburgh to make private inquiries behind the backs of the Governors, and this gentleman was traced by them to the house of the learned Principal, who was understood to be the leader of the opposition to this valuable scheme."

In this address Mr. McLaren's controversy was chiefly with Sir Alexander Grant, and not with the Government, or even with the Commission.  He had little difficulty in showing that the Principal, as yet new to Edinburgh life and imperfectly acquainted with its institutions, had entered into the controversy much too hastily and with inadequate preparation.  He showed conclusively, in contradiction of the assumption of the Principal, that the Heriot bequest was primarily destined exclusively for Edinburgh; that the conditions necessary for the retention of the bequest had been scrupulously fulfilled by successive generations of trustees; that it was an educational endowment intended entirely for the benefit of the poor; and he exposed the one-sidedness and inconsistency of the contention that, on the one hand, an educational endowment administered in the interest of the poorer citizens,

---

[1] "Heriot's Hospital Trust and its Proper Administration."  By Duncan McLaren, Esq., M.P.  Edinburgh: W. Oliphant & Co.

1872

who are numerous, exerted a pauperising influence, but, on the other, produced a stimulating and elevating effect when, in the name of a higher education, it was applied in the interest of the more comfortably situated classes and the comparatively few whose education at the University was practically prolonged into the years of manhood. The pith and marrow of the Principal's essay practically, he said, amounted to this—"That the purposes to which Heriot devoted his fortune should be totally disregarded; that the children of the poor burgesses, brought up under every disadvantage arising from poverty and the death of their natural protectors, should be asked to pay fees to compete in primary schools with the children of those in better circumstances, who have enjoyed all the advantages of paternal home training, and many of them of home teaching, by persons paid for that purpose." He objected to the Principal's proposal to convert the Hospital into a college-hall attached to the University, to grant bursaries and scholarships open to all students out of a fund intended and husbanded for the benefit of Edinburgh, and to multiply endowments for the High School and other similar seminaries attended by the children of the rich, holding that such changes involved a direct breach of the founder's will, a misapplication of the funds, and a spoliation of the poor for the benefit of the rich. The evidence he presented of the high standard of efficiency attained in the primary Heriot schools conclusively answered the reckless statement that the maintenance of these institutions was so much money thrown into the streets; and his reply to Sir Alexander's criticism of the financial administration was, if possible, still more effective.

From this time forwards it may be said, with no exaggeration, that Mr. M<sup>c</sup>Laren, as the champion of the rights of the poor in the Heriot Trust, had the people of Edinburgh

at his back in a way in which few public men have ever
been sustained by any community. The citizens took the
alarm and prepared for combat in self-defence. The Heriot
question entered into municipal and parliamentary politics
and asserted its pre-eminence. Admission to the Town
Council or to Parliament became impossible until a pledge
of fidelity to the Heriot Trust had been given. And nobly
was that pledge kept. The unanimity maintained in the
Town Council throughout a long period of conflict, during
which the enemy frequently changed his tactics and constantly exercised social pressure in the hope of making a
breach in the municipal ranks, was one of the most remarkable illustrations of loyalty to the interests of constituencies
which the history of local self-government has ever supplied.
The Councillors and the Governors were periodically supported by the unanimously adopted resolutions of large and
enthusiastic meetings. They were likewise encouraged by
the unflinching vigilance maintained by Mr. M<sup>c</sup>Laren in the
House of Commons and the wide personal influence he there
enjoyed. The Government, however, refused to yield, and
though they passed the Merchant Company's Provisional
Orders relating to the endowed schools belonging to that
body, they, professed Reformers though they were, stayed
the work of reform in the Heriot Trust, which the Governors
were ready and anxious to begin, until the temporary power
conferred by the Act of 1869 had lapsed. Thus, through
Government obstruction, which no amount of conciliation on
the part of the Heriot Governors could remove, a liberal and
far-reaching scheme of reform was defeated, and the citizens
of Edinburgh were deprived of an enlargement of educational
benefits at the expense of a bequest belonging to themselves
which the guardians of their interests were able and willing
to bestow.

Meanwhile the Governors of the Hospital, anxious to do the greatest amount of good they could, in the absence of the extended powers denied them, established evening classes, and very quickly about 1000 young men and women enrolled themselves as night-scholars. In 1876, mainly for the purpose of strengthening the position of the Trust, and of removing the chief ground of objection taken by the Commissioners, viz., the limited and always decreasing area of selection for admission to the Hospital caused by the burgess rate, Mr. M<sup>c</sup>Laren proposed and carried a bill assimilating the law of Scotland to that of England respecting the creation of burgesses. This Act conferred on all householders, whether men or women, who paid their poor-rates and municipal taxes, and who had resided three years within the burgh, the full right of burgess-ship, and in Edinburgh the number of burgesses was at once increased from 500 to 20,000. It was no longer difficult to find children legally qualified for admission as foundationers to the Hospital, and in a few years it was ascertained that 110 of the 180 boys educated and maintained within the Hospital building, in accordance with the will of the founder, were "puir orphans and fatherless children of decayit burgesses." Immediately after the passing of this Act of 1876, Mr. M<sup>c</sup>Laren addressed a letter "to the new burgesses," clearly and fully explaining its provisions, and reminding them more particularly that George Heriot left his funds for the benefit of the poorer class of burgesses in the city—pointing out that as in Heriot's time "burgess" and "householder" were nearly convertible terms, the new Act brought within the scope of the benefits of the trust the people intended by the founder, "excepting women householders, a class which in all probability he did not contemplate, but one now requiring special sympathy and care, owing in too many cases to the destitute and distressing condition in which they are left as widows with children." He added :—

"I have for many years formed a strong opinion respecting what should be done about the Hospital, but no circumstances equal to the present have ever presented themselves for carrying these views into effect. One of my objects in pressing forward the bill was to facilitate the extensive changes which I thought ought to be made in this institution for the benefit of the whole city. I would, if I had the power, make Heriot's Hospital a great civic school for the clever boys and girls selected from the elementary schools, to be educated along with the boys placed on the Hospital foundation; and from these again I would afterwards select those who wish to pursue a university education, with reasonable prospects of success, and who required pecuniary assistance."

A second Commission.

The Governors of the Hospital were interrupted in the consideration of reforms on the lines indicated by Mr. McLaren by the issue of another Royal Commission in 1878. The constitution of the Commission showed that Mr. McLaren's criticism of its predecessor had not been without effect. It was a Scottish Commission in fact as well as in name; it embraced both Whigs and Tories, and the civic or municipal element was represented. Its members were Lord Moncreiff; Lord Balfour of Burleigh, a young Conservative nobleman, eager to make himself useful to his country; Sir James Watson, an ex-Lord Provost of Glasgow, an honourable and conscientious man, who had had prolonged and varied experience of municipal administration; Mr. Ramsay, M.P. for the Falkirk Burghs, but more closely connected with the commercial capital of Scotland, and a member of the former Commission; Mr. J. A. Campbell, M.P., also a Glasgow citizen, but representing the University

rather than the municipal interest; Professor Tait of
Edinburgh University, a distinguished representative of
science, and Dr. Donaldson, Rector of the High School of
Edinburgh, an experienced educationist, whose efforts as a
reformer were, however, mainly devoted to the establishment of secondary schools, and whose views it was well
known were hostile to the designs of the Heriot Governors. It was therefore sufficiently apparent from the
outset that this second Commission, though its composition
met some of the objections stated by Mr. McLaren to its
predecessor, offered little prospect of reconciliation with the
defenders of the Heriot Trust; and indeed its issue was
generally regarded as a renewed declaration of war on the
part of the Education Department at the bidding of the
spoilers of the heritage of the poor. But this Commission
conducted its inquiries in presence of the press, and therefore of the public, and Mr. McLaren, who was requested
by Lord Provost Boyd to attend and state his views, on the
ground that "the citizens would highly appreciate" the service, at once complied with the suggestion. Accordingly, on
June 7, 1879, he appeared before the Commission. He had
made full preparation for the interview, and the statement
he presented was undoubtedly the ablest and most pointed
refutation of the claims of the University party, and at the
same time the completest and most masterly defence of the
position of the Corporation and of the Heriot Trust, as the
representatives of the citizens, which had yet been submitted.[1]

He was now verging on fourscore years, but his mental
powers were active and vigorous as ever. He was inti-

1878

A renewed
declaration
of war.

Mr. McLa-
ren's evi-
dence.

---

[1] "Evidence before Royal Commission on Endowed Institutions," by
Duncan McLaren, M.P. Edinburgh: Neill & Co.

mately versed in all the details and intricacies of the controversy, and his whole moral nature, his sense of justice,
his fidelity to what he believed to be the rights and interest
of his humbler fellow-citizens, stimulated his intellectual
energies.  He proved more than a match for the adverse
Commission; and his triumph in the conflict was so conspicuous, that many citizens who had long been engaged in
the same struggle and on the same side sanguinely assumed
that the cause had been won.

Outline of
evidence.

Here only the merest outline of the evidence can be
given.   The first conclusion enforced was " that the Trust,
as constituted by George Heriot, was wholly an Edinburgh
trust," designed for the public weal and ornament of the
city; that the claim of St. Andrews University as a
secondary legatee was excluded by the fidelity with which
the primary requirements of the will had been fulfilled;
that the High School had no claim whatever; that ample
justice had been done to the University as regards bursaries; that, in short, the funds of the Hospital had been
and were justly and advantageously applied, and that the
diversion of them to objects outside of Edinburgh or in
Edinburgh in such a way as practically to exclude the poor
of the city, meant spoliation and jobbery.  Mr. M<sup>c</sup>Laren
went further, and showed that even under the Act under
which the Commission were sitting the views for which he
contended were protected, and justified his contention by
a reference to statements made by Mr. Cross, then Home
Secretary, at an interview he had with an Edinburgh
deputation before the bill was passed.  Quoting from a
report of the interview, Mr. M<sup>c</sup>Laren said :—

" 'There were two points in particular on which the inhabitants of Edinburgh held very strong opinions opposed to the
report of the Commission.  The first was that no change should

be made which would make the Hospital a Scotch trust, in place
of continuing to be, as at present, an Edinburgh trust, which
Heriot ordered it to be from the love he bore to his mother city.'
Then there is this interjection by the Home Secretary—'There
I am entirely at one with you.'  The other point, I went on to
speak of was this:—'That no arrangement should be made for
granting bursaries to be competed for from all parts of Scotland
by all classes, rich and poor, mingled together.  The effect of
such a competition would inevitably be, that the sons of the
middle and richer classes, being, as a rule, more advanced with
their education than the sons of the poorer classes of corresponding ages, would carry off all the bursaries, and the working-classes
would thus suffer a great injustice; because Heriot established
the trust for the sons of burgesses who were not sufficiently able
to maintain them.'  The Home Secretary again interposed—
'There I also agree with you.'"

Mr. M<sup>c</sup>Laren next re-exposed, with greater elaboration
and detail than he had employed in his speech in the
Literary Institute, the mistakes into which Sir Alexander
Grant had fallen in his criticism of the financial administration of the trust.  Then he pointed to the Burgess
Act of 1876, as having removed "the main ground of
some of the recommendations of the Endowed School Commissioners made in 1870 respecting the application of the
funds of the Hospital, then confined (apart from the free
outdoor schools) to such a small number of persons."  He
gave statistics and quoted reports illustrative of the pre-
eminent educational success of the elementary outdoor
schools, and of the way parents appreciated the boon of free
education for their children.  Asked by Lord Moncreiff to
state his views as to gratuitous education, Mr. M<sup>c</sup>Laren
answered boldly that he would approve of free elementary
education, not only in the Heriot Schools, but also in the
Board Schools; and he showed that, so far as Edinburgh

was concerned, free education could be provided from the
available surplus funds of the Hospital conjoined with the
Government grant, which the free schools might have
earned so far as educational attainments were concerned,
but which they had never demanded lest Government money
should bring with it Government control and breach of the
requirements of Heriot's will and statutes as respects religious
instruction.   The passage bears so directly on the interests of
the citizens of Edinburgh, and on the question of free schools
throughout the country, which is now being put forward
prominently in the political programme of the Liberal party,
that it may advantageously be here reproduced *verbatim* :—

"I am strongly in favour of gratuitous education, and if I had
my will, I would abolish all fees in the Board Schools of this city,
and I would do so throughout Scotland.  That I may not be thought
very extreme in my views, I wish to say that, so far as I have
been able to find out, the original system of the parish schools in
Scotland was a system of entirely free education.  The parish
school was the same as the church ; they were places open to the
whole inhabitants to come and be taught—in the one to be
taught letters, in the other to be taught religion.  I have carefully read all the School Acts relating to Scotland, and so far as
I can find, I cannot see a trace of any authority to charge fees
till the passing of the Act of 1803 ; and it is my firm belief that
that was done just to save the pockets of the heritors at that
time.  The stipends of the schoolmasters were so scandalously
small that they could not possibly be maintained any longer, and
the heritors by the Act agreed to give a little more ; and, in
order to make the incomes of the teachers something better, in
place of giving a reasonable sum themselves, they got Parliament
to enable the schoolmasters to levy a sum—which the heritors
themselves ought to have paid—from the poor parents whose
children attended school.  Some people whom I have talked to
are startled at the amount of money which they suppose would
be required to do what I have suggested, but really it is not

at all large.  I think the whole Edinburgh School Board fees amount to about £3800.  [*Rev. Dr. Scott.*[1]—The whole fees for the year ending 15th May last amounted to £4044, 5s. 11d.]  Then there is upwards of £700 a year spent in watching those children, to bring them to the school, and about £70 in prosecuting the parents before the Sheriff—altogether about £800 spent in bringing the children to the school; whereas in the case of the Heriot Schools they come without anybody to bring them.  Then the school fees are collected weekly or monthly by the teachers, who account to the Board, and there must be a vast amount of clerks' work and time taken up by clerks and teachers; and it would be a very moderate computation to say that £200 a year might be saved in that way.  Adding these three sums together, I say that £1000 a year is expended by the School Board because of the fee-system.  Well, if you deduct that from the gross income raised by fees, you have £3000 a year as the loss by the abolition of fees.  A penny a pound on the rental of the city yields £5600; a halfpenny a pound would therefore yield £2800: so, if you just increase your school-rate on the city of Edinburgh by a halfpenny a pound, you get rid of the fees and of all the bother connected with them: you get the children to attend better, their education gets on more rapidly, and therefore more successfully, and I hold that great benefits would arise therefrom."

At a subsequent stage of the examination Sir James Watson recalled Mr. M<sup>c</sup>Laren's attention to the loss of the Government grant, and his answer showed he was eager for and hopeful of an arrangement by which the money would be secured to the ratepayers in combination with a complete system of free elementary education :—

" *Sir James Watson.*—If you thought that by taking the benefit of the Government grant, which would amount to £4000, no injury would result, would it not be for the benefit of the institution to get that grant ?—Of course it would be if there were no

1879

The difficulties stated.

---

[1] Then chairman of School Board of Edinburgh.

countervailing evils. But there are just two difficulties. The one is what is called the conscience clause, and the other is the regulation of the Privy Council for setting apart separate hours for religious teaching, and not teaching religion at any other than the hours named. The will and statutes of Heriot are permeated with statements about the religious training and up-bringing of those boys, which are so clearly their intention—perhaps more than anything else—that I fancy the Governors feel they would not be acting in the spirit of George Heriot's will and statutes if they were to give only the minimum of religious training that is required to be given by the Privy Council. However, I speak from general impression, and not as an authority on this subject; but I have ascertained that if these two difficulties were got over there would not be anything to prevent free schools in Scotland—although there is in England—from getting the benefit of the Government grant; that those schools would be just as open to be examined as are the Board Schools, provided the Privy Council were satisfied on those two points. I think the first point I named is already practically settled—that is, about the conscience clause—because I saw in the newspapers within the last six months that a discussion took place in the Hospital on the application of a parent to have his child exempted from being taught the Westminster Catechism, and, after due consideration by the Governors, they resolved that the child should be exempted. I call that a conscience clause. Of course, if right in one case, it would be right in every case, and I call that compliance with the conditions of the Privy Council as regards the conscience clause."

And again, in answer to Mr. Campbell, he explained that the question had been considered when the School Act of 1836 was applied for, and that it was found scrupulous Governors did not like to disregard the hard and fast lines laid down in the old regulations, even to gain a pecuniary advantage. He however added :—

"Such scruples, I have no doubt, are still held, and they should be respected ; but if Dr. Scott, and Mr. Giffen, and Bailie Tawse, and others of the Governors were to lay their heads together, I do not despair of their being able to make arrangements which would comply with the spirit of Heriot's directions, and yet satisfy the Privy Council."

His final words on this subject, in answer to Lord Moncreiff, were these :—

" I would make all the schools in Edinburgh and in Scotland free if I could.   They are free in the United States, and in nearly every country in Europe, and why they should not be free in this rich country I cannot understand ; and I think that while you would pay a halfpenny per pound more to my friend Dr. Scott, you would pay perhaps a penny per pound less to the superin-tendent of police and for prisons."

On other questions raised during the inquiry he showed himself quite as advanced a reformer as any of the members of the Commission.   Of the disadvantages of the Hospital system generally he had been convinced many years ago, and had advised the discontinuance of Hospital training whenever such a change was possible consistently with the conditions prescribed by the founder.   He had given advice in this direction many years previously to the Governors of Gordon Hospital, Aberdeen ; and as regards Heriot's, he had in 1873 proposed that the building should be converted into a great civic secondary school for the poor boys and girls educated in the Hospital outdoor schools who after thirteen years of age desired the benefits of a higher and more advanced education, while bursaries should be provided for the assistance of the pupils who wished or were considered qualified for a university training.

To this graded system, with its ladder from the infant primary school stretching up to the university, he still ad-hered, provided always that the beneficiaries were confined to the sons and daughters of poor citizens of Edinburgh ; and while he told the Commissioners he was not then prepared to advise the abolition of the Hospital as a place of residence, because of the larger number of the poor fatherless children whose claim for admission had been legalised by the Burgess Act, still, speaking generally, he rejoiced that the Hospital system was becoming more and more obsolete. " I do not believe," he said, " it is good to herd together a great number of human beings, old or young, under one management, either as children or as soldiers in barracks, or anything else. I think that the more family life is scattered through the population the better for the good of the country." Further, he quite readily concurred in the proposal made by the Governors, and afterwards commended by the Commissioners, for the development of the Watt College as an expenditure of the Heriot funds in a way fitted to benefit the classes the founder desired to assist.

" ' Do you think,' asked Lord Moncreiff, ' that there are parents who would be desirous that their children should go to the Watt Institution ? '—' Yes,' Mr. McLaren replied, ' and the proof is that they do go. There were about 2000 in attendance last year.' "

He had all along taken an interest in the Watt Institution, and remembering the advantage he himself derived from teaching imparted in the evening after he had begun the business of life, he had, as a Director of this institution, consistently endeavoured to adapt its educational arrangements as to time and character to the wants of young men compelled to work for a living or to help a struggling household. He believed that a portion of the Heriot funds applied in aid of the Watt College would reach a deserving class who needed and would appreciate the help, and therefore this particular part of the scheme of reform secured from the first his warmest support.

1880

But the whole project again failed; and through the obstructiveness of the Commission appointed to facilitate these reforms, the Governors of the Hospital were again baulked of their desire to do good.    Their first Order was stopped because the Home Secretary of the day (Mr. Bruce), guided by the law-officers of Scotland, discovered some technical flaw which other legal advisers afterwards certified was no flaw, and which had neither hindered nor afterwards invalidated the Orders promoted by other governing bodies, notably the Merchant Company of Edinburgh.

Another failure.

The second Order, framed in accordance, as Mr. M<sup>c</sup>Laren and the Governors believed, with the views of Mr. Cross, the Conservative Home Secretary, and Mr. Watson, the Conservative Lord Advocate, were received and generally approved by the Liberal Home Secretary, Sir William Harcourt, who in a letter to Lord Moncreiff, dated 17th June 1880, earnestly urged an immediate and pacific settlement of the controversy.    But this Order also was stopped, and the labours of Commissioners, witnesses, Governors, and Parliament were cast to the winds.    The Commissioners reported that "until the constitution of the governing body was fully inquired into and revised, it was inexpedient to devolve on it new powers or to proceed further with the projected reforms."

The ground of conflict was now to a large extent changed.    The governing body, who had hitherto guarded the bequest as a patrimony of the poor of Edinburgh with conspicuous financial and educational success, consisted of the members of the Town Council and of the city clergy. These two bodies in George Heriot's time embraced the fullest and most comprehensive, and perhaps also the fairest,

Heriot governing body attacked.

representation of the citizens that could have been suggested.

In the course of time, as secessions from the State Church increased and Nonconformist communions grew in strength, the city clergy became less distinctly and less fully representative of the general community. But although several of the clerical Governors always distinguished themselves by the zeal and abundance of their service, as a matter of fact the management was largely in the hands of the lay Governors. It was not, however, to the imperfectly representative element in the constitution of the trust that the Commissioners objected. Their quarrel was with the municipal Governors, just because they were representative of the community and directly responsible to public opinion, as Members of Parliament are. The ratepayers, who approved of the past administration of the trust, and more especially of the application of the funds to the provision of gratuitous education, elected Town Councillors who sympathised with their opinions, and because of the perfect working of the representative system in the constitution of the Trust, the Commissioners declared that until a change was made freeing the governing body from popular control "it was inexpedient to devolve on it new powers or to proceed further with the projected reforms." The *raison d'être* of this desperate plea, which recalls the principle on which the old and rotten close burgh system was defended, was obvious enough. The Commissioners aimed at the abolition of the free schools, while the citizens and the Governors whom they elected desired their continuance. For the purpose, therefore, of the innovators, a governing body was necessary who would not be subject to popular control, and who would be able to abolish the free schools in defiance of the people's will. Incredible though it may appear, a Liberal Government, pledged at the time to the introduction of a large and far-reaching measure of local self-government, and composed of members recognising the supremacy of the democratic principle, submitted to the reactionary dictum of the Commissioners, and in the session of 1880 a new Educational Endowments (Scotland) Bill was introduced by Lord Spencer in the House of Lords, conferring on the Commissioners to be named in the Act the power of " altering the constitution of, or abolishing the existing governing bodies, corporate or unincorporate, with such powers as they think fit."   The bill contained other clauses suggestive of hostility to the Heriot free schools, and of a disposition to protect from inquiry and reform the institutions in which the close and irresponsible system of management had had free and uninterrupted play.   One clause, excluding from interference all endowments which had come into operation within the preceding fifty years, was, rightly or wrongly, read as specially intended for the protection of the Fettes Hospital.   Another clause provided for a de-localisation of funds, that is, the distribution over Scotland, or, in the case of Edinburgh University bursaries, practically over the whole world, of funds destined by will for a particular locality or object ; and further, was so framed as to permit of the diversion of funds, like those of the Heriot Trust, applied in the interest of the industrial classes, to secondary or higher education, which only the middle classes could reach.   In other words, the transference of the benefits of the Trust from the many who are poor to the comparatively few of a higher class.   The clause referred to was expressed thus :—

" It shall be the duty of the Commissioners to reorganise educational endowments, with the aim especially of supplying *the needs of every part and district of Scotland* as regards secon-

1880

Another attack.

Fettes Hospital.

dary or higher education, whether in the industrial arts, or as a preparation for commercial pursuits or for the universities."

Mr. McLaren at once put his finger on these blemishes of the bill, and the warning he sounded quickly called the Heriot Governors, the Town Council, the Liberal Association, the Trades Council, and the citizens of Edinburgh into active opposition.　Fortified by the practical unanimity prevailing among his constituents in support of his position, Mr. McLaren used all his parliamentary influence and skill to secure the desired amendments.　In the House of Lords he obtained the help of the Marquis of Huntly ; but the reception given by the Government to the attempted improvements was so discouraging, that the necessity for resolute opposition to the bill as a whole became only too apparent. Referring to the unbending attitude of the Government on the points mentioned, more especially as regards the alteration of the constitution of popularly elected trusts, Mr. McLaren wrote :—

"I may be permitted to ask why, if George Heriot left, as he did, his property to be managed by the Lord Provost, Magistrates, and Town Council of the city, now forty-one in number, with the addition of the thirteen city ministers ; and if they have managed it so well, as is the fact, that the original capital of £23,000 now yields 'annually £24,000 ; and if these trustees, without one dissenting voice, including men of all political parties and of all religious creeds, are opposed to this bill, backed up as they are by the great body of the people, why should Earl Spencer desire to improve our institutions after the English model ?　Why not leave well alone ?"

But the Government would not let well alone, and their resolution to push the measure through Parliament, practically without alteration, brought them into conflict with a resolution still more unbending and equally watchful. It was the 27th of July before the measure reached the House of Commons, and though the session was prolonged till the end of August, Mr. M<sup>c</sup>Laren's opposition, supported by Mr. Dick Peddie, Mr. Holms, Mr. Grant, and other faithful Scotch Members, proved effectual. Of course, Mr. M<sup>c</sup>Laren was vehemently denounced as an obstructionist by critics who conveniently forgot the effective obstruction, offered by themselves to the Provisional Orders promoted by the Heriot Governors. The responsibility for the prolonged delay in effecting the educational reforms which the finances of the Hospital permitted was serious enough, but it lay with the opponents of the Heriot administration, and not with Mr. M<sup>c</sup>Laren. He was still ready for reform of the right sort. At his meeting with his constituents on the following December he still assumed and encouraged an attitude of expectancy. He believed the amendments he had sketched, and which had been printed on the orders of the day, were faithful statements of Liberal principles, and he had faith in the democratic Liberalism of Mr. Gladstone and his colleagues.

He was willing to assume that the Ministry had at first accepted the bill from the Education Department without giving it the careful examination needed for the discovery of what he regarded as the reactionary and spoliatory provisions hid in its clauses, and that as these had been exposed, the necessary alteration would be made. "I have no doubt," he said to his constituents, "the Government will still further improve the bill when introduced next session, so as to secure its passing without much opposition." Unfortunately, when the amended bill was introduced in the session of 1881, Mr. M<sup>c</sup>Laren was no longer a member of the House, and the various attempts then made, partly

by negotiation and partly by discussion in the House, again
failed.  Mr. John M<sup>c</sup>Laren, then Lord Advocate, who
succeeded his father in the representation of Edinburgh,
loyally assisted these efforts, believing that the differences
between the Government and the supporters of the Heriot
Schools admitted of being arranged by mutual concessions;
but all his official influence and skill were baffled, and the
desired reconciliation was not attained.  Mr. Buchanan, who
was elected Member after the Lord Advocate's elevation
to the bench, made a careful study of the whole question,
and in the session of 1882, and in various interviews with
Ministers, battled bravely for the rights of the citizens of
Edinburgh, and for the Liberal principles threatened by
the Government measure.  After the most important of
these interviews, held on 22nd May, with Mr. Mundella, the
Vice-President of the Council, and Lord Rosebery, the
Under-Secretary of State for Scotland, and when·a closer
approximation to the views of the Governors seemed probable, Mr. M<sup>c</sup>Laren, at the request of Lord Provost Boyd,
embodied in the text of the Government bill all the amendments, whether framed by sympathising Scotch Members
or by the Governors of the Hospital, which he considered
necessary to prevent the de-localisation of funds, the
alienation of their application for the benefit of the poor,
or the limitation of the popular representative element in
the constitution of the Trust.  The Government had by this
time altered the clause which excluded Fettes College
from the scope of the inquiry.  On the 8th of June Mr.
M<sup>c</sup>Laren sent copies of the bill thus amended to each
member of the Heriot Trust, to each of the Scotch Members, to Mr. Mundella, Lord Rosebery, and the Lord Advocate.  He introduced a prefatory statement explaining the
circumstances which had led to his interference, repeating

the expression of his opinion that ninety-nine out of every hundred of the inhabitants of Edinburgh, "who knew the facts well," disapproved of the bill as framed by the Government, and adding :—

"My opinion is, after having carefully studied the history of the Hospital, that it has been one of the best managed institutions in the United Kingdom. There was left by the founder £23,000 in money, but no lands, with which to erect and endow the Hospital; and the annual revenue now exceeds that sum, after having (in addition to fulfilling all the original purposes of the endowment) in the course of the last forty-five years erected and maintained sixteen free schools, now educating about 4500 children, and about 1500 of more advanced ages at evening schools. All these schools are entirely free, even to the extent of furnishing books to the children ; and it may be stated that 91 per cent. of the boys and girls on the roll of the day-schools are in average attendance, which, it is believed, cannot be paralleled in any other schools in the United Kingdom. It only requires to be noticed, to prove the excellent management, that the institution is entirely free from debt."

This composite bill, with the amendments introduced by Mr. M<sup>c</sup>Laren printed in bolder type than the original text, proved most helpful in effecting the ultimate settlement. It guided and steadied public opinion outside, and it facilitated the heavy and responsible task of Mr. Peddie, Mr. Buchanan, Mr. Charles M<sup>c</sup>Laren, and other Members, in labouring to reconcile the clauses of the measure alike with public opinion and Liberal principles. Considerable improvements were effected by the Government. In accordance with Mr. M<sup>c</sup>Laren's suggestion, the Society for Propagating Christian Knowledge, which was being used very largely as a denominational agency in the interests of the Established Church, was specially named as one of the institutions requiring reform; the popular representative element in the governing bodies was increased from "a majority" to "two-thirds;" the right of girls[1] to the benefit of educational endowments was again recognised, and the 15th clause was thus altered as a protection against the de-localisation and alienation to which Mr. McLaren specially objected :—

"In framing schemes, it shall be the duty of the Commissioners, with respect alike to the constitution of the governing body and to educational provisions, to have regard to the spirit of the founders' intentions, and in every scheme which abolishes or modifies any privileges or educational advantages to which a particular class of persons is entitled, whether as inhabitants of a particular area or as belonging to a particular class in life or otherwise, they shall have regard to the educational interest of such class of persons. Provided always that where the founder of any educational endowment has expressly provided for the education of children belonging to the poorer classes, either generally or within a particular area or otherwise for their benefit, it shall continue, so far as requisite, to be applied for the benefit of such children."



But Mr. McLaren was far from satisfied. He knew much had been gained, and for that he was thankful. But he perceived that the clauses were not sufficiently explicit to tie the hands of an unfriendly Commission bent on the diversion of the educational endowments still left in the possession of the poor, and he remembered that while in the Commission[2] the interests of the Hospitals proposed to be affected were not represented, the hostile interests were supreme, "a majority of the Commissioners being members of the association for promoting secondary schools out of

---

[1] This was in the original bill drawn up by Mr. Donald Crawford, and revised by Lord Advocate McLaren.

[2] The members of this Commission were Lord Balfour, Lord Elgin, Sir T. J. Boyd, Lord Shand, Mr. J. A. Campbell, M.P., Mr. Ramsay, M.P., and Mr. J. Ure, then Lord Provost of Glasgow.

the funds of the Hospital." Unhappily his fears were more than justified. In July 1884 the Commission, after having heard evidence, issued their report, which plainly pointed to the suppression of the outdoor schools, and provided for a large transference of the funds to university purposes. Mr. M<sup>c</sup>Laren was at the time residing at Strathpeffer in Ross-shire, and, ever vigilant, he at once challenged the Commissioners' report as contrary to the evidence which had been submitted to them, contrary to the Act under which they conducted their inquiry and prepared their scheme, and contrary to justice and the interests of the poor. From the Commissioners' scheme he prepared a tabular statement, showing that the money proposed to be granted to new objects, and thus to be alienated from the legitimate beneficiaries of the Trust, amounted to £11,370 per annum, or a capital sum of £340,100.

Full of indignation, he denounced the Commissioners' proposals as certainly " the most gigantic scheme of legalised robbery " which had ever come within his observation. He recited the various proofs of successful administration of the Trust, and, in presence of the very doubtful prospects of success in store for the new experiment, he complained that the Commissioners, instead of letting well alone, had upset everything, " turning out the Heriot Trustees who had managed so well, and appointing a kind of conglomerate body in their place," consisting of twenty-one persons, eleven elected by the Town Council, three by the School Board, two by the Established Church ministers of Edinburgh, one by the Non-Established ministers, two by the University Senatus, one by the Royal Society, and one by the Chamber of Commerce. He denied that the University had any claim to the bequest under the will, because, although Heriot in a codicil directed that his trustees should keep "ten bursaries in the College of Edinburgh for ever, allowing yearly five pounds sterling to each," he intended this application of the money as a benefit to the Hospital, and not to the University, for he provided that the professors should take nothing for teaching the bursars. He complained that the Commissioners had acted as if the main object of their appointment had been to take from the poor and give to the rich, and charged them with having in this respect exceeded their power, and transgressed the Act which called them into existence. He reproached them with being the unconscious aiders and abettors of Communism.

"Their action," he sarcastically wrote, "will, no doubt, rejoice the hearts of the disciples of Henry George and other Communists, as well as the more violent section of the Highland Land-Law Reform Association. I fear they will not be able to see any difference in principle betwixt transferring the estates of George Heriot from the poorer to the richer classes, and transferring the estates of the richer classes to the poorer, as has been so much urged of late by certain foolish agitators."



He appealed to the working-classes to take energetic action in their own interests.

"I have seen the day," he said, "about half a century ago, when the working-classes of Edinburgh had public-spirited leaders and good speakers, who would have made the city ring with their demands for protection against the flagrant injustice proposed to be done to them and their families in all time coming by this scheme of the Commissioners."

In a subsequent letter, dated 31st July, and also written at Strathpeffer, he earnestly renewed this appeal. He wrote :—

"I trust the working-classes of Edinburgh will defend their

rights to the magnificent estate left them by Heriot. In his first deed he referred to 'decayed' burgesses as the persons to be cared for, but in his will he cancelled this, and left his estate wholly to the poor and destitute. It is now in the main proposed to be transferred to the comparatively rich."

This appeal stimulated fresh opposition to the scheme of the Royal Commissioners. But the working-classes were at the time keenly interested in the Reform struggle, which had just been complicated by the action of the House of Lords in rejecting the County Franchise Bill, and they were tired, too, of the fight. The enemy had so frequently been driven off, that they failed to realise the gravity of the danger threatening them. Accordingly the response was not nearly so effective or constant as Mr. M<sup>c</sup>Laren had expected, and the scheme of the Commission was, notwithstanding an active opposition in Parliament, in due course passed as a Legislative Act. Mr. M<sup>c</sup>Laren deeply regretted the result, not only because the free schools were suppressed, whereby a check was given to the development of free elementary schools as a basis of our national system of education, nor merely because of the grave injustice done to that class of the population least able to protect their own rights, but also because the ultimate collapse of the opposition to what he regarded as the confiscatory and reactionary policy of the Education Department afforded evidence of a decaying public spirit among his fellow-citizens.

His feeling of regret was, if possible, increased by the very different kind of treatment meted out to Fettes Hospital. In his eyes the administration of this Hospital or bequest was as faulty as that of Heriot's was commendable. He believed Sir William Fettes intended his bequest for the benefit of the poor, irrespective of rank, sex, or locality.

"There are no exclusive words in the will," he said, when examined before the Commissioners in December 1883. "The will does not say, as Heriot's will did, that the children are to be children of burgesses; nor does it say, as Watson's will did, that they are to be connected with the Merchant Company. I apprehend there was no man living who knew better all about Edinburgh than Fettes did. He, I apprehend, said, 'All the world should have access to my Hospital. I will have nothing to do with burgesses, or the Merchant Company, or such, but with every person that comes under the description (1) either of children whose parents are unable to maintain and educate them, or (2) others whose parents are unable to educate them, without saying anything of maintenance.' I think that all these are eligible, and I will give an instance to illustrate the breadth of my view. I think that if a poor man lost his all by such a calamity as the City of Glasgow Bank, and that all was £100, he had just as good a right to benefit from this fund as a man who lost £10,000, if both were equally unable to educate their children."

But in the Fettes administration he saw that this equality of claim was not recognised; that the benefits of the foundation were strictly reserved for persons in the higher ranks of life; that while girls in all conditions of rank and circumstances were rigidly excluded, boys were admitted whose parents were not so destitute of means to educate their children as the description in the founder's will implies; that, moreover, the sons of the wealthiest parents, moving in the highest ranks of society, though paying fees for board and education, were as pupils admitted to the benefits of the scholarships and exhibitions and lodging accommodation, all provided out of the funds destined by the founder for the relief of the innocent victims of misfortune. He complained, too, of the constitution of the governing body; that indeed he regarded as the *fons et origo mali*. He believed that Fettes intended a board of management somewhat similar to the Heriot Trust in its representative character and its open conduct of business. But he saw the powers of the Fettes Trust confined to a practically self-elected body, transacting its business in secret, unamenable to public opinion, and consequently extravagant in its administration and restrictive in the distribution of the benefits of the Hospital. Under an open and representative system of management the Heriot bequest had been so husbanded that in the course of years it had from an initial capital sum of £23,000 risen to a colossal fortune yielding an annual revenue of £24,000 or £25,000, maintaining a handsome Hospital and providing free education for 7000 boys and girls, and gathering a surplus in order to extend its free educational benefactions. Under a close and irresponsible system of management the Fettes original endowment of £166,000 (which between 1836 and 1881 had accumulated to upwards of £450,000, £227,664 having been spent on building, and £230,479 remaining otherwise invested) had been so administered that the net annual revenue was about £6400, while the number of foundationers was restricted to fifty. The former system as regards extent and numbers had produced the maximum of educational advantage with a steadily and rapidly increasing revenue; the latter the minimum of educational advantage, with a steadily declining annual revenue. Adhering to the fundamental doctrine of all his public life, "the greatest good of the greatest number," Mr. McLaren as resolutely and fearlessly condemned the Fettes administration as he championed that of Heriot's; and in the years 1883 and 1884 he laboured most industriously, both by pen and speech, to show the tendencies and results of the two systems. He addressed to the Lord Provost, the Master of the Merchant Company, and the chairman of the Chamber of

1884

Results
free and
close sy
tems co
pared.

Commerce, as guardians of the well-being of the citizens, a series of five letters, afterwards published in pamphlet form,[1] containing a clear and telling exposure of how the rights of the poor had been seized for the benefit of the rich by the self-elected Fettes Trustees.   His pleas for the restoration of the funds of the Hospital to its legitimate object, though warmly sympathised with by the public bodies to whose Presidents he addressed his letters, were not given effect to by the Commission, who were hampered in their suggestions of reform by the unsuitability of the costly college buildings for any other object than that for which the trustees had erected them.   But he was not so disappointed with the failure of his attack on Fettes as with the failure of his defence of Heriot's; and he regarded the elucidation of facts as a necessary preliminary to the reconsideration of the whole question of the relation of the honest and industrious poor to the educational endowments of the city.   So firm was his conviction that justice would ultimately prevail, and so near to his heart did he carry the interests of the people, that even the day before his death he referred to the subject, and expressed the belief that not many years would elapse before a popular demand would be made for a rectification of the unfair and unwise distribution of the heritage of the poor.[2]

---

[1] "Fettes College Trustees and the Rights of the Citizens of Edinburgh," by Duncan M<sup>c</sup>Laren, Esq.   Edinburgh: Oliphant, Anderson, & Co.

[2] An incident characteristic of Mr. M<sup>c</sup>Laren may here be mentioned. When it was proposed by some of the Heriot Governors that his bust should be placed in the Free Heriot Schools, he declined the intended honour, replying: "No; George Heriot did not leave his money to pay for busts of Duncan M<sup>c</sup>Laren."

# CHAPTER XXIV.

## *CHURCH-RATES AND DISESTABLISHMENT.*

Mr. M<sup>c</sup>Laren's public influence was not confined to the older Dissenting denominations. After the Disruption it gradually extended to the Free Church, and as his services, first as Lord Provost of Edinburgh, and afterwards as senior Member for the city, multiplied, it increased and strengthened. Indeed, on the withdrawal from Parliament in 1868 of his friend and political associate, Mr. Murray Dunlop, he was looked to by the Free Church majority as the most reliable of their political friends, and was acknowledged as the chief representative at Westminster of Scottish Nonconformity. His services in connection with the agitation for the abolition of Scottish " Ecclesiastical Assessments," or, as they should be styled in proper English phrase, Church-rates, were specially appreciated by Free Churchmen. Many of the most startling illustrations of the severity of the Church-rates grievance, contained in the effective speeches on this subject which he delivered at St. Stephens and at public meetings, were drawn from the experience of Free Churchmen, and they supplied a case for legislative reform which, from a Liberal point of view, was soon found to be unanswerable. In 1870 Mr. M<sup>c</sup>Laren's bill for the abolition of the rates was rejected by 117 votes, 108 having voted for, and 225 against the second reading. But Liberals felt that moral victory lay with the Member

for Edinburgh ; and the advantage thus gained was pressed
home during the recess.   In the following session the bill
rejected in 1870 was reintroduced, and its second reading
was proposed in a speech teeming with apt and telling illustrations of the wrong done to Dissenters, and the prejudice
created against the Established Church by the operation of
the existing law.   Liberals who had voted for the abolition
of Church-rates in England could not further withstand
Mr. McLaren's arguments and statistics, and on this occasion the second reading was carried by 121 votes against
76.   Lord Advocate Young then undertook to deal with the
question on behalf of the Government.   But other and
more urgent work unfortunately interfered to prevent the
fulfilment of his intention, and by the time Mr. McLaren
was free to resume his independent individual efforts with
any chance of success (for the Tory House elected in 1874
rejected the bill by 210 votes against 155 in 1876, and by
204 votes against 143 in 1877), the question of Disestablishment in Scotland had, or was supposed to have, entered
the region of practical politics.

For the raising of the larger question the Tory and Church
party was responsible.   As forty years previously the aggres-
sive movement of the Establishment for church extension
provoked the Voluntaries into active resistance and reprisals,
so the Patronage Abolition Bill, promoted in the first session
of the Tory Parliament, which lasted from 1874 to 1880, was
resented by many Liberals as a measure intended to " dish
the Free Church," and was met by a counter-demand for disestablishment, in which, for the first time in its history, the
Free Church took a part.   Mr. McLaren was highly gratified
by this development of Scottish Nonconformist policy ; and
to give it free scope, and in order to let the extension and
strength of the now united Nonconformist party be concen-

trated on the one object which embraced the whole Nonconformist claim, he withdrew his Church-Rates Abolition Bill.
Mr. M<sup>c</sup>Laren always maintained that the Church, if freed
from the disadvantages associated with State establishment
and endowment, and from the prejudice against it which
this association fostered, would grow in prosperity and efficiency ; and it was on the ground of direct advantage to
the Church as well as to the community that he advocated
the abolition of the Annuity-tax and Church-rates.   The
prosperity enjoyed by the Establishment in Edinburgh after
1870 was accepted by him as confirmatory of the lessons
taught by the experience of the earlier Dissenting communions and of the Free Church—that compulsory maintenance
was inconsistent with the genius of Christianity, and that
State aid was a hindrance rather than a help to church
work ; and he hoped that this evidence of the advantages
of freedom from reproach would operate on the minds of
Churchmen themselves and materially assist the new Disestablishment movement.   But he never surrendered his
Voluntary principles.   On the contrary, he gloried in them,
as the foundation of his own political creed and of genuine
Liberalism.   He warmly supported in and out of Parliament Mr. Gladstone's resolutions of 1867 for the disestablishment and disendowment of the Irish Church, and the
great legislative measure which he founded upon those
resolutions after the general election of 1868.   He was the
vigilant defender of Nonconformist interests and claims in
connection with minor questions as they emerged in Parliament, such as the appointment of chaplains, the arrangements for the census, the compilation of parliamentary
returns, and the termination of State endowments in the
British Dependencies.   In his intimacy with Mr. Miall,
whose Disestablishment resolution in the House of Commons

1873

he seconded in 1873,[1] his connection with the Liberation Society, and his entertainment at Newington House of English Dissenters during political visits to Edinburgh, he had repeatedly made public proclamation of his Voluntary faith, and given unmistakable proof of his fidelity to the convictions which inspired his first public work as chairman of the Central Board of Dissenters. As earlier chapters of this work testify, his political life had been one of constant conflict against Church Establishments in the root and in the branch, and it is unnecessary here to recapitulate the details of this strife. When, therefore, Disestablishment in Scotland was raised as a practical parliamentary question, he had nothing to conceal and nothing to explain. He was utterly free from the temptation to mystification or evasion

---

[1] When the English Nonconformists began their Liberation campaign in Scotland, they turned to Mr. McLaren as their chief ally. Mr. Miall, then their spokesman and afterwards their parliamentary leader, sent the following letter :—

> BRITISH ANTI-STATE CHURCH ASSOCIATION,
> 12 WARWICK SQUARE, PATERNOSTER ROW,
> LONDON, *October 5,* 1846.

DEAR SIR,—The Executive Committee have resolved upon sending a deputation into some of the more important towns of Scotland before the close of the present year, to awaken public attention to the objects and claims of this Association, and to the importance of diffusing as widely as possible a knowledge of the principles, in prospect of the probable movements of the Legislature in favour of a modified extension of Church Establishments. They have directed me to apprise you of the resolution, and to request your co-operation in carrying it into effect. Perhaps you would favour them, as early as you can make it convenient, with your notions of the following points :—(1.) The towns which it will be most important that a deputation should visit, and the order in which it would be most convenient for them to be taken. (2.) The period of time towards the close of the year which will be freest from local engagements or customary visitations from other societies. (3.) The names of gentlemen attached to this Association who might be acceptably received by Scottish Nonconformists as a deputation.—I am, dear sir, yours respectfully,

EDWARD MIALL.

to which many Liberal Members and candidates at the election of 1880 weakly yielded, under the supposed necessity of retaining Nonconformist support without alienating Liberal Churchmen. He had been elected Member of Parliament for Edinburgh, as a Voluntary; as a Voluntary he had been known in the House of Commons; and as a Voluntary seeking for Disestablishment at the earliest possible moment he wished still to be known to all his constituents. He desired and advocated the formal inclusion of Disestablishment in the platform of the Liberal party. When Mr. Gladstone's " Authorised Programme " appeared during the general election of 1885, he was surprised and disappointed at its evasion of this question; and his influence was thrown into the scale with those candidates in Scotland who were regarded as the exponents of Mr. Chamberlain's " Unauthorised Programme." Fearlessly and unhesitatingly he identified himself with the new movement, in which he was proud to see that Free Churchmen, recognising him as a political leader, were as energetic and resolute supporters as his old Dissenting friends.

"I need make no confession of faith on the subject," he wrote to the chairman of a meeting held in Edinburgh in 1877 ; " for forty years ago I attended a public breakfast in the Waterloo Rooms in support of the Voluntary principle, and subsequently thereafter I had the honour of taking part in a public meeting in this city by moving that the late Mr. Douglas of Cavers should take the chair. I suppose I was asked to do so because I was one of the Magistrates of Edinburgh at both periods. As to Disestablishment apart from the abstract Voluntary principle, I am equally in favour of it, and showed my opinion on the last occasion when my friend Mr. Miall moved the question in the House of Commons, when I seconded his motion by request, and spoke in its favour. I may add that, as regards Disestablishment in Scotland, I am of opinion that when it takes place, the funds now given to the Church should be devoted to education as a substitute for the school-rates now levied in every parish. To prevent misconception in any quarter, I think it right to explain that I would not desire to deprive any existing minister of the Church of Scotland of any advantage which he now enjoys from stipend or manse, or in any other way."

The time has not yet arrived when the history of the elections of 1885 in Scotland can be written ; but it is sufficient to remind the reader that they resulted in the defeat of the Radical Disestablishment candidates through the union of the Tory party with the more reactionary Liberals, such as Mr. Goschen and Mr. Finlay, who were then supported by Mr. Gladstone. Their political alliance with Mr. Gladstone, however, was of very short duration ; and their general attitude towards thoroughgoing Liberal legislation amply justified Mr. M<sup>c</sup>Laren's opinion, that unless a man were sound on Disestablishment his Radicalism could not be of a robust type.



From this time to his death he never missed any opportunity which presented itself of advocating in public, and more especially before his fellow-citizens, complete Disestablishment and Disendowment (subject always to the preservation of the life-interests of the ministers), as an urgent political question, whose settlement could not longer be delayed without detriment to Church and State. The last public meeting he attended was one in favour of Disestablishment, held in the Synod Hall on 15th March 1886, as the Scottish Nonconformists' answer to a bill promoted by Mr. Finlay, the Member for Inverness, which at that time excited public opinion in Scotland as an attempt, though a singularly abortive attempt, to weaken the Voluntary party by modifying, in the direction of comprehension, the powers and the constitution of the Established Church. When the invitation to the meeting reached Newington House, Mr. M<sup>c</sup>Laren was unwell, and the weather was unpropitious. But the veteran of . eighty-six years (who had concealed his illness from Mrs. M<sup>c</sup>Laren, then absent with friends in London), was unable to resist the summons. Physical weakness had not diminished his intellectual force or cooled the ardour of his political aspirations. He was heart and soul with the object of the meeting, and he longed to be with his friends to show his continued sympathy. Too easily he persuaded himself that he was quite capable of the exertion, and by the afternoon of the 15th of March he convinced himself he had not felt so well for many a day. He therefore decided to make one other public testimony of his Voluntary faith by presence, though not by speech ; for he had from the first definitely declined a proposal that he should preside. He was welcomed most enthusiastically by the audience that filled the large building, and he was cheered more loudly still as he rose to nominate the chairman. Highly gratified by the earnestness of purpose shown by the meeting, and believing that the condition had been fulfilled on which he had predicted the early triumph of the Disestablishment movement—that the young men should " take part in the good work, and carry it on with vigour, and in the manner which was done in the old time "—he returned home. But in passing from the heated atmosphere of the crowded hall to his carriage Mr. M<sup>c</sup>Laren caught a chill, though he refused to believe that he had suffered from the exposure. He had, however, rendered his last service as a Voluntary, but he had got a view of the Promised Land.

# CHAPTER XXV.



*RETIREMENT FROM PARLIAMENT.*

WHEN Mr. McLaren entered Westminster to take his seat in the new Parliament elected in 1880, he was again welcomed by those who valued his incorruptibility of character, and devotion to the national service, and who felt that these were actual living influences, commanding the reverence and inspiring the enthusiasm of younger men. In spite of his burden of eighty years, his interest in politics was as keen as ever, and though a growing deafness unfitted him to some extent for participation in debate, his vigour remained unabated. He was, in truth, an embodiment of the Laureate's ideal of the statesman—

> " A life in civic action warm,
>     A soul on highest mission bent,
>     A potent voice of Parliament,
> A pillar steadfast in the storm."

And having given something like fifty years of service to the State, it was not to be wondered at if he felt much gratified that two of his sons were able to take their seats with him ;—his eldest son John, who was elected for the Wigtown Burghs and became Lord Advocate, and his third son Charles, who was elected for Stafford.

The session proved for Mr. McLaren a laborious one. As is shown in another chapter dealing with the Heriot Schools, very special demands were made upon his time and his strength, and in addition to the extra burden of a serious conflict with the Government in regard to educational administration in Edinburgh, his correspondence became extremely heavy. He felt and confessed the pressure of his duties; and his "thorn in the flesh," his increasing deafness, frequently excited in his sensitive mind misgivings as to his power to maintain the standard of efficiency in service he had hitherto exacted from himself. Somewhat sadly he came to the conclusion that his parliamentary days were numbered. At the meeting with his constituents in December 1880, he had intimated that he did not intend, owing to his advanced age, to seek re-election, adding that if he should feel himself unable from impaired health properly to discharge his duties, he would resign his seat even before the expiration of the existing Parliament. An immediate resignation, however, was not expected. But in this case the unexpected happened. Two considerations came into play to suggest a withdrawal from public life. The first was of a public character. As explained in an earlier chapter, Mr. M<sup>c</sup>Laren had in the session of 1880 succeeded in arresting reactionary legislation threatening the Heriot Trust and the Heriot Schools, and had obtained from Government promises which seemed to justify the conclusion that the popular constitution of the Heriot Trust would be maintained, and that the free schools would be preserved. A writer in the public press, who lamented Mr. M<sup>c</sup>Laren's retirement, expressed his conviction that the " electorate would gladly have excused its senior representative, though he had relaxed the rules which regulated his public life, and had consented to take some of the ease which many younger and stronger Members claim without remorse of conscience," but added that he was " too conscientious and too sensitive to be contented with inefficient or partial service." Nevertheless he recognised a certain fitness in the time of the withdrawal. " His work is done," said the writer already quoted. " The Liberalism with which his name is identified is secure. All or nearly all the Scotch Members who support the Government are Liberals in the sense in which, through a long lifetime, he has always been a Liberal—defenders of popular rights and interests, and not self-seeking partisans. Further, the particular measure which, as Member for Edinburgh, and as the reformer of the Heriot Trust administration, he found himself called upon to resist last autumn, has this session been altered in conformity with the liberal principles for which he contended. So far as we are able to judge, the great and much-prized boon which Mr. McLaren years ago secured to his fellow-citizens in connection with the Heriot Trust is no longer endangered ; and he therefore can retire from his parliamentary post with safety as regards the interests of his constituents, and with credit and honour as respects himself." Unfortunately the anticipation of the security of the Heriot Free Schools here expressed was not realised, but at the time Mr. McLaren was led to believe that the struggle was ended, and so the more easily did he reconcile himself to the termination of his parliamentary career.

The other consideration was more private in its nature. His eldest son had succeeded to the office of Lord Advocate, and therefore had to vacate his seat. Unfortunately a slight Tory reaction set in at the close of the general election, strengthened in the case of the Wigtown Burghs by the momentary unpopularity of Mr. Gladstone's appointment of Lord Ripon (then a recent secessionist to the Church of Rome) to the Viceroyalty of India ; and the Lord Advocate, when he asked for re-election on his accession to office, was defeated by a small majority. Later in the year he attempted the still more difficult seat of Berwick-on-Tweed, and was again defeated. The Lord Advocate attended to his duties with great assiduity, and discharged them with skill and ability. But an outcry was raised that Scottish interests could not secure the attention they deserved in the absence of the Lord Advocate from Parliament, and Mr. M<sup>c</sup>Laren, who had himself in former years frequently urged the need for the constant presence of this official, keenly felt the position. A hope was entertained that Government would find some safe seat for their highest political Scotch functionary, but this hope was disappointed. When Parliament resumed in January 1881, Mr. M<sup>c</sup>Laren knew that the Lord Advocate had sketched out for himself important legislative work, but continued absence from the House of Commons was, he was well aware, a fatal barrier in the way of the successful promotion of such legislation. In addition to this, there were other reasons, having reference to various contending interests, into which the present is not a suitable time to enter, that appealed with great force to that sense of justice which was the ruling power in Mr. M<sup>c</sup>Laren's mind. But it may be said that on no other occasion was his adhesion to justice more severely tested, nor more faithfully acted upon. While painfully conscious that he laid himself open to the charge of inconsistency on the part of those not fully acquainted with the whole circumstances of the case, having always maintained the undesirability of Edinburgh being represented by a Government man, he felt called upon to put aside these considerations of self, and, as he believed, in the interest of justice resigned the position he so much prized. He therefore issued the following address to the electors of Edinburgh :—

" I am thankful to say that I was able to attend in my place on the opening of Parliament, and daily since that time as the House met, and to vote in every division without inconvenience ; but circumstances have unexpectedly occurred which seem to make it my duty now to place my resignation unreservedly in your hands, and accordingly I have this day applied for the Chiltern Hundreds.

" I beg to tender you my most grateful thanks for the confidence you have reposed in me during the last sixteen years, and for all the kindness that I have received at your hands.   I cannot refrain from stating that I contemplate with much pain this step, which will sever the connection that has so long subsisted between you and myself.

" When you first elected me to represent you in Parliament, I promised that my efforts would be mainly directed to promote the interests of Scotland generally, and those of Edinburgh in particular ; and I think no one of the 17,807 electors who so zealously and disinterestedly supported me at last election will question the fact that I have redeemed these pledges to the best of my ability."

It was not to be expected that Mr. McLaren could leave that House, the scene of so much interest, without a pang. He had not told any one in the House of his intended resignation, but on the last occasion of his presence there, when a division was being taken late in the evening, Mr. Seely, Member for Lincoln, who was nearly the same age as himself, noticing that he looked troubled and unwell, took his arm, and the two old friends went for the last time into the lobby together ; the one little knowing the pain which the consciousness that it was his last act in that House was giving to the other.

The Lord Advocate offered himself as a candidate for the vacant seat, and the constituency, though deeply regretting their separation from Mr. McLaren, showed their appreciation of the spirit which prompted the self-sacrifice, and in recognition of the acknowledged talents of the first officer of the Crown in Scotland, they placed him at the top of the poll by an overwhelming majority over Mr. Jenkins.

On bidding farewell to parliamentary life Mr. M<sup>c</sup>Laren received an honour unprecedented in the history of the House of Commons. As his last election showed, he had triumphed over all factious opposition in the city of his adoption, and won for himself grateful recognition as the uniting and rallying centre of the different shades of Liberalism represented in the Scottish capital ; so at Westminster a certain primacy among equals, due to his age, his services, and his character, was spontaneously conceded to him ; and a ceremonial leave-taking was organised, chiefly on the initiation of Dr. Cameron, the senior Member for Glasgow, and Mr. Ramsay, Member for the Falkirk Burghs, as typical a Scotchman as Mr. M<sup>c</sup>Laren himself. All the Scottish Members present in the House, with the single exception of the Prime Minister, the Member for Midlothian, signed the following address, and many English Members expressed their regret that they were not eligible to sign, as the presentation was intended to be purely Scottish :—

*" To Duncan M<sup>c</sup>Laren, Esq., late Member of Parliament for the City of Edinburgh.*

" The undersigned Scotch Members of Parliament, of both political parties, desire to express their regret at the termination of your long and useful career in the House of Commons. They have had many opportunities of observing the assiduity and care with which you have performed your parliamentary duties, and of admiring the extent of your knowledge on all questions affecting Scotland, and they desire to express the hope that your life may be long spared to continue, out of Parliament, a career of public usefulness."

This address was beautifully inscribed on the title-page

of an album containing the signatures of the Scottish Members, and the names of the constituencies they represented. At the top of the title-page is a beautifully executed drawing of the picturesque town of Edinburgh. In the foreground the Calton Hill stands prominently out, while in the distance Arthur's Seat and the Salisbury Crags are, with a due regard to perspective, clearly and accurately delineated. In the ornamental border surrounding the address is a medallion likeness of Mr. M^cLaren as Lord Provost of Edinburgh, while at the foot of the page is a coloured sketch of the Palace of Westminster and of the Thames flowing into the distance, designed with the object of showing Mr. M^cLaren's connection with Edinburgh and Westminster. The album itself was enclosed in a richly ornamented box of white Algerian onyx, displaying the arms of the city of Edinburgh in gold, and a chased gold plate bearing the words, " Presented to Duncan M^cLaren, Esq., late M.P. for Edinburgh, by the Scotch Members of the House of Commons on his retirement from Parliament, January 20, 1881." [1]

The presentation was made in one of the committee-rooms of the House of Commons on the 30th of March. Mr. M^cLaren, accompanied by his wife, his daughter-in-law, Mrs. Charles M^cLaren, his two sons then in Parliament, the Lord Advocate and Mr. Charles M^cLaren, and his two brothers-in-law, Mr. John Bright and Mr. Jacob Bright, entered the room, where was assembled a full and representative gathering of the Scottish Members. Mr. Gladstone was absent, but he was not unrepresented. Sir Lyon Playfair, then Member for the University of Edinburgh, and Chairman of Ways and Means, was chosen to

---

[1] This beautiful and appropriate gift was the workmanship of the well-known engravers and lithographers, Messrs. M^cClure & M^cDonald, Glasgow.

preside at the ceremony, and read the following letter from the Prime Minister :—

10 Downing Street, Whitehall,<br>*January 24, 1881.*

Dear Mr. McLaren,—In conformity with the general rule, to which I am obliged pretty strictly to adhere, I have refrained from subscribing a document framed on behalf of the Scottish Members, but I cannot refrain from writing a few lines to state with what sincere regret I subscribed, according to my official duty, another document which opened the door for your exit from the House of Commons at a time when all the qualities you possess have so wide a field for employment in that assembly. Your ability, your application, your stout heart, your facility of clear exposition, will be long and well remembered by your parliamentary comrades; and your great courage in the discharge of laborious duty amidst advancing years will, I trust, have many admirers, even if few imitators. With every good wish for your serene and prolonged old age, I remain, dear Mr. McLaren, very faithfully yours, W. E. Gladstone.

The chairman then continued :—

"Gentlemen, the number of Members who are present with us indicates how much at heart they have the ceremony that is about to take place. I esteem it a high honour to be asked to present this testimonial in the names of the Scotch Members of Parliament. Mr. McLaren has the advantage of many of us in years, although, perhaps, he is not such an old parliamentary Member as some of those who are now present. I think, however, we will all agree that we never knew a Scotch representative who so entirely devoted himself to the duties of parliamentary life. (Cheers.) He never once forgot that he was the representative of our great Scottish metropolis; but he at the same time always remembered that he had even higher duties than those of a Scotch representative to perform, and he took an active interest in all the measures which promoted the social welfare of the people in all sections of the United Kingdom. (Cheers.) As to

the personal qualifications which he brought to his work in the
House of Commons, you all know how great they were. . . . From
the experience which he had derived in his municipal and public
life in Scotland, he brought an amount of exact knowledge,
minute information upon public questions, a large experience both
of Scotch and of general legislation, combined with varied qualifications, to the discharge of his parliamentary duties here, which
enabled him, on all occasions in connection with Scotch interests,
and on many other occasions on subjects of Imperial interest,
to give the benefit of his exact knowledge and lengthened experience, either by private counsel or by general support in the
House. . . . I may say that probably never has any testimonial
to a man's political worth met with such universal approval or
been so generally subscribed to by the representatives of the
nation to which he belongs. (Cheers.) Every Scotch representative has signed this testimonial, saving only Mr. Gladstone, the
most illustrious among all of the Scotch representatives, whose
name is absent on account of official exigency. But the letter
from the Premier which I have read will probably be kept in the
casket, and cherished more dearly than the signature."

Alluding with pleasure to the presence of Mrs. M<sup>c</sup>Laren,
the chairman remarked, amid the cordial and sympathetic
cheers of the company, that " all who have the honour of
her friendship know with what affection she supported
you, Mr. M<sup>c</sup>Laren, in public and private life—a support
which has been a source of admiration to all who have been
privileged to witness it." In concluding he said : " Allow
me now to offer you this testimony of our high esteem, and
to accompany it with the wish that you may still have a
long life to carry out those objects of public usefulness to
which you are still devoted in our metropolis of the North.
We hope that this memorial will convey to Mrs. M<sup>c</sup>Laren
the most grateful of all assurances to a loving wife, that
her husband's character and worth are appreciated as they

ought to be. To you, and your family after you, may it prove a lasting assurance of the esteem in which you are held by your late parliamentary colleagues."

Mr. M<sup>c</sup>Laren, speaking with considerable emotion, replied :—

"Dr. Playfair and gentlemen, I know not how to thank you for this mark of your kindness. I feel that you have over-estimated my services very much in what I have done; but I can say that I came to this House with the intense desire to do what was fair and right and honest to all men. My feelings and my judgment were strongly in favour of the Liberal party and Liberal politics, and I may say even my prejudices were in that direction; but I always endeavoured to act in a fair spirit to those who held different views from my own. The general course of my career in the House was to give Liberal votes, but on several occasions I felt myself compelled to give votes for my opponents in politics. I thank you very much for your kindness and for the personal politeness which I have met with on all occasions. I came to the House of Commons, I may say, unsup-ported by any prestige or any political party, for I got in by fighting and beating the dominant party at the time. (Cheers.) I had no aristocratic or other privilege. I can truly say that, from my earliest youth, I never had a patron of any kind. I am glad to think that so many Members of the House of Commons, during the sixteen years which I have been a Member, are willing to appreciate any services which I had an opportunity of rendering to my country, and of overlooking any faults which I am quite sure I must have committed on many occasions, for no man can assume that he is always right."

After shortly reviewing the different political events of his life in which he had participated, he said :—

"I need only add that I thank you with a full heart for this mark of your kindness and affection, which I am sure my family and those who come after me will appreciate more than anything which has ever happened in the course of my career. I am thankful to Providence that my life has been spared so long, and that it should have been crowned by this mark of your approbation. It is not easy for any one in my present position, with the many things that flow into the mind, to express himself adequately, and I feel that I have expressed myself very inadequately, for I am always more easily overcome by kindness than by opposition." (Loud cheers.)  "But yet," he added, "I feel I can say that, with all the imperfections which have attended my career, I do not believe it was possible for anybody to be more desirous to act fairly, honestly, and truthfully than I have been."

The London correspondent of the Edinburgh *Daily Review*, who witnessed the presentation of the testimonial, described an incident which at once emphasised the remarkable tribute of respect paid by the Scottish Members and illustrated Mr. M<sup>c</sup>Laren's fidelity to the call of duty.  "The scene," said this eye-witness, " was unique and interesting, and it was interrupted in quite an amusing way.  Mr. M<sup>c</sup>Laren, who never erred much on the side of long speeches, at all events in the House of Commons, was drawing his brief and in some respects touching remarks to a close, when the division-bell rang, and a messenger, opening the door, according to parliamentary custom, shouted, ' Division.' The interruption was inopportune, but Mr. M<sup>c</sup>Laren stopped suddenly, and urged that Members should hurry off at the call of duty.  For a moment it seemed possible that there would be a general exodus ; but not a man stirred, and Mr. M<sup>c</sup>Laren was cordially invited to ' go on.'"

It is needless to say that this signal honour afforded the highest gratification to Mr. M<sup>c</sup>Laren's family.  In sending his congratulations from Keighley, his son Walter M<sup>c</sup>Laren drew a parallel reviving old memories, on which his father loved to linger, and which greatly pleased him.  " In your speech," he wrote, " you referred to Lord Grey's banquet, at which so many prominent Liberals from all parts of Scotland were present to do him honour; and I thought what a striking resemblance there was between the banquet and your presentation, and yet what striking differences, according to the differences in Lord Grey's character and your own. The resemblance is plain, for he had all the well-known representative Liberal Scotchmen of the day round him, and you were surrounded by the representatives of every constituency in Scotland, which was a greater honour than Lord Grey received, for his friends were merely Liberals, but you have compelled the admiration of the Tories also. But the contrast is no less striking, for he, being a great peer, had a great banquet, with all the pomp that suited his office, but you received your honour in the much more congenial atmosphere of a committee-room of the House of Commons; and having been all your life a hard worker, who did your duty without any show, it was much more fitting that your presentation should be made in the quiet and business-like way which was adopted. . . . I have had many expressions of pleasure from my friends here in reference to the presentation, and all feel that, though there is no precedent for such an event in the House of Commons, the course taken by the Scotch Members is a well-deserved tribute to you."

The press throughout Scotland was unanimous in its sympathy with this expression of esteem. The *Scotsman* wrote :—

" Mr. M<sup>c</sup>Laren had the confidence of all the Scottish Members, as one whose vigilance in regard to Scottish interests was of service to them all as well as to his country. Diligence such as he showed in the performance of his duties could not fail in approval. His constituents showed what they thought of it by

the ever-increasing majorities they cast in his favour.  So far
as we remember, there is no man who fought a contest at the
last general election whose majority was so decisive against his
opponent and so convincing as to the opinion of his constituency
as that by which Mr. McLaren was returned.  The presentation on Wednesday shows that what the electors of Edinburgh
thought of him in March 1880, the Scottish Members think of
him now. . . . The address, the manner in which it had been
got up, the presentation, the reply, were all calculated to enforce
once more the old moral that he 'who is diligent in his business
shall not be without the honour that is his due.'  The closing
words of Mr. Gladstone's letter will find an echo in Edinburgh
as in all Scotland, where there will be but one wish—that Mr.
McLaren may enjoy a serene and prolonged old age."

Meanwhile a local tribute was being organised.  Lord Provost Boyd called a meeting of citizens interested in public
work, and proposed that Mr. McLaren's portrait should be
secured for presentation to the Town Council, to be placed
in the Council-chamber.  The meeting was numerously and
influentially attended, and the only difference of opinion
which was expressed had reference to the confessed in-
adequacy of the proposed memorial.  Mr. Hugh Rose and
others suggested that a public statue or a bursary should
be conjoined with the proposal for a presentation portrait,
and expressed their conviction that the citizens generally
would frankly and gratefully co-operate if some suitable
memorial of Mr. McLaren's work and character were undertaken.  The answer given to their suggestions was that the
citizens fortunately had Mr. McLaren still with them, and
that meanwhile the portrait for the Council-chamber was the
tribute supposed to be most agreeable to his feelings.  The
presentation of the portrait, painted by Mr. Reid, R.S.A.,
took place on 31st January 1882, when the Council-hall
was crowded with citizens, representing the municipality, the

learned professions, and the public and political life of the Scottish capital. Mr. M<sup>c</sup>Laren was accompanied by Mrs. M<sup>c</sup>Laren and various members of his family, and among the letters of apology for absence which were read was one from Lord Rosebery, who wrote :—" This ceremony, which places him (Mr. M<sup>c</sup>Laren) among the worthies of Edinburgh, may be considered the crown, but not, I trust, the completion, of a long and honourable career, distinguished by an energy and a singular devotion, both as Provost and Member of Parliament, to the interests of your ancient city." The duty of presenting the portrait to the Corporation was intrusted to Mr. Josiah Livingston, then Master of the Merchant Company, who recited the chief facts and events of Mr. M<sup>c</sup>Laren's fifty years of service to the city ; and unveiling the portrait, exclaimed with genuine pride and appreciation, " There is the likeness of an honest man, the likeness of a good citizen, the likeness of a man of great abilities, who laboriously exerted them for the good of his fellow-men,—the likeness of a man who under all conditions of life has done his duty."

Lord Provost Boyd, in accepting the gift on behalf of the Corporation, said, " The unanimous and cordial manner in which the Town Council at their last meeting agreed to receive this portrait to adorn the hall in which their deliberations are held, and in which Mr. M<sup>c</sup>Laren in days gone by played so distinguished a part, is a sufficient proof of the value in which they hold what he has done ; and for myself I may add, that I consider I have been fortunate in occupying the position of Lord Provost when such a well-merited public tribute of respect has been paid to our friend."

Mr. M<sup>c</sup>Laren in a brief speech cordially thanked the contributors, and expressed his appreciation of the honour which had been conferred upon him, noticing with satis-

faction the fact that men of every political party were
present, and he referred especially to Mr. Macdonald, then
Dean of the Faculty of Advocates, afterwards Lord Advocate in Lord Salisbury's Government, and now Lord Justice-Clerk.   Mr. Macdonald had twice on behalf of his
party stood as a candidate for the representation of the
city, and adverting to these contests, Mr. M<sup>c</sup>Laren good-
humouredly remarked, " I daresay he will excuse me for
saying we did not fight with any degree of acrimony, but
more with the gloves than the fists "—an observation to
which Mr. Macdonald afterwards made rejoinder, that notwithstanding the gloves, he felt the blows were extremely
hard, and he was glad that he would never have to respond
to the call of " time " again to face such an opponent as
Mr. M<sup>c</sup>Laren.   Not egotistically, but with a serene satisfaction and enjoyment justifiable and beautiful in old age, Mr.
M<sup>c</sup>Laren recalled several incidents of his public career, and
more especially his introduction to public life in that very
room in which his portrait had that day been placed by his
fellow-citizens.

" Here," he said, " I first learned to take any part in what
may be called public business.   I was associated with many able
and excellent men who were returned at the first reformed Town
Council.   I remember them pictorially in my mind, most of them,
and I think with great pleasure of having co-operated with them.
Here (pointing to portraits on the wall of the chamber) are two
worthies of that time—Sir James Spittal, the first Lord Provost,
and Mr. Adam Black.   Well do I remember that Mr. Black and
I sat side by side for several years, and that I benefited, I am
happy to say, very much by his kindness.   He was greatly my
senior in years and still more in experience of all public affairs.
We always acted together in Town Council matters, and I am
pleased to have an opportunity now of saying how much I respected
him, and how much I was indebted to him on many occasions for

his wise counsel. I should be pleased just to think that my portrait should be in the same apartment with that most valued citizen, and that it will be a sort of ideal continuation of the friendship and respect which I felt for him. In later years, though we differed on certain political questions, I never lost for him that respect; and I have reason to believe that he entertained kindly feelings towards myself."

"The room," writes an eye-witness, "was crowded, and beautifully decorated with flowers. Every one looked as though his heart were thoroughly in the occasion. Looks of love and of homage and of deepest pleasure fell from all eyes on the faithful warrior who had fought so many of their battles, heedless whether praise or blame fell upon himself. One felt that a deep, thorough appreciation of the man on whom this honour was to be bestowed was entertained by all, and that it was no ordinary tribute of affection that was being paid. Mr. Livingston spoke well, and the portrait was unveiled as he spoke. I never saw Mr. M<sup>c</sup>Laren look better; it must have brought solemn thoughts to a matured mind like his thus to see himself, and, as it were, his past life, pictorially represented, to be looked upon and his memory recalled by men and women yet unborn in the city so dear to his heart."

Though now in his eighty-third year, Mr. M<sup>c</sup>Laren was in the enjoyment of excellent health, and interested himself as keenly and as closely in public questions as at any period of his life. Before bidding good-bye to his friends in the Council-chamber he expressed a grateful consciousness of what he owed to Providence for the blessing of health and strength still vouchsafed to him. "I feel," he said, " now that Parliament is approaching, a little like the old war-horse, ' snuffing the battle from afar;' and although I cannot be present, I have the feeling—thank God for His

1882

goodness to me—that I should be quite able to set off to-morrow." But while he had these pleasurable associations with the past, he often spoke of the happiness he enjoyed in the years of comparative repose which followed the termination of his parliamentary career. Yet his presence in the House was sorely missed by Liberals throughout Scotland when such important questions as Disestablishment, Educational Endowments, the reform of the arrangements for the government of Scotland, and the Crofters' grievances were discussed.



But though absent from Westminster, Mr. M<sup>c</sup>Laren was not idle. He continued to take part in public affairs. The period of his retirement became one continued parliamentary "recess" in the meaning in which in these days of superlative political activity the term has come to be regarded by earnest-minded politicians—a period during which freedom from the drudgery of parliamentary attendance gives enlarged opportunities for educational political work among the constituencies. Mr. M<sup>c</sup>Laren made full use of this freedom. His library was his watch-tower and his workshop. In it he read the newspapers and studied blue-books with as much diligence as when he was a Member of the House of Commons; and he maintained a large correspondence with Reformers in every part of the United Kingdom, but in Scotland chiefly with those who were carrying on the war against privilege, in which at different times he had taken a leading part. How vigorously he fought the battle of the poorer citizens in connection with the Heriot Free Schools is elsewhere described. Disappointed with the part the School Board had played in the controversy, he watched its management with a keenly critical eye, and advocated again, as he had previously done, the abolition of the cumulative vote in the triennial elections, with the view of liberating the Boards from sectarian control and placing them more in touch with the opinions of the general body of the ratepayers. Municipal administration, too, felt the healthful influence of his vigilance, and the reforming party in the Parochial Boards, more especially the lady members, were encouraged by the knowledge that his sympathy and advice were always at their command.

Although he had given up attending large public meetings, he occasionally broke through this needful rule. When the citizens met to support Mr. Gladstone's proposals for the reform of the procedure of the House of Commons, he was amongst them. His sympathy with the Crofters also brought him again to the front; but the most noteworthy meeting he attended was the one convened by the citizens in the Free Assembly Hall in defence of the Heriot Free Schools in 1884. The Lord Provost presided, and Mr. M<sup>c</sup>Laren, who spoke with much of his old vigour, was received with the greatest enthusiasm by the vast audience; and as he left the hall shortly before the close of the meeting, the whole audience rose, and he felt that the ovation then accorded to him exceeded in affectionate warmth and earnestness anything which he had ever received.

The last act of his life in London, on the occasion of a visit there in 1884, was when, after a rather severe illness with which he had been there overtaken, he spent the afternoon before his departure for Edinburgh at Barn Elms, an interesting and historic house on the Thames, and at that time the residence of his son Charles, who had invited Inspector Denning and the police usually in attendance at the House of Commons, with their wives and families, to an entertainment in the grounds. His well-remembered face was cordially welcomed by those to whom it had long been so familiar in the precincts of St. Stephens; and the pleasure to him was equally great. At the request of Inspector Denning, he spoke a few friendly words to those who were present, dwelling on the kind attentions he had always received from the men, even in the smallest matters, and remarking that small services were apt to linger in the mind of the recipient long after more important ones had passed away.

His life's battle was drawing to a close. Like all who have to contend with opposing forces, he had developed those unflinching qualities of mind which characterise the reformer. But while consistent to the last, and steadfast in his adherence to the causes he advocated, he emerged from the various conflicts he sustained with a character serene and strengthened, wise, far-sighted, moderate, and just. Thus, in the concluding years of his life he judged old opponents most charitably, and sought only to remember the good they did, thinking and speaking more of their points of agreement with, than their causes of difference from him. The "valiant will to smite the wrong" remained with him to the last, but the "simple faith and truth," the "wisdom deep and calm," which are so beautiful in old age, were his. He frequently spoke with admiration of the serenity of temperament which so well befits declining years, and sometimes alluded to his old and esteemed friend Charles Cowan of Logan House as an example of this. The virtue which he beheld in this honourable representative of an honourable family was by them seen and admired in himself. Referring to this period of Mr. McLaren's life, Mr. John Cowan of Beeslack wrote: "Of late years I have loved to look on his calm and beautiful countenance, so full, as it ever seemed, of rest and peace." Yet these years were not free from disappointments. The abolition of the Heriot Free

Schools was, as we have seen, a specially heavy blow. But as the great electoral reforms of 1884 advanced towards their completion, as he observed the peaceable conduct of the people in their imposing demonstrations, and saw in their use of the franchise in 1885 wisdom abiding with power, his trust in the future ever increased. With confidence and gratitude he descried " above the hill-tops of time the glimmerings of the dawn of a better and a nobler day for the country and the people he loved so well."

1884<br>The better day.

# CHAPTER XXVI.

## *IRELAND AND HOME RULE.*

1835 Mr. M<sup>c</sup>Laren's attitude to Ireland and the Irish question was that of the Constitutional Reformer. He deprecated violent agitation, and wished to take away all excuse for it by the enactment of just laws. That was the keystone of his position during fifty years of his public life.

He was very early convinced of the need of reforms in the administration of Ireland ; but a Unionist—not merely in the party sense in which that term has lately been employed, but on broad imperial grounds—he was not free from suspicion of disloyal motives on the part of the earlier Irish agitators ; and a Constitutionalist, he was strongly opposed to illegal or violent methods of demonstration. Hence, in spite of his own Liberal and reforming sympathies, he kept aloof from O'Connell. When the great Irish orator visited Edinburgh in 1835, Mr. M<sup>c</sup>Laren was invited to take part in the welcome prepared for him. Mr. W. Tait, the publisher of *Tait's Magazine*, wrote : " May I propose your being added to the O'Connell Committee ? From the persons who have purchased tickets, I can see that the company is to be a highly respectable one, and far from being exclusively Radical." The reply sent next day was as follows :—

Edinburgh, September 11, 1835.

Dear Sir,—I am favoured with your note requesting to know whether you may propose to add me to the O'Connell Committee.

In answer I beg to say (although you may think me politically intolerant) that I cannot conscientiously approve of Mr. O'Connell's public life, and therefore do not intend being present at the dinner. Having heard objections stated to his religious creed, I think it right to say that, if I had approved of his conduct in the main, the circumstance of his being a Roman Catholic would have been an inducement for me to attend the dinner to show that I did not approve of the principle of estimating the worth of a public man by his religious belief, which ought, in my humble opinion, to be a matter entirely between him and his Maker.—I am, dear sir, yours very truly,      D. M<sup>c</sup>LAREN.

W. Tait, Esq.

In contradistinction to this repellent attitude towards the Nationalist party, and as an illustration of the kindlier aspect of his relation towards Ireland and Irishmen, another letter, written thirty-seven years afterwards to Mr. M<sup>c</sup>Carthy Downing, may here be introduced :—

NEWINGTON HOUSE, EDINBURGH,
*November* 15, 1872.

MY DEAR SIR,—It was with deep regret I heard of the death of our friend Mr. Maguire, M.P. for Cork; for although, as you are aware, I differed from him in some matters of great importance, I always admired his talents and genial courteous manners, and was especially delighted with the deep interest he took in all questions tending to elevate the sphere of women, and to procure for them, in the medical and other walks of life, equal rights with men. While he was engaged writing his book on "The Next Generation," he applied to me for information respecting the contest going on in this city to enable ladies to get the benefit of a university medical education; and he appeared to be much interested in the information I was able to send him on the subject. I see there is to be a subscription got up to express the great respect in which Mr. Maguire was held by the country at large, and as an expression of deep sympathy with his bereaved wife and family; and I trust the remembrance of his many virtues will call forth a generous response. Not knowing anything of the arrangements for collecting the fund, I take the liberty of sending to your care a subscription of £10 from my wife and myself. I may state that my wife had met Mr. Maguiro, and sympathised with his views on all women's questions, and admired his public character as much as I did, and she has written to some of her friends in London calling attention to the loss the cause of progress has sustained by his death, and suggesting that subscriptions in aid of the fund should be sent by them to your care.—I am, my dear sir, yours very truly,                                       DUNCAN McLAREN.

> Mr. McCarthy Downing, M.P., Prospect House,
> Skibbereen, co. Cork.

Mr. McLaren was a well-wisher of Ireland, but he had no faith in " coddling " treatment. He sturdily resisted every attempt to purchase her good-will by the multiplication and enlargement of Treasury grants. He consistently and fearlessly objected to any special favour shown her in the Civil Service votes, and incurred no little odium by his statistical analyses, which showed that in respect of law and justice, poor-law and police administration, national education, public parks, fisheries, &c., Ireland received more than her fair share of the imperial revenue. But when political or social redress was claimed by the Nationalists by constitutional methods, he was, while in Parliament, one of their most trusted and valuable allies. The first vote he gave as a member of Parliament was for justice to Ireland. At the opening of the session of 1866 The O'Donoghue moved an amendment on the Address to this effect :—" To express our deep regret that great disaffection exists in Ireland, and humbly to represent to Her Majesty that this widespread disaffection is the result of grave causes which it is the duty of Her Majesty's Ministers to examine into and remove." Mr.

McLaren was one of a minority of 25 who voted for the amendment, while 346 voted against it. Along with him in the minority were John Bright, George Hadfield, John Stuart Mill, and T. B. Potter, the other supporters of the amendment being Irish members.[1]

His early association with The O'Donoghue and his friends had exposed him to some injurious comment. He was even spoken of as an aider and abettor of Fenianism, and he was violently attacked by his political opponents in Scotland for this act; but such attacks did not disturb him. Speaking to his constituents at the close of the session in reference to this vote, he said, "If the same question were to arise to-morrow, I would give the same vote with the utmost confidence. . . . I think no man living could say I did it from political or party motives." In pursuance of this policy, he also, towards the close of the session, voted for an amendment moved by Mr. Maguire to the second reading of a bill for suspending the Habeas Corpus, to the effect "that measures of repression, unaccompanied with measures of a remedial character, tend rather to aggravate than to lessen those evils in which perennial discontent and periodical disaffection have their origin in Ireland; and that a wise, generous, and thoroughly liberal policy is that which is alone calculated to promote the material prosperity and contentment of the Irish people,

---

[1] Mr. John Stuart Mill, in his "Autobiography," page 237, refers to this. He says:—"The same idea, that the use of my being in Parliament was to do work which others were not able or not willing to do, made me think it my duty to come to the front in defence of Advanced Liberalism on occasions when the obloquy to be encountered was such as most of the Advanced Liberals in the House preferred not to incur. My first vote in the House was in support of an amendment in favour of Ireland, moved by an Irish Member, and for which only five English and Scotch votes were given, including my own: the other four were Mr. Bright, Mr. McLaren, Mr. T. B. Potter, and Mr. Hadfield."

while adding to the strength and enhancing the moral dignity of the Empire."

At a later period, viz., December 1871, speaking of these votes, Mr. McLaren said, "I have always voted for Liberal measures in regard to Ireland.　I have been more Irish in that respect than some of the Irish Members themselves, for the first vote I ever gave in Parliament was for an amendment to the Queen's Speech in favour of doing justice to Ireland.　There were only five English Members in the minority, of whom I was one, and above 300 members of the House voted on the other side.　For doing that, I was represented in certain quarters as a Fenian ; but I held the principle that until you tried to remove the wrongs of Ireland you had no right to coerce Ireland, and therefore I voted so far as I could to give Ireland the same liberty which England and Scotland have."

In the last speech he delivered to his constituents as Member for the city (December 1880), Mr. McLaren reiterated the doctrine that conciliatory measures ought to accompany special legislation for the enforcement of the law ; and he gave his approval in advance to a scheme of land-law legislation, then attributed to Mr. Gladstone, based on the principle of the three F's—fixity of tenure, fair rents, and free sale of the tenant's interest.　"I think," he said, " with the eminent talents of Mr. Gladstone and his great experience, that if any bill of this kind was prepared by him to be pressed through Parliament, it would meet with great sympathy from honest men of all classes in this country."

Mr. McLaren was also in advance of his party in the advocacy of the Disestablishment of the Irish Church, and he heartily supported the various bills and resolutions proposed for the assimilation of the municipal and parliamentary franchises in Ireland to those in operation in England and Scotland prior to 1884. When the great and latest Reform Bill was proposed by Mr. Gladstone, he cordially approved of the Prime Minister's insistance on the inclusion of Ireland in the scheme, and the equalisation of the franchises and electoral conditions of the three kingdoms. He likewise supported the demand for the closing of public-houses in Ireland on Sundays when it was made by the Irish members and the Irish people; and in his address to his constituents in 1871 he even went so far as to say, "I would deprecate any separation whatever of the nationalities. But if it could be shown that Home Rule for Ireland would be practicable, and that it would please the Irish people, I would be quite agreeable that the Irish people should have Home Rule."[1]

But events occurred between 1871 and 1884 which pained and disappointed him, such as the lack of appreciation on the part of the Irish Members of the efforts made by the Liberal party on behalf of Ireland, and their insulting and contumacious treatment of Mr. Gladstone, Mr. Bright, and their Ministerial colleagues who took charge of the Irish departments of the Government. With the most honest and firm resolution to deal justly and generously by the Irish people, he deeply regretted the apparent irreconcilability of the Nationalists, and more especially their refusal publicly to disavow any connection with the American agitators in the midst of the dynamite conspiracies, even after the assassination of Lord Frederick Cavendish and Mr. Burke through the agency of the secret society of Invincibles. But

---

[1] It is quite certain that in this passage Mr. McLaren was not referring to an Irish Parliament. The Irish Home Rule party at this time had not defined "Home Rule," and the expression was understood by many to mean a large extension of local self-government.

he never had much confidence in Mr. Parnell and the new school of Irish politicians as guides of the Irish people.

When Mr. Gladstone's Home Rule policy was suddenly launched upon the country, the Prime Minister's precipitancy he thought worse than a blunder; he resented it as a fatal stroke at party cohesion, as a virtual assumption of political autocracy or dictatorship. He did not deny that fresh urgency had been given to the Home Rule question by the return of 85 Home Rule Members from Ireland, and he was much impressed by the significance of the strength of the Ulster vote in favour of Mr. Parnell's policy. But he held that the majority given to Mr. Gladstone at the general election which took place in the autumn of 1885 was not commissioned to deal with the question of Home Rule, and that while Mr. Gladstone would have been perfectly justified in entering into negotiations with Mr. Parnell with a view to a just and leisurely consideration of the whole subject in anticipation of needful future legislation, he ought meantime to have made some attempt to carry at least part of the domestic reforms which were confessedly . overdue for England and Scotland, and ought certainly to have consulted his party before he set aside " the authorised programme."

Thus it was that, viewing with distrust the aims and objects of the Nationalist leaders, and resenting also Mr. Gladstone's method of procedure, Mr. McLaren found himself in hostility to the new policy. Recalling the special advantages enjoyed by Ireland from the British Treasury, engaged also at the time in historical studies which led him to the conclusion that the suppression of the Scottish Parliament had proved a great benefit to the country, the more he thought of the new policy the more strongly did he become convinced of its unwisdom and danger. From the point of view of a Scottish Liberal keenly concerned for the accomplishment of various reforms affecting the social and moral welfare of the people, he recognised the loss involved in the disruption of the Liberal party. But regard for party advantage and for the immediate interests of reforms dear to his heart could not shut his eyes to the terrible evils—the intensification of social disorder and the outbreak of civil war—which he thought were involved in the new Home Rule policy.

The unexpected occurrence of a parliamentary election in the Southern Division of Edinburgh by the sudden death of Sir George Harrison in January 1886 compelled Mr. McLaren, as an elector in the constituency, to make a public declaration of his views earlier, perhaps, than he would otherwise have done. Mr. Childers was nominated as a candidate; but while Mr. McLaren held the right hon. gentleman in high esteem, alike for his personal character and his administrative talents, he was not at the time prepared to support his candidature, partly because he desired a Member who would support Disestablishment, but mainly from a wish to keep himself and the electorate uncommitted to Mr. Gladstone's Irish Home Rule policy, at that time as yet only imperfectly explained. Mr. David McLaren wrote him from London on the subject, expressing grave doubts as to the wisdom of the Prime Minister's scheme, and urging his friend once more, in the interest of various Scotch questions which had been put in the background during the general election of 1885, and also with the view of trying to save both the Liberal party and Ireland from the disastrous course on which he feared Mr. Gladstone was entering, to undertake parliamentary service as one of the representatives of Edinburgh.

Mr. McLaren, in his reply to his old friend, dated February 5th, frankly and clearly expressed his own apprehensions and misgivings, but quietly and firmly put aside the call to re-enter Parliament. He wrote:—

"As things have appeared since your letter was written, and in particular since Gladstone's address has appeared, the idea of an Irish Parliament and its command of the armed police is put in abeyance in the meantime. They do not appear on the face of the address, but I have a suspicion that they may be concealed under a multitude of vague words, and may appear in full force some day. However, one can't fairly go on *suspicion* alone.

"As to Mr. Childers, he and his wife called on me as an old parliamentary and political friend. I was out, but they saw my wife. They were aware before they called that I was opposed to any Whig Government man, for I had stated this at a meeting, and some one had told this to Mr. Childers.

"Next day, as a matter of courtesy, I called on them, and, to prevent any misapprehension, the first thing I said was that I was an opponent of his for the reason above stated. He said he was aware of my views, but thought it right to call notwithstanding. We talked about several things, and I said I was glad to understand from his reported speech, although it was not very explicit, that he was opposed to an Irish Parliament with the charge of the armed force of constabulary. He said he was *entirely opposed to such a thing*. I told him how strongly I felt on the subject; he *seemed* to agree with me.

"You would see that Mr. Campbell-Bannerman and Mr. Trevelyan both spoke very strongly against these things, and yet they are now members of the Government, and also Mr. Chamberlain. With my practice through life of calling a spade a spade, I cannot reconcile these things without assuming that Gladstone has told them all that he will not propose this kind of Home Rule. However, I am still by no means satisfied that an Irish Parliament will not be proposed with plausible guarantees so-called, which would be swept away in a short time, and separation or civil war, or both, be the result.

" Of course in such a case, if I were still preserved in health and strength such as I now have, I would do all I could to get some younger and more suitable man, such as yourself, to come forward, and support him by my vote and any influence which I might have, which I fear is not nearly so great as you suppose ; for remember it is fifty-three years since I entered the Town Council, and forty-eight years since I got the city affairs settled, and thirty-five years since I was elected Lord Provost, so that the present generation of active men who *now* move in political matters are to an enormous extent men ' who know not Joseph.' "

Subsequent events quickly showed that Mr. M<sup>c</sup>Laren's apprehensions as to the final shape of the Ministerial pro- posals were well founded, because, in the fuller and more authoritative explanations of the new Home Rule policy, it was made unmistakably clear that the fundamental and vital principle of the Ministerial plan was the concession to Ireland of an independent local Parliament sitting in Dublin, deriving its power from the Imperial Parliament, and in that sense only subordinate to it. Mr. M<sup>c</sup>Laren was greatly disappointed and depressed. He did not readily abandon hope of the discovery of a *via media* which would save the Liberal party from ruinous division. Soon after this his health gave way, but from his sick-chamber he appealed to his most trusted political friend, John Bright, who, perplexed and distressed, was keeping silence when the country was looking to him for guidance. On the 11th April, only a fortnight before his death, he dictated a long letter to his brother-in-law, which he described as " a few rough notes as to what may be called the three kingdoms' part of the question," adding that he was physically unable to write letters with his own hand, and that his dear wife had kindly acted as his amanuensis. " I wish," he said, " I could converse with you for an hour about the details of the bill, or rather *plan ;* but this cannot be." In part explanation of his own views, he enclosed an article from the *Scotsman*, to which he said, " I could conscientiously subscribe, with very trivial exceptions as regards details."   He proceeded :—

" But to my main point—the United Kingdom of Great Britain and Ireland, which it is now practically proposed to dissever; at least it is proposed to take steps at present which, according to all human probability, will either lead to separation in a complete form or civil war.   Gladstone admitted the other day, in answer to your colleague Mr. Chamberlain, that he had made a great mistake regarding the separation of the American United States, and if he lives to my age, I have no doubt he will equally manfully admit that he made a still greater mistake about the separation of the United Kingdoms. . . .



" Is it necessary to legislate in such a way as to require the exclusion of the Irish Members from Westminster ?   I say, *No ;* and I think it the most revolutionary proposal ever made in Parliament during the present century, and one which would do incalculable evil to all parts of the Empire.   The first rough consequence would be a great diminution permanently of the Liberal party in Westminster.   At present Ireland sends 17 Tories and 86 Liberals of various sorts.   Supposing Ireland, when it recovers from its delirium at the last election, were to send 23 Tories and 80 Liberals, the majority of Liberals who would be expelled from Westminster would be 57, which would greatly affect the whole future legislation at Westminster.

" Again, I understand from Gladstone's speeches and those of his party that he is prepared to apply the same principles by giving Scotland a separate Parliament, with equal powers to that of Ireland.   This, I think, would be a great calamity for Scotland ; and if I had the health and strength which I possessed in Anti-Corn-Law times, I would be prepared to do what you and other noble patriots did, and to do what our ancestors used to call ' to testify ' against the proposed injustice.

" To pursue the Irish parallel :—Scotland now returns 12 Tories and 60 Liberals.   But suppose in future years circumstances and opinions might enable the Tory party to return 18 Members, this would leave 54 for the Liberal party. But if you expel the Scotch Members from Westminster, the Liberal party would permanently lose a majority of 36 Members. This number added to the Irish majority would take permanently from the Westminster Parliament a Liberal majority of 93, and leave the Tories of England in what would be called the Imperial Parliament to ride rough-shod as far as they legally could not only over Ireland and Scotland, but over all the colonies and dependencies of the now United Kingdom. It might be called the Imperial Parliament, but it would only be the Parliament of England as a matter of fact.

"And why should it have the exclusive control over all the colonies and dependencies of the present three kingdoms ? Take the case of India for example. It used to be said of the Directors of the Bank of England that they would never admit a Scotchman as a member of their Board, and it was said at the same time that the Directors of the East India Company would never admit an Englishman on their Board. Now it was this Scotch Board that had the merit, as it is generally said, of conquering and annexing to the United Kingdom a large part of our present Indian Empire ; and as the individual members had the power of nominating officers, that body was largely composed of Scotchmen, and many of the most important victories gained were won by armies commanded by officers of Irish and Scottish families. Now I don't mention this by way of approval, for I hold that very many of their proceedings were unjust on the grounds of morality and religion. But I narrate the facts merely as laying a solid foundation for my question—Why should England virtually become the sole governing power over India, to the exclusion of Scotland and Ireland ?

"I remember, as no doubt you do, the law which the illustrious Athenian legislator passed, that when a State was divided by parties on great national questions, as we now are, every upright citizen was bound to take a side, and that any who did not should be expelled from the State. I sympathise strongly with the sentiment implied, although disapproving of the extent of the punishment; and as I now lie on my bed, where I have been over three weeks, and unable to take any public part in the matter, I relieve my conscience by writing to you as a true patriot and an influential statesman. I ask nothing—I suggest nothing; I merely state my opinion, and hope the right cause will win the day, and that the blessings of the Almighty may rest upon the labours of its supporters.—I am, yours very affectionately, DUNCAN M<sup>C</sup>LAREN."

Mr. M<sup>c</sup>Laren signed the letter which Mrs. M<sup>c</sup>Laren penned, and his signature betrayed the emotion under which it was written.

This letter to Mr. Bright was accompanied by the following one from Mrs. M<sup>c</sup>Laren :—

NEWINGTON HOUSE, EDINBURGH,
*Sunday, April* 11, 1886.

MY DEAR BROTHER,—I fear I hardly gave thee an impression in my last letter of how very ill my husband has been for the last three weeks. I did not think then that his being laid aside from all the absorbing interests of life was, as I fear now, a preparation for a longer and lasting rest. I wish I may be wrong, but when the heart is so seriously affected at his age, there must be great danger, and I see our dear invalid is less able for everything than he was a week ago. I never knew him so adverse to any political measure as to these of Mr. Gladstone's. The argument in his letter just written may seem of a very party character, but as he has never rigidly stuck to party lines, it means with him much more than mere party. It means all those advancing questions which come with advancing times. I never saw anything more impressive than his face and whole manner as he dictated the latter part of his letter. I have often called him a *seer*. Whether his views be right or wrong, his eyes in their solemn, piercing expression looked as though they gazed into the future, and his voice assumed a solemnity such as I have never heard in him before. And when he had finished he broke down and wept. It was a most touching scene. I am shut up with my dear invalid, but am where I like to be, but where I would like things to be different. I dare not pray rebelliously for life, but I do pray that suffering may not be great. The doctor says that what he does suffer would appear distressing if borne by most men, but that his great reasoning power, unselfishness, and his power to bow to the inevitable enable him to preserve the wonderful calm which he manifests.—Thy loving sister,

PRISCILLA M<sup>c</sup>LAREN.

Mr. Bright had been in the habit of taking political counsel with his friend; and sensible of his wide and accurate knowledge and genuinely Liberal sympathies, he greatly valued his judgment and advice. The circumstances under which this communication was written, not to speak of the very powerful plea against the rupture of the Imperial Parliament which it presented, must of themselves have produced a great effect on Mr. Bright and strengthened him in his distrust of and hostility to the new legislative proposals. Mr. M<sup>c</sup>Laren himself felt his own course clearer after he had unburdened his mind to his most intimate political friend; and he resolved to keep himself free from all responsibility as a member of the Liberal party for the policy propounded by the Liberal chief. On April 13, the Southern Liberal Association, which had previously chosen Mr. M<sup>c</sup>Laren its Honorary President, adopted resolutions commending the Gladstonian policy, and three days afterwards Mr. M<sup>c</sup>Laren sent the following letter intimating his resignation :—

*To the Members of the Edinburgh Liberal Association.*

GENTLEMEN,—A few weeks ago you did me the honour of electing me Honorary President of your Association, on the understanding that I should not be called upon to do any work.

Being a very old resident in the district, I accepted the honour in the spirit in which it was tendered. I observe from the *Scotsman* of the 14th that the Association met and passed certain resolutions embodying principles to which I have always been opposed, and which compel me to restore into your hands, which I hereby do, the honour you so recently conferred upon me. I need only refer to the first two sub-sections of your resolution. The first expresses great admiration of Mr. Gladstone's talents and sagacity, and refers to his unequalled experience as a parliamentary leader. To this extent I cordially agree with the resolution. When I had the honour of being Lord Provost of your city, I had great satisfaction, thirty-three years ago, in proposing that the Freedom of the City should be conferred on Mr. Gladstone. I greatly admired him then; I venerate him now, as one of the greatest and most patriotic Ministers this country has ever produced. But he never professed to be infallible. He has always laid down his plans for the consideration of the people, and rested his support of them in Parliament on the grounds that he believed they had the approval of the great body of the people. He has now brought forward a bill for establishing a Parliament in Ireland and removing the present Irish Members from the Parliament at Westminster, and it is as regards this bill that I am utterly opposed to the resolution passed by a majority of your Association; and I believe the great majority of the inhabitants, if tested, would be found to be against you, for during the sixteen years I represented you in Parliament I always voted against Mr. Butt's bill for an Irish Parliament, and was never reproved for this. You describe the bill to be—"To set up in Dublin a Parliament chosen by the Irish people for the control of Irish domestic affairs." It seems to me to go greatly beyond this, if we may judge from Mr. Gladstone's speech as to the bill itself; and thus, judging for myself alone, I am bound to say that I consider it by far the most reckless and dangerous measure ever proposed within my experience, and my experience is rather a long one; for I was present at the first great Reform meeting held in Scotland in 1820, usually called the Pantheon Meeting, from the place where it was held, and at which the great Whig leaders of the Scottish bar were the chief speakers.



It was implied by the speakers at your meeting that the bill might be so improved in Committee as to be made harmless to the other portions of the United Kingdom. I doubt the possibility of this. The principle of the bill is radically unsound, in my opinion; but if the principle be admitted, I think the clauses and details flowing therefrom, as now embodied in the bill, are quite logical and symmetrical. One strong objection against the bill in many quarters is the exclusion of the Irish Members from the Parliament at Westminster, and in this I participate, because I altogether disagree with the theory on which the bill is based; but, if we admit the theory of a separate Parliament in Dublin to be right, it seems to me that the exclusion of the Irish Members from Westminster is inevitable—it is a logical sequence. If any number of Irish Members were to be sent to Westminster after the establishment of their own Parliament in Dublin, with substantially the powers conferred by the bill, it seems to me that it would be to admit that the Irish were a superior race to the English and Scotch, and therefore, besides allowing them to manage their own affairs, they were to send a contingent to our Parliament to assist us in managing our affairs also; and bad as the bill now is, such an arrangement would make it still worse. The remedy is like the Highlandman's gun, which required a new stock, lock, and barrel. It is not desirable that Mr. Gladstone should be humiliated by the defeat of the bill, after spending the best part of the session in discussing it, and preventing the progress of other useful measures. The bill should be withdrawn, and some of the wisest heads in the three kingdoms, without regard to party, ought to be employed in devising a measure of Home Rule which would apply equally to each of the three kingdoms, and have a tendency to unite them more and more in one friendly bond of brotherhood, in place of separating them into distinct nationalities.

If an election were to take place at an early period, I hope it will be put on this distinct ground—Should there be a Parliament in Dublin or not? If in our district a candidate comes forward for an Irish Parliament and another against it, if I should be spared in health and strength, I should vote for the candidate against the Irish Parliament, whatever his other political opinions might be, whether Radical, Whig, or Tory, so strong is my conviction of the ulterior evil consequences which would flow from such a measure.—I am, gentlemen, yours faithfully,

DUNCAN M<sup>c</sup>LAREN.

NEWINGTON HOUSE, *April* 16, 1886.

The writing of the letter.

It was not with a light heart, nor was it without the most anxious and earnest reflection, that Mr. M<sup>c</sup>Laren wrote this letter. He estimated the pain and disappointment which his severance of political association with them would cause to men who were in truth his disciples—most of whom had regarded him all their days as their political guide—by the sorrow he himself experienced. But throughout his long life he had placed duty above personal feeling, and this imperious sense of duty asserted its supremacy even in the midst of the physical weakness and suffering which his family and his medical attendant saw were daily increasing.

This letter he was anxious should be in his own handwriting, but some portions of it he was obliged to dictate to his wife. His handwriting was clear and firm; and alternating as it did with Mrs. M<sup>c</sup>Laren's, it was suggestive of the harmony and unity of their public work—the loveliness and pleasantness of their domestic lives. The day after its publication, Mr. M<sup>c</sup>Laren was cheered by receiving a

Letter from Mr. Josiah Livingston.

letter from his friend Mr. Josiah Livingston, expressing much appreciation of his action, and adding that he rejoiced to think he must be much better to be able to write such a letter. Mr. M<sup>c</sup>Laren, greatly touched, at once replied, writing the letter with his own hand. A special interest attaches to it, as the last political message or note he personally penned :—

Newington House, Edinburgh,<br>*April* 17, 1886.

My dear Mr. Livingston,—I had given up personal letter-writing, but cannot resist resuming to thank you for your kind, sympathetic letter. I do not wonder that my published letter has misled you and many others as to the state of my health. I am not so well as you had a right to assume from the publication of that letter. For the last month I have been closely confined to bed, never sitting up for a quarter of an hour; but I am glad to say my medical advisers think I am considerably better than when at my worst. They shook their heads at my yesterday's work, but I felt like our Covenanting ancestors of old on some occasions, that I had a message to deliver, and that I must deliver it, even if it should shorten my days. And accordingly my wife partly acted as my amanuensis, and I got it to the newspapers about eight o'clock, and they all kindly inserted it —even our old *Courant*—having to send it to Glasgow; but of course I did not in any case see a proof, and hence one or two verbal errors.

I am glad to say it does not appear to have done me any harm in the opinion of my medical advisers, who examined me this morning. Am glad to know of your convalescence, and am yours truly, D. McLaren.

My very kind regards to Mrs. Livingston and thanks for her sympathy and inquiries. D. McL.


The letter intimating resolute opposition to Mr. Gladstone's policy and withdrawal from the Presidency of the Southern Liberal Association, while welcomed by many personal friends like Mr. David McLaren and Mr. Josiah Livingston, gave great encouragement to the Scottish "Unionists." They were at the time organising a demonstration in Glasgow in opposition to Mr. Gladstone's Home Rule and Land Purchase Bills; and Professor Sir William Thomson, in ignorance of the conditions under which " the testimony " had been prepared, at once wrote Mr. M^cLaren inviting his presence and co-operation.   He received the following reply :—

*20th April* 1886.

DEAR SIR WILLIAM THOMSON,—I received with much pleasure this morning your note referring to my letter published on Saturday, and inviting me to speak at the great meeting of which you are to be chairman.   Although I have made it a rule to abstain from public meetings for some time owing to my advanced years, I would most willingly have deviated from my rule on this occasion, and I could most cordially have supported your resolutions, if I had been in my usual state of health.   But I am very sorry to say such is not the case.   I have been confined to bed during the last month, and have no immediate prospect of being able to leave my room.

You would naturally infer from my published letter, as many others have done, that I was in good health ; but the fact is that, after considering the question carefully on both sides, the present evils and the future prospects flowing from Mr. Gladstone's proposals seemed to me so overwhelmingly great, that, though quite unable to take any public part in personally rousing my fellow-citizens to a sense of the impending evils, I felt it to be my duty in some form to "testify," as our Puritan ancestors used to say, against the backsliding of the times.   With these convictions pressing on my mind with an intensity which nothing of a political nature ever before approached, I resolved to write a letter of warning to my old constituents, who had so often received my opinions with such kindly consideration.   My wife kindly acted as my amanuensis, and I dictated the letter from a bed of sickness and suffering with not a little risk, but with immense relief to my mind when it was dispatched to the press. —I am, dear Sir William, yours very truly,

DUNCAN M^cLAREN.

In anticipation of the meeting, Sir William Thomson published the letter in the *Glasgow Herald*, and in his introductory note the great mathematician and physicist described the author of the letter as " the veteran, long-tried, and well-trusted Liberal, Duncan McLaren." The letter was read at a crowded meeting in St. Andrew's Hall, Glasgow, and without depreciating in any way the able and earnest speeches delivered at that great gathering, it may safely be affirmed that nothing said or read that night produced a deeper impression than the communication addressed to it from his sick-chamber by the Nestor of Scottish Liberalism.

Mr. McLaren did not quickly or willingly pass into opposition to Mr. Gladstone and his Government. He felt indeed distrustful of the new policy from the moment the first hint of it was given; and though every fuller and clearer explanation of it pointed to the adoption of the proposals he had most earnestly deprecated, he had clung through January, February, and March to the hope that some more or less satisfactory modification would be accepted by Mr. Gladstone. A few days before his last illness he said to a friend, with whom for two hours he had earnestly discussed the subject in all its bearings, with an eager desire to find a common platform on which the unity of the Liberal party might be maintained, and by which Scottish Reformers might be saved from the misfortune of Tory rule under Whig control: " By all means keep your mind open to the last. You are a young man ; and it is right to keep your mind open. I am an old man ; and on this question now, I am afraid, my mind is closed." But deeply though he felt his personal responsibility, and clearly though at last he saw the path which loyalty to his own conscience marked out for him, he kept free from the slightest tinge of intolerance. The separation of friends from him on this new development of policy caused him pain, but aroused in him no resentment. He granted to them, as he claimed for himself, freedom of opinion, and he would not even seek to influence those who owed to him, and who most willingly and heartily owned, filial duty and reverence. Mr. McLaren was aware that his sons (as in the case of so many families) had taken, or were disposed to take, different sides on this question. In conversation with Mrs. McLaren on the subject, the reply was given unhesitatingly and earnestly, "They must think and judge for themselves, and follow their own convictions; I would not think them sons of mine if they did not." A few days before the close his son Charles, then in Parliament, arrived, and at times the great political question of the day and the impending debate and division on the second reading of the Home Rule Bill were discussed by father and son, calmly and earnestly, with strong mutual sympathy, although each was disposed to regard the principle of the bill from different points of view.

The spirit in which Mr. McLaren conversed with his son was in harmony with the following extract from a letter which he had written to him on March 30, enclosing a copy of his "Observations on Memorandum by the Assessor to the Royal Burgh of Lanark," dated March 10, 1886, relating to suggestions for a general reform of Scotch affairs in the direction of the establishment of a scheme of local self-government for Scotland, presented to the Convention of Royal Burghs :—

"Don't make any mistake about my wishing to influence you about the Irish questions. I was *very strongly* urged to give my opinion, and did so. You will notice the date, March 10. It was not *then* generally believed that the Land Purchase scheme was a real intention, and I did not believe so, or notice it, *for that reason.* But I am as opposed to this part as to the other, although that does not appear in my paper. Should you ever talk of the matter with Mr. Bright, please mention this. . . . You will understand from this that, although I tell you my real opinions, I do not wish you to follow mine *unless they shall agree with your own views of what is right.*"

1886

# CHAPTER XXVII.

## *LAST ILLNESS AND DEATH.*

*(This chapter is from the pen of Mrs. McLaren.)*

**1885** IT may not seem unfitting that I should write the closing
chapter of my husband's life.  Though there may be some
things too sacred to lay before the public, I think a few
particulars of his last illness, which no one but myself
could give, may not be unwelcome to those who have
perused the preceding chapters.  To make the record of
the last few months of his life more complete, it is necessary to go back to November, 1885, when he left Inverness to
attend to political and business matters in Edinburgh.  He
caught cold on the journey, notwithstanding all the care
taken to ensure its being safely accomplished, and he did
not return to Inverness, as he had hoped to have done.

During his absence, our son Duncan sent me the following letter from Mr. David Dickson,[1] which urged that a
Memoir of his father's life should be written:—

OSBORNE HOUSE, SPYLAW ROAD, MERCHISTON,<br>
EDINBURGH, November 3, 1885.

MY DEAR FRIEND,—My perusal of Adam Black's Life has
renewed in me the strong desire that your dear and honoured
father would record something of his long and useful life.  I
have kept the paper which gave his address, I think to the

---

[1] Mr. Dickson was City Treasurer while Mr. McLaren was Lord Provost,
and they acted cordially together in promoting civic economy and other
useful public objects.

Cobden Club, some years ago, and it is *very interesting.*  But
what I think would be even more valuable than a narrative of
the incidents of his life, would be *lessons* from his many experiences in *public life* that would be instructive and useful to our
*younger public men,* of whom a large crop seems to be rising
up.  I recall with pleasure and profit some of the lessons I got
from him when associated with him in Town Council business.
Excuse me for urging on you the consideration of this, and
believe me, with kindest regards, yours sincerely,

DAVID DICKSON.

Duncan M<sup>c</sup>Laren, jun., Esq.

One of the characteristics of Mr. David Dickson was that
he was always trying to do good in many unseen ways of
which the public knew nothing, not only for the present
day, but also for the future ; and under the inspiration of
this letter, I hastily wrote and sent my husband a sketch
of his life's work, to convince him that it was only right
that the record of a life so useful should be preserved to
his children, as well as to a wider circle of readers.  The
general election under the new Reform Act of 1885 was
then taking place.  When the polling-day in Edinburgh
arrived, our daughters, Agnes and Helen, who were staying
at Newington House, remarked how vigorously their father,
the veteran who had fought for fifty years in the Liberal
cause, went out to give what proved to be his last vote.
Although no word of disappointment escaped him as some
of the results of that general election were announced, yet,
after the long strain he had been going through, there
appeared signs of reaction.  When I returned from Inverness, I saw with concern some evidence of diminished
strength ; and when Christmas came, he was willing that
the usual family gathering should take place at our eldest
son's house in Moray Place, which was no slight proof of
the need he felt of rest.  On New Year's Day I again

spoke to him about the Memoir, saying that I had ascertained that our friend Mr. Mackie would feel it to be a work of love if he might undertake it. After a short time of silent thought, he looked at me with a smile which I can never forget, and said, " Well, I consent; but it is from no sense of worthiness. It is to please you I consent."

How little did I think what was to be the probable cost of that assent to my wishes! With all his wonted energy he began to arrange the accumulation of papers from 1833 into their different subjects, giving explanations concerning them to his friend who was to undertake the task, and this suggested to both the idea of devoting a separate chapter to each branch of his work. I often expressed my anxiety about the arduousness of the labour, but he treated it lightly at the time. Taking an old and much-esteemed parliamentary colleague who visited him into the room where he was at work, his friend said, " I have a room at home where my papers are stored, but I should not have the courage to attack them as you are doing." But Mr. M<sup>c</sup>Laren never consulted his feelings; where there was work to be done, he did it.

Early in the year he insisted, in accordance with the advice of my medical attendant, that I should go to England to enjoy the cheering influences of my absent children and grandchildren for two or three weeks. Very reluctant to leave him, I went. The day after my arrival in London I was present at the marriage of a daughter of Mr. and Mrs. Pennington, where I was surrounded by many old friends associated with our parliamentary life. " To hear of the warm affectionate way they have all remembered me," Mr. M<sup>c</sup>Laren wrote, " has much compensated for your absence, especially, too, as I know how much you would enjoy it." In a later letter which, though written in a strain of pleasantry to disarm anxiety, and with an apology for being a little egotistical, he told of a two hours' drive 1886 he had taken in the country. The day was cold, and on alighting from the carriage he had a feeling of faintness, attended with pain, which caused him to send for the doctor, but he added that he was again all right and never felt better in his life, which the doctor corroborated, and that he would not have told me, but that he liked me to feel that he never kept anything back from me. He begged I would not return home, as it would make him very unhappy to think of my travelling when there was such constant danger of the trains being blocked by snow. Partly from the almost superstitious regard in which I held his advice, and partly owing to the apparent strength which his daily letters and telegrams evinced, I unfortunately yielded, and anxiously waited for better weather. On reaching Bradford on my way home, I found the line to Edinburgh was blocked. My anxiety became intense. At three o'clock, on March 19, I received word that the line was cleared, and at the same moment a telegram, which had been kept back with intended kindness in the morning, as travelling was reported to be impossible, was handed me stating that Mr. M<sup>c</sup>Laren was unwell. In half an hour I was on my way home. Tidings of improvement met me at the station in Edinburgh; but after the first warm and bright welcome was over, I began to see the seriousness of the change that had come over that once strong frame.

The previous day he had addressed a number of copies of his last work on Local Government, written for the Convention of Royal Burghs. The servants had observed some nervous prostration, but his children had visited him and he had made no complaint. After breakfast next morning he complained of severe pain in his head; other symptoms of weakness followed, from which he rallied.

He was able to converse cheerfully, but what struck me
sadly was that he was quite unaware, even to the last, of
how his illness commenced. In one sense I felt this to
be a mercy, as I could not bear him to remember suffering
when I was not near to endeavour to alleviate it. For a
few hours next day his speech was slightly affected, though
his mind was clear. Telegrams were sent to his absent
children, and his son Walter at once returned from
Bordighera, where he was staying on account of his
wife's health. He overtook what work had been left un-
accomplished in the arrangement of papers. This was a
relief to his father's mind, who never afterwards alluded
with any anxiety to his outward affairs, though with a
smile he said, " If I were well, I should be firing off letters
to the newspapers against Mr. Gladstone's bills." There
was now so much hope of recovery that his son returned
to Bordighera, and he himself was able to enjoy the daily
visits of his sons and daughters in Edinburgh, at which
social and political subjects were freely discussed. Perhaps in the eye of reason the expectation of his recovery
had been scarcely justifiable. The attacks of pain in the
heart rather increased. Still hope was not abandoned;
and this hope in his mind seemed centred in the wish,
which never left him, that he might once more visit the
homes of his children in England, and see once more what
he called his little English grandchildren. This idea led
him frequently to ask his medical attendant whether, in
case of partial recovery, he would ever be able to bear a
railway journey. But he begged not to be buoyed up with
false hopes, saying, " It will be no kindness, and I am ready
and willing to meet whatever is appointed for me." It was
not easy for those around him to discourage hope even in
themselves, for after the spasmodic attacks were over there

was so much apparent strength, that Dr. Playfair, his kind medical attendant, whilst conscious of the extremely precarious nature of the illness, was sometimes encouraged to believe that, if complete rest could be secured, life might be prolonged. But for Mr. M<sup>c</sup>Laren to live was to work, and the needed repose he could not take.

After one severe attack of pain he said, " I have been putting my feelings aside, and looking at my case as dispassionately as though it were that of another man, and I see how little I can expect at my age any but one termination to my illness. I do not anticipate that this will be immediate, though I sometimes feel that I may pass away in one of these paroxysms. I should like to be kept calm and peaceful, so that no disturbing influences should be allowed to ruffle the serenity of spirit which ought to rule at a time like this. I wish to prepare for the change whenever it may come." There was cheerfulness and life in the sickroom, and the inward peace which was nourished by this conformity to the Divine will was beyond the reach of worldly discord. Disappointment could not cloud it, nor could physical suffering destroy it.

I remarked to him one day that I thought it was more easy to die when young than old. He said, " Yes, I think so too; we have struck out so many roots when we are old, and they are all so dear." He asked his medical attendants if they thought the effort of arranging his papers could have affected his heart. " For," he said, " to go over one's life's work in that way causes much feeling." His anxiety lest I should suffer by close attendance upon him was great, and when resisting his entreaties that I should drive out, saying I had no pleasure in going without him, and expressing my sympathy with him in his confinement to his room, he said, " You will have to learn to go out without me. I should enjoy being up and going out with you into the fresh air, and seeing the beauty of the coming spring ; but I have much to be thankful for.   My life is not and has not been a dull one ; I have had many joyous times, many blessings, and much happiness, though mingled with trials, which fall to every human lot."

On the 15th of April he was reminded that the 16th would be the birthday of his dearly loved grandson Harry. " Then," he said, " I must write him a letter with my own hand, as it may be my last."   I was afraid of such an effort. The letter was so characteristic that it may be inserted here :—

*To Henry Duncan McLaren.*

NEWINGTON HOUSE, EDINBURGH,
*April* 15, 1886.

MY VERY DEAR BOY,—Grandmamma tells me to-morrow is your birthday.   I thought I would try to write to you a few lines on your seventh birthday, but I have not written any letters for ten days.

I write this in bed, where I have been constantly for twenty-six days, and have often been very ill, and have suffered much pain, which I hope you will never suffer.

You know I love you very much, and believe you have been a good boy, obedient to father and mother, and to grandmamma Pochin, and grandpapa, and loving and very kind and affectionate to your two little sisters, whom I also love very much.

I want you to understand that I am *very, very* old, and it may be the will of God that I shall never get better of this illness, but that I may die and be buried without ever seeing again my dear Harry or his loving little sisters ; but it may be otherwise ; and if so, I should like very much to go to London to see you all and your parents and grandparents ; and perhaps it may be God's will so far to prolong my life.

And I want to explain about the difference between old age and young children like you, if you will do what I tell you.

First take seven little pebbles from the lawn and lay them down in a row thus :—

* * * * * * *

You would think "That's myself—Harry."

Then you would lay down another row opposite it, and you would say, "That is for the first seven years of grandpapa's life, when he was as old as I am now." Then you would put down another and another, till you had put down ten rows altogether, and you would see that ten rows of seven would make seventy. That would represent me as *ten times older than you are* now, when I was seventy; and people often talk as if men when they are seventy would soon die, as that is the general expectation.

But to complete the picture by the little stones, of comparing my life with yours, you must lay down other two rows of seven, and that would be twelve times as old as you are, and show me to be eighty-four. But you cannot stop there. You must begin another row and lay down two stones and then stop. That will represent my age, eighty-six. This will show what a long distance in age there is between us, and how old I am; and that I cannot expect to live long.

Now, my dear boy, be good and affectionate and kind to everybody, but especially to your little sisters, and fear God in all your doings, and that the blessing of God may rest on you is the sincere prayer of your loving grandfather,

Duncan M<sup>c</sup>Laren.

His love for all his grandchildren was intense, as was his desire for their highest and best welfare. He often said, " How I long for the right training of their spiritual being, and that they may have the moral courage to help on what is right."

When it was needful that a nurse should be engaged, I told him that one of those recommended was an Englishwoman. He replied, " *You* cannot think this could be an objection with me." . . . . Ultimately a Highland nurse was engaged, and it was interesting to see how much his

heart turned towards her when he heard what he called
"her good honest tongue;" and one could see how his
thoughts turned to his own early days as he discussed with
her subjects of Highland interest.

On the 15th April he was much cheered by the arrival
of his daughter Helen, her husband, Dr. Rabagliati, and
their eldest boy, Andretto; and again, closely following
upon this, by the visit of his son Charles, bringing with
him little Harry. These additions to the home circle
brightened the latter days of his life. He always warmly
and affectionately welcomed to his bedside these two dear
boys, enjoying their conversation, and remarked, "How
much more boys of seven know now than they did at that
age when I was young."

As the paroxysms of pain became more distressing, it
would be impossible to describe the expression of submission
and fortitude which seemed to illumine his countenance,
and many remarks can be recalled which we now believe
were intended to prepare his anxious attendants for the
change which was drawing near, but which they refused so
to interpret at the time. His daughter Grant (Mrs. Millar),
had presented him with a little book, "Daily Light on the
Daily Path," which entirely consisted of texts of Scripture
admirably selected and arranged. He liked it because, as
he said, it contained the pure water from the pure fountain.

On the 24th Dr. Rabaglaiti was called home to Bradford.
Mr. M<sup>c</sup>Laren's farewell words of grateful appreciation of his
visit, and of his valued professional services in conjunction
with those of Dr. Playfair, were touching. He told him
how great a comfort his presence had been, but that it was
quite right he should leave him. It was affecting to see how
much pain the parting cost him, and we could scarcely regret
that, as it proved, he was spared any other parting words.

At the commencement of his illness a deputation of men from the Blind Asylum wrote to ask for an interview, as they wished to lay before him some questions of interest to them. This request, which he was not able to grant at the time, he did not forget, and it was almost the last act of his life to request his son Charles to write to them to say how much he regretted that he had not been able to see them or to render them the assistance they had asked for.

On the morning of the 26th, after a night of suffering, during which he had repeated some of the Saviour's words of love, he seemed to have much to say to us. His memory was clear, and after giving his son Charles directions about some papers and other matters, he told him to bring a sheet of foolscap paper, and place it upon his table, saying he wished to dictate a letter to one who had caused him much irritation, but he added, " That is all past ; I feel no irritation now—none." As he said this a beautiful expression of love and peace settled upon his countenance. He told his son to wait for half an hour, when he should be ready for him. He then spoke to me about the Memoir, and said that if it should ever be written, he wished that nothing should be inserted that could give pain to a single individual. After some other things of touching interest, he said, if in case of his death there should be any proposal made for a public funeral, he thought we ought to discourage it. He told me to sit near him ; then asked for some flowers which had come the night before from Walter and Eva from Bordighera. He took a few out of the glass, saying, " How very beautiful they are! Place them where I can see them. Now let me rest—let me rest." The rest was of short duration ; what he had foreseen as probable came to pass. A spasm came on. His head turned towards the light. The hand whose loving pressure was never before withheld, gave no response to the



1886

grasp of affection ; there were a few deep breathings, and the loving watchers by the bedside knew that the brave and faithful spirit had passed from them to join in the higher life the "just of all generations."

---

Notwithstanding Mr. McLaren's advanced age, and although the fact of his illness had been known, the news of his death stunned his fellow-citizens. The letters bearing his signature, which had appeared in the newspapers a few days previously, gave evidence of so much mental activity and moral courage, that it was difficult for those outside his home to believe that the physical powers of the writer were nearly exhausted ; and when the earlier reports were circulated, the townspeople refused to think it could be possible that "the good grey head which all men knew" would never more be seen on the street or on the platform. When the truth was realised, and when they comprehended the circumstances under which the last public letters had been written, admiration of the heroism and fidelity to conviction displayed in the closing hours of life mingled with and deepened the feeling of sadness inspired by the consciousness of irreparable loss.

After days of cloud and rain, the morning of the 1st of May opened with brilliant sunshine, and Nature seemed in harmony with the popular tribute, given with every mark of distinction and honour, to the "plain and simple citizen" whose remains were that day to be laid in their last resting-place. In accordance with the universal sentiment, the funeral was a public one. The coffin, which was borne on an open car, was so covered with wreaths of flowers, the offerings of affection from all parts of the kingdom, as to be almost hidden from view. Friends from many parts of England came to be present on the occasion. All places of business were closed, and all classes and creeds united to do honour to the dead. Spectators looked out from the windows of the storeyed tenements, and lined the crowded streets from Newington House to St. Cuthbert's Churchyard, a distance of more than two miles.

Religious services were conducted at Newington House, at Rosehall Church, and at St. Giles Cathedral, where official representatives of the University, the learned societies, and other public bodies of Edinburgh, and deputations from other parts of Scotland, assembled to await the *cortège*. As far as the Cathedral the car was preceded by the officials of the High Constables and the Merchant Company of Edinburgh, and by the Lord Provost, Magistrates, and Council. There the procession, now over a mile in length, was joined by the other public representatives, and slowly passed over the Mound and along Princes Street to St. Cuthbert's Churchyard. Those who witnessed the scene from the slopes of the Castle Hill can never forget it. Everywhere as the coffin passed the onlookers reverently raised their hats, and as far as the eye could reach, the procession moved through an avenue of sympathetic mourners. Within the churchyard boys from the Heriot Schools lined the path to the grave. Here the pall-bearers took their places—his four sons, two sons-in-law, the eldest grandson, and his brother-in-law, John Bright. Professor Calderwood having offered a prayer, the coffin was lowered, the twenty-third Psalm was then sung, and, by an interesting and accidental coincidence, it was sung to the old Gaelic tune with which Mr. McLaren's mother used to soothe him to rest as a child. Mr. Bright, who had first brought his sister into the presence of his friend, now led her from the grave which held all that remained to her on earth of the husband she had so much honoured and loved; and the relatives and friends left the scene through a crowd of solemn mourners.

As was remarked by a distinguished statesman present, no man, however exalted his position might be, could desire a higher mark of esteem and affection than had that day been given to Duncan McLaren.

> "And now he rests; his greatness and his sweetness
> No more shall seem at strife,
> And death has moulded into calm completeness
> The statue of his life."

IN ST. CUTHBERT'S CHURCHYARD.

MONUMENT TO THE MEMORY OF
DUNCAN McLAREN
On the Site of the Cottage at Tullich near Dalmally
where he spent his School days.

ERECTED BY HIS WIFE.

# APPENDIX.

—‡—

The following is the letter referred to on page 26, Vol. I., a copy of which is given to each winner of the M<sup>c</sup>Laren-Robertson Prizes at the Watt Institute :—

## A QUIET HEROIC LIFE.

**To the Students who may gain the " M<sup>c</sup>Laren-Robertson " Prizes at the School of Arts.**

The title of this little paper may seem paradoxical to some of you as we usually associate the word "heroic" with deeds of fearless and valiant action. Perhaps, when all shall be revealed, it may be found that a self-denying life in conscientious obedience to some high principle, though passed in comparative obscurity, will be deemed the highest heroism.

Such a life was that of Charles Leopold Robertson, and it is my wish that some further record of it shall be given than that of his mere name being attached to the M<sup>c</sup>Laren-Robertson prizes. I regret that this record is of necessity so short. Mr. Robertson's mother was a Pole. His father was the captain of a trading-vessel. His upbringing and his education devolved entirely upon his mother. Mrs. Robertson had to practise much self-denial in order to give her son a good education, which enabled him to obtain a situation in the bank of Sir William Forbes & Co., Edinburgh. He became a student at the School of Arts, and it was whilst there that a warm friendship was formed betwixt him and Duncan M<sup>c</sup>Laren. They had some experiences in common ; each had a noble mother, and each out of a small salary helped to support his mother.

Mr. Robertson was soon promoted from the bank in Edinburgh to a higher position in an English bank, and ultimately he became manager of the Wilts and Dorset Banking Company at Frome in Somersetshire, where he passed the remainder of his life. When he left Edinburgh on the occasion of his first promotion, one of

Mr. M^cLaren's family said to him, " We shall hope, Mr. Robertson, to see you soon back again in Edinburgh." " Yes," he replied, with a smile—unconsciously verifying the proverb that " many a true word is spoken in jest,"—" I'll come back when your brother is Lord Provost." He did not return for more than twenty years, and Mr. M^cLaren was then Lord Provost of Edinburgh.

Mr. Robertson had become a small shareholder in the Forth Marine Insurance Company. It was before the time of limited liability companies. The company was unsuccessful, and Mr. Robertson, like many others, was brought to poverty, having to pay up the calls made upon him. He resigned himself to his fate. Burdened with a debt for which he was in no way responsible, he denied himself everything except the bare necessaries of life, and what most men prize, a married home and children to carry on his name. His sterling integrity and social nature, combined with a womanly tenderness of character, brought him congenial companionships, and made him a welcome guest in some of the happiest households in Frome, where his memory is still held in affectionate esteem. When, at last, his long-standing and cruel debt was discharged, with the first money he could call his own he took the train and came down to Scotland, and was warmly welcomed at Newington House by his old friend, the Lord Provost of Edinburgh, and by those who had twenty years before hoped for his speedy return. The meeting was a very touching one. Old memories were revived, and old friends and acquaintances inquired after, but there were few to remember the unobtrusive youth who had left the city so long ago.

Mr. Robertson paid his friend a second visit when there were still fewer to recognise him, and one day coming in late for the family dinner, he made the affecting apology that he had been wandering through the cemeteries of the city to see what names of old friends he could find on the tombstones !

When the British Association was held at Bath in 1864, Mr. M^cLaren and some of his family who were attending it went over to Frome to see Mr. Robertson in his English home. He was greatly gratified by this visit, which proved to be the last time the two friends met.

Knowing what fidelity to principle had cost his loving, social nature, I have had the two friends photographed together from *cartes* taken about the time Mr. Robertson was last in Edinburgh, twenty-eight years ago, which have been kindly allowed to be hung in the Library and Students' Room of the Heriot-Watt Institution, so that the students may know something of the outward man whose honesty of life and great integrity I hope each may imitate in his or her own walk in life.

Mr. Robertson's frugal habits enabled him to save a little money, which he divided into equal portions, and left by will to chosen friends who had cheered him in his self-denying life. One portion of £400 he left to my husband, Mr. McLaren. It seemed only right to use this money, so conscientiously earned and saved, to preserve the memory of so good a man in his native city, and nothing would have gratified him more than by having it associated with that of his life-long friend for the benefit of others.

Though the prizes are small, if the example of the lives of Charles Leopold Robertson and Duncan McLaren should help those who gain them to meet the varying fortunes of life with a noble Christian integrity, they will not have been given in vain.

In Holy Trinity Churchyard, at Frome, is a grave with this simple inscription on the stone cross at its head—

CHARLES LEOPOLD ROBERTSON,

Died 16th October 1875,

Aged 76 Years.

This short notice of a virtuous life is accompanied by true sympathy with all who aspire to do what is right. It may often be through much difficulty; but the promise is sure of blessing to the upright. That this blessing may be yours is the prayer of Mr. Robertson's friend and yours,

Priscilla Bright McLaren.

Newington House, Edinburgh,
   *May* 11, 1888.

# INDEX.